The Duke of Windsor Conspiracy

A Novel By

David Philips

Black Rose Writing | Texas

The author grants the final approval for this literary material.

First printing

ISBN: 978-1-68513-397-9
PUBLISHED BY BLACK ROSE WRITING
www.blackrosewriting.com

Printed in the United States of America
Suggested Retail Price (SRP) $23.95

The Duke of Windsor Conspiracy is printed in EB Garamond

*As a planet-friendly publisher, Black Rose Writing does its best to eliminate unnecessary waste to reduce paper usage and energy costs, while never compromising the reading experience. As a result, the final word count vs. page count may not meet common expectations.

PRAISE FOR
THE ERROL FLYNN CONSPIRACY

"Once again, David Philips has produced an intriguing counter-history in a narrative that would rival the efforts of Hollywood legends."
–Carolyn Korsmeyer, author of *Little Follies*

"What happened or could have happened at that fateful meeting in Washington, D.C., when Hedy Lamarr and George Antheill attempted to persuade the top Naval officers to use their invention that would have jammed the signals of the torpedoes? Was it truly that the top "brass" could not take seriously the intelligence of a beautiful movie star and an eccentric composer? Or were there more sinister forces operating behind the scenes -- maybe even closely linked to a popular movie idol? We may never know for certain, but it is entertaining to speculate!"
–Rebecca H. Augustine

PRAISE FOR *THE*
DUKE OF WINDSOR CONSPIRACY

"Another brilliant work of fiction based on real historical characters, Edward VIII and Wallis Simpson."
–AJ McCarthy, bestselling author of the *Charlie & Simm Mystery* series

"The tightly-constructed novel keeps many balls afloat in an exciting race to see who will benefit and who will end up frustrated by the narcissistic and naive royal couple."
–Carolyn Korsmeyer, author of *Little Follies and Charlotte's Story*

This book is dedicated to the memory of those brave servicemen and women of all races and nations and religions who gave their lives to protect us from the scourge of Nazi-ism.

Lest we forget.

ACKNOWLEDGEMENTS

As I have written elsewhere, writing is a solitary pursuit, the author's enforced seclusion broken only by those periods when he/she needs to tend to their basic needs.

However, in contradiction to the above statement, it is also very much a collaborative process. After all, for the vast majority of writers, where would we be without our agents, our editors, our publishers, and our literary 'sounding boards,' those poor unfortunates on whom we foist our embryonic works, expecting no less than complete admiration of our writing skills?

To this end, I am eternally grateful to my agent, Kirsten Schuder of Apex Literary Management, for her kind words of support and encouragement, her incredible editing skills and her market knowledge.

I am also thankful to my A.L.M. writing buddies, Mark Mc Quown and Al Stoffel for their helpful advice and suggestions which helped to make the finished work infinitely better and far more polished than it otherwise might have been.

And finally, once again, I am grateful to Black Rose Writing for accepting this manuscript for publication.

The Duke of Windsor Conspiracy

INTRODUCTION

To students of British contemporary history, 1936 is known as The Year of the Three Kings. In January, the reigning monarch, George V, died, to be succeeded by his eldest son, Edward. In December of that year, Edward abdicated in favor of his younger brother, who became King George VI. On his relinquishing of the position, Edward was given the title, The Duke of Windsor.

Before he succeeded to the throne, Edward was known as the Playboy Prince, and liked nothing more than holidaying in foreign resorts, being seen at all the best places, and was generally known as 'A Man About Town.' He was well liked and often acted as an unofficial ambassador, promoting Britain's interests abroad. He was particularly welcomed in the United States, perhaps due to his easy charm and flamboyant lifestyle.

Edward, however, had a darker side. He was an ardent admirer of Adolf Hitler and Nazism, and an anti-Semite, often blaming all the world's problems on Jews. His experiences, albeit limited, of trench warfare in the First World War, made him a lifelong pacifist, and dedicated to preventing another conflict on such a massive scale. When Hitler came to power, and all the way through the 1930s, Edward preached a constant cry of appeasement, and was often at odds with many in his own government, especially his friend, Winston Churchill.

Despite the disapproval of the British government, Edward and Wallis even visited Germany in 1937 and had a secret audience with Hitler. One can only speculate about what might have been discussed at this meeting.

As the Second World War was coming to an end, and Allied forces closed in on Berlin, a cache of documents was discovered in a town called Marburg in Germany. Some of these documents purport to contain correspondence between Edward and Hitler in which the dictator promises that he will depose the reigning monarch and re-install The Duke of Windsor as King of the United Kingdom once he has conquered the country. As many of these files were suppressed, and have never been released, no one can say for certain what damning indictments they may contain.

Closely inspired by actual events, this novel explores what might have happened if Edward had returned to Germany at the height of WWII to ally himself to the Nazi regime to be used as a willing pawn by Hitler to service his own selfish ends.

August 1939

The German leader sat behind his desk in the Reich chancellery. All had been prepared, and soon his forces would drive east into Poland. Now, it was all about waiting. It had been so easy to dupe Daladier, the ass Chamberlain and even his erstwhile ally, Benito Mussolini. Still, eight months later, after signing that ludicrous document at Munich, Hitler pinched himself to be sure he was not hallucinating. These men had proven themselves to be nothing more than craven cowards, willing to put their names and their reputations to any agreement that would prevent war. Well, good luck to them. Despite his own signature on the Treaty, Hitler had no intention of abiding by its terms, not when he now knew he could acquire even more territory than he had claimed. Poland would only be the start. Soon, other countries would follow, and all would be gathered into the Greater German Reich – *his* Reich. But Hitler knew he could not have accomplished all that he had without the assistance of others, and it was to one of these patrons that he was now writing.

With his personal private secretary, Johanna Wolf, sitting before him, Hitler composed a letter.

"Your Royal Highness, I hope this communication finds you and your wife well. As we have previously discussed, matters will shortly come to a head. Whether or not France and England will honor their commitments to Poland, I fully intend to carry out my plans. Soon, we will cleanse this nation and every country which comes under our authority of its undesirables, the

Bolsheviks, the Jews, the religious fanatics, the physically and mentally handicapped. None of these will have a place in the new Aryan society we seek to build. Those men and women of superior physical and intellectual capabilities who will forge a new empire such as the world has never seen. But all these ambitions would not be attainable, nor would I even have been able to contemplate such possibilities without the help of certain people, yourself not the least of those.

'Just as I never forget those who sought to thwart my plans, so I always remember those who have supported me in my bitter struggle. For this reason, it will be my pleasure and my honor to install you to the position which is rightfully yours. I will ensure that those titles of which you have been deprived will be restored once we have eliminated the political establishment and their lapdog church. I, personally, will ensure you take your rightful place as the King of England. With your Royal Highness as the monarch and myself as the political head, there will be no limits to what we might achieve together.

'I fully understand your Royal Highness's anger, frustration, and feeling of helpless impotence at this moment, but I would crave your Royal Highness's patience for just a little while longer.

'Please extend my best wishes to your charming wife, and I expect it will not be too long before you can return in triumph to England to take up your royal duties.

'With all best wishes, A,'

Hitler asked his secretary to read back his notation. Satisfied by what he had dictated, he instructed her, "Ensure this message is sent through the appropriate channels."

Johanna Wolf uncrossed her stockinged legs and got to her feet, laying down her pen and notebook at the edge of Hitler's desk. Smoothing down her gray, pleated skirt with the palms of her hands, she nodded in compliance of the orders she had just been given. "*Sehr gut, mein Führer,*" she acknowledged as she lifted her pen and pad, turned smartly round, and left the room.

CHAPTER 1

Rome, Italy - London, England, June - July 1936

It was late in the evening, and most of the staff in the Palazzo Montecitorio had gone home. In another part of the building, only the janitor remained cleaning and tidying the detritus left by those government members whose portfolios had not been taken over by their leader himself, Benito Mussolini. The windows of Mussolini's study looked out onto the darkened streets below. The only illumination in the room came from the electric wall lamps that adorned the walls of the richly decorated interior, whose subdued lighting cast eerie and sinister shadows of the two men still there. The mood and the ambiance were, perhaps, appropriate for the subject they were discussing.

The Italian dictator paced the floor of his study. His chin was tucked into the top of his chest as he contemplated the strategy about which they had been speaking. The decision he would make could have far-reaching consequences, not only for him but his son-in-law, Galeazzo Ciano, who was in the room with him. As well as, or perhaps because of being a family member, Ciano was also Italy's Minister of Foreign Affairs. It was he who had initially suggested the plan they were now mulling over. Raising his shaven head, Mussolini looked at Ciano and asked, "Are you sure this operation will work, Galeazzo? So much rides on its success if we are to propel our country into the forefront of European politics. I cannot even begin to contemplate what might befall us if anything goes wrong, especially with that paranoid little corporal sitting on my shoulder. We also have to consider the League of Nations and their blasted sanctions. I understand they are due to lift them, but this will not happen if the slightest indication of what we are about to do is made public."

"Everything is in place, *Il mio Duce*. Our subject knows what he has to do, but has no idea why we have asked him to do it. He has only been motivated to believe that in doing what we have asked of him, he will be helping not only our cause but the cause which is also dear to his own heart."

"And you are sure he is not also working for the Nazis?"

"Quite sure. We have had him under discrete observation for some time and are well aware of his antipathy towards Hitler. No, *Il mio Duce*, he is quite sound."

"Yes, but is he of sound mind?"

Ciano smiled respectfully. "Mostly, as far as we know. He is believed to be a trifle eccentric, a bit of a – how do the English phrase it? – fantasist, but that is to our advantage, is it not? Who would believe a person like that if he is apprehended? They would most likely commit him to a sanatorium."

Mussolini had confidence in his son-in-law, but had not been the sole ruler of his country for over fourteen years without taking some precautions. Without the knowledge of his Minister of Foreign Affairs, he had instigated some safeguards of his own, should their strategy not go as they intended. Quickly changing the subject, Mussolini asked, "So, what did you learn from von Neurath? Does Hitler really seek to have England as an ally?"

"Without a doubt. His Führer speaks very highly of the country and would like nothing more than to come to a peaceful accommodation with them. He sees Britain as another bulwark against Stalin's expansionist policies and a partner in preventing the spread of Bolshevism throughout Europe. War with Britain is the last thing on Hitler's mind."

Mussolini banged his hand down on his desk, rattling the pens and inkstand in their ornate green onyx holders. "I knew it. What did I say right from the start, eh? I told you that little bastard with the lopsided mustache couldn't be trusted. Look how he turned against me when we invaded

Abyssinia last year. I never again thought I would see the day when Italian troops, my army, would be fighting German forces. Yet, it happened."

Ciano did not think it would be politically expedient or do his career much good to remind his leader that Italy and Germany were on opposite sides in the conflict of eighteen years ago. "Of course, he wants to be friends with Britain – for the moment. Britain is the only country that has the might to stand up to him. As soon as he thinks he has military superiority over them, Hitler will treat them with the same contempt he has shown everyone else, including us! It will not stand! I will show that treacherous hound who he is dealing with. So, he believes he can make a pact with the British, does he? Does he think we in Italy all go around with our eyes closed? Does that scoundrel believe we know nothing about the naval treaty he signed with Britain last year, eh? He would sideline us to ally himself to the former enemies of his country, would he? We'll see about that!" The Italian dictator banged his hand down on his desk once again. "Very well, let's make it official. I'm giving you the go-ahead to do what we planned. Obviously, there will be nothing in writing, neither will you discuss this operation with anyone else. Do I make myself clear?"

"Very clear, *Il mio Duce*. I'll get onto it at once."

"One other thing...."

"Yes, sir?"

"On no account must Dino Grandi be made aware of what we are planning. He has a loose tongue, especially when he is in the arms of some beautiful and seductive woman. If he finds out about our intentions, he may do or say something ill-advised, and right now, I need him to be exactly where he is."

* * *

July 16th. was a warm and sunny summer's day. The man in the shabby brown suit edged and elbowed his way through the London throng. They had gathered along the tree-lined Constitution Hill to see their monarch, King Edward VIII riding by, flanked by his household guard, going from Hyde Park toward Buckingham Palace. It was a grand parade, and Edward smiled to his cheering subjects as he rode sedately past. Many of them were carrying their lunch, intending to take advantage of the fine early afternoon weather, and eat their picnic in one of the adjacent parks.

As the procession neared Wellington Arch, the man ran out from the crowd, holding a revolver and shouting, "*Sieg Heil, Heil Hitler, Long beo Eire, Saoirse don eirinn*!" As he made to fire his weapon, a policeman, acting almost on impulse, knocked the gun from the man's hand while a woman spectator tugged at his other sleeve to try and restrain him. Rather than attempt to flee or resist arrest, the man merely shrugged himself free of the woman's grasp and held up his hands, exclaiming to everyone in a broad Glaswegian accent, "It's me! Ah'm the person! Ah'm the one!" Within seconds, he was surrounded by police officers and the King's own security team before being hustled away from the terrified onlookers. The King looked on, almost indifferent to the tragedy that might have befallen him as the gun was retrieved from under his horse. Even his mount seemed to sense that the danger had passed and remained calm and docile despite the furor going on around it. As they were leading him away, some of the policemen heard him mutter, "I tried tae tell them! I tried tae tell them, but they widnae listen!"

The shabbily dressed man was called Jerome Bannigan, who also went by the name George Andrew McMahon. He was taken to New Scotland Yard and interrogated by several officers, including the Assistant Commissioner, James Whitehead. Whitehead had previously served in the British Army, reaching the rank of Brigadier. During his time in India, he had interrogated insurgents, men who would go to any lengths to achieve independence for their country, but never one who had attempted to kill his sovereign. For the time being, he had left the questioning of the Glaswegian to the officer sitting to his left, Detective Inspector Alan Bentley.

In his early forties, Bentley was outwardly a career officer who should have risen further than his current rank. It was a source of constant contention between him and Deborah, his wife. She was more ambitious for him than he appeared to be for himself. It was not the first time she had told him, demanded of him, to give his senior officers an ultimatum. Either promote him to the rank he deserved, or he would leave the force. As much as he would have liked to have done just that, he couldn't. His lack of promotion was not simply because he was good at what he did in his current post, and his superiors were reluctant to take him away from regular detective work. Unbeknownst to Deborah and almost everyone else at New Scotland Yard, he was not only a D.I. with the Metropolitan Police. He was also the eyes and ears of a little-known branch of the Intelligence service with a remit that went way beyond his authority as a humble police officer. The only other person within New Scotland Yard who knew his dual role was the person sitting beside him, Brigadier James Whitehead.

Since Hitler came to power in 1933, German espionage and destabilization activity in the United Kingdom, especially around London, had increased almost exponentially. The security agency had acquitted themselves well and had proved more than a match for the *Abwehr*, who had agents stationed across the capital and the south-east of England. Their English Nazi supporters accomplished little more than effecting nuisance value and were not worth wasting the time and resources of the professional domestic security services. Although their activities were not so serious as to warrant investigation by the Agency itself, neither were they quite innocent enough to ignore completely. It was also becoming apparent that Hitler's policies were influencing police officers themselves. Several of them had been spotted at meetings of Sir Oswald Mosley's British Union of Fascists.

This was Bentley's other purpose. To gather intelligence on those subjects who did not quite fall into the realm of being serious contenders for security surveillance and also to monitor the activities of Metropolitan Police officers who had pro-Nazi sympathies. Bentley was also the only Metropolitan police officer outside the Special Branch who was authorized, albeit secretly, to carry a weapon at all times. It was a Colt Police Positive .38 caliber revolver, given to him by an F.B.I. officer on a recent trip to the United States.

McMahon ran his fingers through his thinning ginger hair in exasperation. Sweat was running down his rugged-lined face, which was caused not only by the temperature in the room. "Ye's urnae listenin.'

Ah'm tellin' ye's, Ah wis pit up tae dae this. Ah hid nae intention o' killin' the King. Ah hid nae intention o' killin' anybiddy! Why are youse no' listenin'?"

Whitehead and Bentley winced from the smell of cheap whisky coming from McMahon's breath. Mingled with the overpowering stench of his body odor, the effect was almost unbearable. The detectives sat as far back from him across the other side of the desk as space permitted. On the table in front of McMahon sat a buff-colored folder with an amber stripe running diagonally across it, stamped 'Confidential' with his name and a file number stenciled underneath. "So, let's get this straight. A couple of Italian gentlemen of your, ah, acquaintance asked you to kill the King, and you said 'yes,' just like that?" Bentley asked this question skeptically. McMahon grimaced. "Naw, no' jist like that. Dae you think Ah'm that fuckin' stupid? If Ah hid agreed too quick, they wid huv been bound tae become suspicious. Ah hid tae let them think Ah wiz against the whole idea at first, well, Ah wiz against their crackpot scheme, ye understand. But Ah had tae let them believe that Ah could be talked aroon' like, ye know?"

Bentley drew on his cigarette and exhaled a plume of smoke through his nostrils before continuing. "But they never said why they wanted you to assassinate the King?"

"Ah told you. They said Ah wid be strikin' a blow for Irish freedom. You know, return the six counties back to the rest of Ireland, an' aw' that."

"And how would killing Edward the Eighth have helped the cause?"

"Can you no' see it? Are you that fuckin' dense? Can you imagine the outcry there wid hiv been if Ah really hid murdered Edward, shoutin' thae Irish freedom slogans? The British public wid hiv been so disgustit an' demoralized at whit Ah'd done, they wid have screamed at the government tae gie the province back tae the Irish Free State, and be done wi' it. Then Ireland wid finally be united again, and De Valera wid be happy." McMahon shrugged his shoulders. "That's aboot it."

Bentley cocked his head to one side, reminding McMahon of an inquisitive spaniel. "But they, the Italians that is, wanted you to shout Nazi slogans to make us believe the Germans had sent you? Is that what you're trying to tell us?"

"Aye, Ah s'pose it is." McMahon shrugged his shoulders.

"And why would they do that, I wonder."

"Ah've nae idea. Ye'd huv tae ask them yersel'. Aw' Ah know is that they said Ah should shout Nazi slogans, an' then the Irish wans. That's aw' Ah kin tell ye's."

"And you never thought to ask why the Italians should ask you to shout Hitlerite platitudes?" McMahon shook his head."And another question comes to mind. Why should the Italian government, which I suppose means Mussolini, take such an interest in the affairs of Ireland? That's what I'd like to understand."

"Aye, Ah know. That wiz botherin' me, tae. The only thing Ah kin think of is that both Italy and the Irish Free State are Catholic countries. An' if it comes tae that, maybe the Pope had a hand in it tae, somewhere."

Whitehead had intended to remain silent, but at McMahon's last remark, he spluttered, "The Pope? Are you seriously suggesting that Pius the Eleventh was complicit in the attempted murder of the British King? Have you gone quite mad, sir?"

"All Ah'm sayin' is that Edward is the heid, the *head* o' the English church, the Protestant church, is he no'?" McMahon argued. Without waiting for either man to concede the point, he continued, "Ah'm no' sayin' he wiz behind this, ye unnerstand, Ah'm only suggestin' he might huv been. It makes sense when you think aboot it, Ah suppose."

Both police officials shook their heads. Each was thinking the same unwelcome thought. This is preposterous. It has to be, but what if there's actually some truth in what this lunatic is telling us? With no evidence, of course, all they had was speculation. It was bad enough thinking Mussolini might have been the driving force in the attempt on the King's life, but to implicate the Pope? Both men looked at each other. No, neither officer was inclined to pursue this avenue of inquiry any further, not without some hard proof. Whitehead slowly drew McMahon's dossier toward him. He had already scanned the Glaswegian's history but made a show of reading it as if for the first time. "George Andrew McMahon, also known as Jerome Bannigan...is there not an 'r' missing here?" he asked no one in particular.

"No, sir. Many folk've asked me the same thing, but we've always been Bannigan. Maybe we couldnae afford the extra letter, eh?" McMahon's attempt at levity did not go down well, and neither officer even acknowledged the joke. Whitehead continued, "Born in Northern Ireland, I see. County Tyrone, eh? I once had the dubious pleasure of visiting Omagh. My God, Bentley, if you think he's hard to understand," nodding toward McMahon, "you should hear them speak over there. It was easier to understand the bloody natives when I was stationed in Abbottabad." Whitehead went on, "I notice you worked for Harry Longbottom. I can't think of a bigger anti-Catholic than Alderman Longbottom. Would you care to explain why a good Papist like yourself would have anything to do with someone like him?"

McMahon sighed heavily. "Oh, so you know about that, do you?"

Whitehead smiled. "There's not very much about you that we don't know, Mr. McMahon. Now, I'd like an answer to my question. Why would someone like you associate yourself with him?" McMahon tapped his forefinger against the side of his nose.

"Ah, I see," nodded Bentley slowly. "You were feeding information about him to... who? Special Branch? Thames House? the Irish Republicans? Which one was it?"

"Does it really matter?"

"Yes, it bloody well does matter. If it was to our security boys, that's one thing. If it was to the terrorists, that's a whole different game, and I'll tell you this now. If you were forwarding any intelligence about anyone, even an evil bastard like Longbottom, to the I.R.A., not only will I make sure you hang, I'll pull the fucking lever myself. Are we clear?"

Bentley would soon find out from his security colleagues if they got any information on Longbottom from the man sitting in front of him.

"I see you're no stranger to the inside of His Majesty's prisons. Done several stretches for fraud and embezzlement, eh?" Turning over the folio, Whitehead remarked, "Hello, what's this? You have been a naughty little Scotsman, haven't you? Running guns into Abyssinia in the middle of a war? Really? You actually smuggled weapons into North Africa? You? I'm surprised you know where the blasted country is!"

"Aye, well, Ah did, an' it's no' somethin' Ah'm particularly proud of. Mind you, the money wiz good."

Bentley undid his tie and loosened his top button. Scratching the back of his neck, he said, "I don't know, Brigadier. This all sounds so bloody far-fetched; it's like a penny dreadful." The detective-spy reached into the ashtray for his cigarette, then saw he had smoked it down to the butt. It had gone out. He made to light another but thought the better of it. "If you didn't want to carry out their instructions, why didn't you just disappear? Run off somewhere?"

"Aye, sure, an' dae you know whit wid've happened if they'd found me?" McMahon drew his forefinger across his throat. "You don't say 'no' tae these guys. That's why Ah hud tae make it look real. At least they wid think Ah'd tried. That might jist be enough tae keep me frae bein' kil't."

"By them perhaps, but you do realize that attempting to assassinate the reigning monarch is classed as treason. That offense carries the death penalty," said Whitehead.

"How often hiv Ah got tae tell ye? Ah never wanted tae kill King Edward. Look, Ah kin prove it."

"Oh, this should be interesting. What is it? A letter from the plotters with their names, addresses, and dates of birth, requesting you to kill the King at your first available opportunity?" smirked Bentley.

"There's nae need tae take that tone, ya English gomeril! Naw. Ah don't have a letter frae anybiddy. Ah wrote letters. Ah wrote tae the Home Sec'tary, Ah wrote tae the security services, an' Ah even met wi' yon detective, John Otway. Ask him yersel'. He'll tell ye."

Whitehead looked as astonished as he felt. "You... you met with John Ottaway?" he asked incredulously.

"Aye, Ah did, an' all. He gave me short shrift. Sent me packin' after aboot two minutes. Looked at me like Ah wiz shite aff his shoe, so he did. Just ask him."

"Oh, don't worry, Mr. McMahon, we surely will," Bentley promised. Turning to Whitehead, Bentley whispered, "I've got a bad feeling about this, Brigadier. Can we have a word outside?" Rising to his feet, Bentley signaled to the two other detectives in the room, telling them to keep McMahon amused until they returned.

Once they were out of earshot, Whitehead asked Bentley, "What's on your mind, Alan?"

The detective exhaled loudly, before replying, "I can just about understand Mussolini wanting to drive a wedge between the Germans and us. It makes sense from his standpoint, especially in light of the naval treaty and everything, but even so..." He hesitated before continuing, knowing that his next words would make his boss very uncomfortable. "If, and I mean if McMahon is telling the truth, why didn't Ottaway take this claim further? No matter how unbelievable it sounded, he would have been duty-bound to alert the King's security team at the very least, yet it seems he did nothing. Why?"

"Sadly, Alan, I know the answer to that, and what's more, I think you do, too."

THE WINDSOR CONSPIRACY

August 1939

The Duke re-read the message for perhaps the fourth or fifth time. Despite the repeated number of occasions he had scanned the paper, his feeling of pride and self-satisfaction had not diminished. To think that the most powerful man in Europe, indeed, one of the greatest men who had ever lived should not only feel a debt of gratitude to him but to take the time to express his appreciation in writing was almost more than he could imagine.

He could hardly contain himself at the thought of finally being recognized as the true and only monarch of his country, the country of his birth. Soon, the establishment, those who had denied him his birthright and had stripped him of his titles, would be made to pay for their disloyalty. Those who were still alive, that is. He knew that others were already thinking of deserting the sinking ship that was Great Britain. How long would the government and its forces hold out against the *Wehrmacht's* power, especially once they had overthrown not only Poland, but France, Belgium, and the Low Countries? In a perverse way, he hoped the British would not seek terms with Germany. He would have liked nothing more than to see their country's forces humbled before the might of the new Germany; a Germany filled with a renewed sense of purpose and determination, whose troops would surely crush all before them, even the once proud and mighty British army. How fitting it would be if Britain had to sue for peace on Germany's terms.

Of course, this outcome would mean taking the throne of a country militarily defeated for the first time in its recent history. The population would be cowed and demoralized and certainly unwilling to recognize a monarch installed by its country's conquerors. But that time would pass, especially when the penalty for sedition and treason would be swift and final.

The Duke wanted to show his wife the document he had just received but thought the better of it. Although the letter did not state it as such, he was sure the Führer would prefer him to keep his own counsel for the time being. He would be the King, and his wife would finally get what she had always craved; not just to be his Duchess and consort. She would be accorded the title she duly deserved – Queen of England.

CHAPTER 2

London, England, July 1936

Detective Chief Superintendent John Ottaway, head of Special Branch's Detective Division, sat uncomfortably in the brown leather chair. His hands were clasping his knees while his ashen face was looking toward the floor. He was in serious trouble, and he knew it. Despite the faults and the incompetence of others, it looked like it was he who was being set up to take responsibility for the debacle over the failed attempt on the life of Edward the Eighth. He was the only one sitting in Whitehead's office. Whitehead himself and Alan Bentley stood in front of him, towering over the seated figure. Ottaway knew how the game was played – he'd done the same thing many times to intimidate the subject, making him (it was almost always a 'him') feel threatened and under pressure. He knew all this, but it did not make him feel any more at ease.

"You have to understand," Ottaway pleaded, "we get crank calls and letters every day, telling us about some plot or other, to blow up the Houses of Parliament, London Bridge, or to assassinate the Prime Minister, the Archbishop of Canterbury. You name it; we've heard it. We can't possibly investigate every crackpot who has a grudge against us. We'd never get any real police work done if we spent all of our time chasing shadows. Surely you can understand that. You're both police officers yourselves. You must know what I mean."

Whitehead responded acidly, "In normal circumstances, I'd agree with you, of course. But these are anything but normal circumstances." The Brigadier held up his hand, counting off each finger. "Firstly, he came to see you personally. The fact that you agreed to meet him means that you must have already known who he was. I'm sure you don't allow any Tom, Dick, or Harry just to waltz into your office to pass the time of day. So, you knew he had links to the Security Service, yes?" Ottaway nodded. "Secondly, he not only told you of the plot to assassinate the King, but he also told you who was behind it." Ottaway nodded again. "Thirdly, and this is the bit I really don't understand, he even told you where and when it would happen and that he would be the one who would pull the fucking trigger. Yet, you still did nothing!"

At this point, Ottaway became animated, standing up to confront the two men face-to-face. "You don't understand. There are larger issues at stake here, issues you don't understand. I... I wish I could tell you, but I can't."

"You do realize who you're speaking to, Ottaway," snarled Whitehead. "I'm not some fucking office boy. I'm the Assistant Commissioner of the Metropolitan Police, and he's..." nodding toward Bentley, who gave him a warning look before Whitehead could go any further, "he's... one of my best officers, so if there's anything you know, now's the time to say it. Right now, your career's hanging by a very fine thread, which is fraying by the second."

"If we had stopped him, it would have blown his cover," Ottaway whispered too quietly for the other men to hear. Bentley asked him to repeat louder what he'd just said. Ottaway complied.

"So, you did know that there was substance to his claims?"

"Yes!" Ottaway shouted, "I knew! I knew, but I... I had to let it go ahead. You need to understand. As hard as it is to believe, McMahon was feeding us some good intelligence about the Italians. We couldn't just allow that information to stop coming. Please believe me; I didn't want this to happen. I swear I didn't."

"I've never heard such a load of sanctimonious nonsense in my life," sneered Whitehead. "Why didn't you just fill his gun with blanks? Then, he could have blasted away as much as he liked. No one, least of all the King, would have been harmed."

"Yes, but the Italians aren't that stupid. They'd quickly have seen his gun was not loaded. That really would have put the cat, well, the Italians' cat, well among McMahon's pigeons."

"Tell me something, Chief Superintendent. Did you believe McMahon was really going to kill the King?"

"No, I didn't. Why would he have told me their plans if he was actually going to assassinate Edward? It doesn't make sense. Despite everything, I think McMahon is a loyal subject."

"When exactly did McMahon come to see you?" asked Bentley, trying to work out a timeline.

"It was on the thirteenth, I think."

"The thirteenth of July. Three days before he was due to pull the trigger."

"Yes."

"So, you had three days to do something about it, and you want us to believe you did nothing?"

Before Ottaway could answer, Whitehead asked, "Did he tell you why they wanted him to kill Edward?"

Ottaway shook his head slowly. "I'm afraid I didn't give him a chance. I dismissed him without hearing him out.

"But you didn't take his warning further?" Bentley insisted.

Ottaway hesitated a heartbeat too long.

"You did! You did notify someone else. For God's sake, why didn't you tell us?"

"I couldn't! They told me to say nothing to anyone.

"Who, Ottaway?" Whitehead asked quietly. "Who are 'they?'"

"I... I can't. Don't you understand? My career will be over if I divulge who it was."

"Your career will be over before I leave this office if you don't tell us," warned the Assistant Commissioner.

Silence filled the room. No one wanted to be the first to speak in the hiatus, but Ottaway knew it would have to be him, whatever he said. Finally, he broke. "I told MI5. They knew."

"So, you're saying that the most senior security network in England knew about the intention to murder the King and did nothing about it? Just as we suspected, eh, Bentley?"

"They told me they had the situation under control and that I should stand down. They would take care of it."

Whitehead glanced at Bentley. Obviously, his own Service had even kept this intelligence from him.

"And yet, they didn't. Why do you think that is, Chief Superintendent?"

"I... I don't know. How could I know what MI5's reason was for allowing...?"

"Oh, but I think you do. We do, don't we, Detective Inspector?"

Bentley nodded in agreement. Ottaway shook his head adamantly. "No, I don't," he insisted.

"Well, allow me to enlighten you, Chief Superintendent Ottaway. The reason the government's main security organization allowed McMahon to try and kill the King was that they didn't want a Nazi sitting on the throne of England!"

CHAPTER 3

London, England, July 1936

Through discrete, diligent, and patient investigation, Bentley discovered that McMahon had been working for his organization for almost a year. He was attending Communist and Irish Republican meetings and reporting back to his national security handlers. The Glaswegian claimed his uncle had a farm near the border with the Free State and that gun-running between the two countries was a regular occurrence. Bentley also discovered that Liverpool Special Branch had taken a keen interest in Harry Longbottom's activities. It was to their London counterparts that McMahon was sending what information he could gather on the politician and Protestant pastor. So, at least, he would not be tried for passing intelligence to a foreign power, well, the Irish at any rate.

As with most security organizations, intelligence gathering was compartmentalized. No agent would be aware of any activities outside their own particular mission. That way, any operative who was compromised could reveal little about anything more than their own current investigation. Other colleagues controlled McMahon, and only Colonel Vernon Kell, 'K' to his staff, and his deputy, Sir Eric Holt-Wilson, had a complete overview of all of the security service's operations.

The weather was still warm. Neither man felt like sitting in a stuffy, badly ventilated office, so they decided to continue their conversation while strolling through Hyde Park. Neither Whitehead nor Bentley had spoken for a while, each police officer wrapped up in their own particular thoughts.

Eventually, it was Whitehead who voiced what both men had been considering. "What d'you think, Alan? Should we tell His Majesty that his own security force was prepared to allow him to be assassinated? Can you imagine his outrage and indignation? He'll want to have someone's head, not that I can blame him. We could give him Ottaway, make him the sacrificial lamb, and all that, but it's really Vernon Kell whose neck should roll. Not that it will, naturally. Once we tell Edward, of course, we can't untell him, and he's not the most stable of people at the best of times. How do we know he won't even peach to his friend Hitler about the botch-up? How do you think that will go down in Berlin, I wonder?"

"You know, this could work to our advantage, given the King's admiration for the Nazi dictator."

"How so?"

"Well, Edward must have heard Bannigan or McMahon, or whatever his name is, shouting 'Heil Hitler' as he raised his gun. What's he supposed to think now? He believes that this odious regime that he's been cozying up to and getting all pally with has just sent an assassin to kill him. What must be going through his head right now? If we play this right, we might convince Edward that he's been supporting the wrong side after all. For whatever reason Mussolini had for wanting to kill Edward, he could have given us the very opportunity we need to get the King to see the light – our light! He's so impressionable and gullible, if you told him the moon was made of green cheese, he'd probably believe you. It shouldn't take too much persuading to convince him of Hitler's culpability after what happened."

"Yes, I agree with you, but you can bet that right now as we speak, someone, probably Goebbels, is composing a memorandum denying any involvement in the incident and blaming us for staging the whole event to destabilize Edward's relationship with Hitler. Why wouldn't they? For once, they really weren't responsible for this mayhem. And who is Edward more likely to believe – us or them? In his unstable position, the more we deny it, the more he'll believe it really was us."

"Yes, maybe you're right. Think of the ammunition that would give the little German tyrant. Even if Edward asked him to keep it quiet, d'you think Hitler would honor his request?"

"No, I don't. It would just give him incentive to sow even more discord and disharmony in the country, and that's the last thing we need right now. That bloody American woman's got Edward's head tied up in knots. He doesn't know if it's raining or Wednesday. No, it's best if we all keep this debacle to ourselves for the time being. The less Edward knows, the better."

* * *

Julian DeVere Musgrave was on his second bottle of Pol Roger 1914. He could afford it; well, his father could afford it, and a lot more besides. It was a rare vintage. Only a relatively few bottles had been produced before the outbreak of war, but he knew a little vintner just off Mayfair who had the foresight to buy up as much of the precious wine as he could. There weren't many bottles left now in the old fellow's cellar, but a judiciously placed pound note now and again made sure that what remained would be for his consumption only.

He was drunk and getting drunker by the glass. He couldn't help it. This latest assignment was pure boredom; keeping an eye on some heathen Jock who was supposed to be a security threat? Do me a favor! These people could barely walk upright, and didn't they all walk about in skirts? Skirts, for God's sake? Who did Kell think he was kidding? He knew why he had drawn this mind-numbing job. O.K., so maybe he wasn't the best operative in the Security Service, but he certainly wasn't the worst – not if half the stories he heard had any weight to them. He was surprised Britain still had an empire, judging by the number of mistakes his colleagues had made and those in the S.I.S. So, it just wasn't bloody well fair that he had to babysit this Godforsaken Scotsman when he should have been out catching some real spies.

Musgrave considered ordering a third bottle, but even in the state he was in, he knew it would be too much. And he still had a job to do, one he detested, but one which, despite his misgivings, had to get done. Bidding his host a drunken farewell, the secret service operative staggered out of the wine bar. A few steps along the road, he stumbled and knew he was going to hit the pavement. He instinctively tensed himself for the inevitable impact, but just as his body was about to meet the concrete, an arm gripped his shoulder. "Can't have you making a mess of the King's highway now, sir, can we?" a Cockney accent asked from somewhere above Musgrave's head.

The agent allowed the stranger to help him to his feet. "Thank you," Musgrave mumbled, brushing invisible road dust from his Anderson and Sheppard pants. He was trying to focus, but found it difficult. "Do you live far?" the stranger asked him.

The question seemed to confuse Musgrave. "Live far? Far from what? How far away should I be? I mean, how far from home, that's it, how far from home am I? Is that what you mean?" He couldn't see the smile on the stranger's face. "Yes, that's exactly what I mean."

"It's, ah, I... no, not far, and Musgrave pointed vaguely in the direction of his apartment block. "Right, then," laughed the man, "let's get you home and sleep off your bender then, shall we? You'll need to direct me. I don't come out this way too often."

"Just my luck, then, wasn't it, that you happened to be passing by?"

"Yes, I suppose it was," the stranger replied, only the smile had now left his face.

At the end of the road, they came to a 'T' junction. Musgrave was uncertain. Was it left or right? He wasn't sure. "Um, right, I think," he suggested.

"No, left is the way we need to go," the stranger replied.

"Well, if you're sure, then left it is." agreed Musgrave.

This was going to be easier than they had planned for. It was all falling nicely into place. Soon, the mystery of why the demented Scotsman had tried to kill the King would be solved, and the stranger would be a much wealthier man.

CHAPTER 4

London, England, July 1936

Whitehead and Bentley had returned from their afternoon stroll through the park. Feeling refreshed, Bentley sat opposite his superior officer, lighting up a cigarette. "I don't know if I altogether accept McMahon's story about the Italians being complicit in trying to achieve Irish unity. It's a bit, oh, I don't know, a bit funny."

"He seemed authentic enough to me," countered Whitehead, referring to their earlier interrogation of the Glaswegian.

"And yet, when you wheeled in Dino Grandi for questioning, he appeared to be truly shocked by our allegations. It was as if he was only hearing about all of this for the first time."

"Oh, come on, Alan. You know how theatrical these Italians can be. You only have to look how they always overact in their bloody operas. Every scene filled with passion and pathos, even when they're emptying out their privies."

Bentley laughed. "I don't think I've ever been to an opera, Italian or otherwise, where I've seen that. You must take me some time."

"You know what I mean," Whitehead chided. "Of course, he's not going to admit to being part of a plot to assassinate the King. I agree he's a fool, but he's not an idiot."

"No, Brigadier. I stand by my belief. I honestly think he was as dumbfounded as we were when we told him what we knew. The color drained from his face. I don't care how good an actor he is; you just can't fake a reaction like that. He really was shocked."

"So, what are you saying? That it wasn't the Italians at all?"

"No, I'm pretty sure they were behind it. McMahon had no reason to lie about that, especially when we got confirmation from John Ottaway about McMahon's involvement in the whole thing. Oh, no, they were up to their necks in this. You can be sure about that."

"So, what you're saying is...?"

"What I'm saying is, whoever ordered the killing, they made sure Grandi was kept well out of it. That way, he couldn't dishonestly deny anything about a situation of which he truly knew nothing. And if we accept Grandi's repudiation as genuine, then were we being asked to believe that the Italians weren't behind the scheme at all?"

"You're throwing more questions at me than I have answers to, Alan. But I sense you believe more than you've just told me. Would I be correct in that assumption?"

"Yes. My sources tell me that nothing happens in Italian politics and intrigue without the knowledge and consent of *Il Duce*. You can bet he's behind this somewhere, but the reason McMahon gave us about the Irish situation is just eyewash. McMahon wasn't lying. That was the line they fed him, and he swallowed it, but there's more to it, I'm sure. I just hope we find out what it is before it's too late to do anything about it."

* * *

With Musgrave's arm draped around his shoulder, the stranger carry-dragged the intelligence agent up the two flights of stairs to his front door. He fumbled in the operative's pockets until he found his door keys. Juggling the dead weight of his new 'friend' with finding the correct key, the stranger eventually opened the door to the apartment, staggering in with Musgrave still in a drunken stupor. He lowered the agent onto a kitchen chair, removing his jacket one arm at a time. Removing some rough hessian rope from his inside coat pocket, he tied Musgrave's hands behind his back and his feet to the chair legs before slapping his face to revive him. "No, Mr. Musgrave, I don't want you to go to sleep quite just yet. First, you're going to answer a few questions, and then you can snooze as long as you like." He took a small package from his inside jacket pocket. Unwrapping his parcel, he took out a syringe filled with a clear liquid. The stranger rolled up his captive's shirt sleeve while tapping the glass to get the bubbles to float to the top, then injected the agent with its contents. Musgrave shook his lolling head from side to side, mumbling incoherently. The stranger lifted his head with his forefinger, searching the agent's eyes for signs of alertness. There were none. A few more seconds should do it.The stranger watched as the second hand of his wristwatch ticked slowly round. Right. It was time. He slapped Musgrave hard twice, three times, then again until the helpless man showed a faint gesture of recognition. "I've never injected anyone with this solution who's been so affected by alcohol. Should be an interesting experience for one of us."

Musgrave sensed he was in trouble but could not formalize his concerns. He thought he was in his flat, but did not recognize the man standing over him. Yet, he did, and from the recent past. If only he could remember...

He had no time to think any further. The stranger stood in front of him, smiling, but even in his drunken state, Musgrave knew it was not a smile of friendship. "Right. Down to business. Who is McMahon working for? Really working for?"

"McMahon? Who...?" The stranger punched Musgrave in the stomach. "I've got no time to play these stupid games. Now, tell me what I want to know, or I'll teach you a lesson in pain you'll never forget. Oh, actually, you will forget it, but I'll still enjoy inflicting it. Now, answer my question. Who is the Scotsman working for?"

"The Scotsman. McMahon?"

"Yes, him."

"The Italians. He works for the Italians. I've seen him slip into the embassy many times. He doesn't know we're watching him, naturally."

"Who is his handler there? Who's controlling him?"

"I…I am." The stranger punched Musgrave again. The agent groaned. "Not MI5, you idiot. The Italians. Who is controlling him from the Italian embassy?"

"I don't know. We asked him, of course, but he said they never used any names in front of him."

"Why did they instruct him to pretend he was a German supporter? Why did he shout '*Sieg Heil*?'"

"I don't know. Obviously, it was to stir up trouble between Germany and England, but I don't know the specifics."

"Who else in MI5 is involved with McMahon's case file?"

What was happening? Why did this man want to know about a no-account drunkard like McMahon? Why did he keep punching him? What had he done to upset this man? The agent tried to loosen his bonds, but the man was a professional. Musgrave couldn't budge them. "I'll ask you one more time; then I'll really start to get angry. Who else controls McMahon from within the security service?"

"I don't know; I swear I don't. Punching me any more won't make me tell you something I don't know."

"No, it won't, but it will give me a good deal of satisfaction nonetheless." Musgrave was telling the truth. The fluid in his captor's syringe was foolproof. A mix of chlormethiazole, chloral hydrate, and some unknown barbiturate. It was the creation of some American doctor Nazi sympathizer. Guaranteed to loosen the tongue but leave no memory afterward. This was the ideal solution. If they killed Musgrave, the security service would know they had been breached and take appropriate action. This way, they could find out what they needed to know, and no one would be any the wiser. Perfect. But this idiot knew next to nothing, yet… "Did anyone say why they let the assassination attempt go ahead?"

"They didn't want Edward to remain on the throne. They wanted a change of monarch."

"Why? Why did they want to depose Edward?"

"Because of his links to Nazi Germany. They were frightened he was getting too pally with Hitler."

It was just as they had thought, but now they had the proof. There was no way the British establishment would allow a Nazi supporter to remain on the throne of England. Well, we'd see about that. "Dino Grandi. Do you know who he is?"

"Of course I do. He's the Italian ambassador."

"What part did he play in all of this?"

"Part? What part?"

"My God, the Secret Service must be desperate when they employ morons like you. What part did Grandi play in the attempted assassination of King Edward the Eighth?"

"As far as I know, he played no part at all. He knew nothing about it."

"Are you telling me that Mussolini planned to execute the English King and didn't tell his ambassador?"

"I suppose so. I say, I'm getting beastly tired. Would you mind if I shut my eyes, just for a few minutes?"

"Soon, my friend, very soon. Just another few questions, then we'll be finished. Who gave the Scotsman the gun?"

"It was someone at the embassy, some lowly official, but I don't know his name, honest."

"So things are happening within the walls of the embassy that the ambassador is unaware of?" It was a rhetorical question, not requiring an answer.

Musgrave's eyes were now drooping, and he was struggling to stay awake. "Does McMahon report to anyone else in the security services? Apart from you, that is?"

"Please, I just want to go to sleep."

"Soon. Give me a name, and then you can close your eyes."

"We never know who's doing what. That's how they work. I don't know about anyone else in the Security Service, but one name did crop up. He doesn't work for us. I overheard it by accident. I don't think they meant me to, but I did." Musgrave nodded his head, pleased that he could help his new friend, who would soon let him find that elusive sleep he so desperately needed.

"So, tell me, Julian. What's the name of this mysterious person?"

"Bentley. Detective Inspector Alan Bentley."

CHAPTER 5

Berlin, Germany – London, England, August 1936

Admiral Wilhelm Canaris looked thoughtful. His agent believed he had done good work and was looking for approbation from the head of the *Abwehr*. Canaris was in no mood to show any appreciation for the information the man had provided. He had given his organization few details they did not already possess. The burning question remained. Why did the Italians want to kill the British monarch and blame the crime on his country? What was so important to Mussolini that he was prepared to incite a war between Germany and Great Britain, a war in which Italy would inevitably become involved, whether or not *Il Duce* wished to be? The Italian leader was playing a very dangerous game. He did not know why, but the stakes had to be high for him to perpetrate an act of such extreme violence. So Canaris asked himself the same question again and came up with the same answer. It just did not make any sense.

The British newspapers had reported on the incident, of course. They could hardly do otherwise, the event having been witnessed by hundreds of people. But very little was being said of the Italian or German connection. The British public was being asked to believe that a lone gunman was responsible—a fantasist who saw himself as an Irish freedom fighter with Nazi sympathies. No, there had to be more to it than the newspapers were saying.

Although the British public had been kept largely in the dark about Edward's endorsement of the Reich, Hitler and his echelon were well aware that some members of the government were concerned over having such a monarch on the throne. If it hadn't been for the confirmation that Mussolini was responsible, he would have believed that the Agency itself had invoked McMahon to commit *lèse majesté*.

Now the head of the *Abwehr* had to ask himself another, altogether more awkward question. What, if anything, should he tell the Führer? Canaris knew about the close relationship between Hitler and Edward Windsor. How would he take the news that his friend the King's own subjects had conspired to see him murdered? The admiral doubted his leader would be best pleased, and with his unpredictable and volatile nature, who knew what the Führer might do? Would he even go so far as to expose the plot and publicly shame the British prime minister, Stanley Baldwin, as part of the conspiracy? It did not bear thinking about. Not when Hitler was trying to foster better relations with England. But still and all, Edward did have the right to know. What he did with this information would be up to him and his advisors if he chose to share this knowledge with them. The dilemma was how to get this information to Edward discretely, without the knowledge of Hitler. Contacting the King directly was out of the question. The only person who could do that was Hitler himself.

A thought then struck Canaris. Of course. It was so obvious. He would reach out to one of the King's advisors himself, a confidante he communicated with personally and one who would know how to be discrete. He had to be. He was a lawyer by profession.

* * *

It was an apoplectic Vernon Kell who had a nervous and confused Julian DeVere Musgrave sitting across from him. The young agent was glad there was an oak desk separating them; otherwise, he thought Kell might actually strike him. This action, if it happened, would do the careers of neither man any good, but right now, the young agent believed that his ultimate superior wouldn't give a damn. "You're his caseworker!" Kell screamed, then he corrected himself. "You *were* his caseworker," he corrected himself. "barely a handful of people knew we were prepared to let the Scotsman put a bullet into Edward. The Home Secretary, John Ottaway, James Whitehead, one of his D.I.'s, Alan Bentley, Holt-Wilson and myself; and you!" the Director barked. "I've spoken to each one of them. They have accounted for their whereabouts to my satisfaction during the times when this information might have got out. And believe you me, even John Simon quivered when I questioned him. Do you know the damage you've done? Do you? Can you even contemplate the ramifications of what you did, eh?"

"Sir, I..."

"Don't you dare try to deny this, Musgrave. There was no one else it could have been. And let's face it, after the last balls-up you made, you're lucky you're still in the Service at all. But hopefully, not for much longer."

"My father will...."

"I know who your father is, Mr. Musgrave, and if you think you're going to intimidate me by using your father's name and his connections, you really don't have the measure of me. Now, let's get down to brass tacks. Who did you blab to about our little problem? And don't faff about. I don't have time to play games."

Musgrave recalled his days at Harrow school. He would have been about fourteen or fifteen. Some pupils, him included, had decided to bicycle the three miles from the school to Pinner. It was a Saturday afternoon, and they had planned their trip to be back in time for supper. As boys do, they joked and carried on as they rode towards the town, steering their bikes into each other, forcing their friends to cross onto the opposite side of the road. It was all so innocent, just a few boys enjoying their afternoon off.

Then it happened, the tragedy out of the literally clear blue sky. Cars were so uncommon on that road that none of the boys thought that a vehicle might be driving from Pinner toward Harrow. It was at a bend in the road when a playful friend, Reginald Rhodes-Willingham, rode his bike into the frame of another one of the group, Peter Capsall. Even as he lost control, trying to straighten his steering to compensate for Reginald's bicycle push, Peter was laughing. He was still laughing when the oncoming car slammed into him, sending both bicycle and rider into the air.

The driver, Albert Stockton, later admitted that he was traveling too fast, but the accident would never have happened at all, except for Reginald's foolish actions. Stockton rushed the stricken youth to the local hospital, but the young boy's injuries were too severe, and he died on the operating table.

Peter was a gifted student. His parents were both hard-working people but could not afford the cost of tuition fees the school required. Despite this financial handicap, they wanted the best for their bright son and managed to get him enrolled in the elite establishment under a fully-funded scholarship. His ambition was to return to the school as a teacher to repay in some measure the generosity they had shown him.

The following day, Sunday, young Reginald Rhodes-Willingham found himself sitting in the headmaster's study. His father had been summoned, and also present were two policemen from the local station, and Peter Capsall's parents, Maud and Cyril.

Peter's friends had already been questioned, and all agreed that it had just been a tragic accident. Reginald certainly never meant to harm his friend. They would all swear to that. Nonetheless, a boy was dead, and accident or not, there would have to be an inquiry, and charges would almost certainly be brought. It was a scandal the school could hardly afford. It relied on the fees paid by some of the most well-known and wealthiest families in the country. Who would want to send their son here now when such disgrace had fallen upon the prestigious institution?

It was then that Lord Montague Rhodes-Willingham, Reginald's father spoke up, and gave an eloquent discourse. Yes, he agreed, a tragedy had occurred, and he had every sympathy for Peter's parents. He could not begin to imagine what it must be like to lose a son under such terrible circumstances, but as he reminded them, his son had never meant any harm. It was bad enough that their son had died, but no amount of punishment would bring him back. Lord Montague agreed that some form of retribution was required, but did they need to involve the police? And what would his son be charged with? Murder? Hardly. The incident was not planned with malice aforethought or premeditation, nor was there any intent to harm, injure or impair the victim. There was certainly a case for manslaughter, at which both police officers nodded obligingly; too obligingly, Lord Montague thought.

But the car driver, Stockton, was also partly culpable, admitting that he had been driving above the speed limit for that stretch of the road. Stockton, too, had a wife and children. He lived in Pinner, and it would not take long for rumors to start. His life would be in tatters also, and maybe even his job, his livelihood, would be at stake. Would it be fair for him to suffer punishment for the fault of another? No, it wouldn't, but it would be unavoidable if the case went to trial.

Lord Montague also delicately reminded Maud and Cyril that the school had been very gracious in allowing Peter to study there on a full scholarship. Harrow had never, nor would they ever, seek any payment for their son's education. Yes, it was so sad that he would never reach his potential, but bringing his own son to court would not change that. Wouldn't it be better all-round just to allow everyone to forget this tragic incident?

Naturally, Lord Montague would see that their son got a decent burial and would defray any other expenses that might occur. Peter had a younger brother, Percy. Lord Montague would ensure Percy would not need a bursary. He would pay all of the boy's tuition fees for his time at Harrow. He would also make a sizeable donation to the school's trust, so that future generations of impoverished students would not be disadvantaged simply by an accident of birth.

The headmaster, Lionel Ford, smiled approvingly. The two officers discretely replaced their notebooks into their uniform pockets. This incident would die and be forgotten by the end of the week, at least by Lord Montague. Yes, he would make good on his promises, and Reginald would certainly get a good dressing down. But his name and the school's reputation would not be tarnished. That was the main thing. He did not see the troubled looks on the faces of Cyril and Maud Capsall. Is it not better to say nothing to anyone, suggested His Lordship, and allow their son to sleep in peace without the ignominy and unfavorable publicity a trial would cause. That their son's memory could be bought so cheaply was somehow disturbing to them. They could just not determine why that should be so.

Reginald's father had made that problem disappear, like a rabbit in a magician's hat. But it did not go away. A local paper had somehow got hold of the story, to the dismay of everyone. They wanted to know the identity of the boy who had caused the accident. Rhodes-Willingham was incensed. Yes, his son had been partly responsible for the boy's death, but now a filthy rag wanted to besmirch his family name all over London. No, this would not do. This would not do at all.

Rhodes-Willingham found out the names of the other boys who had been involved in the incident. The youngest was a brat called Julian DeVere Musgrave. He would do. He knew the Musgraves by reputation. Greville Musgrave was a minor politician, a back-bench M.P. with one of the main parties. Rhodes-Willingham could make or break a man's career by a simple word in the right ear. Musgrave senior would toe the line. At least, he would toe the line if he wished to be considered for advancement to a front-bench seat at the next cabinet re-shuffle.

And so it was done. Musgrave got his promotion but lost his integrity and his son's love on the same day. Sadly, Julian could no longer carry on his studies at Harrow, but they would find somewhere else for him to continue his schooling. So it was all arranged.

It was now fifteen years on, and this problem was much bigger. The defense of the realm was at stake, all because of him, and once again, his father would be unable, maybe even unwilling, to help him. He was on his own.

"Sir, I swear to you, I told nobody about McMahon. I mean it. Absolutely nobody. I know I've let you down, let everyone down, and I suppose if you've already spoken to everybody else, and they didn't do it, then it must have been me, but as God's my witness, I told no one. That's the truth. I swear it."

"Not some sweetheart you were trying to impress, perhaps?" asked Kell. "Some girl you wanted to become better acquainted with, eh?" his Director said suggestively.

"I... I'm not seeing anyone at present, sir. Haven't had a girlfriend for some time."

Against his better judgment, Kell almost believed his subordinate. It was in his eyes. You could fool people with your lies and the timbre of your voice and even your mannerisms, but your eyes always betrayed you. They really were the windows to the soul, and this young man sitting in front of him was just not that good an actor. Either he was telling the truth or he believed he was telling the truth. Yet somehow, their operation had been compromised, and Musgrave was the most likely, the only one, in fact, who could have blabbed. And someone had definitely blabbed.

* * *

Edward was currently on holiday on the eastern side of the Mediterranean Sea, sailing through the Adriatic with Wallis Simpson, unaware of the drama that was about to unfold about him. The newly-knighted Sir Walter Monckton did not share his employer's fondness for Adolf Hitler and his gang of Nazi thugs. To him, they were the anathema of all that he stood for. In his view, the King was playing a dangerous game, appearing to condone and support such a ruthless and warmongering regime. As Edward's counselor and legal advisor, he delicately tried to steer his monarch's sympathies and concerns to more positive and productive values, but to little avail. Edward showed no inclination to follow his lawyer's advice, always a dangerous practice for someone with so little knowledge of the outside world.

There was also the likelihood, the near-certainty, of His Majesty having to abdicate if he did not rid himself of his silly infatuation for that American woman. The government and the church were united in their disapproval of his relationship with a divorcée, and he had been given what had amounted to nothing less than an ultimatum. Marry Wallis Simpson, or keep your throne. As titular head of the English Church, you cannot be seen to flout its most sacred laws and traditions.

Despite Monckton's disdain for the Nazis' odious regime, he harbored a certain degree of admiration for their inventiveness and ingenuity. He had received a greeting card from a 'friend' in Berlin. A small red dot was at the top left-hand corner of the envelope, signifying that a secret message was enclosed. Extracting the card, he carefully tugged on a slightly ragged edge at its back fold. Carefully peeling away the top layer of the thin card, he found a wafer-thin folio. The paper appeared blank, but when he rubbed it gently with some lemon juice, a coded message slowly appeared. This had to be important. Typically, they did not bother with such subtleties, rightly believing that the cipher was secure enough as it was.

Although the security services may have been monitoring their sovereign's activities, it was unlikely they would be applying the same level of surveillance on his lawyer, hence the message being sent to Monckton's home rather than to the King at his office in the Palace or at Fort Belvedere.

Edward was sorely trying Monckton's loyalties. Usually, one's allegiance to the state corresponded to one's devotion to its monarch; usually. But by aligning himself with what ultimately may turn out to be an enemy of his country, he made Monckton's patriotism very difficult. And the message he had just read did not help his feeling of indecision about his divided loyalties.

Could it be true, or was this just some sort of Nazi propaganda thought up by that horrid little man with the game leg, Joseph Goebbels? Monckton would have indeed dismissed it as just so much mischief-making, but for one pressing fact. It had come from no less a person than Canaris himself. The head of the *Abwehr* was no fan of Goebbels and would not allow himself to be a party to anything designed purely to stir up division between the Monarchy and the State. No, he had to take this intelligence seriously. Did the security service actually intend to allow a crazed gunman to assassinate his King? His friend?

If he merely asked Vernon Kell if the allegations were true, Kell would undoubtedly refute the accusation. Then he would be no further forward. No, the only way to confirm or otherwise this astonishing information was to confront the Agency director head-on. So that's what he would do.

* * *

By the grim expression on Monckton's face as he walked into the office of the Director, Kell knew it was not going to be a pleasant meeting, but he had no idea of the bombshell the King's counselor was about to drop in his lap. There were no niceties or polite formalities. Monckton sat down and got straight to the point.

"Director, I have had information from a very reliable source that your organization intended to allow someone to assassinate the King. I'm not going to ask you if this intelligence is accurate. I know it's true. Now, would you mind telling me what the hell is going on?"

Inwardly, Kell was seething. How could this knowledge have reached the Palace? They had taken such great care to keep anyone even remotely connected to His Majesty at arm's length from their machinations. Now, no less a person than the King's legal adviser had come storming into his office, not just asking if these allegations were true. He knew they were. But how?

Despite his discomfiture at Monckton's anger, Kell appeared unfazed by the lawyer's outburst. "My dear Sir Walter...."

"Never mind 'my dear Sir Walter,' I want to know why you tried to kill the King. Don't deny it. My source is unimpeachable."

Kell attempted to bluff out Monckton's assertions. "My dear, er...Sir Walter, I don't know where you heard this nonsense, but I assure you no one in the Service ever contemplated any such action, to the best of my knowledge. I must ask you, where did you hear this?"

Kell's blank denial unsettled the King's advisor. Like Monckton, Kell was at the top of his profession and did not trip up by simply rolling over when asked tough questions. Yes, he was lying, but the country's security was at stake. To the Director-General, that overruled any other considerations, even being untruthful to the King's representative. Monckton might not see that at the moment, but one day he would.

Monckton was not finished, not by a long way. "Well, I'm sure Sir John will be delighted to hear it. I must say, he wasn't so effusive in his response when I discussed this situation with him not an hour ago."

Now Kell was rattled. He had not reckoned on this. "You've been to see the Home Secretary?"

"Why? Is that a problem for you?" Monckton asked blithely.

"No, of course not. It's just...what did he say, if I may be so bold?"

Monckton felt the same way he did in court, when he caught out a witness who had lied. Perjury was a serious offense, punishable by a term of imprisonment. He always enjoyed seeing the expression on the witness's face when he presented them with irrefutable evidence that what they had just stated was not truthful. And now, Kell had exactly the same look on his face. It was priceless. "Let's just say he was not so outrightly contemptuous of my accusations as you are, Colonel Kell. If I were a gambling man, I'd say Sir John hedged his bets. Now, I'm going to give you one more opportunity to tell me all you know. If you don't answer my questions, all my questions, to my satisfaction, you will find yourself in the dock. Do I make myself clear?"

Facing such a challenge to his position, there was only one answer Colonel Vernon Kell, Director General of Britain's main security agency, could give.

CHAPTER 6

London, England, August 1936

Despite his best efforts, Kell could not prize from Walter Monckton, the source of his knowledge. This situation was all getting so bloody complicated. Why did they have to have a king who seemed to be more in agreement with a foreign power than he was with his own country? Whatever way this went, it would not end well for Edward. Kell could live with that. His monarch had shown himself to be a selfish, weak, and foolish man who had no place to be on the throne of the greatest country on earth. It was not Edward's fate that concerned the Director.

Winston Churchill and Leo Amery were correct. The government could bury its head in the sand as much as it liked, but it could not be denied. Under Adolf Hitler, Germany was re-arming at an alarming rate and had changed little from its belligerence of twenty years before. It must be something in the German psyche, Kell supposed, that made them want to wage war every twenty years or so. If Britain did not maintain its vigilance and increase spending on its own armed forces, it might find itself outgunned by a very dangerous and predatory enemy. And Edward, as King, would not show the leadership and fortitude the country would need to keep morale high and determination strong in the event of another conflict between the two nations. Far from it. With his strong ties to Germany, Edward would find himself with an insurmountable conflict of interest. Might he even capitulate to the Nazis at the first opportunity? Then where would we all be? Under the Nazi jackboot, that's where. Not on my watch, thought Kell. Not on my watch.

But these ruminations were not getting him any closer to discovering who had disclosed the plot to Monckton. Despite his anger and frustration with Julian Musgrave, Kell believed he had not deliberately or maliciously breached protocol. He was not a traitor and had not knowingly revealed McMahon's role or the Service's involvement in the whole affair, yet word had got out. By process of elimination, the only weak link in the chain was the young security agent. It could not have been anyone else. Yet still, Kell felt Musgrave was telling him the truth as he knew it. There was only one explanation. The operative must have somehow allowed himself to give away the secret without knowing he had done so.

This situation was too sensitive to involve anyone else in the Service. He would have to investigate it, to get to the bottom of how this explosive information had gotten into the hands of someone so close to the King. But not by an internal inquiry. It would have to be conducted by someone not connected to the security agency, or, at least, someone not connected officially. For the first time that day, Kell smiled. He knew just the man for the job.

* * *

On hindsight, Monckton believed he had made a big mistake. He had allowed his emotions to override his legal training. By revealing his knowledge of the plot, he had put himself right into the firing line. Monckton dared not tell Kell that he was in regular contact with the head of the *Abwehr*. Then it would not be Kell, but Monckton himself who would face trial. And Kell would not just let this go. He could not. He, Walter Monckton, had to have acquired this intelligence from somewhere, and Kell would not give up until he discovered the source of such damning information. There was absolutely no doubt the two men would meet again, and when they did, Monckton knew Kell would not be alone. As much as he did not want to, Monckton now realized there was only one course of action open to him. He would have to tell Edward. Everything.

* * *

Musgrave had been suspended from duty pending an inquiry. He expected to be dismissed – hadn't Kell said as much? – and was aimlessly wandering the streets pondering his future. He had friends, but they were all successful, all 'something in the city,' courtesy of their well-placed and influential fathers. All had stable careers, long-term prospects, glamorous girlfriends and wives, some with both, and little to trouble their privileged lives. Right now, he hated them all.

How could he have been so stupid? But had he been as careless as his Director had said? He told Kell the truth. He hadn't peached to anyone. Not that he knew. And how could they be so sure it was him? Nobody would admit to doing what his superior had accused him of. They all had too much to lose; far more than him. Perhaps they were using him as the sacrificial lamb, being made to take the blame for their shortcomings, whoever 'they' were. That had to be it. No, damn it, that was it! Well, this wasn't Harrow School, and he wasn't a callow fourteen-year-old schoolboy anymore. No more would he be forced to take responsibility for someone else's actions. Somebody had talked, but it wasn't him. And he would prove it.

He found himself walking in the direction of his apartment, so decided to go home and start to work out what had happened. How he could have done what Kell said he did. He was so absorbed in his thoughts, he did not notice a man standing outside his block, smoking a cigarette. "Good afternoon, Mr. Musgrave; my name's Bentley." Taking out his warrant card, he went on, "Detective Inspector Alan Bentley. Do you think we might have a word?"

Unnoticed by Bentley, a green-bodied Austin 10 had been following him for the past hour. He may not have recognized the driver, but his new companion might. Possibly, but unlikely. It was the man who had helped him home on that last occasion when he had drunk too much of the Pol Roger 1914.

It had been a puzzle to the stranger why a detective inspector should be involved with national security. A quick check from his source within the Metropolitan Police confirmed that Detective Inspector Alan Bentley was merely a serving officer in the C.I.D. He was not attached to Special Branch, so why was he involved with MI5's conspiracy to assassinate the King? And now, here he was meeting with that young agent, Musgrave. It might be time to pay Bentley a visit with his little hypodermic...

* * *

"I kept telling Colonel Kell, I didn't say anything about McMahon to anyone. That's the truth, but he doesn't believe me; I know he doesn't."

"No, Julian, you're wrong. That's why I'm here." They were in DeVere's apartment. It was the middle of the afternoon, and the young agent wanted a drink. He asked Bentley if he would join him, but the detective-spy declined for them both. "I need you to have a clear head, and booze isn't going to do anything to help that, all right?"

"Yes, I suppose so, but I only want one...."

"One will lead to two, which will lead to... well, I'm sure you can count. You do realize how much trouble you're in, don't you?"

"I only..." Musgrave whined.

"Enough!" Bentley was now losing his temper. He was here to try and help this young man, and it seemed as if he cared more for Julian's career than the agent did. "I need you to be sober if we're going to try and work out how you did what you did."

"I was thinking about that, Detective Inspector. I've come to the conclusion it wasn't me at all." And Julian then expounded his theory.

"Well, it's an interesting hypothesis, I'll give you that," agreed Bentley. "It's one we can return to later if we don't get anywhere with you, O.K.?"

"I suppose so," Julian accepted reluctantly.

"O.K. Let's make a start. Bentley took out his notebook and pencil. "When were you given the brief to take care of McMahon?"

Julian gazed up at the ceiling scratching behind his ear in concentration. "Well, he tried to... you know... on the sixteenth of July, didn't he?" Bentley nodded in assent. "So it must have been the following day, the seventeenth, after Brigadier Whitehead and you had interviewed him."

"Who else was handling him?"

"You know how it works. We never..." Julian suddenly stopped talking. He looked bemused as if unsure where he was. "You know, I've just had the oddest feeling."

"What is it?"

"Well, I know it sounds absurd, but I feel as if you've asked me that question before."

"Don't go acting all strange on me, Julian. Just answer my question, then we can...."

"No, I'm serious. I know it wasn't you; it was the way you asked. You know, like an interrogation. I'm sure someone has already asked me the same question, like the way you just did."

"Julian, we don't have time..."

"Please, just give me a minute, let me think." The young man massaged his temple, trying to stimulate his memory. Yes, he had been asked the same question, not by Bentley but by someone... someone who he knew yet didn't know. A familiar stranger. It was there, somewhere. In the back of his mind.

"It was here!" he exclaimed.

"What was here?" Bentley asked, now becoming impatient.

"Here, he asked me that question here. Well, not in this exact chair." They were sitting in two floral upholstered armchairs on either side of the fireplace. Julian pointed toward the kitchen. "It was in there. He asked me in there." The young agent began to shiver uncontrollably. "He punched me in the gut. Yes, I... I remember. He hit me, hard. He... he tied me up..."

"Julian, do you know what you're saying?"

"I'm not making it up, honest. I can't recall everything, but I definitely remember being struck."

It was Bentley's turn to stroke his forehead. "O.K. Let's say you're not imagining it. Let's assume for the moment that what you say happened, happened. Let's work back. I need you to...."

"Oh, God, I need a drink. I need to sleep; I really need a drink."

"And I told you, later. Let's try... wait a minute. What did you just say?"

"I need a drink. Can't we...?"

"No, you said something else. You said, 'I need to sleep.' Are you tired? It's only just after three o'clock in the afternoon."

"No, I'm not tired. Did I say I needed to sleep? Why would I say that?"

"Yes, why would you? Do you mind if I take a look in your kitchen?" Without waiting for permission, Alan stood up and walked into Julian's cooking area. His examination of the first chair yielded nothing, but his second inspection showed scratches near the bottom of the front legs. Calling Musgrave over, the detective asked him if he knew what had caused them.

"No idea. I never even noticed them until you pointed them out." Bentley bent down to peer more closely at the markings. He then repeated the exercise on the other two chairs. There was only one with such scrapes. Hefting up the chair to get a better look, his eyes confirmed his suspicions. These marks were fresh. They showed no signs of discoloration. The detective breathed a sigh of resignation. It was now clear what had happened. Musgrave's involvement with the Service was compromised. Someone knew what he did for a living, and that someone told someone else, et cetera, et cetera. "Julian, I need you to think very carefully. Outside the Service, who knows you work for MI5? Anyone you can think of; friends, parents, anyone."

The young agent sat down on one of the kitchen chairs, making sure it wasn't that chair. "I... I..."

"Julian, this is no time to be coy. Who knows?" "Only one person, I promise."

"For God's sake, man, do I have to drag it out of you? Who knows?"

"My father. I told my father."

* * *

It was a decision he had to make. Did he go to Kell now or interview Julian's M.P. father and see what that discussion turned up? To hell with it. There had been enough foul-ups by the Service already. He would handle this situation his way. Frankly, the whole of the organization was filled with amateurs. Well, maybe not the whole Service, but too many to make him feel comfortable sharing what he knew with anyone else, and that included Kell. It was true they had been successful in tracking and foiling German attempts at infiltration, but Bentley believed that had been more by luck than judgment.

The House was about to go into a Division when Bentley arrived. Even he did not have the authority to disrupt the workings of the world's greatest democracy, so he waited until the vote was over. He then sought out Greville Musgrave. It was unlikely, although not impossible, that Julian's own father would have disclosed his son's position with a potentially hostile power, but someone had. If it wasn't Musgrave himself, then it had to be someone the M.P. had told. A careless word, a casual, unguarded reference, who knew? After asking a few Members, Bentley tracked him down. Musgrave looked to be in a serious discussion with a fellow Member, but the detective's mission was much more urgent.

Inserting himself between the two men, Bentley pulled out his warrant card, offering his apologies for interrupting their impromptu meeting. "Mr. Musgrave, might I have a word with you in private? It won't take too long, sir." Musgrave looked nonplussed as he glanced from Bentley's identification to his parliamentary colleague. "It is rather urgent, sir, if you don't mind." The detective insisted.

As Musgrave's fellow M.P. politely moved away, Musgrave asked, "What's this all about? Couldn't it have waited until after we had concluded our debate?"

"I'm afraid not, Mr. Musgrave. It's about your son."

Musgrave turned pale. "Julian? Is he alright? Has something happened to him? What's...?"

"No, it's nothing like that. Your son is fine. Is there somewhere we can talk privately?"

Musgrave led them to his private office. After they were seated, Bentley asked, "Mr. Musgrave, do you know what your son's occupation is?"

The M.P. looked taken aback at the question. "I... I don't know what you mean exactly," he stammered.

"It's not a difficult question. Do you know who your son's employer is?"

"I'm not sure if I should tell you, but if you're asking me, I suspect you already know the answer. Would I be correct?"

Bentley smiled reassuringly. "Please, just answer the question, sir."

"Very well. He works for the Security Service, and that's all I'm telling you until you let me know what this is all about."

"I can't tell you too much at the moment, but what I can say is that your son is in some trouble, and perhaps you can help him."

"Yes, of course. Whatever I can do."

"Who else did you tell that your son works for the security services?"

"Who else did I tell? That presumes I told anyone at all, and I assure you, I did no such thing. I don't have to be reminded of...." Musgrave bristled.

"Mr. Musgrave, I make no apologies for asking you again. Who else besides you knows of Julian's involvement with the Security Service? Please think, sir. It's very important."

"And I told you, I..." he trailed off.

"Yes?"

"Well, naturally, I may have mentioned it to Lord Rhodes-Willingham – Viscount Rhodes-Willingham. We go back a long way. He... he helped me gain my start in government."

"Yes, I know. Julian told me the whole thing." Bentley said without emotion. "When did you tell Viscount Rhodes-Willingham about Julian?"

"About six months ago, I think. But His Lordship is a sound man. He's a member of the Upper House, for God's sake. If you think he's involved with whatever Julian is mixed up in, you're quite mistaken, I assure you."

"So that would have been around February, yes?"

"I suppose so. Perhaps earlier, January, maybe."

"Could it have been earlier?"

"No. I only found out myself around the middle of January."

"Now, I need you to think very carefully, Mr. Musgrave. Apart from His Lordship, is there anyone else, anyone else," he emphasized, "in whom you may have confided? Think. Take your time. This is most important."

For perhaps half a minute, Musgrave stared into the middle distance. "No. I can definitely say that apart from His Lordship, I told no one."

"Fine. I must ask you not to discuss this conversation with anyone, even your wife, and especially the Viscount. Do I make myself clear?"

"Yes, but..."

"No 'buts', Mr. Musgrave, no exceptions. Your son's career, perhaps his life, might depend upon your silence. Do you understand?"

"Yes. You've made your point. Can't you give me even a hint of what's wrong?"

"No, sir, I'm afraid I can't." Although Bentley displayed no interest in Musgrave's information, alarm bells went off inside his head. Rhodes-Willingham was known to have been an infrequent visitor to the German embassy, and it was rumored that the incoming ambassador, Joachim von Ribbentrop, had spent at least one weekend at Rhodes-Willingham's country estate in Northamptonshire. It could, of course, all be coincidental, but then again...

After thanking Musgrave for his help, Bentley went in search of the viscount. It did not take long for the detective-spy to discover that he spent most afternoons at *Boodles* on Pall Mall. This establishment was an exclusive club mainly frequented by the aristocracy and senior politicians. It had a strict policy of not admitting any women as members.

It was only a drive of a few minutes for Bentley to park his car outside the Georgian building. Despite showing his warrant card to the duty attendant, the flunky showed no urgency as he deigned to see if His Lordship would consider giving the detective inspector a few minutes of his time. It did not take long for the attendant to return and announce that it was not convenient at the moment. Perhaps some other time might be better. Bentley whispered a few words into the servant's ear, causing him to hurry off in a panic. The man was back within a few seconds, deferentially escorting Bentley into the Viscount's presence.

Even before the peer uttered a single syllable, Bentley knew who was striding purposefully toward him. His manner, his bearing, and his expression of arrogant aloofness reflected his aristocratic personality. Standing at just over six feet, the Viscount sported a mane of black hair, graying at the temples. He was clean-shaven, his deep-set eyes two pinpricks of undisguised contempt as he approached the police officer. "I must say, Detective Inspector, I do not take kindly to anyone strong-arming my man to get an interview with me. There was really no need to threaten to send several black Marias down here. We don't tolerate that sort of thing, you know. I have a good mind to make a formal complaint to your superiors about your behavior."

"Well, I'm glad Your Lordship was able to get that off his chest. Now, can we please get down as to why I'm here?"

"And why are you here, exactly?"

"Your Lordship, with the greatest respect, I think you'll find this interview will go much quicker if you allow me to ask the questions and you to answer them."

"How dare you?" the peer exploded. "Do you know who I am?"

Yes, thought Bentley acidly, and I also know what you are. He retorted quietly, "Your Lordship, I am here on a matter of national security. I need to ask you a few questions."

"Questions? What questions? And if it's a matter of national security, why is a lowly detective inspector here, and not someone from Special Branch, or the security services?"

"That's a good point, sir. I can, of course, arrange for someone from either of these two branches to attend instead, but then it might, well, might get to the ears of certain people of your standing, so to speak. Become official, if you see what I mean, with a record of the meeting being kept and all that. I thought it would be better to handle it this way. More discrete, you understand. That way, it might stay just between the two of us."

"So this is an unofficial visit then, is it?"

"You could put it like that, sir." Yes, you could, thought Bentley. You could put it like that, but you'd be dead wrong. This was as official as it could get.

"What is it you want to know?" the peer asked impatiently.

"How well do you know Greville Musgrave?"

"Musgrave? Yes, I know Musgrave. We see each other occasionally. Meet for drinks and a bit of a catch-up now and again. Why, what's he done?"

Ignoring the question, Bentley went on, "How well do you know his son?"

"Julian? Yes, well, I've met him a couple of times. Nice young man."

"Do you know what Julian does for a living, Viscount Rhodes-Willingham?"

The peer hesitated. "Why do you want to know?" then it dawned. "Ah, you do know, and you want to see if I do, too, is that it?"

"Please, Your Lordship, I don't have time for this. Just answer my question. Are you familiar with Julian's occupation?"

"Yes. He works for MI5. His father told me; in confidence, you understand."

"Might you have told anyone else? Casually, perhaps? In passing, you know? Just a slip of the tongue, maybe?"

"How dare you?" Rhodes-Willingham spluttered. "Get out! I want you to leave right now or, by God, I'll have you thrown out!"

"I'm not ready to leave just yet, Your Lordship, and all your bluster won't change that. Now calm down. I've got a few more questions for you."

"Well, ask your damn questions and be done with it. And I'm still going to complain to your Chief Constable, who I know personally, by the way."

"Let's get on with this, shall we, sir?" retorted Bentley, ignoring the peer's threat. "I believe you're friendly with the incoming German ambassador. Would that be correct?"

"Who my friends are is of no concern to you!" Rhodes-Willingham snapped.

"Just answer the question please, sir."

"Yes, I know von Ribbentrop. What of it? Are you suggesting that I told a foreign power, even a benign foreign power, that the son of one of my acquaintances is an MI5 spy? That's absurd. Preposterous. I would never do such a thing. I am a loyal subject of His Majesty."

It was very telling, thought Bentley, that he referred to the soon-to-be German ambassador as a friend while talking about Musgrave as an acquaintance. And thinking Germany was a benign nation under that warmongering tyrant, His Lordship was deluding no one but himself. "How often have you visited the German embassy, Lord Rhodes-Willingham?"

"Now, see here...." He could see that the detective was not to be deflected. "Oh, I don't know. Three, four times, perhaps."

"And what do you discuss?"

"I don't know. Just general day-to-day issues, nothing you can't read in the newspapers or hear on the wireless."

"So, nothing of import. Nothing that you might debate in the Upper House or in Committee?"

"I've already told you, no. I'm always cautious what I discuss with the temporary ambassador, just as I shall be with Herr von Ribbentrop when he takes up his appointment. I am well aware of my duties to the Crown."

"Quite so. And has the new ambassador visited you at your home?"

"Yes, he's been to my place in Northampton as my guest once or twice."

"Which is it? Once or twice."

"I don't like your tone, Detective Inspector. I'm complying with your request, so please don't take that high-handed attitude with me if you'd be so kind."

'High-handed attitude?' That was a laugh, coming from him, smiled Bentley to himself.

"To answer your question, I believe he's been up twice. Yes, twice," the peer confirmed.

"And was anyone else there, when von Ribbentrop was a guest?"

"No. Only him, and my family, of course."

"And that would be your wife Marjory and your younger son Reginald, yes?"

"Yes. My older son, Clarence, is some sort of finance guru in the City. Not quite sure what he does," Rhodes-Willingham sniffed. "He'll inherit my seat eventually. Still, it keeps him out of mischief, I suppose. He's got a place in Knightsbridge. Handy for Harrods and all that."

"But your younger son still lives at home?"

"Yes. He's tried moving out once or twice, but it's never seemed to work out. He's like a bloody Australian boomerang. No matter how far you throw it, it always comes back."

"I believe Reginald and Julian Musgrave were at Harrow together."

Rhodes-Willingham coughed. "Yes, for a short while. Julian left after about two years, I seem to recall."

"And would you remember why that was, sir?"

"Why are you asking me? You should ask him, or his father. They'd have a better idea than I."

"I've already spoken to Julian, sir. He told me the whole thing."

"Then why the hell are you asking me?"

"Just for confirmation, sir. Corroboration's a great thing. And you swear you never mentioned Julian to von Ribbentrop or anyone at the German embassy?"

"I've already told you. How often do I have to repeat myself?"

"Very well. I may need to speak to your wife and younger son, sir. What's the best place to see them?"

"You'll do no such thing. Now, I think this interview is concluded. Will you please leave."

"In a minute. I will want to speak to your family, sir. I'll ask you one more time. Where and when can I meet them?" The peer gave Bentley an address in Mayfair.

"Tomorrow, sir. Two o'clock, if that's convenient."

"No, it bloody well is not convenient, but they'll be there. It's where we usually stay when the House is sitting."

"One more thing, sir, then I'll go."

"Yes, what do you want to know?"

"Does your son still see Julian?"

"No. We felt it was better for the boys not to come into contact with each other after the... incident. As far as I know, Reginald and Julian haven't met or spoken for almost sixteen years."

Maybe that was true, or maybe it wasn't, but one thing was for sure. The key to the mystery of how Julian's cover was blown was in the hands of Lord Rhodes-Willingham, whether or not he knew it.

CHAPTER 7

London, England, August 1936

King Edward had now returned from his vacation and was looking tanned and fit. His attitude to his royal duties and responsibilities, however, had not changed. He barely glanced at the documents sent to him in the red cases, detailing the important briefings discussed in parliament of which, as monarch, he needed to be aware. They were mundane, boring tractates of which he had little interest.

With his friend's character so unpredictable, Sir Walter Monckton wasn't sure how he would react to the news. He would have preferred not to have disclosed the Security Service's seditious intrigue against Edward, but Kell was not the kind of man to let this go. Monckton would be in serious trouble for collaborating with a foreign power, albeit in his King's service. He doubted if Colonel Kell would see it that way. Despite Kell's known dislike and distrust of the King, Monckton would need the support of the one man who could put the spymaster in his place. It was the only way.

Sitting in the blue drawing-room which adjoined the cross gallery to its south, Monckton cleared his throat before starting. "Your Majesty, a situation has arisen of which I believe you should be made cognizant."

"For heaven's sake, Monckton, how often do I have to tell you? Titles are only for formality. When we're alone, you may address me by name. We've surely known each other long enough to forego such tiresome protocols."

"Very well, David, as I said, a situation has come to my attention of which I think you should be aware."

"Oh dear, is it going to be one of those tedious and boring political things?"

"No. I'm afraid it's something much more, er, personal."

"Well, you've got my full and undivided attention. Now, what's on your mind?" So Monckton told him everything. It took the King a few seconds to process the information his counselor had related to him. Monckton was well aware of the King's lack of intellectual acuity. He had failed miserably at university, having left Magdalen College, Oxford, without attaining any degree or diploma. Despite Edward's lack of academic brilliance, Monckton thought he would at least be smart enough to understand the news he had just imparted; the fact that his own intelligence organization was complicit in the plot to assassinate him. But all Edward could do was to stare blankly at his friend. "I don't understand, Walter. Why would they want to have me killed? What harm have I done them? I'm their King, for goodness' sake. I could have them all hanged for treason."

"Yes, but it would probably be for the best if you didn't," Monckton quipped, trying to lighten the atmosphere.

"And they were all in on it?"

"Well, Kell was in overall charge, but I believe Sir John Simon also knew. It might even have been him who gave the go-ahead. At any event, it would have to have been a political decision taken at the highest level."

"I am the highest level!" Edward screamed.

"Of course, Your Majesty, er, David. I only meant...."

"I know what you meant, Walter. I'm sorry I lost my temper just now. Everyone! All of them, treacherous and disloyal. To their sovereign, their monarch, their King! Apart from you, I don't know who to trust anymore."

But for how much longer, Monckton thought. For how much longer?

* * *

Things were now getting much more serious. So the detective, Bentley, had been to interview Rhodes-Willingham at his club. The policeman was now becoming a dangerous liability and would have to be silenced before he could become even more troublesome. But first, he would need to reveal what he knew before they could take care of him. The peer would have told him nothing. Of that, he was sure, but Bentley was not the type of officer to give up that easily. He had a solid reputation as a dogged and relentless investigator. If he were Bentley, what would he do next? Follow His Lordship; that's what he would do. So the stranger decided to take his own advice. If Bentley did, indeed, follow the peer, then he, too, would have a shadow. A shadow with a much higher calling and with more deadly intent.

* * *

Monckton had been correct. Colonel Vernon Kell, 'K,' was not the type of man to give up easily and had summoned the King's lawyer back to his office, and this time, he was not alone. Sitting with him were James Whitehead and Sir John Simon. But Monckton had also brought someone with him. His friend, King Edward the Eighth. If this had been a game of chess, thought Monckton, it would be hard to predict whose 'king' would be the one to be toppled.

Trying to disregard the presence of his monarch, Kell addressed Monckton directly. "Sir Walter, we all know why you're here, so I'll come straight to the point. This is no longer a request. You must answer my question. How did you know about the Service's involvement in, er, the situation regarding His Majesty?" deferring to the King who was sitting nonchalantly with his legs crossed beside his mentor and who remained noticeably silent.

"I'm afraid I'm not prepared to answer any questions of that nature, Colonel Kell. Quite frankly, I've come here out of a sense of courtesy, but I doubt we'll get much farther than the last time we spoke."

"And I'm afraid I'm not prepared to put up with any more of this sanctimonious hypocrisy. One of my officers was beaten and probably drugged to get him to reveal his knowledge of this situation. I'm convinced beyond all doubt that it was he who divulged this intelligence, but I'm just as equally certain that he did not do so willingly. With the greatest respect to His Majesty, no one in this country, even him or you, is above the law. Now, In the presence of the King, and the Home Secretary, I demand you divulge where this knowledge emanated from – unless you, yourself, wish to confess to the assault on my man."

"Don't be so ridiculous."

Brigadier Whitehead interjected. "Sir Walter, while we are within this office, only we five know of your involvement. I would like to keep it that way, naturally, but you know how these things eventually find their way into the newspapers. I'm sure the public would not wish to see their monarch embroiled in the discreditable case of a British man, a member of the intelligence service, no less, being beaten up and drugged by the confederate of a close adviser to His Majesty."

"But I don't even know who this man is. I was completely unaware of the circumstances you've just described."

"I'm afraid that's not how the press will see it. I'll make damn sure of that. Let me make it as plain as I can." Turning to the King, Whitehead continued, "Your Majesty may know that in certain quarters he is not held in the high esteem that befits his position as ruler of this country. This situation is mainly due to Your Majesty's association with a certain American lady. Your Majesty's position is precarious enough at the moment without a further scandal to jeopardize your reign. We are also not unaware of Your Majesty's association with a certain foreign power whose ideology and philosophic policies are diametrically opposite to those of the British people."

"You would stoop to blackmail? You would seek to coerce the sovereign of the British people?" Monckton shouted.

"Sir Walter, there is no action I would not take to safeguard the safety and welfare of the people of this country. No action. Do you understand?"

For the first time since entering Kell's office, Edward spoke up. "Now see here...."

"No, Your Majesty. I will not 'see here.' Your lawyer has been involved in some serious underhand activities, which I'm going to get to the bottom of, with or without his help."

Monckton now accepted that his ruse to involve the King had drastically backfired. Kell was made of sterner stuff than he had believed. "May I have a word with His Majesty in private?"

"You have two minutes," Kell assented.

As was customary, all remained seated until Edward rose from his chair. The other men then stood in courteous deference, although neither Kell nor Whitehead felt respect for their dissolute monarch. Monckton followed Edward out of the room into the reception area, where they were alone. Monckton then discussed some issues with his friend before returning to Kell's office.

It was a few seconds after the allotted time when they went back into the room. Monckton took off his round-framed spectacles and polished them before he started to speak. "I must first make it clear that His Majesty knew nothing of the matter I am about to discuss. I wish that to be duly noted."

"Very well, it is duly noted," replied Kell impatiently. "Now, let's have it."

So Monckton gave it to them. All of it.

After he had finished, Sir John Simon said, "But it still doesn't answer the question as to who told Canaris that young Musgrave worked for the Security Service. We're still no further forward on that score."

A very contrite Monckton added, "And on that matter, gentlemen, I cannot help you. I am truly sorry for the upset I've caused, but I don't know who betrayed Musgrave's name."

"I accept what you say, Sir Walter, but you are by no means out of the woods. This is a grave breach of security, receiving secret messages from the head of German intelligence." Kell shook his head. "It is only because of your loyal devotion to His Majesty that I'm not having you taken away right now. But I will be instigating a formal inquiry, and I expect your fullest cooperation. Is that clear?"

"Yes, Colonel Kell." The security director could not help but notice that the King stayed silent during this time. He did not intercede on his lawyer friend's behalf. It might have meant nothing, but then again, it might have meant something far more significant.

* * *

The stranger kept a close, unobtrusive watch on Bentley. He was surprised when the detective did not appear to be acting in the manner he had anticipated. Far from keeping covert watch on the peer, Bentley drove away after leaving *Boodles*. He did not remain close by, as the stranger had expected him to do. Did this mean that Rhodes-Willingham had said something useful enough to allow the police officer to pursue his investigation elsewhere? This was now becoming worrying. He could put it off no longer. It was time to act, and he would need to act tonight.

Finding Bentley's home address had not been difficult. The stranger also found out that Bentley was married. It was always good to know these things. Knowledge was power, and the more one knew about one's adversary, the easier it would be to defeat them. But it still troubled him how an officer from the Metropolitan C.I.D. had become involved in national security matters. Surely that was what the Special Branch was for. Had he been seconded to them for some unknown reason just for this investigation, or were there other factors at play, of which he knew nothing? Well, he'd soon find out. Then he would kill Bentley and his wife.

CHAPTER 8

London, England, August 1936

It was 11.30 p.m., and the lights in the Bentley household had been out for almost an hour. They would be asleep by now in their semi-detached villa in Barnet, north of London. He doubted it would be as easy to subdue Bentley as it had been with the young intelligence agent. But then again, Bentley had a wife...

He parked his Austin 10 a short distance away and walked through the dark, deserted streets until he stood across the road from Bentley's home. There was no way an experienced policeman like Bentley would leave his front door or downstairs windows unlocked, especially at night. Bounding stealthily across the road, the stranger crept up the side of the property along the driveway until he came to the rear of the house. As he knew it would be, the back door was also locked and probably bolted, but a drainpipe a few feet away provided a possible way in. Glancing upward, he saw that the pipe went past an upstairs window, which looked only around six inches away from the cast iron conduit. The window appeared to be of a casement design, meaning that it slid up and down and would be secured by a simple bolt at the bottom. Releasing the catch would be child's play. His employers had taught him well, and he had been a willing student. Like most people, including time-served officers, Bentley would not have thought to secure an upper-story window. The risk of entry was remote, and many households had become complacent, often to their cost. Even if he had locked them, they would not be as steadfast as the windows and doors at ground level. Of this, he was sure.

Gripping the drainpipe with both hands, the stranger scaled the wall, using his rubber-soled shoes as counter purchase. When he drew his body level with the upper-floor window, he slipped a blade from his inside pocket, sliding it silently through the wafer-thin gap between the bottom of the window and the frame. The titanium-hardened blade sliced across the narrow space, seeking the latch which secured the window. As he thought, it was not fastened as securely as it should have been, and the stranger had no trouble in sliding the bolt away from its retainer. Carefully withdrawing his tool, the intruder slowly slid the window upwards. His success would now depend on how well Bentley maintained his home. These old wooden windows had a habit of warping due to rain and moisture if they were not adequately protected. To avoid weather damage, it was usually necessary to paint or varnish them once or twice a year.

It seemed that Bentley did, after all, take care of his property. The window slid silently up, and, using his back as a brace against the window sliding back down, the stranger stole into the darkened house before quietly lowering it again. The room he found himself in was empty, save for a bed and a chest of drawers. It was no doubt a spare room used only when they had staying guests. He waited a few seconds to allow his eyes to become accustomed to the darkness before venturing out of the room. He carried a flashlight but dared not use it in case the unusual glare disturbed the sleeping incumbents. There would be time enough for illumination later. Creeping gently around the landing, he heard the measured, rhythmic breathing of the two occupants in the main bedroom. The door was ajar. It would be even easier than he anticipated.

As he pushed the door open, Deborah Bentley snored, unintentionally kicking her husband as she turned restlessly around. Being the light sleeper he was, the detective instinctively opened his eyes for a second as the stranger lunged toward him. Unsure if he was hallucinating or was momentarily awake, he nonetheless instinctively pushed his hands out in front of him at the dark shape coming toward him. Before he could react further, the stranger was on top of him, forcing him down on the bed with his left hand while searching for his hypodermic with the other. Bentley's legs were becoming more entangled in the bedclothes as he strove to free himself while the stranger pulled out his syringe.

The tussle awoke Deborah, who screamed at the sight of the two struggling men, distracting the stranger for the merest of seconds. As he turned to look at the terrified face of the detective's wife, Bentley punched him, but his fist hardly connected with his assailant's jaw. The stranger swatted Bentley's clenched fist aside as he reached for the detective's arm to insert the needle. As he was about to plunge the hypodermic into Bentley's muscle, Deborah stabbed the stranger's hand that held the syringe, causing him to drop it in pain and shock. His blood was pouring onto the bedclothes as he arched back, pulling out a knife of his own with his other hand, one longer and more deadly than that used on him. But it was too late. He had lost the element of surprise, and Bentley was now fully awake and galvanized into action. Grabbing the stranger's wrist with his hand, he twisted it outwards, not stopping until he heard a satisfying snap as the weapon fell onto the floor. The stranger yelped in pain, shouting as he tried to retaliate ineffectually with his other wounded hand. Bentley threw himself out of the blankets and head-butted the stranger as both men rolled off the bed.

This time he did connect, and blood immediately flowed from the stranger's nose, his eyes losing focus as he hit the floor. Bentley was on top of him now, punching him remorselessly about the face. Again and again, he struck his would-be interrogator until the stranger's face was nothing but a bloody mess of flesh and tissue. His eyes were almost punched out of their sockets, his nose an obscene pulpy mush gushing with blood and snot, and his mouth and lips hanging loosely, showing the few remaining teeth the detective-spy had not knocked out.

Bentley had tired himself out in his frenzy and was slowly calming down while still sitting astride the unconscious man. He had accepted danger as part of his job. The phrase he had heard was 'an occupational hazard.' But not for Deborah. She was a civilian, an innocent bystander who had no place in his world, a world of violence, malevolence, and death in its many brutal forms. It took a few minutes for his adrenalin to return to anywhere near normal. Looking up at his wife in the darkness, he asked her if she was alright.

"No, I don't think I am," she replied, and then she swooned back onto the bed.

She recovered a few minutes later, by which time Bentley had hoisted their attacker onto the only chair in the room and switched on both bedside lamps. He had doused the stranger with water, then slapped him a few times to arouse him. There was no need to tie him. He was in no condition to cause trouble. Bentley had seen to that. To be sure, the detective had searched his pockets, removing the sharp tool he had used to gain entry along with another knife and, of all things, a garrote. This made Bentley shiver all the more, not for himself but for the woman who was now standing behind him. "Alan..." he heard her mumble.

He smiled as he turned to face her. "Never let me scold you again for taking fruit into bed, darling." He said softly.

* * *

They were sitting in Whitehead's office the following morning. In the room was Whitehead himself, Bentley, Colonel Kell, and Julian Musgrave. They had tried to interrogate the stranger last night, but he had been in no condition to answer any of their questions, even if he wanted to. Bentley had beaten him so savagely, the man could barely talk. Earlier this morning, all the stranger demanded, when they could finally understand him, was that he should see someone from the German embassy. They would demand his release, and if this was not forthcoming, great friction would occur between Britain and Germany. Colonel Kell had brought the belligerent man down to earth with the unwelcome truth that when they had explained to the German ambassador what he had done and had attempted to do, they would probably deny any knowledge of him.

"So, is he the man who beat you?" asked Kell of Musgrave.

"I... I'm not sure. I think so, but I can't be certain."

"I think we'll have to assume it was," suggested Bentley. He had found the syringe which had rolled under the bed. It was now beyond doubt that this was how they, whoever 'they' were, found out what they had and how the assailant had been aware of Bentley's involvement. The stranger had somehow befriended Musgrave and then beaten and drugged him. "I might find out more when I see Lady Rhodes-Willingham and her son this afternoon."

"Are you O.K., Alan?" Whitehead asked solicitously. "You've had quite a night of it. How's your wife? Is she alright?"

"It's thanks to her that I'm here. Yes, she's over the worst of it, I think. No, I need to see Her Ladyship and their son as soon as possible. It's even more urgent now, don't you think?"

"Well, if you feel up to it."

"Up to it? You bloody well bet I'm up to it. That bastard might have killed us last night, and I think Rhodes-Willingham's up to his neck in it. Oh, I'd love to get His Lordship for something, just to take that smug, supercilious look off his aristocratic face."

"We'll keep questioning your attacker and see if he tells us anything else, though I doubt he will."

"Me neither, but you never know. If we convince him that his embassy's disowned him and that he'll most likely spend a good deal of time in a British nick with loyal, patriotic villains who'd like nothing more than to repeat what I did to him, he might have second thoughts," Bentley said hopefully.

* * *

The detective-spy arrived at the Mayfair address a little before two o'clock. He assumed it would be just Lady Rhodes-Willingham and her younger son, Reginald, who would be in, but the Viscount was also there.

"Right, let's get this over with, then you can leave. After this afternoon, I wish never to see you again. Is that understood?" Rhodes-Willingham demanded.

"I will try my hardest to accommodate Your Lordship's request," replied Bentley, wondering if the peer would appreciate the irony. "If I may so bold as to ask, why did Your Lordship feel it necessary to be here. I believed we had concluded our discussions yesterday. I was not expecting you, not that I would ever tire of Your Lordship's charm and noble grace."

The peer either did not notice or chose to ignore Bentley's acerbic compliment. "After the way you tried to bully and cajole me yesterday, I felt it necessary to be here to safeguard my wife and son from your strong-arm tactics. I believe I am within my rights to be in my wife's presence when you speak to her."

"I would have it no other way, Your Lordship."

"Right, let's begin. I have some important meetings later."

Bentley suggested they would all be more comfortable seated, suggesting four of the dining chairs placed around the formal table. Grudgingly accepting the detective's advice, the peer pulled out a chair for his wife before taking his place beside her. A sulky-looking Reginald sat at the other side of his mother, and Bentley chose the seat across the table facing directly toward Lady Rhodes-Willingham.

Last night's adventure still played heavily on Bentley's mind, and he wondered just how much the peer knew about the incident. Did he really have no involvement in Musgrave's attack, or was he a supporter of Hitler? Facing the Viscount's wife, the detective took stock of the woman sitting in front of him. He estimated her to be in her mid-fifties, which meant she must have had her older son when she was about twenty years old. Rather young for a lady of such high nobility to have borne a son at such an early age, he thought. She certainly had her husband's haughtiness and arrogance, barely able to keep from looking anywhere but at him directly. He was making her feel uncomfortable. Good. That was just how he wanted her to feel, and he hadn't even opened his mouth yet.

She was wearing what looked like a Norman Hartnell creation. A postbox-red calf-length dress with black piping and shoulder-length bouffant sleeves. It was quite a striking outfit. Deborah had seen it, or something similar, in a fashion magazine a couple of weeks earlier and had pointed it out to her less-than-interested husband. His only response was how she had expected him to afford such a garment on a copper's wages. The peeress's neck was adorned with a double string of pearls accompanied by a set of matching earrings. Her make-up and hairstyle were subtle but effective, and people who had not had his training might take her for ten years younger. She had probably been striking in her youth, but Bentley doubted that she had ever been beautiful, not like Deborah. The detective began gently. No point rushing in like a bull at a gate if she was unaware of anything. It would only antagonize and alienate her, and this was the last thing he wanted. He might need her as compliant as possible if his instincts proved correct.

As he was about to start, he noticed that she was clutching not her husband's arm but her son's. "Lady Rhodes-Willingham," Bentley began before the woman interrupted him. "Detective Inspector Bentley, we'll get along much quicker if you just call me by my first name – Marjory – otherwise, we'll be here all day." She smiled.

Bentley returned her smile. Maybe he had been wrong about her. Perhaps she wasn't as big a snob as he'd taken her for. Her husband turned to her, giving her a look of disdain, but said nothing. "Very well, Marjory, I understand you have played hostess to the incoming German ambassador, Joachim von Ribbentrop. Is that correct?"

"I already said as much." Her irate husband interjected. Bentley turned to face the peer. "As you and I discussed a moment ago, Your Lordship, we had our little conference yesterday. I'm now addressing your wife. Will you please allow her to answer the question by herself?" His Lordship harrumphed but otherwise remained silent. He knew that despite his exalted position, this detective was not going to be intimidated by him. Returning his gaze toward Marjory, he nodded for her to continue. "It is as my husband says. Herr von Ribbentrop has been to our home in Northampton once or twice. Twice, I think."

Reginald spoke up for the first time. He would have been about thirty years old, with short, sharply Brilliantined hair parted in the middle. He also smelled as if he used cologne. Only a certain type of man uses scent, thought Bentley to himself, but then again, this was now the nineteen-thirties. Times were changing. Maybe he just wanted to smell nice. Above-average height, he sat as erect as he stood. Bentley wondered if he had had any training at Sandhurst military academy. He certainly had the bearing and the mien of a soldier. He wore a gray, two-piece business suit, which looked like it cost more than Bentley made in a year. "Is all this questioning strictly necessary?" he asked impatiently. "My father told us how you treated him yesterday. I must say, I don't know what the world is coming to when men of the lower orders speak to their betters in such a discourteous manner."

Bentley turned his attention to Reginald. "Sir, I have a job to do, and I must confess there are some aspects of it that I find distasteful, but the job still has to be done. Now can we please get on? I am sure you have better things to be getting on with than to be interrogated by a member of the 'lower orders.'"

"Yes, well, just don't go upsetting Mother too much."

Bentley looked at his watch. His message was clear. His time, also, was valuable, too valuable to be wasted on speaking to people whose wealth was matched only by their vanity and sense of entitlement. Returning his attention to Viscountess Rhodes-Willingham, he continued, "I understand your husband is friendly with Greville Musgrave, the M.P."

"Yes, I believe he is."

"And are you friendly with Mrs. Musgrave?"

"There is no 'Mrs. Musgrave.' I believe she died a short while ago. I would have thought you would have known that."

Yes, agreed Bentley inwardly, I bloody well should have. And I've got the cheek to call myself a detective. Just as well Whitehead's not here. He'd have my guts for garters for making a blunder like that. Allowing her barbed retort to die away, he asked her, "And you never see Mr. Musgrave on your own?"

The Viscountess clutched at her pearls in mock distress. "I'm not sure what you're suggesting, but I take great exception to what I think you are implying. I have only met Greville Musgrave twice and was with my husband on each occasion. How dare you insinuate otherwise? The whole idea is utterly preposterous." She gasped. Her husband nodded sagely. The lady doth protest too much, methinks, thought Bentley, remembering Hamlet. "I was suggesting nothing of the kind, Your Ladyship. A member of the security service's identity has been compromised, and highly confidential information was forcibly extracted from him, probably while he was drugged. This situation is a serious breach of security and could harm the safety of this country. Only a very small number of people know what he does for a living. Now, I've already established that your husband is one of that small group, so you will understand that I need to find out how many more there are. Please understand me when I tell you that I will get to the bottom of this, no matter what, and I have the support of the top echelon to do so. That's how important they are taking this, so please let's have no more histrionics." It may have been his imagination, but Bentley could have sworn that he saw Reginald visibly squirm.

"I give you my word that neither Greville Musgrave nor my husband, nor anyone else ever disclosed any information to me about Julian Musgrave. I cannot make it any clearer than that."

"No, indeed, Your Ladyship, you cannot." In a more conciliatory tone, he added, "And I'm sorry for any upset I may have caused you just now. It was not meant, I assure you."

Turning to address Reginald, the detective asked him what he did for a living. The question seemed to amuse the peer's younger son. "Do for a living? Work, you mean? Well, I..."

"Reginald is still considering his options. He has various avenues open to him, and we are currently deciding which would be the most suitable." The Viscount answered for his son.

"Yes, that's it exactly," the young man concurred. "Still considering my options. Can't be too hasty to rush into anything I might regret later, what?"

"Quite so, sir," the detective responded without further comment. He then asked Reginald, "Do you still keep in touch with Julian Musgrave?"

Reginald hesitated before he answered. "As I'm sure my father will have told you, there was a bit of an, er, misunderstanding when we were at Harrow together. I haven't seen him since he had to, that is, since he left. Once again, I fail to see why you're asking me the same question you asked Father. Musgrave will also verify we haven't seen each other for many years. There. Does that answer your question?" he asked defiantly.

Bentley scratched the back of his neck. "The fact remains that someone betrayed Musgrave to a potential enemy..." He saw Lord Rhodes-

Willingham bristle at this remark, "and the number of people who could have done so is exceedingly small. Outside of the Service and those who needed to know, only two individuals were party to Julian Musgrave's occupation. His father and Your Lordship. I'm convinced that it wasn't his father, so..."

"What makes you so sure it wasn't his father who let something slip? The alternative would have to be that it was my father, and I will not believe that for a second."

"Sir, I have been doing this job for a long time, and I've developed what my bosses have called a 'copper's nose.' I spoke to Greville Musgrave at some length, and I'm absolutely certain he was telling me the truth."

"Which can only mean that you believe I have not," retorted the peer with asperity.

"You see, that's the thing, Your Lordship, I believe you as well. That's what's troubling me so much. If you did reveal Musgrave's job, I honestly believe you were not aware you had done so, but from speaking to you yesterday, I do not think that is the case, despite your familiarity with the new German representative. If it wasn't Musgrave or you... I'm sure the answer's staring me in the face, and I just can't see it. I must confess, I'm stumped.

"Well, perhaps you can be 'stumped' elsewhere. If you're quite finished...." The Viscount's son smiled without humor.

Turning to her son, the peeress asked him, "Did you tell the detective that you've also been to the German embassy? We need to be open and transparent; otherwise, it will look as if we have something to hide." She looked to her husband for confirmation.

"Mother, I..." the Viscount's son floundered, lost for words. Bentley did not fail to notice the look of contempt her son drew his mother. "I... it was nothing. It was a social call, nothing more." Reginald looked as if he were about to cry. "I wished to improve my German and thought someone there might be able to tutor me. There was nothing sinister in my visit, I assure you." The peer's son had now lost some of his earlier cockiness. He was fidgeting in his chair and made to stand up, but thought the better of it and remained where he was. He glared disapprovingly at his mother, who merely returned his gaze sweetly before turning toward the detective.

"My son is innocent of any impropriety, I am sure. Why should I not disclose his appointment at the embassy? It was all above board. Indeed, he even showed me the appointment in his diary. Would he have been so open if there had been anything furtive about his visit?"

Bentley's expression gave nothing away. If he looked as though her explanation didn't entirely convince him, he did not show it. But he was now convinced. He knew who had betrayed Julian Musgrave, and what was more, he thought he knew why.

CHAPTER 9

London, England, August 1936

Bentley sat in his car, making notes of his conversation with the Rhodes-Willingham's. It was all coming together, although he had no proof of his deductions. Right now, it was all 'copper's nose,' and how the family had comported themselves during his visit. As he was talking to the peer's son, he started to become convinced that it was he who had undermined his former friend's occupation. It seemed so obvious; Reginald Rhodes-Willingham had become mixed up with the Nazis. The young were much more influenced by Hitler's rhetoric and were easier swayed by his extreme ideals. It was also curious that he had not mentioned his visit to the German embassy. This could, indeed, have been viewed as suspicious, but Bentley finally believed it was as just as the peer's son had explained. No, his suspicions had been aroused much earlier and from a different source.

It started the first time he had mentioned the German ambassador. Although she must have known he was bound to refer to von Ribbentrop, Lady Willingham could not stop herself from touching her pearl necklace when Bentley spoke his name. She had done the same thing, of course, when she believed he had tried to imply a romantic connection between her and the M.P. But this was different. Bentley played poker and could spot a 'tell' when he saw it. An unconscious sign that a player had a good hand. In Lady Rhodes-Willingham's case, he believed it was something altogether different. Her face reddened when he mentioned von Ribbentrop's name, appearing flustered and shaken, further convincing him there was a romantic liaison between them. The necklace may also have been a secret gift from the German diplomat, hence her unconscious desire to seek comfort from it when confronted with his name. Even her dress gave her away. Red and black - the colors of the Nazi emblem. She was taunting her husband right to his face, and he did not see it. He was as loyal to his country as he claimed. Unfortunately, it looked as if his wife were not so patriotic.

There was one more reaction that convinced him of her duplicity. When he, Bentley, admitted he was 'stumped' but implied the answer was close by, Marjory lost no time in trying to implicate her son, her own son, to deflect attention away from herself. All circumstantial, unfortunately, but his 'copper's nose' was seldom wrong. He was as sure as he could be that it was Lady Rhodes-Willingham who had somehow found out about Julian Musgrave and had given this intelligence to the *Abwehr*.

He had been honest when he said he believed that Lord Rhodes-Willingham had not knowingly betrayed young Musgrave. But what about unwittingly? It had been the Viscountess herself who had given him the idea of how she had been treacherous to her husband. She had tried to insinuate that Reginald was the guilty one by claiming that he had shown his mother the diary entry confirming his appointment at the German embassy. Was it possible that the Viscount kept a diary? No doubt he would have an official one to keep track of his appointments and engagements. But did he also keep a personal one, a journal that was meant for no eyes but his own? And if so, would he have written such sensitive information in it? If the answer to these questions was yes, then the case was almost closed. He would just have to confirm his suspicions. But how?

* * *

He drove back to New Scotland Yard, confronting Whitehead with his observations and suspicions. The Assistant Commissioner was thunderstruck. "Lady Rhodes-Willingham is a German spy? You can't be serious, man. Her lineage goes back generations. She's as British as you can get. It's outrageous."

"She may be British in body, but all my instincts tell me she's a traitor in spirit. We need to prove it, though. Will you help me?"

"Of course, I'll help you, but if you're wrong...."

"I'm not wrong." Bentley insisted.

"If you're wrong, we'll both be looking for new jobs."

"I know I'm right. Trust me."

"You sound like a snake oil salesman," smiled Whitehead. "What do you want me to do?"

"Well, I doubt Viscount Rhodes-Willingham will want to speak to me again after the way I... never mind. You'll have to do it. Phone him and ask him if he keeps a diary. A personal journal, not an official one."

"And if he says yes?"

"Ask him to bring it in."

"And if he tells me to get lost?"

"Tell him it's to do with the defense of the realm. Tell him both the Prime Minister and the Home Secretary have been apprised of the situation. Don't worry; he'll comply if he knows what's good for him. We need to see his diary, his unedited, unexpurgated diary from January this year. But don't tell him why, just that we need to see it."

"And what will you be doing while I have His Lordship in here?"

"Don't worry, Assistant Commissioner. I'll not be at home with my feet up, I assure you."

* * *

Bentley sat outside the Mayfair flat until he was sure the peer and his diary would be on their way to Whitehead's office. The detective had briefed the senior policeman on the questions he should ask, although he already knew the answers. He trusted Reginald would be out, doing what young wealthy and spoiled loafers with indulgent parents usually did – loaf. He needed Marjory Rhodes-Willingham to be by herself. He knocked on the door, surprised at how quickly she opened it. "I didn't think you'd be here so...," she began and then stopped abruptly, startled at seeing Bentley. "I... oh... Detective Inspector, I wasn't expect... I mean... I... you'll have to leave. I believe I answered all of your questions earlier. Why have you returned? This is not a good time." She was flustered and obviously embarrassed.

"On the contrary, Lady Rhodes-Willingham, I would say this is a very good time. Mind if I come in?" and, without waiting for a reply, stepped into the apartment.

"You can't stay. You have to go. You're trespassing. You're a police officer. You should know you can't come into my house without my consent. Now leave, or I'll...."

"Call the police?" Bentley suggested helpfully. "They're already here, in case you hadn't noticed, but I'll be more than happy to stay until my colleagues arrive. Then we can all have a nice little chat."

"What do you want?" she asked in evident distress.

"Who did you think I was just now? It wasn't your husband, and I notice you're wearing a different perfume from when I was here the last time. Is that the one he prefers?"

"He prefers?"

"Oh, come now, Marjory. Don't be so coy. We both know who you thought I was. You were expecting Herr von Ribbentrop, weren't you?"

"How dare you?" she challenged him. What do you mean by coming here to my home and making such outrageous allegations? You've really overstepped the mark this time, Detective Inspector. When my husband gets home, I'm sure he'll have plenty to say about this. Now leave my house this instant, do you hear me?"

"It's no use, Lady Rhodes-Willingham. I know about your, er, dalliance with von Ribbentrop. You as good as told me earlier on."

"I did no such thing!" she stormed back. "I've got no idea what you're talking about. Now you must leave at once."

Bentley could see that although she still spoke with spirit, some of her earlier bluster had gone.

"You can refute it as much as you like, but it won't change the fact that you've been having an affair with Joachim von Ribbentrop. I know this, and there's no use in denying it. You're only delaying the inevitable."

"Having an affair with Joachim von Ribbentrop? Have you completely taken leave of your senses, Detective Inspector? That's absolutely ludicrous." The Peeress countered dismissively.

Bentley replied softly, "Lady Rhodes-Willingham, there is no use in continuing to deny it. I have irrefutable evidence you have been seeing the German." He shook his head sadly. "Unfortunately, you have not been as discrete as you thought you were."

"But you can't have. We were so careful. How...?" The Viscountess finally crumpled. "How do you know? How did you discover...?" she sobbed. "If my husband finds out, I...."

"You've been playing with fire, Your Ladyship. Fire burns. Your only hope to salvage what's left of your marriage is to be honest with me. I can help you out of this mess, but you must answer my questions truthfully. Do you understand?"

The Viscountess glanced at the ornate mantlepiece clock. "Never mind the time. How did you find out about Julian Musgrave? You read your husband's diary, didn't you? Then you passed on the information about Julian Musgrave to the Germans. Quickly, we don't have much time." He was guessing, bluffing as he had never bluffed in his poker-playing life, pushing her to respond, but it was the only answer, he was convinced.

"No!" she screamed before collapsing onto a sofa. "It wasn't like that. I... it was Reginald." She was staring straight at him, but Bentley got the impression that he was not the focus of her attention. It was as if, for that brief second, she was pleading with her husband. She looked almost relieved to be getting this terrible secret off her chest. "I tried to get him to confess when you were here. That's why I mentioned his going to the German embassy. I hoped he would tell you himself, but he lied, and I'm afraid I did not correct what he said. It was Reginald who read my husband's diary then told the Germans. He has become infatuated with the Nazis; he is so impressionable. He... he...oh, God, he worships that horrid little man. Some of the things he says... I can't believe he's my son anymore. He sees them as the way of the future. Please believe me, Detective Inspector, they may be his future, but they are certainly not mine. But he was smart, oh, yes, he was so smart," she said bitterly. "von Ribbentrop has always felt... something... for me. He... he said if I was not... nice... to him, he would see that word got out about Reginald's treachery. Even a hint of his unpatriotic behavior would be disastrous for our family, and Reginald himself, of course."

"Does your husband know any of this?" Bentley asked her.

"No, Montague is completely oblivious to it all. Neither is Reginald aware of the pressure von Ribbentrop has put me under. It will kill him when he finds out that his actions have turned his mother into nothing more than a... a..." The peeress could not finish the sentence as she broke down completely. "What am I to do, Detective Inspector? Please tell me, what can I do?"

Bentley bent down and put his hand on her shoulder. "I have done you a great disservice, Lady Rhodes-Willingham, for which I am truly sorry. I knew it was either you or your son who had betrayed Julian Musgrave, and to my shame, I thought it was you. But you need not worry. A short while ago, I arranged for a telegram to be sent to the incoming German ambassador, advising him that some information has come to light regarding a certain lady of high standing and *Herr von Ribbentrop*. It was made clear that the lady's husband had been made aware of the relationship, and it was an association of which he disapproved. I doubt you will hear from him again."

"But his threat to expose Reginald. How...?"

"I'm afraid von Ribbentrop is the least of your son's worries. He faces a spell in prison. This cannot be avoided, and, quite frankly, after what he did and what he put you through, it is no less than he deserves."

"What about Montague? If he finds out about von Ribbentrop...?"

"He will not hear about it from me, and I doubt Herr von Ribbentrop will rush to admit to his highly disreputable and salacious part in the whole affair. Your secret is safe – Marjory," he smiled.

"I don't know how to thank you, Detective Inspector. But what about Reginald? As much as I abhor what he has done, he is still my son. Is there nothing you can do for him? Please?"

"I'm sorry, Lady Rhodes-Willingham. It is out of my hands, but honestly, even if it were in my power to do something to help him, I would not do it. He has behaved despicably, and even his father's title will not save him, nor should it." She nodded her head in acceptance. The police officer was quite correct. Her son had done a terrible thing. It was only fitting he should pay the price.

"It's funny, Detective Inspector. I suppose strange would be a more appropriate word."

"What is?"

"Many years ago, my husband used his station and title to do a great wrong to Julian."

"Yes, I know about it."

"Don't you see the irony? My husband did what he did to protect the family name and Reginald's expulsion from Harrow. Now it seems as if that name will be forever associated with a far worse crime. I have never believed in divine retribution, but now I'm not so sure." She almost managed a rueful smile.

There wasn't much Bentley could say to that, so he kept quiet. Then he asked her if he could use her telephone. He dialed the main switchboard number at New Scotland Yard, WHI1212, and asked to be put through to the Assistant Commissioner. When Whitehead answered, Bentley asked him, "Is His Lordship with you, Brigadier?"

"He's sitting across from me right now. What did you find out from his wife?"

"I was dead wrong, Brigadier. It wasn't Her Ladyship at all." He heard Whitehead groan.

"My God, Alan, do you know what you've done?" Whitehead's voice rose an octave as he gripped the instrument in his hand. "How am I going to explain this to...?" He didn't mean to be so vociferous in front of the Viscount, but couldn't help himself. Rhodes-Willingham got to his feet, preparing to vent his anger at the Assistant Commissioner. They had obviously got it wrong, whatever it was, and by jingo, someone would pay and pay dearly.

"It was Reginald. And there's a lot more I've got to tell you, but I'll give you the dubious pleasure of advising His Lordship that his son is going to jail."

CHAPTER 10

London, England, December 1936

The stranger had kept silent and refused to say who he was working for, although they already knew who his paymasters were. The security service discovered that his name was Eric White, real name Erich Weiss, a member of the Berlin Nazi party and a suspected *Abwehr* agent. Weiss had a German father and a mother who had grown up in Hackney, hence his ability to mimic a Cockney accent. Thanks to the intelligence supplied by the peer's son, the German embassy notified the *Abwehr* that they had unmasked a British security agent. Canaris organized a watch on Musgrave, awaiting the ideal moment when he would be ripe for interrogation. They did not know why he held back for six months before importuning the young agent. Perhaps they were waiting to see if the Viscount's son could unmask any more British spies.

It had gone so smoothly to begin with, and they might even have been able to use Musgrave again without his knowledge or consent. Yes, it would have worked out well had Weiss not taken it upon himself to attack the Scotland Yard detective. As Whitehead had predicted, the German embassy denied all knowledge of Weiss, suggesting he was nothing more than a violent thug and denied any involvement in his crimes. Bentley himself was called to give evidence, but only his role as detective inspector was read out as his occupation. No mention was made of his connection to the security services.

Von Ribbentrop had conveniently been recalled to Germany just before the start of the trial to be a signatory with the Japanese to the *Anti-*

Comintern Pact. He was not expected to return for some time. No one else from the embassy was in any mind to help the Nazi agent, and he was tried and convicted for breaking and entering and attempted murder. His lawyer pled in mitigation the beating he had taken at the hands of the detective and that he had been traumatized since the assault. The prosecution pointed out that it was every man's right, indeed, it was his obligation to protect himself and his loved ones from serious assault by an intruder whose intent was nothing less than to cause harm or worse. This fact was evidenced by the weapons found on the defendant, to wit, two knives, one of which he attempted to use, and a garrote. The fact that he was the one who had sustained most of the injuries cut no ice with the jury.

In passing sentence, the judge made a telling statement. He said that sometimes the courts dealt with not only the law of the land but also the law of unintended consequences. Had Weiss/White not entered the detective's home intending to commit the felonies for which he had been tried and convicted, he would not have sustained the injuries he had received. He hoped the German would spend at least some of his time in prison reflecting on what he had done, and on his release, might decide to lead a law-abiding life. As the judge passed sentence, Weiss stood up and stared straight ahead. Proudly extending his right arm straight out, he shouted '*Heil Hitler,*' as he was led away to start his prison term of fifteen years.

Although he vehemently refuted the allegations to begin with, Reginald Rhodes-Willingham eventually admitted under questioning to passing Julian Musgrave's activities to the German embassy. After Whitehead told him of von Ribbentrop's monstrous demands of his mother, it did not take long for her son to break down and confess to everything. How the Germans had known of his infatuation with Nazism, and how they manipulated him to spy on his father hoping to secure confidential government information. In his journal entry for January 22nd, the peer did detail his luncheon with the M.P. He disclosed in confidence his son's recruitment by the Security Service during his final year at Keble College, Oxford.

Despite his father's connections, Reginald Rhodes-Willingham stood trial for treason which was held in camera due to its sensitive nature. Court reporting was restricted, and a D-notice was issued requesting the newspapers not to publish any of the trial details. Although not compelled to do so, the press complied with the directive. Any publisher who printed an account of the proceedings could find themselves frozen out of any future War Ministry briefings. It was not worth any newspaper editor's while to find their rivals had acquired major stories to which they were not invited.

As Reginald would plead guilty, there was no need for a formal trial. The hearing was mainly to determine the sentence the young man would face. Despite hiring top barristers from the Inns of Court and the best K.C. money could buy to plead in mitigation, the evidence against the peer's son was damning, especially in light of his confession and his mother's sworn testimony.

Despite the government's attempts to censor details of the trial, Reginald's Nazi sympathies and his connections to British fascists and his support for Sir Oswald Mosley became public knowledge, much to his father's disgust. The prosecution had established all three elements for a successful conviction; means, motive, and opportunity. The Viscount spent only the first day of the week-long hearing in court, preferring to spend the rest of his time at his Northamptonshire estate. Lady Rhodes-Willingham endured the whole week and burst into tears when her younger son was sentenced to six years imprisonment in Camp Hill Prison on the Isle of Wight for his part in the Musgrave episode.

George McMahon's trial was held at the Central Criminal Court, more commonly known as the Old Bailey, on the previous September before Justice Walter Greaves-Lord.

McMahon was charged on three counts. 'Unlawfully possessing a firearm and ammunition to endanger life.' 'Presenting near the person of the King a pistol with intent to break the peace.' 'Producing a revolver near the person of the King with intent to alarm His Majesty.'

Although McMahon had been branded as no more than an attention-seeker, the Crown thought the charges against him serious enough to be prosecuted by the Attorney-General, Sir Donald Somervell. By coincidence, Somervell, like Edward, had also attended Magdalen College but with a great deal more academic success. McMahon was defended by his solicitor, Alfred Kerstein, and his barrister, St. John Hutchinson, who implied that it was not the Italians but the Germans who had been complicit in the attempt to assassinate Edward.

Having read the charges and as the trial continued, Greaves-Lord instructed the jury to acquit McMahon on the two accusations that concerned the King. He intimated that although there was no doubt that McMahon did produce a loaded pistol, there was no direct evidence to prove that he had intended to discharge it at the King. Sir Donald Somervell rose to protest, but Greaves-Lord merely raised his hand. His decision was irreversible and final. McMahon would be tried only on the lesser charge. Had the Judge been suborned by higher powers who did not wish the Agency's involvement to be made known? That was the question on everyone's lips, but which no one would dare voice.

McMahon gave evidence in his own defense. He claimed that far from trying to kill the King, or anyone else, he had attempted to prevent his part in the attack and had even contacted a senior police officer and the Home Secretary. On cross-examination, Somervell contemptuously tried to dismiss McMahon's claims by asking if he wanted the jury to believe 'someone like him' would be given the time of day by either of the two parties to whom he alleged he spoke?

McMahon became so incensed by Somervell's arrogant tone, he uttered his response in such broad Glasgow demotic, his language was incomprehensible.

The jury found the Scotsman guilty of the lesser charge, and Greaves-Lord duly tariffed McMahon to one year's hard labor. In passing sentence, the Justice remarked that he was lenient in his judgment as he did not wish to turn a figure such as McMahon into a 'fancied hero.' There would be no martyrs of any persuasion in this judge's court.

* * *

Edward was seething. Thanks to that meddling bishop and his bible-thumping rhetoric, the government, the church, the judiciary, and even his subjects had turned against him since his relationship with Wallis had been made public. How dare they? How dare that unwashed and ignorant rabble who call themselves patriotic show him such contempt? Baldwin, Simon, the whole cabinet seemed to want him gone, or worse, they wanted him dead. The Judge, Greaves-Lord, persuaded the McMahon jury to disregard the prosecution charges of attempted regicide. This decision was, no doubt, to safeguard the blushes of the secret service. How would the public react, considered Edward, if they knew that even his security organization was implicated in the duplicity? And they dared to call him traitorous? He would show them. He would show them all. He was still the King, but not for much longer, of course. His mind was made up.

Royal obligation or not, nothing would stand in the way of him marrying the woman he loved. He was prepared to give up his throne for her, but it would only be for the short term. Hadn't Hitler assured him that he would restore him as King once he sat in Downing Street, and he, Edward, would install Wallis, not just as his consort, but as his Queen. Once he had retaken his rightful place as monarch, he would show all those who had conspired against him. He would let them see what it truly meant to betray the King of England.

CHAPTER 11

Paris, France – London, England, May 1937

Edward and Wallis were living in Paris, having fled the United Kingdom after Edward's abdication the previous December. The wedding of the former King, now the Duke of Windsor, and his fiancée, Wallis Warfield Simpson, was scheduled to occur on June 3rd. It would take place at Château de Candé, the luxurious and palatial home of their friend, Charles Bedaux in Indre-et-Loire, just south of Tours, France. The Duke was unhappy at the restrictions his brother had imposed and gave vent to his feelings to his wife-to-be. "How dare he? How dare that bumbling, stuttering, nincompoop of a brother dictate who I may and may not have at my wedding, *our* wedding," he hastily corrected himself. "It's an outrage; that's what it is, a bloody outrage." Edward was referring to the new King's instruction that no member of the royal family was to attend the forthcoming celebration. No one was to go, and there would not even be a token presence from the Palace to vindicate his union to such an unworthy person. "I'll show him. I'll invite whoever I damn well please, and if Albert doesn't like it, he can go to hell! They can all go to hell!"

But deep down, he knew that it was all bluster on his part. No member of the Royal Family would dare defy the express wishes of His Majesty. "Darling, you must calm down. All this aggravation is not good for your blood pressure. We just have to bitterly accept that they don't want me as a queen. I told you before; I would have been quite happy for you to remain on the throne and for us to continue to have our relationship as it was. You could have married someone more suitable to them, and we could have seen each other when circumstances permitted. I would not have been happy with this arrangement, but...."

Edward interrupted her. "There you are, then. That was all I had to hear. You would not have been happy. Don't you understand, my darling? All I want to do is to make you happy for the rest of our lives, and if that meant relinquishing the Crown, then so be it."

"Oh, Edward, I..."

"I even offered to enter into a morganatic marriage, but still that ass Baldwin dug his heels in. Let's face it; they didn't want you, a twice-divorced American, at any price. What more could I have done?"

"Nothing, my sweet. There was nothing more you could have done."

"And don't think I don't know," he continued, almost to himself. "It wasn't just because they didn't consider you to be suitable marriage fodder for me, oh, no. They thought me a security risk just because I spoke the bloody truth."

"Darling, please..." Wallis pleaded.

"No, it's no use. Can't they see it? Are they so blind? Adolf Hitler doesn't want a war with us; anything but. He sees us and the Americans as allies in the war against the Bolsheviks. It's not us he considers as the enemy; it's Comrade Stalin and his great unwashed horde of malcontents. So they think I'm a security threat, do they? Well, I'll show them how much of a threat I can be, don't you worry. At least Adolf Hitler has never tried to kill me. Not like my own so-called security establishment. I'll show them; I'll show them all." These words were not just the petulant rantings of a spoiled, self-indulgent adolescent. They were the determined utterings of a man who was so far gone in his own delusional beliefs, he could, indeed, pose a danger to the very country he once ruled as King.

Unknown to either the Duke or the Duchess of Windsor, they were not as alone as they thought they were. Someone else overheard his remarks, someone far more loyal to his King and his country than the man who appeared to want to betray everything he was meant to stand for.

* * *

The man sitting before the Prime Minister had been crying, making his primly trimmed mustache glisten with teardrops. Although he had composed himself as best he could before he met with Stanley Baldwin, it was apparent he had been, and probably still was, in great distress. His eyes were red-rimmed and baggy, and it took him a minute or so to compose himself before he started to speak. The fact that he stammered when he was upset did not help him voice his concerns. "Prime Minister, thank you for seeing me. It... it is a matter o... of great import th... that I wished to speak with y... you about."

Baldwin smiled sadly. There was only one reason why Sir Dudley Forwood, equerry to the Duke of Windsor, would be in his office at Westminster. The former King had said or done something irresponsible again or was planning on doing so. Seeking to put Forwood at ease, Baldwin seemed not to want to rush the young man, although his diary for the day was full. "Very well, Sir Dudley. Please take your time. I'm surprised to see you here. I thought you were with the Duke and Duchess in Paris. Would you care for a cigarette?" and proffered his gold case across the desk. "I don't know why you're here, but whatever the reason, it must be very painful for you."

Forwood declined Baldwin's offer. "Y... yes, Prime M... minister, it is. The Duke requires s... some of his belongings from F... fort Belvedere. As both he and the D... duchess are unfortunately considered by... by the government to be *personae non-gratae*, th... that task has fallen to m... me. I have taken the liberty of seek... seeking a... a private audience with y... you for a r... reason of the g... greatest im... import...."

Baldwin could see that his visitor was struggling with how to proceed. "Go on," he prompted.

"I was accidentally privy to a conversation I sh... should not have overheard, and one half of me wishes to God I had not been so. The other half is glad that I was." And Forwood related the discussion he had accidentally eavesdropped on between his employer and the Duchess.

Baldwin considered Forwood's information for a few seconds in silence before replying. "Do you think he is likely to cause trouble or embarrass the government, Sir Dudley?"

"From the vehe… hement way he spoke, I sh… should not be sur… surprised if that were the case. The problem is, Prime Minis… ster, the Duke cannot reconcile himself to… to the f… fact he is no longer K… king. He s… still expects to b… be treated with th… the same def… deference he was when he w… was monarch. N… not only for h… himself but also for the Duch… duchess. He is ab… absolutely liv… livid that his b… brother has s… seen fit not to permit any roy… royal to be at his w… wedding."

"Yes, I can see why the Duke would be so upset, but he must understand he has made his bed and must now lie in it. He has no one to blame but himself. Unfortunately, and I trust I am not speaking out of turn, someone like him can never accept the consequences of his actions and always seeks to lay the blame anywhere but at his own doorstep. I'm sorry, Sir Dudley, but I take a very dim view of this whole affair. I'm not quite sure what you expect me to do about it."

"I… I'm sorry, P… Prime Minister. I may not have made m… myself clear. It's not just the Duke's bitterness at how he… he perceives he is be… being treated by the est… establishment. It has gone way be… beyond that. I fear that the former k… king may be getting ready to co… commit treason. You… you have to stop him before he does some… something truly awful!"

"I appreciate your concern, Sir Dudley, but now that he and the Duchess are exiled, as they would see it, in France, they are outside of our jurisdiction. I suppose we could ask the French authorities to keep an eye on them if they're not already doing so, but that would mean washing our dirty linen in public, and I am not really of a mind to do that. I'm not dismissing your concerns; I'm just going to have to give it some thought. I'll have a word with a couple of people, and see if there's a way we can monitor the Duke's activities without his being aware of it." Baldwin looked at his watch. "Now, if there's nothing else…."

Sir Dudley rose dutifully, mindful of the time he had already taken. He hesitated as he looked at Baldwin, unsure whether or not to reveal his other piece of information. Once it was out in the open, there was no way back, and things would change forever. After a few more seconds, he made up his mind. This intelligence was too important for him to keep to himself. He had to tell someone, and who better than the man sitting in front of him? He sat back down before continuing. "Th... there is s... something else I need t... to tell you, Prime Minister," and this revelation shocked Baldwin even more than the information the equerry had already disclosed. It showed just how far the Nazis had penetrated into Edward's inner circle. There was now no doubt about it. The former king was about to play Judas on his country.

CHAPTER 12

London, England, May 1937

Sir Stanley Baldwin did, indeed, give much consideration to the information disclosed by the King's equerry. It seemed that even living in France, having been ostracized by the British establishment and his own 'society' friends, Edward was still able to be a thorn in the side of the government. It was just a pity that Edward had not been more forthcoming about how he planned to be even more of an irritation than he already was. At least then, they might have been able to forestall whatever actions the Duke was contemplating. Without this information, all the Prime Minister had to go on was speculation and supposition, not enough grounds to warn him off whatever he was planning.

Baldwin thought about the problem. As it could be a matter of national security, he felt it would be best to advise the domestic intelligence service, so he telephoned Vernon Kell. Kell was walking back into his office when the call came through. Sitting ramrod-straight behind his desk, he adjusted his pince-nez before lifting the mouthpiece. Foregoing the formalities of politeness, the intelligence chief asked, "Yes, Prime Minister, what can I do for you?"

Responding in kind, Baldwin replied, "Good day, Colonel Kell. It's about our ex-king. It appears he's thinking of making mischief of some kind. I just thought I should let you know unofficially. We may need to do something about the situation."

"What sort of 'mischief' are we talking about?"

"That's the trouble. I don't know. I only know that he is furious with us for what he sees as a great injustice done not only to him but to that Simpson woman. It seems he won't rest until he gets some sort of retribution. I don't know what he has in mind, but considering who some of his friends are, anything is possible, I suppose."

"How did you come across this not altogether surprising information?"

"His equerry, Sir Dudley Forwood, came to see me. He was very agitated. It must have been a great conflict of interest for him to speak out against his friend. He's worried the Duke will do something to harm the interests of this country."

Baldwin then told Kell the other disturbing news imparted to him by the Duke's equerry. The Intelligence man could not believe his ears. Sir Dudley Forwood had been invited to Claridge's Hotel to meet Charles Bedaux, millionaire businessman, friend of Edward, Duke of Windsor, and well-known Nazi supporter. Bedaux had tried to recruit Forwood into working for him, implying that the equerry's employer was already helping Bedaux in his dealings with the Third Reich. The French-American was not specific in what he expected from Forwood, merely explaining that he would benefit from the association if he agreed.

Kell pursed his lips, looking vaguely into the middle distance, his mind seeming to be momentarily elsewhere. "I was afraid something like this might happen," he eventually said. "That man is not fit to run a hot bath, never mind a country. I remember his father, the late King, God rest him, saying that once he was gone, Edward would ruin himself within the year. His son has exceeded George's worst fears. It has only taken him eleven months!"

"I was hoping you might be able to, er, monitor his activities somehow. I hesitate to use the word 'clandestinely,' but I can think of no other way to put it. Is there any way you can secretly watch him? It would certainly put my mind and that of the cabinet at rest."

"Short of getting Sir Dudley Forwood to listen in on his conversations deliberately rather than by accident or read his mail, I don't see what we... oh, wait a minute. I have an idea." Kell smiled. Wagging his forefinger as if to emphasize his point, he said, "I think I know a way, and what's more, the Duke is going to help us himself."

"What do you have in mind, Colonel Kell?"

"I'd rather keep my plans to myself, for the time being, Prime Minister, if you don't mind. It's probably better if you don't know at this stage," Kell replied.

Baldwin took the hint. "Very well. I just hope we can nip Edward's plans in the bud, before he does something we might all regret."

"Quite so, Prime Minister; quite so." After ending the call, Kell lifted his telephone again and dialed a local number. When the call was answered, he asked one simple question. "How's your French, Detective Inspector Bentley?"

* * *

"So you want me to go to France to snoop on the former King?" Bentley asked. They were sitting in a café just off the Strand. It was a little before eleven in the morning. The breakfast crowd had dispersed, and the lunchtime clientele was still to come in for their mid-day meal. The place was quiet, with only one or two tables occupied by customers who had stopped in for a mid-morning 'cuppa.'. The two men sat well away from the other diners, their conversation not meant for the ears of anyone else. "Just for a little while. Since his abdication, he's been bleating on about the lack of personal security. For some reason, he thinks his life or Mrs. Simpson's is in danger; God knows why. I suppose it's because of that debacle a few months ago. Anyway, he's miffed that his brother has withdrawn his protection officer. The King's quite right, of course. I don't see why we should pay for his security when the blighter has buggered off abroad. If he wants to live in France, let the bloody Frogs look after him. But having said all that, it's a Heaven-sent opportunity for us. We can say that having given careful consideration to His Royal Highness's concerns, we have decided to re-instate his nursemaid, that is, you, if you're interested. I can't officially order you to do this, of course, but you'd be doing me and the country one hell of a service. What do you say?"

"It may have escaped your notice, Colonel Kell, but I am rather busy at the moment. A lot is happening right here in London, without my chasing ghosts over in France. Is there no one else you could send?"

"I won't lie to you, Alan. There are other more qualified agents I could use, but I chose you for a reason."

Bentley's eyes arched. "Oh, yes? And what reason is that?"

"I need someone who's not accountable to me officially. If I use any of my team, and this operation goes belly-up, we, well, I, will be in big trouble. If that idiot discovers that our security service is still watching him, can you imagine what he'll make of that? Nothing would be surer to drive him even further into the waiting arms of Herr Hitler. And think what a coup that would be for the Nazis. No, we can't become officially implicated. It has to be someone from outside the Service, or at least, someone he thinks is not connected to us."

The detective-spy sipped his cooling coffee, buying time before he had to answer. "Yes, I see your point, Colonel Kell. But do you think they'll buy the story of us returning his security officer? I mean, it's a rather obvious ploy, don't you think?"

"Not to him, it won't be. Sir Dudley told Baldwin that Edward behaves and wishes his staff to treat him as if he were still the monarch. He can't seem to grasp the fact that he's not 'His Majesty' any more. No, he'll accept it, alright."

"It's not him I'm thinking about. From what I know of his paramour, she's a very shrewd operator. I'm sure she'll smell a rat."

"No, I think you're quite safe on that score. If anything, she sees herself even more as the 'Queen who never was' than Edward does as the ex-Sovereign. Apparently, she abuses the servants appallingly and insists they address her as 'Your Royal Highness.'"

"Oh, thanks. That's all I need. I get enough of that treatment at home," Bentley joked.

"So, will you do it?"

"Yes, I suppose so. Will you confirm my new posting with the Brigadier?"

Kell patted Bentley's arm. "Already done, old boy; already done."

CHAPTER 13

Tours, France, May 1937

King George the Sixth was apprised of the situation regarding his brother and duly authorized the Duke's revised security arrangements. Edward was overjoyed that he was finally being accorded at least some of the deference to which he felt entitled. "You see, my darling, if you show enough determination, you always get what you want in the end. I'm glad Albert has seen sense. You never know who might be lurking in the bushes these days. The last thing we need is another mad Scotsman taking potshots at me."

"Yes, my sweet, but if they think they can buy us off with one single police officer, they can think again. It still breaks my heart when I think of the sacrifice you made for me. One lousy detective isn't much of a consolation. Oh no. I want much more out of those people than that."

"What do you mean?"

"I don't know yet. Let's wait until after the wedding; then we'll see what we want to do. I want as much from those swine as we can get."

The Duke of Windsor smiled. "My sentiments exactly."

* * *

Bentley arrived to take up his new duties a few days before the Duke and Duchess's wedding. The couple's host allocated him a room in the servants' quarters but superior to the chambers he used for the rest of his staff. The detective allowed himself a day to become acquainted with the layout of the sixteenth century, eight-bedroom property and its grounds before commencing his duties.

The staff was preparing everything for the big day, and the closer it came, the more imperious and bad-tempered Wallis behaved. Neither of their hosts, Charles Bedaux nor Fern, his wife was anywhere to be seen, preferring to spend as much time away from their home as possible. The Duchess was putting a strain on their friendship they had not foreseen. "Please be patient with them, Fern. They've been through a lot in the past few months. It won't be long now until the wedding, then we'll have the house to ourselves again, just like before." Bedaux said plaintively in his French-American accent.

"I know they're our friends, and I do like them very much," his wife replied, "but Wallis is becoming so irritating; sometimes, I wish they would just elope and get married elsewhere." Her husband smiled but said nothing. His friendship with the Duke was too important to the businessman to be sidetracked by the behavior of his wife-to-be.

As if on cue, they heard Wallis shouting downstairs, no doubt haranguing some poor maid. "No, no, no! How many times must I tell you, you stupid woman, the orchids are to go in the blue vase over there by the escritoire. My God, do I have to do everything myself? Can you not take simple direction, you imbecile?"

"But Madame, earlier you said...."

"How dare you contradict me? If you were in my employ, you'd be walking out of this house right now with your tail between your legs. Now, do as I say!"

"*Oui, Madame, Je suis vraiment désolé pour ça.*"

"Never mind speaking in your execrable language. Talk English, girl. I've no time to learn how to speak French. I have a wedding to prepare for, in case you hadn't noticed!" The Bedaux couple shook their heads in disgust as they heard this exchange from their vantage point at the top of the stairs. Many fences would have to be mended with the staff once Edward and Wallis left for their honeymoon.

Pretending not to have heard the heated conversation, the couple walked down the staircase, appearing surprised to find their guest standing in the foyer. Fern studied Wallis, hoping her pretense at seeming concerned looked genuine. "What's wrong, my dear? You're looking terribly flustered. Is everything alright?"

Nothing would have given the Duke's consort greater pleasure than to vent her disgust at their servant, but she was, after all, a guest in their home, and there were some things guests did not do. Criticizing your hosts' staff was one such custom.

Composing herself, Wallis lied, "No, nothing's wrong. It's just that there's so much to think about before the wedding; I don't know if I'm coming or going."

Fern smiled, "Well, it's not as if this is your first time, is it, dear? I'd have thought you'd be used to all the formalities by now. So many men, so little time." Bedaux coughed to hide the laugh he was trying to suppress at his wife's remarks. She had a wicked sense of humor, and he made a mental note to ensure she did not disgrace herself at the reception.

Wallis kept silent, merely returning her hostess's smile, and appeared not to notice Fern's barbed comments.

"We'll have to go over the guest list again, just in case we've missed anyone out," Madame Bedaux suggested.

"Missed anyone out?" Wallis brayed. "There are so few attending, we could have held the ceremony in the public telephone box in the village and spared the expense. We invited over three hundred people, and do you know how many have confirmed?" Madame Bedaux did know, but kept her own counsel. "Less than twenty, that's how many! The King has forbidden any of the royal family to attend, much to David's disgust. Even those who Albert cannot prevent have declined so as not to offend His Majesty. This was not how I imagined our wedding would be. Even Winston has found that he cannot make it due to some pressing prior engagement and is sending his son instead. It is so depressing. Well, at least Herman and Katherine are here. I don't know what I would have done without them after the... you know... I just had to get away, of course, from all the unwanted attention, and their home in Cannes is just so idyllic, it was perfect. It's just a pity that more people aren't as loyal as they are."

"Yes, indeed, but I'm sure it will be an exciting affair just the same." Madame Bedaux remarked.

After hearing the heated tirade of Wallis toward their unfortunate servant, the Bedaux couple decided that if they wished to keep their sanity and retain their friendship with the Windsors, it would be for the best if they just allowed the bride-to-be to attend to her nuptials the way she saw fit.

Bentley kept a journal, locked safely away in his valise, of his interactions with the couple he was ostensibly detailed to protect. The Duchess was not present at his first meeting with Edward, presumably bullying some other poor member of the Bedaux staff. "Thank you for coming, Detective Inspector Bentley. You have no idea how relieved my fiancée and I are that the government and my brother have now relented their previous decision. It's comforting to know that we finally have some protection. One cannot be too careful these days."

"No, your Royal Highness, indeed one cannot. When your Royal Highness sees fit, perhaps you would be kind enough to furnish me with an itinerary of your proposed visits until the day of the wedding. That will help me to prepare any measures I might need to put in place."

"Is that strictly necessary? I doubt I shall be going anywhere, to be honest. I usually leave that sort of thing up to Wallis. I'll ask her what the arrangements are and let you know."

"That would be fine. Thank you, your Royal Highness."

It was a short, informal meeting, but it told Bentley a couple of things. Firstly, it was plain to see who ruled the roost in this relationship and who would continue to do so after they were married. This fact was evident by the way he spoke her name with such awe and reverence. It also made him wonder just how fearful he was for his safety if it took him two days to summon the detective to an audience.

He was doing his rounds later that evening. It was around eight-thirty, and the sun was beginning to set in the west. It had been a dry, warm, and slightly humid day, and the detective was thankful for the cool breeze brushing his face as he strolled through the grounds. If only Deborah could be here, he mused. However, the only problem with that thought was that having had a taste of how the other half lives, he might never get her back to their semi-detached in Barnet.

Suddenly, he heard a rustling in the bushes to his left. His first thought was that it might have been the same gentle wind that was caressing his face or a small animal or bird hiding in the undergrowth. Then the movement happened again, this time with a greater intensity. Without being obvious, he trained his eyes in the direction of the disturbance, continuing to walk peacefully along the graveled path. He reached into his outer jacket pocket and pulled out his packet of cigarettes. Putting one to his mouth, he then reached into his inside pocket for his lighter. Then he saw it. Something or someone definitely moved, as if keeping up with his own walking pace. Yes, it was a person, wearing a cream-colored jacket. Not the best camouflage for hiding in such verdant greenery. Either an amateur or someone not as well-trained as he was.

He pretended to have trouble lighting his cigarette while slowly ambling toward the source of the movement. As he approached the edge of the shrubbery, he threw his lighter to the ground while reaching for his pistol, all in one fluid motion. With his free hand, he pushed aside the bushes directing his revolver at the crouching figure. Bentley found he was pointing his gun at a man in his mid-twenties, medium height, with dark, slicked-back oily hair. He was clean-shaven but with a neatly-trimmed mustache. The stranger gasped in astonishment, his eyes saucer-like as he stared at the weapon aimed at him. He raised his hands, saying, "*Ne tirez-pas, Monsieur Bentley. Je ne suis pas un assassin. Je suis avec le Deuxieme Bureau.*"

Keeping his weapon trained on the stranger, Bentley demanded, "*Voyons une identification*!"

The Frenchman replied in good English. "Very well, Detective Inspector, I am going to reach into my pocket...."

"Do it very slowly. If I suspect any trickery, there will be a bullet hole where your brain used to be. *Comprenez*?"

"*Oui, Monsieur Bentley. Bien sur.*" The Intelligence agent gingerly searched for his wallet and pulled out his ID, offering it to Bentley for inspection. Satisfied that he was genuine, the British detective returned his papers and lowered his pistol. Extending his arm, he helped the Frenchman to his feet as the hidden man hand-brushed forest detritus from his clothes. "Olivier Betancourt. Well, Monsieur Betancourt, you'll need to practice a lot harder at concealment in enemy territory if you don't want to get your head blown off. What if I had been a German instead of an Englishman? Do you think Fritz would have waited to see the whites of your eyes before he fired? Unlikely. Then where would you be?"

"It is as you say, Detective Inspector. I will need to do better next time." Betancourt smiled ruefully. Despite just meeting the French Intelligence man, Bentley was immediately attracted to him. He saw much of the Frenchman in himself as he was twenty years earlier. Eager, but so naïve.

"How do you know my name, Monsieur Betancourt?"

"Your security department notified us of your imminent arrival. My chief told me to keep watch on you, among my other duties. Observe only. Do not overtly interfere."

"Well, that's very considerate of your boss. I must remember to thank him when we meet. Oh, and I'll also be having words with my own people, don't you worry. Talk about not telling the left hand what the right hand is doing... What do you mean, 'other duties?' So you weren't sent just to spy on me, then?"

"Oh, no, Detective Inspector. You are the least of my concerns. At least, I hope you are."

"So, what is your assignment here, Olivier?"

"It is to keep watch on the incumbents of the château. To make sure they do nothing that will affect the interests of France."

"Why would the Duke and Duchess wish to harm the country that is offering them refuge?"

"Ah, non, Monsieur Bentley, you have misunderstood me. It is not Edward and Madame Simpson I am tasked with keeping watch on. It is Monsieur Bedaux. We believe him to be an agent of the Nazis."

"Yes, we're already aware of Charles Bedaux and his activities on behalf of the Third Reich, but I don't understand. What good are you doing skulking in the bushes? You'll not learn much from leaves and twigs."

"You are quite correct, of course, but that is not why I spend my time among the undergrowth. It is to monitor who comes and goes into the château. Betancourt pulled out a small Ermanox camera with a telephoto lens. "Sadly, I fear it is all a waste of time. I have been doing this for the last two weeks, and most of the people are tradesmen or those connected to the upcoming wedding, apart from one person I did not recognize, and whose photograph I have given to my boss. He is probably just a local dignitary, come to pay his respects. I may have to tell my *chef du département* that it is not worth the manpower. Surely, my time would be better spent elsewhere, *n'est-ce pas*?"

Bentley remembered the English security man, Julian Musgrave, and how he was assigned duties that would not get him into harm's way, yet it had. He wondered if this young man in front of him was Musgrave's French Intelligence counterpart. Well-meaning but inept. But if that was the case, why keep him on the Service at all when he could still be a danger to himself or others? The answer was sadly obvious. He was the Judas goat. Used when the situation was probably hopeless. Easier to blame a rookie like him than to apportion responsibility where it really belonged.

"When are you due to finish?" Bentley asked the young man.

"Midnight. They reckon no one will come at that time of night, so I can go home then."

And that's why the French are so successful at losing wars, thought Bentley. Your enemy doesn't just work from eight a.m. to six p.m. Monday to Friday. If Bedaux were planning anything illegal, he wouldn't do it in the glare of the mid-day sun. He'd do it when there was less chance of being noticed. How the French ever built a colonial empire was a mystery to the bemused detective. "I'm going to continue my walk," Bentley informed the Frenchman. "I'll be back in half an hour. It'll be after nine o'clock by then. If nothing happens, just call it a night."

The French Intelligence man was shocked. "Monsieur Bentley, you are asking a member of the French security service to abandon his post. That is unthinkable. I must never... I mean..."

"Don't you have a sweetheart, Olivier?"

"*Oui, bien sûr, mais, je ne pourrais jamais quitter mon poste...*" Betancourt lapsed into his native tongue, so astounded by Bentley's seditious suggestion."

"Very well, Olivier, as you wish. I'll be back soon. Just keep pointing your camera at the entrance. You never know, or as you might say, '*On ne sait jamais.*'"

Olivier smiled, waving the detective away and returning to his hide. By the time Bentley returned, twilight had fallen, and the mansion was shadowed in gloom, the only illumination coming from the château's courtesy outdoor lights. The detective called softly, "Olivier, it's Alan. I'm back. Have I missed anything?" The only reply was chirruping from the crickets who had made the bushes their home. He shouted again, slightly louder, but not strident enough to be heard from the house. "Olivier, it's Alan. I'm back. It's O.K.; there's no one else here." Again, there was no reply from the Frenchman.

A cold dread spread over Bentley as he rushed to the last place he left the *Deuxième Bureau* man. Sweeping away the greenery, he searched in the dark, knowing that it would not be good. Betancourt had already remonstrated with him that he would not leave under any circumstances, so... and there he was, barely a foot from where the detective had last spoken to him. His lifeless body lay sprawled on top of the bushes he had secreted himself behind. He was face-up, his open eyes staring into eternity. The Frenchman's neck was a bloody mess, and even in the fading light, Bentley could discern his blood still oozing from two small puncture wounds just below his Adam's apple. He had been stabbed not with a knife, but with a blade much thinner. Slimmer, perhaps, but just as deadly – a stiletto. An assassin's weapon. Death must have been swift.

Whoever had attacked him had come from the front, not secretly from behind. Did this mean that Olivier had known his assailant, had known him so well, he trusted him? Or had someone from the house seen the two men talking, one hidden in the shrubbery, and pretended to be Bentley before taking the young man's life? Christ, what was he going to do now? Then he realized something else. Brushing aside the earth and bushes, the detective searched for his camera. It was gone. Had he been killed for what or who he saw and had the photograph to prove it?

It was now too dark to search for clues to the young Frenchman's death without using a torch. This activity would only inflame the curious minds of those in the house and lead to all sorts of unwelcome questions. He would ensure the man got a decent burial, only not just yet. He still had work to do to unravel this mystery, and sadly, for the time being, young Betancourt's body would have to remain where it was. He covered the corpse with more leaves and twigs, ensuring no one could see the body from the gravel path. The only two people who knew there was a body there and exactly where it was located were Bentley himself and the killer.

So just who had murdered the Bureau man, and perhaps even more importantly, what was so important that it merited killing an officer of the French security service?

CHAPTER 14

Tours, France, June 1937

Bentley hurried up to his room, where he washed off the blood from Betancourt's body. He then quickly changed his clothes and shoes, stuffing the stained garments into his valise before returning downstairs. None of the guests seemed perturbed by his presence. Everyone looked and acted naturally. Either no one in the room was aware of the tragedy that had occurred not a hundred yards from where they were standing, or someone was an outstanding actor… or actress. This was becoming nothing less than an Agatha Christie whodunit. For country house, read 'château,' and for a cast of seemingly upright Home Counties citizens, substitute a mélange of upper-middle-class English and French aristocracy. For the deductive sleuth who has everything wrapped up in a red ribbon bow by the second-to-last chapter, consider… him? Detective Inspector Alan Bentley? Yes, he was a good policeman, but no one, not even Hercule Poirot, was that good.

Herman Rogers was mingling with the crowd, ostensibly greeting everyone with equal aplomb, but Bentley saw that his eyes never strayed far from Wallis Simpson. He knew the rumors, of course, that they had had an affair while they were both in China, him on business, she seeking a quick divorce from her first husband, Win Spencer. By the way he followed her with his gaze around the room, even with his wife Katherine present, Bentley had to believe the gossip was more than just innuendo. But surely Rogers or even Wallis Simpson would not have killed the young *Deuxième* agent for catching them having a quick fumble in a quiet area of the château? That was unthinkable. Almost.

He was so wrapped up in his own thoughts that he only caught the last few words of the conversation taking place a few feet from where he was standing. "...yet I could have sworn I saw him not two minutes ago. Yes, I'm positive I did." The slurred accent was Irish with the clipped tone and delivery of military authority. Turning around to discover who had uttered the words, he saw it was Major Edward Metcalfe, a confidante of the Duke of Windsor and a known supporter of Sir Oswald Mosley. My God, they were all here tonight. Bentley would not have been surprised if Adolf Hitler himself came strutting through the double oak doors.

Bedaux gripped Metcalfe by the shoulder, tugging at his tuxedoed arm to separate him from the other guests. The host smiled affably as he guided a slightly drunken Major to a seat, tugging at his sleeve to force him to sit down. The thought raced through his head faster than his mind could process it. Was it... could it have been the leader of the British Union of Fascists that Metcalfe saw or thought he saw? But even if it was, why would his presence here cause anyone to want to keep it quiet? Well, it would confirm Edward's flirtation with extreme right-wing politics. So far, only the top echelon knew of his admiration for Adolf Hitler. That was a well-kept secret that the British public was not aware of.

But what if it did become known? How would that affect not only Edward's relationship with his former subjects but the peoples' view of royalty as a whole? Were they all supporters of that odious little man and his horrible racial policies? Yes, Bentley could see how it would all play out. No wonder they wanted Betancourt killed. If word of Mosley's visit to the former king leaked into the open, there would be hell to pay on both sides of the Channel. But hold up. Mosley couldn't be here as an official guest, could he? Even Edward would not be stupid enough to invite such a controversial figure to his wedding. If he did, George would not only disown him; he would at least cut off his not insubstantial royal allowance. He might even demand the French return his brother to be tried for treason. So why was Mosley here, if not for the nuptials? Was this what Kell and Baldwin were so concerned about? Mosley and Edward in the same place at the same time. Oh my God! This could mean only one thing. They were using the wedding as a cover. Edward was planning a coup. They were somehow going to topple the government, replace Baldwin with Sir Oswald Mosley as Prime Minister and reinstate Edward as King. Hitler wouldn't have to go to war with Britain, not when he would be welcome with open arms by the new Fascist regime and its puppet king.

Bedaux's next statement changed everything. Everything he had just considered, every horrifying possibility, was thrown to the winds. As he sidled over to where Metcalfe was sitting with Bedaux standing beside him, he heard the French industrialist hiss into the Major's ear, "Be quiet, you fool. No one is supposed to know he is here. Everyone thinks he is in Paris. If word gets out that he is with us tonight, it will ruin all our plans. You must forget you ever saw Axel Wenner-Gren...."

CHAPTER 15

Tours, France, June 1937

Excusing himself from the party, Bentley hurried up to his room. He had no idea who Axel Wenner-Gren was, but he'd soon find out. Lifting out his other traveling case, he opened the lid before taking out his Vibroplex Morse code transmitter. During his induction into the security service, he had been trained in its use but had scarcely ever had to employ it. One beat for a dot, three beats for a dash, wasn't that what his instructor drilled into him? He found the cipher code and prepared to tap in the message by identifying himself with his call sign, E2G6, and then await the corresponding confirmation.

He had not memorized the encoding pattern to transfer letters of the alphabet into their equivalent Morse binary alternatives. Bentley knew he was slow, but accuracy was more important than speed. This drawback was his one vulnerability. It would be easy for anyone to not only intercept his message to locate its source. A skilled operator could find him to within a hundred feet. At that radius, there was only one place he could be. He did a few practice strokes to gain some confidence and build up speed.

Finally, he was ready. After a few seconds, he received his acknowledgment. Slowly at first, he abbreviated his meeting with the young French agent and its hideous aftermath. Then he relayed the question he was burning to ask – who is Axel Wenner-Gren? The British intelligence operator was as mystified as Bentley. They would find out and get back to him. They arranged a call time with an alternate one should circumstances dictate. If Bentley did not respond to either instance, contingency measures would be put in place. The operator would make a third try at midnight on the day after the second attempt at contact. If this failed, he would be considered lost. The detective could, of course, initiate a further transmission himself any time if conditions allowed.

Bentley signed off. There was nothing he could do now but wait. Wait and think. This must have been the reason why the young French agent had been murdered. He had not only seen but had photographed this man, whoever he was, as he entered the château, presumably by a side entrance. Somehow, he had made himself conspicuous to either the man or, more likely, his bodyguard, who dealt with the situation the only way it could be dealt with. Bentley shook his head, his face bent low as he sat on the bed. Why hadn't he listened to wiser counsel? If only Olivier had stayed buried in the shrubbery and kept as quiet as the grave, he would not now be waiting to be buried in one.

He would not get a callback tonight. It was too late, and anyone who could have helped him would have long since departed the office.

The detective-spy returned downstairs to rejoin the party. Some guests had already retired, including the inebriated Major. Edward and his bride-to-be, the Bedaux's, and Mr. and Mrs. Rogers were still talking and appearing to enjoy each other's company. It did not look as if they had missed Bentley in his absence. He kept discretely in the background, not wanting to make his appearance too obvious. Of the secretive man, there was no sign. Finally, Edward called him over. "I say, my dear chap, isn't it past your bedtime? Don't you think you should call it a day? If anyone needs their beauty sleep, I'd say it's you, old boy," the Duke guffawed.

There was plenty that the detective wanted to say but merely replied, "It's my job to see you safely to bed, your Royal Highness." Then he added mischievously, "We don't want to see you attacked by any bogeymen before your wedding. I don't think the Duchess would ever forgive me."

Edward stood stock-still for a few seconds. He was not used to being addressed in such a cavalier, off-hand manner, especially by one of the lower orders. He was about to speak when the Duchess interrupted him. Turning to the police officer, she remarked, "Yes, you're quite right, of course. I would never forgive the man who allowed my fiancé to come to any harm."

With a vulpine smile on her lips, she continued, "Much as I will never forgive the man who speaks to the Duke like that again. If I ever hear you address my husband-to-be in such an offensive and disrespectful way in the future, Detective Inspector, your tenure as my husband's protection officer will be over. I, personally, will ensure that your next job will be cleaning the toilets at the worst police station in England. Do I make myself clear?"

"Yes, Madam. I am sorry for any upset I may have caused. It was entirely unintentional, I assure you."

The Duke piped up, "Yes, well, see it doesn't happen again, or..." he elbow pointed toward Wallis, "I'll sic her on you. Do you hear me?"

"Yes, your Royal Highness. Once again, I offer my apologies."

"Fine. The matter is now closed, and we'll say no more about it." It may have been Edward's final word on the matter, but Bentley wasn't so sure if the same could be said for his bride-to-be. She may have threatened to have him cleaning out the privies, thought the detective, but that task wouldn't be so inappropriate considering all the shit he'd just taken from them. But Bentley was still kicking himself. Why did he have to make such a stupid remark, when it wasn't necessary? Now all he'd done was to put the Duchess's back up, and he reckoned she was a woman who held a grudge longer than she held a gin and tonic. And this sideshow wasn't getting him any closer to finding out who the enigmatic Axel Wenner-Gren was or why he was here when he was supposed to be in Paris.

They had left him on his own again. It seemed that they were happy to have chastised him, letting him know in their own, not-too-succinct way, who the bosses were around here. Having accomplished that, they executed what they considered to be the worst slight possible; they chose to ignore him. This situation suited Bentley just fine. He would have been happier to be in the company of some of the miscreants he'd put away over the years than this bunch of arrogant, treacherous, ignorant, self-entitled snobs.

* * *

Bentley arose early the next morning, just as day broke over the château. Stealing out of the house from the staff entrance, he made his way back to where he found the dead agent. Hunkering down, he saw that some of the gravel was disturbed, as well as the shrubbery. The way the stones had been hastily arranged, it appeared as though the young man had been dragged from his hiding place, stabbed very quickly, probably, the killer then taking his camera before throwing him back into the foliage. The whole exercise could not have taken any more than a few seconds. He pushed aside the bushes, moving Betancourt's body to feel the ground with his hands in case there were any clues the murderer may have left. There were none. This man was a professional.

Edward had called Bentley into his private quarters earlier. "Look here, Detective Inspector. I won't be going anywhere today and will remain in the château. I'll be surrounded by guests who are above reproach and utterly trustworthy, as well as Monsieur Bedaux's own staff. Why don't you take some time off? Tell you what, I'll see if I can swing it with our host to allow you to take his car into town. Why not buy something for your wife? You are married, I take it? I'm sure she'll appreciate you bringing her a nice gift from Tours, eh?"

The detective surmised that this was not a benign gesture on the ex-King's part. He or they wanted him out of the road. Well, they were going to have to try a damn sight harder than that if they wanted to be rid of him. "Thank you, your Royal Highness, but my duties have been made clear to me. I'll just continue to do my rounds. I'm sure you'll be as safe as the Bank of England, but I'll always be within hailing distance, just in case."

"Very well. Just as you wish," Edward replied with ill humor. That exchange was a little while ago. Wenner-Gren had still not made an appearance, even well into the afternoon. He was keeping himself to himself, and probably none of the guests, apart from Metcalfe, who had been told to forget he saw him, had any idea he was even there. There might even have been a meeting happening right now in a private part of the house between Edward, Bedaux, Wenner-Gren, and God knows who else. But to what purpose? There had been no sign of Edward or Charles Bedaux for over an hour, probably nearer two. Where the hell were they?

Bentley's authority gave him access to parts of the mansion cordoned off to everyone else, even to most of the other guests. However, there were limits to where even he was permitted to wander. He came upon such an area as he was making his regular tour of the property, and it was this discovery, above all else, that convinced him that something was afoot. Out of idle curiosity, he tried the handle of a door he believed merely to be a cupboard, but when the detective pulled it open, he saw there was not just a small press but a hallway leading to another part of the building. This layout was not on the schematics he had read.

Just as he was about to explore, a voice behind him said, "*Arêtes immediatement. Que faites-vous ici? Qui est-vous*?" Bentley turned to find a tall, stocky man with blonde hair and eyebrows in his mid-forties standing four square, a gun aimed at his back. Slowly completing his maneuver so as not to alarm the guard, he turned to face him. "*Je suis un détective Anglais. Je suis ici pour protéger le Duc de Windsor et la Duchesse aussi. Je m'appelle Alain Bentley*," the Englishman replied, using the French version of his first name. He mimed to say he was going to reach into his pocket for his identification. The stocky man gestured with his pistol, flicking it to agree. Bentley pulled out his warrant card, holding it in front of him. Keeping his weapon trained on the detective, the Frenchman scanned it closely before signaling him to put it away.

"So, you're here to look after that worthless piece of shit and his whore, are you?" the stranger asked in accented English. His accent wasn't French, although he could easily have passed as one. It was more Scandinavian, Norwegian, perhaps.

"I tend to lose my voice when someone points a gun at me," Bentley responded. The man returned his weapon to his concealed holster and offered his hand. "Arvid. Arvid Arvidsson. My parents didn't have much of an imagination," he smiled. The English detective automatically shook Arvidssons's hand just as it dawned on him that he could be greeting young Betancourt's killer. "So, what are you doing here, Arvid?"

"Much the same as you. Guarding someone. Someone with far more to offer than that waste of good fresh air you've been detailed to protect." Arvidsson replied dismissively.

"Mind if I ask who? None of these people look as if they need nursemaiding."

Arvidsson smiled inscrutably. "I doubt it's anyone you know, Detective Bentley."

"What's 'Arvid?' Norwegian? Swedish?"

"Swedish. Why? What's it to you?"

"Nothing; nothing at all," Bentley offered noncommittally. But it was. Although it wasn't a certain deduction, the English detective had a mental bet with himself that if the bodyguard was Swedish, then probably his charge was, as well. Men, especially wealthy and influential ones like Wenner-Gren had to be, tended to put their safety and security in the hands of their fellow kinsmen than trust to foreign assets. There was one way to find out. "So, are you Swedish police, or...?"

"Strictly off the books. Some call it 'mercenary.' Me. I term it as 'additional unofficial assistance.' It has a nice ring to it, don't you think?"

Well, that gambit led nowhere, but he was still sure that Arvidsson's principal was also a Swede. "It's a bit wordy, but, hey, that's just my opinion. I would have thought that your client, whoever he is, would have enough clout to get his country's security organization to provide protection instead of just one man."

"You're just one man also, don't forget. Sometimes it benefits my client not to let the authorities know where he is. It can be...awkward, if you get my meaning."

"So, just who is your client?" Bentley ventured.

"That is for me to know, and you...not to. Believe me, my new friend, it is probably better if he remains anonymous to you. The less you know...."

Bentley nodded sagely. He understood the meaning all too well. He wondered what his new 'friend' might do if he discovered that he already knew the identity of his patron. This man might know all the right defense moves, but he liked to talk too much. He could be a good protection asset, but he'd never be an outstanding one. Would he take a bullet for his employer? Perhaps; perhaps not.

Bentley gestured with his head toward to corridor. "So, what's going on down there?"

"All I know is that they're having a meeting of some kind. They don't let me in on all their dirty little secrets. I'm just the hired help, same as you."

No, you're not, thought Bentley. You're nothing like me, and I'm nothing like you. Still, it told him enough. His suspicions were correct. Wenner-Gren, Bedaux, and our charming Duke, no doubt, were having a confab of some kind. He tried his luck. "Listen, it's part of my job to check on the Duke once an hour to make sure he's safe." Bentley made a show of consulting his watch. Pursing his lips, he added, "Almost time. If I don't give him a wave, he'll think I don't love him anymore. I'll just...." The Englishman made to move down the hallway but was stopped by Wenner-Gren's bodyguard. "Wait here. I'll see if my client says if it's O.K.. You've got your job to do, and I've got mine."

"For crying out loud. I don't intend to barge in on them. I only need to set eyes on the Duke. That's all. That's it. Can you imagine the fool you'll make of yourself when it transpires that you didn't let the Duke's protection officer see if his Royal Highness was good? You'll be a bloody laughingstock." Arvidsson stood hesitant and undecided. Finally, he relented. "You've got thirty seconds, and then I'm coming after you, laughingstock, or not. Do you hear me?"

"Loud and clear, my friend. Loud and clear," Bentley intoned quietly as he bounded noiselessly down the hall. Yes, Arvidsson might be a good bodyguard, but he'd never be a great one. Bentley slowed down to a walk as he approached the doorway to the room from which he heard voices. Believing they would not be interrupted or overheard, the group had left the door open. The outside air was warm and muggy, sending its heat into the room. The open door provided much-needed ventilation.

He would have barely five seconds to glance into the sequestered apartment. Although he had little time, he stopped for a moment to try and discern how many voices were speaking. It seemed to be only three. Good. He reckoned he knew who two of the incumbents were. It only remained to get a look at the third to corroborate any description London would send him about Wenner-Gren. He stealthily walked past, hoping they would not notice him. As expected, he spied Edward and then Bedaux. There was a third man seated at the conference table. A cursory glance told Bentley that his target was in his early-to-mid fifties, with a good head of silver-gray hair and the appearance of a noble intellectual. He was wearing a dark monogrammed blazer and a pale-blue open-neck shirt. Although he was sitting, Bentley estimated him to be well under six feet in height.

He was running a few seconds over his time and could see Arvidsson getting anxious. He held out his hand, clenching his fist with his thumb extended upward. It was the universal signal to show that all was well. He could see the Swede visibly relax. Christ, what he had to do for King and Country.

"Well?" Arvidsson asked expectantly.

"Yes, it's all fine. The Duke was being his usual obsequious, obnoxious self."

"Obsequious...?"

"It's the Duke of Windsor we're talking about here. What do you think it means?"

"I really don't know, my friend, but I have a pretty good idea." The bodyguard smiled.

"Probably best if we kept this little drama to ourselves, eh?"

"Yes, I do not think my employer would like it if he knew I went against his wishes. Did you see him, by the way?"

"See who?"

"My employer. Did you see my employer?"

"I've no idea, old son. I had only had eyes for the Duke. You won't tell the Duchess, will you?" They shared a compatriot smile before the English detective removed himself from the secret doorway. Did this burly Swede really do for poor Olivier? All Bentley's instincts told him no, and yet the man was dead. Someone was responsible, and if it were Arvid Arvidsson, he, Detective Inspector Alan Bentley, would see that justice was done, one way or another.

CHAPTER 16

Tours, France, June 1937

Bentley took out his Morse code box. It was almost time. A minute later, the return call sign came in. Yes, it was definitely London. He listened as the Morse operator relayed the intelligence he requested. Firstly, the description. Yes, there was no doubt. The third man in the room had, indeed, been Axel Wenner-Gren. There was so much information on him, they would have to break it up into two or three messages, so they would start with the essential details. *Multi-millionaire Swedish industrialist and arms dealer, reckoned to be one of the wealthiest men in the world. He is a close friend of Hermann Göring and frequently travels to Germany, ostensibly on legitimate business. He is, however, suspected to also organize covert financial and economic institutions for Nazi supporters in foreign countries to gain access to local currencies to finance sabotage and insurrection operations. Seems to think he can play both ends against the middle and come out on top. Sources close to Göring indicate he is more of a nuisance than anything else, always trying to get an audience with Hitler and bypassing official channels. Can you discover what he's doing there? More to come.*

So this was, indeed, the third man in the secret room. An acolyte of Hitler, supporter of the Third Reich, financial backer of Nazi Germany, and now he was here, sitting across the table from the former King of England. Strange bedfellows, indeed. Can I discover what he's doing there? Yes, of course. No problem. I'll just waltz up to the Duke of Windsor and ask him nicely why he had shared a table in a secret room with an out-and-out Nazi. Did Kell understand how the espionage game was played? This individual is a man I am not supposed to know, turning up on another Nazi's doorstep when he should be a hundred and fifty miles away. And that's not to mention trying to find out who killed young Olivier Betancourt.

There was one ploy he could try. He would put his plan into operation in the morning when he was fresher and more awake.

* * *

After breakfast, the detective was about to knock on the door of the Windsors' quarters when he heard raised voices coming from within. He did not have to strain his ears too much to catch most of the conversation. "...care who I'm bloody offending. After what they've done to us, I don't care anymore. I simply don't care. Do you hear me?"

"Yes, my sweet, and I do understand, but do you think it's wise to antagonize them any more than you've already done?"

"Let them stew. He was never a father to me, anyhow. We were always left in the care of abysmal nannies while Mama and Papa swanned around the globe, strutting about as if they were Mr. and Mrs. God Almighty. Then, when they did decide to come home, what did they do? I'll tell you. They got us tutors. We were the Royal Family, too good to mingle with the *hoi polloi* like other children. Always packing us off to our rooms with our private tutors, hardly ever giving any of us praise when we did something we were proud of. So, no, my dearest one, I honestly don't care if our wedding coincides with my late Papa's birthday. Tell me something. If he were still alive, do you think he would have come? You don't need to answer that. We all know what the answer is, don't we?"

"Yes, I suppose so."

"And here's another thing," he began. Oh, dear, his bride-to-be thought. He's off on one of his rants again. I shall have to treat his ravings like a summer squall and just let it blow itself out. "Don't think I don't know why my brother bestowed a dukedom on me. He has effectively emasculated me politically. He is well aware that as a duke, I have no right or authority to sit in the House of Lords, as my peerage is not hereditary. It was a smart move on his part; I'll say that for him." Edward conceded grudgingly.

"Well, it was a smart move on someone's part," retorted Wallis, but I doubt it was your dope of a brother. He's not clever enough to have come up with that strategy."

Bentley had heard enough. He had no more time to waste on these two self-entitled fools moaning about how life was so unfair. Had the Duke learned nothing from his visits to the deprived areas of Britain? Had he not seen with his own eyes the deprivation, hunger, and homelessness that was being allowed to fester in the streets and cities of one of the wealthiest countries in the world? And all he could think about was destroying the memory of his late father and his exclusion from the best club in London. It was pathetic. Yes, that was the word – pathetic.

Waiting a few more seconds, he coughed loudly enough for them to hear him before knocking at the door to their chamber. After getting permission to enter, Bentley stepped into the room, bowing deferentially to the soon-to-be-married couple. From the way they reacted, it was clear that the pair were expecting someone else. They were quick to hide their disappointment, however, as the Duchess asked indifferently, "Yes, Detective Inspector, what can I do for you?"

It was all the detective could do to keep his expression straight. It was not 'what can we, or what do want my husband for? The reaction, or lack of one, from Edward was another sign of his diffidence toward her and the irrational hold she had over him. "I was just wondering, Your Grace, if you had the final numbers for the guest list?"

"And why is that any concern of yours?"

"Because I need to familiarize myself with everyone who will be present. That way, I can keep an eye out for anyone who should not be here. Someone who may not wish His Royal Highness and Your Grace the same goodwill as your other guests."

"I say, old boy, do you really think anyone would try to bump me off in the middle of my wedding vows? It's unbelievable."

"Maybe so, your Royal Highness, but I would ask you to recall the events of last July. Who would have thought anyone would have been so bold as to shoot at you while you rode down Pall Mall, not five hundred yards from Buckingham Palace?"

"My God, Wallis, he's right. Anyone could sneak in, pretending to be a guest or a cook or a tradesman, or a ..."

"Yes, yes, yes, David, I get the point." His mistress replied tartly. "So what do you suggest, Detective Inspector?"

"As I've already said, Your Grace, it would be most helpful if you would furnish me with a complete list of guests and tradespeople. Perhaps Monsieur or Madame Bedaux could help."

"I'll have it ready by the end of the day or tomorrow morning at the latest. Is that suitable, Detective Inspector?"

"Yes, Your Grace." Smiling at her, he concluded, "that will do nicely."

* * *

It was just after supper when the Duke and Duchess sent for the detective. Written on two sheets of foolscap paper were the guests' details as well as the catering staff and all the other people who would make the couple's day so memorable.

As he scanned the document, he noticed two omissions. One he expected and one he didn't. As he suspected. Axel Wenner-Gren's name did not appear on the guest list, so he would probably have left by the time of the celebration. The other missing name was the minister who would be officiating. Glancing up from the papers, he asked the Duke, "Your Royal Highness, I don't see the name of the clergyman who will be conducting the ceremony. Would you mind if I...?"

The Duke's face had turned puce. "Yes, I bloody well would mind, Detective Inspector." The Duke replied angrily. "You are now taking the extent of your remit too far. What? Do you seriously believe I am to be murdered by a senior member of the Church of England? I appreciate your concern and attention to detail, but I assure you that there will be no danger from that direction. Now you may leave us. I'm sure you have other duties elsewhere."

"No, your Royal Highness, my duties are solely to look out for your welfare and safety and for the Duchess too, of course."

"Yes, well, I'm sure we will be safe enough in our quarters. Now, will you please leave us? That is a direct order."

Bentley gave a small bow before saying, "As you wish, your Royal Highness. Good evening," Nodding to Wallis, he added, "and to you, Your Grace." He wasn't sure of the protocol, whether he should take the customary three steps backward before exiting the room. Bugger it, he thought, as he turned abruptly round, his back facing toward them as he left their quarters.

Christ, he hadn't half touched a sore spot. It was obvious from the way Edward reacted that they were not going to get the celebrant of their choice. For such a royal occasion, they would normally have been married in Westminster Abbey, like his brother Prince George, the ceremony conducted by the Archbishop of Canterbury, or someone of equal standing. But the government and the clergy itself had put paid to that dream. Well, Edward was right about one thing. It was unthinkable that someone from the Church would attempt to assassinate him. Then again, with all the upset, confusion, and soul-searching the pair had caused, nothing was impossible.

Whether they wished to tell him or not, he had to know who would be conducting the wedding service. London would know. He would get a name from them along with a description of whoever had the unenviable task of joining these two souls in holy matrimony. He would leave nothing to chance.

It was time. He contacted London to find out more about the enigmatic Wenner-Gren, and confirm the clergyman's identity and description. It took barely twenty minutes, slightly faster than his attempts of the night before. He was getting better. Time to get ready for bed. It was the thirty-first of May. They would be tying the knot in three days, then disappearing on honeymoon. After that, his work would be done, and he could bid a not-so-fond farewell to all the covert machinations of these dreadful people. But he couldn't. Not yet. Betancourt's body was still lying in the shrubbery. Why had no one called to investigate his disappearance? This was very odd, very odd indeed.

He had three days to solve the young man's brutal slaying. Bentley had no idea what he would do if the case remained unsolved. These thoughts troubled him as he lay on the bed. Was the agent's death linked to Wenner-Gren after all, or was it just a coincidence? Either way, he had to find out. He was snapped out of his reverie by a quiet tapping on his door. Who the hell was this, at eleven-thirty at night? Making to move off the bed to answer, he nudged against his Morse code machine. Bloody hell, he had been careless. He had been so wrapped up in everything, he had forgotten to stow it away. Quickly unlocking his carry case, he called out, "Just a minute. I'm not decent," as he hastily shoved the valise under his bed.

He had no idea who might want to pay him a call so late in the evening, but whoever he thought it might be, he was unprepared for the person standing there, her fingers sensually running up and down the door frame. Barefoot, with her dark lustrous hair running free and wearing nothing but a diaphanous light blue negligee stood the Duchess of Windsor.

In a husky voice, unlike her usual imperious tone, she asked, "Are you going to let me in, Detective Inspector, or am I going to freeze to death out here?"

CHAPTER 17

Tours, France, June 1937

Acting on instinct, Bentley pulled her toward him, quickly closing the door behind them both. The Duchess raised her eyebrows, smiling at his effort to keep anyone from spotting them. "My, my, Detective Inspector, so manly. Do your treat your wife in the same dominant manner? I suspect she has no, ah, issues with your… er… performance, eh? I wonder if I would say the same thing. My appetites are more, ah, exacting, if you get my meaning."

Bentley grabbed hold of her elbows and held her out at arm's length. He had seen a lot in all his years as a policeman and a security operative for His Majesty's government. However, he had never been propositioned by an American lady, twice-divorced, and about to be wed for the third time to the former King of England, no less. "What is it you want, Your Grace?"

"I might have thought a man of the world like you would be all too aware of what I want." She looked at her reflection in the full-length mirror. Do you not find me attractive… Alan?" She began to stroke her body, fondling her breasts, and Bentley could see the swell of her nipples rise under the gossamer-thin material. She took his left hand and guided it with her own, pulling it slowly down toward her groin. The Duchess unclamped his other fist, opening his palm and licking his fingers one by one. He pulled his left hand away but could not stop the American from continuing to run her tongue over his other outstretched hand. Despite his refusal to play her game, the detective found himself becoming aroused. He was only wearing pajamas, and his discomfort was plain to see. He was a loyal and faithful husband and had never cheated on Deborah. She would have to find someone else to satisfy her passionate nocturnal desires.

It was at that moment he realized he had been handed a Heaven-sent opportunity. He allowed her to let him gently massage her opening, his fingers seeking to find her erotic spot. She began to sigh and moan as he caressed her sex organ, feeling her becoming moister with each stroke. She lifted her leg and wrapped it around his waist, kissing him on the mouth with her lips and her tongue. "Oh, that's it. Oh, yes," she gasped, her rapture now all-encompassing. "Oh, I know what you're thinking, you gorgeous man. Shall I tell you?" she asked breathlessly, teasing him, licking his ear and neck in ever-increasing acts of sensual stimulation.

"If you must," he replied, unsure what she would say next.

"I'll only... *gasp*... go so far, just to... *gasp*... take the edge off." Am I right?"

"Oh, God yes... yes, you're right." He replied as he continued to rub her and to allow her to explore his manhood.

"But that... *gasp*... won't be enough, will it? So you'll need to get a bit more, but... *gasp*... that won't be enough either. So you'll... *moan*... have to get more, and then more until only one thing... *oh*... will satisfy you." She caressed his enlarged member, feeling it grow even stiffer as she stroked it between her thumb and forefinger. "Don't fight it, Alan. Let it embrace you, give yourself the pleasure you deserve; give me the satisfaction I desire. Let me show you delights you... *gasp*... can never have... *oh*... thought possible." She pulled him over to the bed, throwing him backward on top of the bedclothes. Untying his pajama cord, she pulled down his bedtime pants, lowering her face until it was barely an inch from his erection.

Her tongue darted all over the top of his legs until finally, she softly bit his engorged member. Before he could react to the sudden pleasurable pain, her mouth was over it, sucking him as if her life depended on his achieving climax. But she was not ready to allow him to satiate himself. Not yet. Like a gymnast, she turned herself around one hundred and eighty degrees while her lips still caressed him. Now her womanhood was against his mouth. His tongue entered her organ, while his fingers augmented her pleasure as he stroked her at the same time. She was undulating in time to his maneuvers, her rhythmic pelvic movements becoming more strident with each touch of his fingers and every wash of his tongue. "Oh, my God," she intoned breathlessly. "Now! Do it now! Take me, fuck me as hard as you like!" Turning herself around once more, she quickly sat astride him, her carnal urges becoming uncontrollable. But now, it was Bentley who was not ready. He would not allow her to cover his penis with her dampness. "No! Not yet." He murmured ardently.

"Now! I'm ready. I need to feel you inside me," she panted.

"Soon," he sighed hoarsely. "Very soon."

"Oh, God, what is it? You're still big. Why won't you put it in?"

"I need something from you," he whispered, continuing to stimulate her aching body.

"Anything, anything! I must... oh, God, what do you want? I can perform in positions that would make your eyes water. Just tell me..." she pleaded.

He nibbled gently at her ear and continued to caress her but slowed his pace. He did not want her to reach orgasm until he had the information he needed. She pressed her glistening body against him, pulsating in time to his hand movements. It required an extreme level of self-control on his part not to give her what she begged for. "Wenner-Gren. What's he doing here, when he should be in Paris?" He angled his erection even nearer to her vagina, but not close enough for Wallis to let him penetrate her.

"Oh, God, he... oh, please, I need to come right now. Put yourself inside me, then...."

"No, Your Grace, I..."

"*Your Grace*?" she almost screamed. "We're just about to fuck, and you're calling me by my title! My God, I thought I'd seen all there was to see of your English formalities, but... are you going to screw me or not?" she insisted.

"Wallis, I'll take you to heights you never imagined, but first, I need to know what Wenner-Gren is doing here. He could pose a security risk." He kept pressing her.

"I don't know how you found out about Axel, but I assure you he's the last person who means me or Edward harm."

"It still doesn't answer my question. What is he doing here?"

"If I tell you, will you take me to those heights you promised?" she asked him breathlessly as she writhed sensuously in time to his gently probing fingers.

"Absolutely, Your, er, Wallis." Bentley had not stopped caressing the Duchess, and she was now at boiling point.

"Oh, God," she exhaled. "He's here to arrange a trip for the two of us. Quickly, now!" she moaned.

"A trip? To where?"

"To Germany. He's going to get Edward and me an audience with Adolf Hitler. Fuck me now!" she commanded him in the loudest whisper he had ever heard.

"When? When are you and Edward going to Germany?"

"Oh, sweet Jesus, I... I don't know the exact dates. Sometime around October, I think. Now can we please get down to business? God, I've never been as horny. You *promised*." She pouted desperately, gasping and out of breath.

He let her guide his still enlarged organ until he felt himself slipping into her. "So I did, Your Grace. So I did...."

CHAPTER 18

Tours, France, June 1937

The bright morning sunshine streamed in through his window as he awoke, causing him to screw up his eyes in reaction to the light. His mouth felt dry as he fumbled for his watch on the bedside table. He squinted at the dial as his sight slowly became accustomed to the brightness. The hands showed it was just past seven o'clock. A slow realization returned to him, and he jerked his head to stare at where she had been lying after their frenetic bout of lovemaking. Wallis was no longer there. She must have stolen away once he had gone to sleep. He wondered if there would be any repercussions from their nocturnal encounter. He thought not. As much as what he did could have been considered a gross dereliction of duty, the consequences would have been far worse for her. To have been found to be engaging in intimate relations with a relative stranger two days before she was due to be married would not have sat well with anyone, least of all, her husband-to-be. It might even be grounds to call off the whole affair, 'affair' being the operative word.

He thought of Deborah, his wife. He had never cheated on her in their fifteen years together. How would she take it if she ever discovered what had happened between her husband and a woman so despised by much of the British public? It would ruin his marriage, no doubt. Bentley's feelings of guilt at his betrayal of his wife were tempered by the acceptance that, as distasteful as the encounter had been, it had provided him with the intelligence he wanted. So Edward and his unfaithful shrew were to be the guests of the leader of the Third Reich in a few months' time. What did it all mean? As private citizens, there was nothing to prevent them from visiting whoever they chose but to wish to associate themselves with that dreadful regime said much about their loyalties to the United Kingdom. And what was the purpose of their trip? He doubted it was solely to foster better relations between the two countries. If that were the case, why couch the meeting in such secrecy?

The detective had no time now to contact London. He should soon be starting his duties, and the last thing he needed was for anyone to wonder why such an efficient police officer was late. As Bentley washed and shaved, he considered how the Duchess would explain her absence from Edward. Likely, this was not the first time she had engaged in such activities, and no doubt, they had come to an 'arrangement' over Wallis's nighttime excursions. He would not ask her where she had been, and she would not satisfy his curiosity.

An hour later, he was conducting a tour of the grounds, his mind constantly wandering to the dead body buried in the bushes. Why had no one from the Bureau turned up to find out what had happened to one of their agents? It had been two or three days since the incident. Surely, he would be missed by now. It did not make sense.

As these thoughts ran through his head, he suddenly noticed someone a few yards in front of him. This new person had not heard Bentley behind him or had given any indication he was aware of the detective's presence. Whoever this man was, he seemed to be acting strangely, furtively creeping closer to the shrubbery where Betancourt's body lay. Was this the killer, returning to see if anyone had discovered his victim and discretely removed the corpse? Or was it, indeed, someone from the Bureau secretly searching for their missing agent? As Bentley drew closer, he was able to get a better look at his quarry. It certainly was not one of the guests, and he was too well-dressed to be a tradesman. Somehow, he seemed familiar, yet the Englishman would have sworn that he had never seen him before. Then it struck him.

The stranger matched the description of the parson sent to marry the Duke and Duchess. Late middle-aged, slightly stooped (weren't all parsons slightly stooped?), somewhat paunchy with thinning sandy-gray hair.

As Bentley approached, the parson turned, confirming the detective's supposition. He was dressed in clerical garb, ruddy-complexioned, with bulbous eyes and a large nose. Yes, there was no doubt. This was Robert Jardine, Vicar of Darlington, self-appointed wedding celebrant to the Duke and Duchess of Windsor.

Then Bentley saw the reason for what he surmised was Jardine's suspicious behavior. There was nothing sinister at all in his actions. He held a notebook and pen and was bending down to examine the local flora, while sketching the leaves and jotting down notes of his findings. Turning to face the detective, he asked with a vacuous smile, "Simply beautiful, don't you think? We don't get anything like this in the North-East, you know. Such a beautiful climate here."

He could wax lyrical all he liked about the château's vegetation as far as the detective was concerned, but he was getting too close to Betancourt's body. Taking Jardine's elbow, Bentley steered him away from the locus, saying, "You don't want to be stooping over for too long, vicar. You'll seize up. Can't have you complaining of stiff joints just before such an important occasion, eh?"

Jardine was startled by Bentley's comments but only momentarily. Slowly rising to his feet, he conceded, "Yes, I suppose you're right. And you are, sir...?"

"Bentley," the detective smiled before enlightening the cleric. "Detective Inspector Alan Bentley. I've been detailed to look after the Duke and Duchess for the next couple of days."

"Oh, my. Do you think that's necessary? Are they in any danger?"

"Not that I'm aware of, but better safe than sorry, eh?"

"Yes, indeed. It's a sign of the times, I suppose. Such a lovely couple, don't you think? If ever two people were meant to be together, it is the Duke and Duchess of Windsor."

I doubt you'd be saying that if you saw what the Duchess got up to in my bed last night, Bentley thought.

"It's such a pity that the Establishment is blinded by its own petty prejudices to see that it doesn't matter to God," the vicar pontificated. "if two people are in love, why should it concern anyone if it's not the first time for either of them? Are we permitted to care for one person only in a whole lifetime? I cannot believe our Lord would be so insensitive to our earthly feelings not to allow us more than one chance at happiness. It hardly bears thinking about."

"Perhaps you're right, vicar. I leave theology to the theologians and philosophy to the philosophers. My task is to care only for their physical welfare, not their spiritual wellbeing."

"Well put, young man. Now, if you don't mind, why don't you accompany me back to the house? It's almost time for elevenses."

* * *

Having found what he thought was a fellow intellectual compatriot, Jardine was reluctant to leave Bentley to his duties. It was only with barely disguised impatience that the detective finally announced, "I'm sorry, Reverend Jardine, but I really must get on," making his meaning perfectly clear, even to the obtuse vicar. Reluctantly, the cleric allowed Bentley to leave, but not before almost imploring him that they should sit together at dinner.

When he was safely out of sight of the Anglican minister, he raced up to his room. Extracting his Morse device, he contacted London with the information he had gleaned the night before and sought answers to a few questions he'd posed on an earlier transmission. He had to disappear for a while but knew his absence would be noticed, if not welcome. There was only one thing for it. He had to see Edward. Finding the Duke in conversation with Bedaux, he politely interrupted the discourse. "Your Royal Highness, if I may have a minute of your time..."

"Yes? What is it? Can't you see I'm busy?"

"It will only take a moment, sir."

Smiling condescendingly at his host, Edward turned to face his protection officer. "Well, what do you want? I'm not used to being waylaid in the middle of an important discussion."

"Your Royal Highness, I've been giving some thought to what you suggested the other day."

"Yes? And what was that? Remind me."

"Would I have your Royal Highness's permission to take a couple of hours off just now? Your wedding is in a day or two, and then I must head back to England. I thought it would be nice to bring my wife back a souvenir of my journey, but I may not have time before I leave."

Edward's tone softened. It wasn't often that anyone listened to his opinion, never mind act on his advice. "Just a minute, and I'll see if Charles will lend you his car."

Bentley saw the two men chatting, and Bedaux nodding his head in agreement. It was done. Tours was only about thirty minutes' drive from the château. He would, indeed, buy a gift for Deborah to salve his aching conscience, but that was not the main reason for his drive to the town.

Forty minutes later, he walked into the local *Gendarmerie Nationale* in the Avenue de Grammont, the local office of the *Deuxieme Bureau*. It was a fine colonial-style two-story building with a central construction flanked on either side by matching symmetrically winged structures. A fine piece of architecture, indeed, thought Bentley with respect as he approached the exterior. He entered the premises and walked up to the counter. "*Salut. Je cherche Monsieur Georges Monpamon, s'il vous plait,*" He addressed the duty sergeant. Without looking up from his desk, the gendarme replied, "*Il n'y a personne ici sous ce nom.*" It was the standard response to anyone casually looking for a member of the French security agency. No one knew anyone, *et cetera, et cetera*.

Bentley took out his identity card, only this time, it was not the warrant he used with the Metropolitan Police. This ID was his British security services authority. "*Je n'ai pas le temps de pisser. Obtenez Monpamon maintenant.*" The surly French gendarme stared indifferently at the document but did not dismiss him. He had finally gotten his attention, but the officer was not about to show deference or courtesy to a British secret service agent. "*Attends ici. Je verrai s'il est disponible.*"

"*Vous avez exactement trente secondes pour faire venir Monpamon ici ou je contacte Guy Schlesser à Paris. Comprenez?*" This abrupt demand seemed to focus the desk clerk's mind. Lifting the phone to his side, he dialed a single digit. Turning his face away from Bentley, he spoke into the mouthpiece. After a few seconds, the gendarme replaced the handset. "*Il sera a terre dans un instant. Attends ici.*"

A few seconds later, a door marked '*Privé*' opened to Bentley's left, and a tall man walked through. Bentley aged him around fifty with a strong military bearing. He gave the appearance of looking about six inches above your head as he addressed you. "Detective Inspector, what a pleasure to finally meet you. I apologize for the misunderstanding just now. You know how it is...."

Bentley gave a non-committal nod in reply. "Can we speak in private, *Monsieur Monpamon*? It's very important and urgent." Monpamon's face grew grave. "Is everything O.K. with the Duke? Has he been... harmed?" Monpamon asked hesitantly, not wanting to hear the answer.

"No, the Duke's just fine. Please. We need to talk." The detective urged.

Monpamon led Bentley back through the door from which he had emerged. They had entered a large vestibule area with various doors indicating different department offices around the periphery. To his left, an ornate balustraded staircase ascended to the floor above, which was where Monpamon headed, indicating for the English detective to follow. At the top of the stairs, the Bureau agent took them both around to the office, which was situated directly above the front door to the main building. It had a small, decoratively railed balcony that looked onto the street below.

They were in a sparsely furnished office with a single filing cabinet, a hat stand, two old oak desks facing each other across the room, behind and in front of each of which sat bare wooden chairs. On both desks sat a telephone. Bentley noticed the top of one desk had files stacked neatly in various trays, whereas on the other desk, the dossiers were strewn haphazardly across the surface in an untidy heap. Taking his seat behind the tidier desk, Monpamon indicated to Bentley to sit down in front of him. The Bureau man apologized for the poorly equipped room. "Unfortunately, the Bureau budget has been cut again. How they expect us to operate on such meager... I'm sorry, you did not come here to listen to my rantings. Now, what can I do for you, Monsieur Bentley?"

Foregoing formalities, Bentley came straight to the point. "When was the last time you heard from Olivier Betancourt?"

"Betancourt?"

"Yes, your agent, Olivier Betancourt."

"Last night. He called in to report as usual around midnight, just before he finished his shift. That is the usual routine. May I ask why? Please don't tell me he's got himself into trouble again."

"How did he deliver his report? Did he come here in person, or...?"

"No. We now have radio communication in our vehicles. He calls in from his car. It is such a blessing, don't you think? Now we can communicate so easily without needing to find public call boxes. You still haven't answered my question. Why do you wish to know about young Olivier? Is he in any sort of trouble?"

"How often did he call in?"

"Please, Monsieur Bentley. What has Betancourt done?"

Bentley's face turned solemn as he replied. "I'm sorry to have to tell you, Monsieur Monpamon, but you could not possibly have spoken to Olivier Betancourt last night."

"Why ever not?"

"Because the night before last, I found Betancourt in the bushes of the Château de Candé. He was dead. Someone had pierced his throat with a stiletto."

Monpamon's complexion turned white. "*Mon Dieu. C'est incroyable.*" The local *chef de bureau* stood up, staring Bentley in the face. "Dead? How can he be dead? I only spoke to him last night. It's impossible. No, you must be mistaken, *mon ami*." The English undercover agent explained his impromptu meeting with the young French security officer and its dreadful sequel. Once he had finished, Monpamon covered his mouth with his hand, remaining standing across the desk from Bentley. "And Betancourt's body. Where is it now?"

"I left it in place. I didn't see what else I could do without alarming everybody. But we will need to remove it, of course. Probably best if it was done late at night when the château is asleep."

"Yes, I suppose so. I cannot get over it. Why would anyone want to kill him?"

Although he felt sorry for Betancourt's superior officer, his display of grief might all be an act. Bentley could not be sure and did not believe the time was yet right to tip his hand. Not unless he, too, wanted to suffer the same fate as young Betancourt. For the time being, he would keep his thoughts and his suspicions to himself.

"I don't know, but presumably because of something he saw or heard that he shouldn't have, and they discovered he was hiding in the bushes."

Monpamon could still not get over the news. "But I... that is... we spoke...." The distraught Bureau officer could not find the words to express his shock and sorrow. "But if I did not... if I could not have spoken to the young man because he... then who impersonated him?"

"Presumably the killer, which means he must have been aware of your contact arrangements."

"No. I cannot believe that... I refuse to accept that anyone in the service of the *Deuxième Bureau* would do such a dastardly thing." Monpamon shook his head. "This cannot be happening."

"How did he sound? The killer, I mean. Did he seem... different from the last time you spoke to Betancourt in person? Was there anything unusual, not the same?"

"Oh my God, what a fool I've been. When we spoke, his voice sounded hoarse. I jokingly chastised him for smoking too much, but he said it was the hot and spicy meal he had had earlier that had gone for his throat. Oh, God, why did I not see it then? I must have been blind." Monpamon punched himself on his thigh.

"Why do you say that? You couldn't possibly have known what had happened to him."

"No, you don't understand, Monsieur Bentley. Olivier liked spicy meals, but his stomach could not tolerate them. They gave him awful indigestion and heartburn, and he suffered badly whenever he ate them, so he avoided those types of foods. Why did I not think to query him, the killer, that is?"

Bentley tried to comfort the tormented security officer. "It was too late by then, anyway. Betancourt would have already been dead. There was nothing you could have done. Our mission now is to discover who killed him, and why. I already have a couple of ideas that I will need to investigate."

"Then tell me," begged Monpamon. "For the love of God, and the sake of this young man's poor family, what is on your mind?"

"Apart from you both, who else knew about your routine?"

"No one. We kept this arrangement strictly between the two of us, I assure you."

"Apart from the killer's call at midnight pretending to be Betancourt, did he not call in earlier in the day?"

"No. And before you ask, I told him only to report if he saw or heard anything unusual. When he did not call in, I assumed it was because nothing had happened in the interim. Other than that, I only required him to call me to tell me he was going off-shift."

"Did he tell you who he saw or what he heard?"

"Yes. As soon as I hung up, I contacted the Avenue de Tourville."

"Who did you speak to?"

"What difference does it make? You're hardly likely to know him."

"Just the same; what was his name?"

Monpamon rummaged through the papers on his desk, triumphantly holding up an official memo pad. He proffered the page to Bentley. No, Bentley did not know him. Remembering his run-in with the desk officer at reception, he said, "But what if there had been an emergency and he could not contact you, or you him? Was there no contingency plan?"

"Sadly, no, Monsieur Bentley. You are quite correct, of course. Even such a simple field operation as a locally organized routine surveillance mission should have had a, how would you say, backup plan. Still, I did not consider it necessary, and now because of my lack of professionalism, this young man is dead. I shall never forgive myself. I don't know how I shall be able to look Betancourt's family in the face and tell them his death is on my conscience. I shall have to resign."

Bentley was becoming tired of this maudlin self-flagellation. "No, Monsieur Monpamon, you fucking well won't resign, at least, not yet. If you want to honor your agent's memory, you will help me find his killer. Do you understand?"

Monpamon looked up at Bentley, smiling bleakly. "Yes, you are right, of course. The time for recriminations will come later." He paused, inhaling deeply before speaking again. Bentley thought it was a sigh, but Monpamon seemed to have suddenly acquired a newfound sense of purpose. With a steely tone the English officer had not heard until now, the Bureau man declared, "Very well, Inspector. Our investigation begins right here, right now! How do you wish to proceed?"

"Firstly, my friend, this is not our investigation; it is yours. I am merely here in an advisory capacity, if you understand me. I do not think it would go too well for anyone if your people thought you were not efficient enough to handle this case on your own. Officially, I am at your disposal only to offer advice and support as the officer who just happened to find poor Betancourt's body. Unofficially..."

"Yes...?"

"Unofficially, I will do everything I can to see that Betancourt's killer is brought to justice, even if I have to drag the bastard into the court myself."

"Please do not think I do not appreciate your assistance, but may I ask why an English law officer should concern himself so much with the murder of a French security agent?"

"I only met Betancourt very briefly, but I took an instant liking to him. That he was dedicated, I have no doubt, and he might have risen far in the Bureau. To think that someone should kill him only a few minutes after I had spoken to him offends me greatly. To put it another way, he died on my watch. That is something I cannot tolerate. For that reason, if for no other, I, too, feel a sense of responsibility."

Monpamon smiled grimly. "*Mais oui*. So now we both have a mutual interest in bringing Betancourt's murderer to justice. That is good." Gesturing with his palm up in a 'stop' motion, he went over to the filing cabinet. From the top drawer, he took out a bottle of brandy and two glasses. Pouring out the amber liquid into both tumblers, he offered one to Bentley. As both detectives were about to drink, Monpamon declared, "Let us toast to our early and complete success, my English friend. *Vive l'Entente Cordiale*. Someday I hope I may be able to return the favor."

"With the greatest of respect, Monsieur Monpamon, I sincerely hope you never have to."

"Quite so, *mon ami*. Now, I suggest...."

"Before we start," Bentley interrupted him, "How many other Bureau agents operate from here?"

"Well, there is one other, but he is on assignment elsewhere." Pointing across the room, the French detective continued, "That is his desk over there. The untidy one. I cannot discuss this case with you, as it is rather a delicate matter, but I assure you, he is many kilometers away from here. He has been out of town for the past two weeks. I believe we should concentrate our efforts at the guests and staff at the château, *n'est-ce pas*?"

Just as Bentley was about to answer, there was a knock at the office door. "*Entrez*," Monpamon shouted.

The duty sergeant from downstairs stepped into the room, clutching a sheet of paper. Speaking softly, he whispered his message to his superior. Showing respect and courtesy, Bentley turned discretely away as the officer spoke. He caught only a few words before Monpamon retorted, "When was this? Why was I not told?" The officer muttered again, with Bentley picking up a few fragments of the exchange. "Very well, sergeant, you may go." Monpamon ordered him with impatience. The officer saluted, turned smartly around marched out of the room, completely ignoring the visitor. Monpamon apologized for the interruption and was about to resume their conversation when Bentley asked, "I wonder if you would do me a great favor, Georges? Several favors, actually."

"Anything, my friend. What can I do for you?"

So Bentley told him.

* * *

Just over an hour later, the English security agent left the offices of the *Gendarmerie Nationale* and walked toward his destination. It was an old two-story mid-terraced building on Rue du Metz, only a few streets away.

Alphonse Albinetti, the third member of the local Bureau squad, lived in the narrow little thoroughfare, barely a five-minute drive from the *Gendarmerie Nationale* office. Monpamon had warned him it might be difficult to park in the compact street, suggesting he leave his vehicle where it was and travel the distance on foot. It would take him no more than fifteen minutes. Bentley thanked him for his advice. Not only would it save him trying to find a parking space, but it would do something else. It would give him some extra time to consider how he would handle Albinetti, assuming it was, indeed, him who he was going to meet.

Bentley found the address easily thanks to Monpamon's explicit directions and the agent's Renault *Nervastella Grand Sport* parked outside. The *Deuxieme Bureau* must pay their agents a lot more than we do, he thought, not without a pang of envy. He waited at the door for a few seconds, listening for any sounds of activity within. When he heard none, he rapped on the door. As he expected, there was no response, so after a few more seconds, he knocked again, this time a little louder, shouting in French, "Monsieur Albinetti, I have come from the office of the *Gendarmerie Nationale*. Monsieur Monpamon has sent me to see if you are alright."

Short moments later, Bentley heard footsteps padding softly down the stairs. Then a muffled voice from behind the door asked, "Who is it? What do you want?"

"As I said, Monsieur Monpamon has requested me to come around to make sure you were O.K.. Is everything well?"

"What on earth is going on?" shouted the local Bureau agent. "I only spoke to the Paris office a little while ago. I told them I was recovering well and would be back to my duties within the next day or two. Now please go away. I'm trying to rest."

The English detective heard the same footsteps begin to shuffle away. "I'm sorry, Monsieur Albinetti. Monsieur Monpamon requested that I see you face to face to ensure you do not intend to return to work before the virus has left you. I need to see for myself and report back that you are not suffering from the effects of the disease."

"Oh, for goodness' sake, this is quite ludicrous. It's not much more than influenza. It's not fatal if that's what he's thinking. Can you not just tell Monpamon that you've seen me, and everything is good? You've heard me speak. Surely that will be sufficient, will it not?"

"If it were for myself, Monsieur Albinetti, yes, I would say so, but I have to answer to Monpamon as you, yourself, do. I am under strict instructions to see you do not show any outward signs of the virus, and I must carry out my instructions. Monpamon was very explicit on that point. I have a wife and six children, Monsieur, for whom I must needs provide. I cannot afford to be without employment. Please. It will take but a few seconds. Then I will leave you in peace."

"Oh, very well. Just a minute," came a sigh of resignation. From behind the door, the detective heard the sounds of ill-humored mutterings mingled with the noises of a deadbolt being withdrawn and a mortice key being turned in its lock. Bentley braced himself. No matter who opened that door, he was coming in, regardless. As the door creaked inwardly open, the detective pushed roughly against it, shoving the incumbent back inside before he had time to react. "What on earth...?" the startled occupant staggered backward as the door swung in against him. Before he had time to respond, Bentley pulled out his Police Positive revolver, aiming the barrel at Albinetti's head. "Who the hell are you? What gives you the right to...?"

"Shut up!" Bentley barked, peering at his victim, satisfied that from the description Monpamon had provided, this was, indeed, Alphonse Albinetti.

"You obviously know who I am, so you'll also know just how much trouble you're in, whoever you are. Who are you? What are you doing here? What do you want?"

"I don't think you've quite got the hang of how this game is played, Monsieur Albinetti. It's the guy with the gun in his hand who asks the questions, and it's the other guy, the one with the barrel pointing at his head, who answers them. Do you understand?" Bentley showed his British security ID.

"Don't think you can intimidate me, you worthless piece of shit. If you wanted me dead, I'd already be on the floor with a pool of my own blood around my face, and you'd be dust in the distance. So obviously, you don't want to kill me. At least, not yet. Now, I'll ask you again. Who are you, and what the fuck are you doing here?"

He was good, thought Bentley with a grudging respect. He was showing no sign of being under pressure at all. Someone had trained him well, but who was it? "Betancourt. Olivier Betancourt. How well do you know him?"

"Who says I know anyone by that name?"

In one swift movement, Bentley switched his finger from the trigger, to the middle of the barrel, gripping it around his fist, and pistol-whipped Albinetti around the head. Blood immediately spurted from a gaping wound to the French-Italian's temple, the crimson fluid running freely down the side of his face. The Bureau agent instinctively thrust his hand to the ragged gash, his eyes bulging in fear and anger. "Now you've really done it, you filthy bastard. When word gets back to Monpamon what you did, he'll throw the book at you."

"You let me worry about Monsieur Monpamon. Now, we're going to start again, and this is what's going to happen. I'm going to ask you some questions to which you are going to give me truthful and accurate replies. I already know the answers to some of them but not to others. If you tell me anything I know to be a lie, you know what'll happen, don't you?" and the Englishman raised the gun as if to strike at him again.

"Alright, alright, put it down. What do you want to know?" Albinetti asked, taking out a handkerchief and pressing it to the wound to stem the flow.

"Do you know Olivier Betancourt?"

"If you've just come from Monpamon as you say you have, you'll know the answer to that one."

"Where were you two nights ago?"

"What right do you have to...?"

Bentley glared at the man, hefting his weapon. "Alright, alright. Two nights ago, I was on assignment. I'm not allowed to discuss it. If you want to know where I was, you'll have to ask Monpamon, whom you seem to know well, Mr. Englishman."

"He told me. I just need to hear you confirm it."

"How do I know you're not lying, just to get me to open up?"

"Fair point. Fine. I'll tell you, and you can contradict me if I'm wrong. Two nights ago, you were, correction, you were supposed to have been in Paris. Yes?" The French agent stayed silent. "Like your colleague Betancourt, you were on surveillance duties also, weren't you?" Again, Albinetti did not respond. "It was an assignment you asked for; am I still on target?" When Albinetti did not reply, Bentley continued, "Did you know what mission Betancourt was on?"

"What's with Olivier again? What's the stupid prick gone and done now?"

With a hard edge in his voice, Bentley repeated his question.

"No. I didn't know what he was doing. Why? And why are you here? What's an English special agent doing interrogating a French citizen about a matter involving a French intelligence officer. What gives you the right to...?"

"I was the one who found his dead body, not half-an-hour after I had been speaking to him."

"Dead body? What do you mean, dead body? Olivier isn't dead. He's...no, I don't believe you. You're lying. For some reason, you're lying."

He was good, thought Bentley. He's almost got me convinced; almost. "How did you know about the Paris assignment?"

"What d'you mean?"

"It wasn't an assignment. You weren't assigned. You volunteered. How did you even know there would be such a mission?"

"I...I don't remember," Albinetti stammered. "I must have heard about it through the grapevine. You know how these things work."

"You're over two hundred and fifty kilometers from Paris. Why would they need to bring someone from Tours for their purpose when they have plenty of agents much closer in Paris itself?"

"If you must know, I'm sick of Tours. Sure, it's a nice place, but nothing much happens here. I thought if I could get a job there, it might enhance my chances of being transferred to Paris permanently. I want to make a career in the Service, and that's not going to happen if I'm stuck in a backwater like this place. Just look at old Monpamon. D'you know how long he's been doing the same job here?"

"No, I don't," Bentley answered testily, "and quite frankly, I don't care. I'm not here to discuss your boss. I'm here to discuss you. I'll ask you again, how did you know about the Paris assignment?"

"And I'll tell you the same thing I told you before. I don't remember."

"Let me tell you, then. Someone from the Avenue de Tourville called you and told you. Does that explanation ring any bells?"

"Could be. Now you mention it... but what about Betancourt? And what's it got to do with you?"

"I'm helping your boss out. He's kindly allowed me to consult with him on the investigation into Betancourt's death."

"And you think I had something to do with it, you bastard? If you didn't have that gun in your hand, I'd show you right now what I say to that suggestion. I'm truly sorry for what I said about him just now. I meant no disrespect. I didn't know... but wait a minute. What's an MI5 man doing investigating the assassination of a *Deuxième Bureau* agent. One of us should be conducting this inquiry, not an outsider, a foreigner. I should be helping to find Betancourt's killer, not you!"

"Because I was the one who found the poor sod. I'm here on protection duties for the Duke and Duchess for their wedding. I was on the spot, and your Monsieur Monpamon is more than happy for me to be involved. You can ask him, yourself."

"Don't you worry yourself on that score, you worthless piece of crap. When this is all over, and you've not got a gun in your hand, we'll see if you're still so happy to be involved."

Ignoring Albinetti's rant, Bentley continued, "Where were you two nights ago, Albinetti?"

Albinetti looked shocked. "You think I murdered Betancourt?"

"I don't know. Did you?"

"You bastard. How can you say such a thing?"

"You still haven't answered my question. Where were you?"

"I wasn't feeling well and asked to be excused from my duties in Paris. They didn't want me infecting any of the other agents, so they told me to go home until I recovered. Two nights ago, I was nursing a temperature of almost forty degrees. I was in no fit state to go anywhere else."

"They told you to drive home with a virus raging inside you, almost three hundred kilometers away, when you could have quarantined somewhere in Paris? That's crazy."

"Crazy or not, that's what I did."

"Did the Bureau not have a doctor examine you?"

"There was no need to. Everyone could see how ill I was."

"Or how ill you pretended to be, perhaps."

"Now you're the one who's crazy."

"Can anyone confirm you were here that night?"

"Look around you, Inspector. Do you see glamorous movie stars and underwear models coming and going from my bedroom? If you do, I'll gladly share them with you. To answer your stupid question, no, I was here by myself – alone."

Christ, he was really good, or maybe he wasn't really good. Maybe he was being truthful. He certainly wasn't fazed by the detective's bombardment of questions. A guilty man would look much more troubled, yet Bentley was so sure. There was just something about this man. Something so unlikeable. Maybe that was why he thought he was guilty. Because he wanted him to be.

"I told you, I wasn't anywhere near the Château."

Oh, yes you were, you bloody liar. I just have to get you to say it, the detective said inside his head. The Englishman smiled confidently. "Are you sure?" he asked smugly. For the first time, there was a moment of apprehension on Albinetti's face, and Bentley noticed it, fleeting though it was.

Albinetti was still trying to brazen it out, but Bentley could see he was worried. It was time to bring this charade to an end. "I was in Monpamon's office when I heard your name being mentioned. Something about a virus. When I heard the name, Albinetti, it rang a bell with me, in the back of my mind. I'd heard it before, somewhere. I acted on a hunch and asked Monpamon to make some phone calls before leaving his office. Have you ever heard of anyone called Guglielmo Albinetti? He's a real nasty piece of work. He's a killer for hire, and he's done some contract work for the Italian SIM. He was in London a year or so ago when an Italian politician opposed to Mussolini was murdered. His weapon of choice is a stiletto. We investigated quietly but couldn't prove it was him, so we had to drop our inquiries. As soon as I came across Betancourt's body and saw how he'd been dispatched, he was immediately my first choice, but it didn't make sense. Your colleague, your friend...." Bentley spat out the word, "was stabbed in the front of his neck, not from behind. I had just met him and told him he needed to brush up on his camouflage skills. He would have been far more careful after I left him. As naïve as he might have been, I don't think he was stupid enough to allow himself to have been seen so easily again within a few minutes of our chat. He would have been on his guard and wary of anyone who came too close to where he had secreted himself. Wary of anyone except a fellow Bureau colleague. He trusted you, and you betrayed that trust, you treacherous bastard.

"We pieced it together, me, Monpamon, and my friends back in the UK an hour ago. We found out that Schlesser suspected he had a traitor somewhere in your HQ, but he did not know who that person was. He knew only that information was being passed to people who should not have had such knowledge. All Bureau agents' reports are sent to your HQ for analysis, recording, and documenting after your local offices have actioned them. Two days ago, Betancourt sent his earlier report to Monpamon, who, in turn, relayed it to Paris, where it is filed. Imagine the horror on the traitor's face when he sees a photograph of the person you are supposed to be keeping under surveillance being spotted at a location hundreds of kilometers away by a fellow Bureau officer. This target is supposed to be in Paris. Why has the Bureau agent following him not reported that he is no longer in the Capital? Because he has been paid to turn a blind eye to this target's movements, but now, a fellow officer has seen him in Tours. Not only has this target been seen, but the agent has proof of what he saw. He has taken photographs of the target at the location. Steps must be taken. It is all the fault of the agent who allowed this lapse to happen. He must rectify his mistake.

"They instructed him to remove the image of the target from the files, then drive to the Château de Candé at all speed, through the night if necessary, and eliminate the agent who took the photograph. He does all of this, but now he has another problem. Monpamon will be expecting reports from Olivier and will become worried if he does not hear from him. What to do? There is only one solution. The murderer has to pretend to be him. He has to find a reason to stay out of Paris for a spell, so concocts the virus story, a virus only he and one other person seem to know about. Does the name Giscard Duvalier mean anything to you?" Without waiting for a reply, Bentley pushed on, "He's one of the section heads at Avenue de Tourville. Monpamon and I searched your desk and found his name on a memo sheet in one of your drawers. He was the agent who 'suggested' you apply for the posting, wasn't he? He knew you, knew you could be bought. Maybe he was aware of your connection to the Italian. He's your cousin, I believe. Duvalier knew that your target would have a free hand on your watch. Schlesser now reckons he was the one passing information. He's going to be arrested, so we'll soon find out. What's the betting he'll sacrifice you to save his own neck?

"And the person you were supposed to be keeping watch on? None other than Axel Wenner-Gren, known Nazi sympathizer. The man who, despite the best efforts of the Bureau, still managed to evade surveillance; surveillance that was your responsibility. Your job and your lucrative second income as a traitor to your country were at risk, not to mention your life, if you couldn't sort this mess.

"The murderer, you, banked on his victim lying undiscovered until Wenner-Gren had left Château de Candé and you had recovered from your non-existent virus and returned to Paris. It was just your bad luck that I had stumbled across Betancourt when he was still alive only a short time earlier. Betancourt's killer and I must have just missed each other by a few minutes.

"Unfortunately, Monsieur Albinetti, you've now not only lost your freedom, you...." The treacherous agent had heard more than enough. As Bentley was about to spell out what was in store for the Bureau man, Albinetti was slowly drawing out his stiletto from its concealed sheath strapped to his back. Just as the detective was about to tell him his fate, a fate he already knew, Albinetti struck. From behind his right shoulder, a long, thin knife sliced through the air, arcing sideways to cut Bentley across the stomach. Bentley was unprepared for the speed and viciousness of the deadly assault. A split second more, and the stiletto would have found its target. The detective instinctively danced back, pulling in his middle just in time as the steel blade sliced past. He knew what Albinetti would do next. It's what he would have done in the same situation, and the only move open to the killer from the Bureau. Swing back from the opposite direction, pushing forward even harder, taking care not to overextend his reach and topple forward. But that two-second gap was all Bentley needed. Firing his Police Positive revolver at point-blank range, two quick shots to the chest blew the assassin off his feet. The impact threw the murderer backward into the wall, a pool of his crimson fluid coalescing around his lifeless body as he slumped slowly to the floor. If there had been any doubts that Albinetti was guilty of Betancourt's slaying, the last few seconds had allayed them.

The *Deuxieme Bureau* man had escaped the ultimate humiliation. Well-publicized trial, universal condemnation, inevitable conviction, and the worst indignity of all, public execution by guillotine. Now, there would be no official police investigation or account of Albinetti's death. Monpamon would attribute his agent's demise to a highly virulent strain of the non-existent virus and arrange for a quiet, discrete burial without the formality of an autopsy. Albinetti's fellow Bureau officers would never know that he had betrayed them for nothing more than a few thousand francs and a swanky French car.

CHAPTER 19

Tours, France - London, England, June 1937

The morning of June 3rd. 1937 dawned bright and clear over the grounds of the Château de Candé. This was the big day, the local society event of the year, if not the decade. The wedding of the Duke of Windsor, former King of Great Britain, Edward the Eighth, to his bride, Wallis Warfield. She had changed her name from 'Simpson' to avoid that surname being used on their marriage certificate, aware that her former identity caused such controversy.

Edward was dressed in a dark morning suit with gray pinstripe pants, and his bride-to-be was adorned with a soft crepe 'Wallis Blue' dress and matching halo-style hat made by Mainbocher, one of the leading New York couturiers.

The first part of the ceremony was performed in the green-paneled music room, whose windows overlook the Indre Valley. According to French law, a civil and a religious service were required to legalize the union. This function was conducted by the Mayor of the local town of Monts, Doctor Charles Mercier. At the same time, in an adjoining room, sixty-one-year-old organist, Marcel Dupré, played works by Bach and Schumann and one of his own compositions. Cecil Beaton, the well-known British society photographer, was commissioned to take the official wedding pictures.

After the formal ceremony was over, the bridal party returned to the music room, where the religious Sacrament was conducted. An oaken chest in an alcove of the room served as a makeshift altar. A solitary lit candle at each end of the chest, with a cross in the middle, were the only adornments.

The Duke and Major Metcalfe walked on ahead to await the bride-to-be, with the melodic strains of Schumann echoing through the corridors. Abruptly, the music changed to the short overture to the traditional wedding refrain, part of Handel's oratorio, Judas Maccabeus. Everyone in the music room held their breath as Wallis Warfield, accompanied by Herman Rogers, who had offered to give her away, strode majestically and slowly into the room, walking in time to Dupré's music.

Edward could not fail to notice one unsetting and disturbing thing. On their parade into the music room, Wallis did not take her eyes off Rogers as she clutched him tightly by the arm. As the couple was halfway across the floor, Edward turned and whispered something into Metcalfe's ear. The major shook his head and whispered a brief reply. This answer, whatever it was, seemed to mollify the Duke, but every time Metcalfe caught sight of his friend, a worried frown still seemed to be across his face. Then all was still.

Jardine conducted the religious part of the ceremony without incident, as Dupré softly played Sir Joseph Barnby's 'O Perfect Love' during the benediction.

After Beaton had finished taking his photos, the couple and their guests adjourned to the formal dining room, where a buffet luncheon was served, toasts and speeches were said, and the Duke and Duchess cut the three-tier wedding cake.

This was a day for Bentley to be as unobtrusive as possible, and he stayed discreetly in the background but was ever alert to any sudden or unusual disturbance. He was thankful that his services would not be required. He had not had much sleep. In the very early hours of the night before, he and Monpamon quietly removed Betancourt's body. Both men had assumed correctly that everyone would want to get a good night's rest before the morning's celebrations. It had all gone to plan, and no one had challenged them as they put the agent's dead body in a hessian sack before carrying it to the Bureau man's car, which he had left just outside the gates of the spacious front approach. Unlike his killer, Monpamon would ensure that Betancourt would get a proper burial, honored by his family and all those who came to offer their last respects. The agent had died, his epitaph would read, in defense of his country, and all French people everywhere would owe him a debt of gratitude they could never repay.

There was a scare early in the morning of the wedding when the Duchess sought out Bentley on the pretext of confirming there were no last-minute security issues to deal with.

"I... looked for you last night, but you weren't in your room. Where were you?" She asked quizzically.

For one of the few times in his life, Bentley was flustered, but quickly recovered. "I was... I was doing some last-minute checking to make sure everything was secure," he lied.

"What? At three o'clock in the morning? Really?"

"A good security agent never sleeps, Your Grace. How do we know someone from, oh, I don't know where, but someone who just wanted to spoil your wedding, wouldn't steal into the house to disrupt the proceedings? You wouldn't want that, would you?"

"No, I suppose not," she agreed.

"So that's what I was doing, O.K.?"

"Yes, my sweet, if you say so." But Bentley knew she did not believe a word of it. Too bad. Let her think what she liked. She could hardly reveal that her protection officer wasn't in his bed in the early hours of the morning, could she?"

The Royal couple drove off in the early evening, bound for the train that would take them to Austria, where they would spend the next three months, ostensibly on honeymoon. Once the couple had departed, life began to return to normal in the Château de Candé. In his room for the last night, Bentley concluded his written report before contacting Thames House on his Morse device to advise them of all that had happened since the evening before. He had just stowed away his machine when there was a knock on his bedroom door. Had it not been for the fact that he had seen the newly-weds drive off, he might have fancifully believed it was the Duchess desiring one last romp. But, no, it was not Wallis Windsor. It was Charles Bedaux, the owner of the property. After the formalities were done, Bedaux said, "I just came to express my thanks and gratitude for all you have done to facilitate a smooth and seamless affair. I cannot bear to think what might have happened if there had been any... disturbance."

Keeping an impassive demeanor, Bentley's imagination went into high gear. Did Bedaux know anything about the death of the young French agent? Was this his way of letting Bentley know that he was aware of what had transpired in the bushes a few days ago and that he was willing to stay quiet if there were no inconvenient investigations that could implicate him or any of his guests? Bentley stayed silent as Bedaux continued, "You have behaved with exemplary efficiency and professionalism, despite your verbal tussle with the couple the other night." Bentley made to speak, but the millionaire entrepreneur halted him, smiling. "Please don't concern yourself, Detective Inspector. They are our friends, yes, and I know that at times they, especially Wallis, can be insufferable, but they are good people at heart."

That depends on your definition of 'good,' Monsieur Bedaux, thought the detective.

"Wallis took quite a shine to you, I hear. So much so, in fact, that I believe she's become quite infatuated with you." Despite himself, Bentley couldn't help blushing. "Oh, yes, if your little nocturnal escapade the other night is anything to go by, you've set her heart aflutter."

"I..." Bentley stammered. So there were going to be repercussions after all. The only thing he could do was wait and see what Bedaux said or did next. He was about to find out.

"I don't think it would do your career any good if your superiors found out that you had had a, how shall we put it, a dalliance with the woman you were meant to be protecting. Our promiscuous little Duchess said you gave an excellent account of yourself. You should be pleased. She does not rate even her new husband as highly as she spoke of you." Bedaux was no longer the smiling, jovial host. His face had adopted a vulpine leer as he continued, "If you want to keep your job and not have to end your career under the most God almighty cloud, you'll listen to me."

"Wait a minute, Bedaux. If you shout out about what the Duchess and I... did, you'll implicate her as well. I don't think the Duke would be too happy about that, do you?"

Bedaux grinned mirthlessly. “Little David will say and do exactly what we tell him to. As for the Duchess, she is well used to... situations of this nature. It would be nothing new to her. She will shrug it off as she has done in the past and move on to her next lover. She is a free spirit in many ways and cares nothing for what people think of her, especially as she has been cheated, as she sees it, out of her rightful place as Queen of England. So no, Detective Inspector, the only ones who will suffer in this tawdry little scandal will be you and your lovely wife. Am I beginning to make myself clear?”

“What do you want from me, Bedaux?”

“Good, Inspector. You’re a fast study. First of all, in her throes of passion, Wallis told you things we would prefer to keep to ourselves for the time being. How you discovered that Axel was in the mansion, I do not know, but you will keep this fact to yourself. As for the Duke and Duchess’s proposed trip to Germany, you will not divulge this to anyone. Is that clear?”

“Perfectly,” Bentley responded through a mouth that had gone dry.

“That was the easy part. Now comes the part that will perhaps be more difficult for you, but one which you will accommodate us in, anyway.” Without giving Bentley time to respond, the French-American continued, telling the English detective what he required.

Bentley nodded slowly, his head downcast, appearing reluctant to agree to Bedaux’s terms but realizing he had little option but to do so.

“Very well. You will return to London tonight, but I expect to see you back in a couple of days. I don’t care how you do it, but if I do not hear from you within forty-eight hours, you know what will happen.” Without waiting for a response, the French businessman turned around and left Bentley’s quarters.

* * *

The following day, three men sat in the New Scotland Yard office of Brigadier James Whitehead. Colonel Vernon Kell, Detective Inspector Alan Bentley, and Whitehead himself. “So Bedaux wants you to be the

Duke and Duchess's full-time protection officer, does he? What right does a bloody Frog have to demand anything from New Scotland Yard? He might own a bloody castle in France, but he does not own the Metropolitan Police. How dare he? Who does he think he is?" Spluttered Whitehead.

"There are a couple of things I haven't told you," Bentley admitted. They heard him out, then Kell said, "You have been a busy boy, Alan. I'm not sure if I would consider it a perquisite of the job, mind you, and it goes against protocol. But if that was what it takes for us to get inside their scheme, whatever it is, I suppose we'll all have to turn a blind eye. So Bedaux thinks he's got you where he wants you, does he?"

"Yes. He thinks I won't let you in on my night-time adventure with the Duchess for fear it would ruin my career and my marriage. I didn't think you would be too concerned about my lapse of judgment, but I'm not sure if Deborah would be so forgiving."

"Well, we'll just have to make sure she doesn't find out then, won't we?" suggested Whitehead. "I've been doing some more digging on Axel Wenner-Gren. I think he's someone we're going to have to keep an eye on in the future. When he's in London, that is. He seems to be getting even more friendly with Göring than he already was. This situation could be troubling to us in the future, considering his wealth and enormous influence. I'm still not clear why Bedaux is so keen for you to be the Windsors' full-time security officer, though."

"I think I am," Offered Kell. "Edward has been whining about not having enough security, although who would want to kill him apart from the rest of the Royal Family, the hierarchy of the Church of England, the British government, and countless numbers of his former subjects, I've no idea." Kell joked. "Seriously, from what Alan tells us, it seems like they want someone they think they can trust. Someone who'll keep his mouth shut if he sees or hears anything he shouldn't."

"Yes, no doubt you're right, Colonel." Agreed Whitehead.

Turning to Alan, he asked, "Are you alright with this? It'll mean spending quite some time away from home. How will you explain that to Deborah?"

"I'll think of something."

Bentley worked on the old maxim, 'when all else fails, tell the truth.' Or, in this case, a near approximation. He explained to his wife that the Duke and Duchess were so impressed by his handling of their security in Tours they had requested that his tenure as their security officer be extended. Sir Samuel Hoare had agreed to the request. He would, naturally, be rotated from time to time to allow for breaks and time off, but he would be on duty most of the time. Whether it was the way he said it, or his demeanor, he felt as if she did not entirely believe him. Or was it merely his guilty conscience? Either way, a small souvenir from wherever he was guarding the Windsors would not be good enough this time, he told himself.

Bentley called Bedaux on the number the French-American had given him, telling him that his superiors had authorized the detective to become Edward and Wallis's permanent protection officer.

"The couple are honeymooning at Wasserleonburg Castle in Austria. I'll telegraph you instructions on how and when to get there. I won't be there, but I'll arrange for someone from the Castle to pick you up from the local train station." Then Bedaux hung up. Abrupt and to the point. Was this how his life was going to be now and into the foreseeable future? An inconvenient necessity, to be utilized and exploited as nothing more than a government-approved bodyguard to two of the most loathsome people he had ever met?

Something Bedaux said troubled him. It took him some time to recall what it was and why it had concerned him. Then he remembered. '*Little David will say and do exactly what we tell him to.*' Wallis, Bedaux, Wenner-Gren, and probably others were bending the weak-willed Duke to their purposes and manipulating him for some nefarious reason. Whatever it was, could only be to the good of the Third Reich, which, conversely meant it would be detrimental to his own country. They wanted him to be the Windsors' protection officer. So be it. He would make sure he was never far away. In fact, an idea was forming in his head, one which might see him ensconced in their inner circle, ready to thwart whatever plot the enemies of his country were hatching.

CHAPTER 20

Saak, Austria, June 1937

Bentley arrived a few days later at Nötsch im Gailtal, the nearest railway stop to Wasserleonburg Castle, to continue his duties. As Bedaux had promised, a driver was on hand to take the detective to his destination, a short but winding drive away through Saak. The Duke and Duchess had rented the entire Castle for the duration of their three-month stay. The only other guests would be those invited by the couple themselves. After the unhappy prelude to their wedding, they wanted privacy above all else, and this remote Schloss was ideal for their needs.

After being shown to his quarters and settled in, he sought out the couple to alert them of his arrival. Neither of them seemed that keen to see him, a servant merely informing him that the Duke and Duchess were aware of his presence and would send for him as and when they wished. Bentley shook his head impatiently. If he did not assert his independence now, his life would not be worth living. Not if the pair of them thought they could treat him like they did the staff of the Château de Candé.

To the flunkey who gave him the news, he said, "Tell the Duke and the Duchess it is my responsibility to see that they are well and to confirm in person that they are aware that I am here. Now go!" The liveried servant hesitated, unsure who had the greater authority. His reason told him it had to be the royal couple, but this man acted with such command, he merely nodded nervously a few times before withdrawing.

He returned less than five minutes later, having obviously been chastened by them for overriding their instructions, but indicated Bentley should follow him, nonetheless.

"Is this how it's going to be for the duration of your stay, Detective Inspector? We give orders which you promptly countermand? I won't have it, you know. You can be dismissed from your post just as easily as you came." This was from Edward. His attitude was so transparent, it was risible. He had to put on a show in front of Wallis, pretending that he was the dominant partner in the relationship, while everyone knew she was the puppet mistress who pulled his strings.

"Yes, Your Royal Highness, I am aware I breached protocol by going against your instructions, but I have my duties just as the rest of the staff do. You can, of course, dismiss me if you choose, but you may find it difficult to obtain another officer when I put in my report, short as it will be."

"Report? What report?" asked Wallis.

"We all have to report to someone, Your Grace. Present company excepted, of course. But when I say that I could not perform my duties how they needed to be conducted due to the obstructive nature of my protectees, the Home Office and the Metropolitan Police may not wish to replace my position so quickly." It was now or never. If he had overstepped the mark, they would send him back by the next train, but he had decided before setting out from London that he would not allow them to treat him as they had tried to do a few days ago. Not again; ever.

"And I should, with the greatest respect, also point out that Monsieur Bedaux was especially insistent that I return to continue my duties as your protection officer. I'm sure you would not want to displease the man who so graciously opened his beautiful home to you for your nuptials barely a week ago."

"Yes, that's all good and well, but…." Edward began, but Wallis placed a restraining hand on his forearm.

"The detective has a valid point, of course. If we do not take his advice on matters of security, what's the point of having him here in the first place?" she smiled softly.

"No!" shouted Edward. "Dammit, I will not be spoken to like that by a member of the lower orders. It's damn well not good enough. Does this man not know his place?"

"Oh, I think the inspector knows his place all too well, doesn't he?"

"Sir, Ma'am, I'm here to do a job, a job that you asked me to do, through your friend, Charles Bedaux. If I cannot do my job the way I see fit, I can be of no use to either of you. Do I make myself clear?"

While Edward sat fuming, Wallis replied in her native Baltimore drawl, "I suppose we are in your hands, Detective Inspector." Bentley could not be sure, but he could have sworn he saw Wallis almost imperceptibly raise her open fist up and down while winking at him. Oh, God, was it going to be like this for the next few months? Just what had he let himself in for?

* * *

The first couple of weeks passed uneventfully. Edward kept out of Bentley's way as much as he could, and, despite his apprehension, Wallis made no more evening excursions to his room. It seemed she had done what had been required of her. Make love to a man they thought would be useful to them to coerce him by whatever means necessary to act in their interests rather than those of his employers. Despite his display of independent defiance, they were sure that he would do what they would demand of him when it was necessary.

Towards the end of June, the Windsors threw a party to which they invited many of the local aristocracy and politicians. One of them was George Messersmith, U.S. Ambassador to Austria and a friend of the Duke. Suspicious of Edward's political allegiances, President Roosevelt had given Messersmith a watching brief to monitor the Duke's activities. During one of those rare moments in the evening when his guests did not surround him, Messersmith approached his host. The man seemed to be moving toward Edward purposefully, and Bentley suspected that the diplomat might be about to cause trouble. As he approached the two men, however, he saw that the American merely wished to reach the Duke before other members of the party could buttonhole him. Trying to make a good impression on his host, he grasped Edward by the hand. "Your Royal Highness, it's so nice to meet with you again. Thank you for inviting me to your dinner party. I trust you and the Duchess have settled in to your temporary home. If there's anything you need, please let me know."

Edward smiled pleasantly, thanking Messersmith for his offer. As he was about to respond, the diplomat leaned forward, whispering into Edward's ear. The Duke smelled the alcohol off his breath. It was clear Messersmith had indulged just a little too much and had taken advantage of his host's generosity. "I have some news that might amuse you," he confided softly, but not softly enough, "it certainly gave us a laugh or two, I can tell you."

His interest now piqued, Edward stayed silent and allowed Messersmith to continue, assuming he was about to be privy to some harmless embassy gossip. "Those Italians are pretty dumb, don't you think? Why, we've just cracked their cipher codes. Imagine that! Nothing they say will be a secret from us any longer. Thanks to our Intelligence boys, we've decoded their signals. We'll know what those Eyeties are up to before they do! We've just found out that a freight train carrying illegal weapons from Germany to Italy has crashed in Austria. That'll set the cat among the pigeons, I don't doubt."

The Duke merely smiled and nodded approvingly. They engaged in some more small talk before Edward politely excused himself and moved away.

Bentley had stayed close to his charge and had overheard the conversation. This was a worry. Of all the people the naïve young man could have confided in, he had to pick the Duke. A short while later, whether with intent, or due to careless exuberance, Edward approached another guest, the *chargé d'affaires* at the Italian embassy, no doubt intending to gloat about the devastating secret the young diplomat had just given him. Before Bentley could divert the Duke from his intended target,

Bentley's worst fears were realized when the Duke quietly blurted out to his Italian guest the information Messersmith had just given him.

Accepting he had not acted swiftly enough, the detective-spy knew that there was nothing he could now do to prevent this betrayal of trust from having devastating consequences. What the Italian would do with this intelligence, Bentley could only guess at. But one thing was for sure. Under no circumstances should Edward or his wife be given any information that could be harmful to Britain or her allies. The ramifications could be damaging beyond repair. He had to let London know as soon as possible what had transpired. Whether they chose to relay this unwelcome news to the Americans was not a matter for him to decide. A higher authority would need to make that call.

Casually strolling around the reception chamber, Bentley slowly made his way out of the room and headed for his quarters. The nearer he got to his bedroom, the quicker he raced. Bending down, he reached under the bed to pull out his valise. He searched with groping fingers only to find that his case was not there. Frantically, he ran his hand along underneath the bedframe, eventually touching it a few feet from where he was sure he had left it. A worse shock awaited him when he pulled it out from where it had been laying, only to find that one of the hasps had been opened. Evidently, someone had been in his quarters, someone who was either an amateur, or someone who wanted him to know that they had been there.

Were the Duke and Duchess, or someone close to them, playing a double game? Was he merely the public face as their protection officer? Was there another person, or persons, perhaps known only to a select few, secretly watching the watcher? Putting his fears aside, he sprung the other lock. Opening the lid of his case, he was relieved to see that his Morse machine appeared untouched, but this proved nothing. Using the usual protocols, he contacted Thames House to alert them to the Duke's lack of discretion. He would not mention the potential lapse in his own security. Not yet. Not until he knew who, singular or plural, had invaded his room. London had no new instructions for him, so he signed off and went to rejoin the hosts and their guests.

The gathering finally came to an end in the early hours of the morning as the Duke and Duchess saw off their last visitors.

"Well, that all seemed to go off rather splendidly, I thought," observed Edward as they climbed the stairs.

"Let's leave the post mortem until tomorrow," yawned Wallis as she took his arm. "Right now, all I want to do is sleep. It's been a long day."

"Yes, it has, but an enjoyable one."

Turning to her husband, Wallis said suddenly, "You go on ahead, my sweet. I just need a quick word with our protection officer. I shan't be long." Edward gave her a quizzical look. Reluctantly, he replied, "Can't this wait until the morning? Dammit, what am I saying? It's already morning. Come on, my love, whatever it is, surely it can wait a few more hours. I'm sure our loyal security officer needs to get to his bed as well."

"It won't take a minute," Wallis insisted. "Just while I have it in my mind. I may have forgotten it by tomorrow."

Without querying what was on her mind, Edward climbed wearily on, while his wife retraced her steps back down the stairs. Bentley was helping the staff to tidy up a little before he, too, returned to his room. Gliding over to him, she said so the other servants could not overhear her, "I was in your room earlier." The detective made no reply. She continued, "Don't you want to know why?"

"I have a pretty good idea, Your Grace," he replied as he continued to collect all the empty champagne and wine bottles. The staff would pick up all of the detritus before stopping for the night. They would complete the vacuuming, polishing, and dusting in daylight. By the time the Duke and Duchess surfaced, no one would ever tell there had been a party in this large reception room the night before.

"Don't flatter yourself, Detective Inspector. The first night was a... necessity. The second night had there been one, would have been a... reward to myself. They were singular events, never to be repeated. No, the simple truth is, you intrigue me. A Metropolitan Police officer who is not afraid to speak his mind to, if I may say so, others who are way above his station. I have never come across that situation before, at least not outside of America. The upper classes over there are rather more tolerant than their English counterparts."

"Your Grace, it is very late, and I am quite tired. If there is a point to this discussion, I would be most grateful if you would get to it."

"My point is this, Detective Inspector. I would like to know what a humble police officer is doing with a gadget which, if I did not know any better, would say looks like a Morse code transmitter? How do you explain that, eh?"

"And, Your Grace, how do you explain knowing about the device in the first place. That is a gross infringement of my privacy." Bentley stormed.

"In my home, Inspector Bentley, I decide what is and what is not private."

"With the greatest respect, Your Grace, this is not your home. It is one which you are only renting temporarily. It does not give you the right to...."

"Oh, stop being so pedantic, Inspector," Wallis bit back dismissively. "Whether or not I own this house is beside the point. While my husband and I are the main incumbents, we decide what is and what is not secret. You are merely a paid employee, like the rest of the staff. You would do well to remember that. Now, I will ask you again. Why do you have a Morse transmitter hidden in your room? Tell me, or...."

"Or what, Your Grace? Fire me? Sack me? Throw me out? Yes, you can do all of those things, but then you will be without a bodyguard. Who will protect you from those bogeymen your husband seems so fearful about? It really is such a pity...."

"A pity? What's a pity? Please do not pity me, Inspector. Trust me; I am someone who does not need your compassion. Far from it."

"No, Your Grace, I didn't mean it to come out like that. I meant... the more I am in Your Grace's company, and the Duke's, of course, the more I can understand... I'm sorry, I was about to overstep the mark again. Forgive me. I should go to bed. It's very late."

"No, Inspector, now you've really gone and intrigued me. What were you going to say? Please speak freely. This revelation sounds as if it may be interesting."

"Well, Your Grace..."

"Wallis. Please call me Wallis, but only when the Duke is not around. That will be our little secret; well, one of them, eh?"

"Thank you. I was only going to say that just before you got married, I bumped into Reverend Jardine in the grounds of Candé. He lamented the fact that the Church of England was, as he put it, myopic, if they could not see that sometimes we get the opportunity to love more than one person in our lifetime. Despite our, ah, short romantic interlude, I can see that you care for each other very much. I must confess I have changed my own opinion since being involved with you both. Jardine was right. Love can happen more than once in a lifetime. You and the Duke have proved that, if I may say so."

"That is very kind of you, Inspector. Yes, David and I are very much in love, despite what you may hear from other quarters. I am sorry if I was a bit harsh with you. I know you are only trying to do your job, and we haven't always made that easy. I will try to be more accommodating in the future. I am feeling fatigued. Would you mind escorting me to my room?"

"Not at all, your... er... Wallis." Bentley gently guided the Duchess up to her and Edward's suite. As he was about to leave, she whispered, "You still haven't told me...."

"In the morning, Your Grace. I promise."

Despite the lateness of the previous night, Bentley was up, shaved, and dressed by seven a.m. The Duke and Duchess did not appear until sometime in the afternoon, and when they did, it was apparent that they had been arguing. Both were stony-faced and barely acknowledged each other as they sat down to luncheon. So much for true love, thought the detective, remembering the conversation of the night before.

Without uttering a word, the Duke lay down his cutlery before dabbing at his lips with his napkin and leaving the dining room. Wallis smiled over at Bentley, who was sitting at another table in the otherwise empty dining room. "Yes, Inspector, even two people who are as much in love as David and I still have our disagreements from time to time, as I'm sure you do with your wife. I suspect, however, judging by your, ah, performance, you do not argue about...." Bentley stayed silent as Wallis continued, "Sometimes

David starts what he cannot finish, if you get my meaning. It can be quite... unsatisfactory."

"I'm not sure if you should be discussing such intimate details with someone like me, Your Grace. These are very personal matters that I...."

Quickly changing the subject, Wallis asked, "So... Alan... about last night; are you going to answer my question?"

"Yes, I will. As I mentioned to you the other day, I have to submit a regular report to my superiors. We're now living in the nineteen-thirties. We don't need to use pen and paper anymore. They will soon be as outdated as the carrier pigeon. My superiors don't like to wait for weeks to receive my reports, which would be hopelessly out of date by then, anyway. This merely allows me to update them almost instantaneously if the need arises. It's as simple as that."

"So why all the secrecy last night?"

"I wasn't being secretive, just tired."

"Yes, it was a late-night, wasn't it? So what happens to it at the other end?"

"I assume someone transcribes it somewhere in the bowels of New Scotland Yard and forwards it somewhere, where it will no doubt be filed away. If that's all, Duchess, I..." Bentley made to leave the table.

"Just one more thing, Inspector."

"Yes, Your Grace?"

"That second evening at the Château de Candé, when I came looking for you."

"I believe you mentioned it."

"You said you were patrolling the grounds at some ridiculous time of night, if I recall."

"Yes, indeed."

"And did you find anything suspicious on your travels?"

"No, not as I remember. It was all quiet."

"That's funny. I happened to glance out of the window and could have sworn I saw you and another man carrying a sack between you. It looked like the shape of a body. It was very late, of course, and I could have been mistaken. The eyes do tend to play tricks at that time of the night, don't they? Was that all it was, Detective Inspector? Were my eyes deceiving me?"

Bentley was stunned by this revelation. There was no time to dissemble or think of a reasonable explanation that Wallis might believe. There was only one thing for it. He had to tell the truth without telling the truth.

"If I tell you, Duchess, I can't untell you. Do you understand me? Right now, you don't know anything. Please believe me, for your sake, it would be better to keep it that way. What I can say is that anything you saw or thought you saw does not impact you or the Duke in this hypothetical event that you may or may not have witnessed. Does that answer your question?"

"Inspector, contrary to popular belief, I was not born yesterday. What you're saying is, I can't be held liable for something I know nothing about."

"Quite so, Your Grace."

"My, we are becoming a dreadful pair of conspirators, aren't we, Detective?"

"It's for your own good, I quite assure you, Your Grace."

"Very well. I shall forget we ever had this conversation – for the time being," she added ominously as she dismissed him.

Bentley thought it unlikely that she would tell the Duke about their discussion, but who else might she disclose it to? And what would be the ramifications? Time would tell.

CHAPTER 21

Paris, France, September 1937

The Windsors returned to Paris in September where they took a suite at the Hotel Meurice on the Rue de Rivoli. There had been no further repercussions regarding Wallis and Bentley's exchange about the Château de Candé and, indeed, after that discourse, the relationship between the detective and the Windsors seemed to improve. By the time they had settled in at their hotel, their initial hostility to each other had turned into a cautious familiarity. The detective appeared to understand the stresses they were under and expressed his appreciation for their position at various times while they were in Austria.

A few days after their arrival, Bentley committed an act that could have led to his instant dismissal and possible prosecution. He tentatively approached the couple, clearing his throat before speaking. "Your Royal Highness, Your Grace, I don't know if you're aware, but you, we, seem to be being observed by certain people. It's my job to look for unfamiliar as well as familiar faces, and I'm sure that whenever you are in the hotel foyer, the same two or three men are always present. I just thought you should be aware."

"Yes, well, it's probably the first arrondissement gendarmerie looking out for us. We are something of celebrities, you know, Inspector." Edward opined.

"I don't think our protection officer means the local police force," countered Wallis.

"No, Ma'am, I don't. If you will pardon my bluntness, you are not the only famous people to stay at the Meurice. I do not think those men are from the gendarmerie. I believe they are from the French *Deuxième Bureau*."

"What makes you say that, Inspector?"

"I've had run-ins with our own secret service from time to time, Your Grace. The country and the language might be different, but some things do not change. Their manner, their stance, everything about them screams 'intelligence.'"

"Why would they be following us, Inspector?" asked Edward.

"Regrettably, your Royal Highness, your links to, ah, certain, um, international figures, is not unknown. They fear you may be, that is, you...."

"...might be up to no good. Is that it, Detective Inspector?"

"Something like that, Sir."

"Of all the damn cheek. How dare they spy on two British citizens like that? I have a mind to put in a complaint to...."

"That would not be wise, your Royal Highness."

"And why not, pray?"

"Because if they know you are on to them, they will change their routine, and the next time, they will be more discrete. Even I may not spot them. Surely it is better to let them believe you do not know of their presence and just behave as you would normally do. Then we can play them at their own game."

"Our protection officer has a point, David."

"Yes, I suppose so," the Duke conceded.

"Well, it does prove one thing, I suppose. Our detective knows where his loyalties lie, doesn't he?"

"I'm only doing my job, Your Grace."

"No, Inspector. If I'm right, you're doing far more than that."

Bentley demurred, lowering his head away from Wallis. The Duchess indicated for the three of them to sit in the red velvet upholstered regency chairs. "May I, that is, may we, have a confidential chat, Inspector? It won't take too long."

"I'm at your disposal, Your Grace."

The protection officer and the Windsors spoke for almost half an hour. At the conclusion, Wallis said, "So it's done, Detective Inspector. David will arrange for you to accompany us on our visit to Germany next month. We have still to work out the final details, but we are meeting with Monsieur Bedaux and Wenner-Gren in this apartment within the next day or two. They have already been in contact with certain figures from the German government to facilitate our trip. Thanks to your vigilance, we can ensure that no one, apart from us, will know they are here."

"Yes, Your Grace."

"David and I would like to spend some time on our own, so you may leave us for the time being. One last thing before you go."

"Yes, Your Grace?"

Turning to face Bentley full-on, she smiled. "Thank you."

* * *

Two days later, Bedaux and Wenner-Gren sat in the Windsors' suite, assured that they had arrived without the knowledge of the *Deuxième Bureau*. They were accompanied by Captain Fritz Wiedemann, Hitler's personal adjutant, and one of the main organizers of the proposed trip. Despite the reluctance of the Swede and the French-American, Wallis was insistent that Bentley should be included in their itinerary. He was, after all, their protection officer and had to know how they would be traveling to Germany, where they would be going, and who they would be meeting. The pair reluctantly accepted Wallis's argument, and Bentley was summoned to join them, the Duchess assuring them that the detective was 'one of us.'

The discussion took several hours, which was punctuated by Edward periodically calling down for drinks and food. By the end of the afternoon, every facet of their trip down to the last detail had been finalized. With or without the blessing or consent of his brother or the British government, Edward and Wallis were going to Germany.

CHAPTER 22

Berlin, Germany, October 1937

Edward and Wallis arrived in Berlin on October 12th., alighting at *Friedrichstrasse* Station to a tumultuous welcome. Although they were no longer considered part of the Royal Family in Britain, the crowd flocked to them as if they were on a State visit. They were met off the train by Robert Ley, leader of the *Deutsche Arbeitsfront*, or German Labor Front, the only official trade union permitted under Nazi Germany. Officially, the Windsors had been invited at the behest of the German government to tour new housing projects, a subject which the former King had taken an interest in back in the United Kingdom. As they were cheered away from the throng in their official Mercedes limousine, Edward said to his wife, "This is what I'd hoped for in Britain. What a pity that the only ones who recognize us for who were truly are, who we might have been, are the German people. I wanted so much for you, my darling, so much."

"Don't distress yourself, so. Let's just enjoy the trip and see what the future brings. I think our friend has big plans for us; in fact, I'm certain of it. He couldn't have made it any clearer if he'd spelled it out in ten-foot-high lettering."

"What do you mean?"

"Didn't you hear Doctor Ley? He addressed me, me as 'Your Royal Highness,'" she answered exuberantly. "If that doesn't signal *Herr Hitler*'s intentions towards us, nothing does."

Edward allowed himself a contented smile. Yes, it was all going to work out just fine. At least for him and Wallis. As for the rest of the traitors back in Britain, they would face whatever fate was in store for them.

They arrived at their hotel, the *Kaiserhof*, conveniently situated next to the *Reichschancellery*, to more crowds wanting to catch a glimpse of the man who gave up his throne, the greatest throne in the world, to marry the woman he loved. Their schedule was a heavy one, the Nazis wanting to make the most of their high-profile British guests. As they entered the hotel foyer, surrounded by their entourage, the staff bowed to Edward and curtsied to Wallis, also addressing her by her unofficial royal title. Wallis smiled graciously as the hotel manager escorted them to the lift to take them to their suite.

Bentley, as usual, was glancing around the hotel, on alert for any possible danger. He saw nothing to alarm him, apart from two men in identical long black leather trench coats and dark fedora hats. They stared menacingly at him but did not attempt to approach him or the Windsors. He knew who and what these men were. He had nothing to fear as long as he did not assert his authority too much. They were no longer in Wasserleonburg Castle or at the Meurice. These men would not think twice to harm him if they believed he did not play by their rules.

The detective-spy went with the Windsors into their hotel apartment, together with Wiedemann. They chose to unpack their belongings themselves, being tired of staff who 'accidentally' found a personal item of the Duke or Duchess and which they kept as a souvenir. As they were beginning to empty their valises, Wiedemann said, "May I remind you both that you have a dinner engagement at *Horchers* this evening with the Foreign Minister and the Minister of Propaganda and his wife. The meal has been booked for seven-thirty. Formal dress will not be required."

"Oh, really," the Duke complained. "Can't you see that we're both exhausted after our train journey? Could we not...?"

"No, your Royal Highness, we cannot postpone it. This appointment has been planned for weeks, and it cannot be altered to suit Your Royal Highness's fatigue. May I remind Your Royal Highness who is paying for this lavish hotel, not to mention the entire trip? You will both please make yourselves available to be collected no later than seven p.m. That will give you a couple of hours at least to rest up, refresh and change."

"I say, that's a bit sharp, old boy."

"I am not your 'old boy,' Your Royal Highness. I am the adjutant to our Führer." He retorted disparagingly. "I will now leave you to prepare for this evening." And with those parting words, Wiedemann left the chamber.

"When in Rome..." observed the Duchess wryly.

"We're not in Rome, in case you hadn't noticed. We're in Berlin."

"Never mind. Let's get some rest. I fear it's going to be a long night."

* * *

The limousine arrived to take them to *Horchers* at precisely seven o'clock, driven by Robert Ley. The restaurant was located in *Martin Luther Strasse*, a fifteen-minute drive from the *Kaiserhof*. Their dinner guests were already seated when the Duke and Duchess arrived. Observing formalities, they stood to welcome the pair, addressing them both by their spurious royal titles. Von Ribbentrop was particularly attentive to the couple, especially the Duchess, who returned his familiarity with polite amusement. Edward was not unaware of the rumors which had circulated among London's elite that his wife had had an affair with the Foreign Minister when he was the German ambassador in London, and continued seeing him even during their own relationship. Some had suggested that he had frequently sent her seventeen carnations, one for each time they had been intimate. Edward could only look on and smile graciously as von Ribbentrop engaged in small talk with his wife, with whom he was dominating the conversation.

"I hope you don't mind, Your Royal Highness, but I also invited one of our Führer's friends, Albert Speer, to join us. Knowing your husband's fondness for the arts, I thought they might indulge in their shared passion for opera."

As he spoke, the restaurant door opened to admit the man himself. As well as being one of Hitler's closest adherents, Speer, an architect by training, was also the General Building Inspector for Berlin. Greeting everyone at the table, Speer took his seat next to Edward as the rest of the assembly ordered their meal. While Wallis and von Ribbentrop engaged in animated conversation, discourse between Edward and Speer was stilted, mainly due to the Duke's ire at the attention being accorded to her by the Foreign Minister.

The party broke up just after midnight when Ley returned to drive the Duke and Duchess back to their hotel. Conversation was muted between them on the way back, with Edward still smarting from his wife's apparent over-friendliness with her former lover. The Duke was well aware that anything they said would be reported back to Hitler, and even possibly von Ribbentrop himself, so he kept his temper in check until they were in their suite. "I must say, I think it was a bit much for Ribbentrop to monopolize you for the entire evening. What must the other guests have thought?"

"It doesn't matter what they thought; there was nothing they could do about it. Don't be jealous, my sweet. You know I only have eyes for you. We were just catching up on lost time, that's all."

"Well, as long as that was all you were doing. We're married now, Wallis. I can't have you cavorting about with other men, you know. It wouldn't be seemly, even if there was nothing in it. You know how tongues wag, especially in this place. I must ask you to keep a more demure profile while we're here. Do you understand me?"

"Oh, yes, I understand you, alright. You listen to me, Edward." Wallis only called him by that name when she was angry with him. He had upset her, but what was a husband to do? He had to assert his authority. He was the Duke, after all. "I shall have conversations with whoever I like whenever I like. I promised to stay faithful to you, and I shall honor that vow, but I will not be subjugated to the extent that I cannot have friendships of my own. Now, do you understand me?"

A chastened Edward could only reply meekly, "Yes, my dear. I do. I'm sorry." It was only then that Edward noticed a scrap of paper on the escritoire desk. He was sure it had not been there before he left. He had done some writing and had tidied up, not wishing to leave any trace of his work behind. Lifting it, he turned it over to find a note. It read, '*Your Royal Highness and Your Grace, although I have not been able to find any evidence, I believe your conversations are being overheard elsewhere. Please do not say anything which might compromise your stay in the country. I will discuss this with you more in the morning.*' It was initialed, A.B. The detective must have left it just before they went to *Horchers*. Oh, God, why hadn't they seen it earlier? Now someone knew of his jealousy and quiet animosity toward von Ribbentrop. They had dismissed their protection officer on their return, and he had gone to bed. There was no more he could do tonight, but how could Edward repair the damage he had done? Perhaps Bentley might have an idea. The detective was becoming more indispensable to them with each passing day.

It was a troubled Edward who lay down next to his wife. He was still to have official, 'informal' meetings with other high-ranking members of the government, including the Führer himself. How would this bode for him if word got back to Hitler that he, Edward, had been concerned about his wife's supposed unfaithfulness with his Foreign Minister? Sleep would not come easily after what he had just read. He turned to face his wife, hoping to receive a few comforting words. Wearing her eye mask and breathing rhythmically, Wallis was already slumbering peacefully.

Bentley had not gone to bed. He had telegraphed Thames House with as much information as he had been able to overhear while sitting at an adjoining table, not that there had been much to report. He also related other items he thought Colonel Kell should be aware of while omitting more details he was not yet ready to impart. Only when he had finished and had secreted his equipment did he turn his mind to the Duke and Duchess. He hoped they'd read his note and that the Duke had said nothing indiscrete. Too bad if he had. It was late, and he was going to sleep. Anything else could wait until the morning.

CHAPTER 23

Berlin and other locations, Germany, October 1937

Edward awoke early. He was up and about by nine in the morning, a practice he was not used to. Wallis was still asleep, and he knew from prior experience it would not bode well for him to rouse her unless in an emergency. He found Bentley, ushering him down to the breakfast room on the ground floor. Once they were safely ensconced, the Duke said quietly, "It was you who wrote that note, wasn't it, Inspector?"

"You don't have to whisper here, Sir. I doubt even the Gestapo could plant listening devices so covertly and securely in such a large room. I think we may talk freely."

"What makes you think they are listening in on our conversations?" Edward asked, still keeping his voice low.

"I don't know for certain, but it's how they operate. That much I do know, and I doubt Your Royal Highness's lofty position and goodwill will prevent them from eavesdropping in on anything you say which they may feel is contrary to what they want you to believe. I'll have another look later, with your Royal Highness's permission, of course."

Edward nodded vigorously. "I... I may have said some things last night which... oh, God, do you think they know?"

"Know what, Sir?"

"What I said about... about Wallis and von Ribbentrop. I mean, I... it was nothing, really."

Bentley smiled reassuringly. "I don't think you have anything to worry about on that score, Sir. That was not the type of conversation they would be interested in if you don't mind my saying so."

"No? You really think so?"

"I think they are more concerned that you should say, or even think anything detrimental about the government or the Reich, especially Hitler himself. You didn't…?"

"Oh, good heavens, no." Edward breathed with a sigh of relief. "So you don't think I've blotted my copybook with them, then?"

"I don't believe so, Sir. Fortunately, *Herr von Ribbentrop* already has a reputation for his, ah, associations with women. I doubt this will give them any cause for concern."

"I hope you're right."

"I'm sure I am, Sir." Quickly changing the subject, he stated, "I believe you are going to visit a car plant at some point. Is that correct, Sir?"

"Yes," the Duke sighed. "Why on earth they think I'm interested in traveling hundreds of miles to see how they make their blasted cars is beyond me. I came over here to see how they're applying themselves to building new homes and improving conditions for the workers, dammit. That's what this trip is for, not to see some bloody stinking factory."

"Well, Sir, Daimlers and Mercedes are considered to be some of the finest automobiles in the world. It would be interesting to see how they assemble all the bits together."

"I don't give a fig how they build the bloody things," stormed the Duke. "All I need to know is how to drive the blessed things, and I can do that already. Still, it has to be done, I suppose. We're going there in a few days. It's about four hundred miles away from here. You'd think they'd find a factory a bit closer to civilization for me to visit, wouldn't you?"

"That's not for me to say, Your Royal Highness, but I would have thought that to foster goodwill between our own country and Germany, they might have allowed more time for you to get down to the nuts and bolts of why you came if you don't mind my saying so. There are far more important things for you to be getting on with if you catch my meaning."

"Quite right, Bentley. I'm glad at least one other person can grasp the nettle. Good man. Let's just hope that they've allowed us enough time to do what's necessary instead of having us gallivanting halfway around the country to visit some old car factory. I'm only going because they've promised that Richard Seaman will be there. He's a racing driver, you know."

"Indeed, Sir."

"I believe we are going to see a new housing development later today. That's more like the reason why I came, apart from the other thing, of course."

"Yes, your Royal Highness. Do you know when you will be meeting... *Herr Hitler*?"

"Not yet. They're keeping their cards very close to their chests on that one. I expect they'll tell me in their own good time."

"Quite so, Sir."

* * *

Edward and Wallis did visit a new social housing scheme on the outskirts of Berlin. They marveled at how quickly the buildings were being constructed, with much of the work being prefabricated before being shipped to site. Bentley was surprised to see the Duke take out a notebook and jot down some notes after speaking to the clerk of works. His estimation rose with regard to the Duke. He really did care about those less fortunate, despite his superior airs. Maybe he would be able to do some good after all if he was ever allowed back into Britain. The couple spent more time than had been allocated to them so Edward could inspect all aspects of the building process. He seemed genuinely interested in all facets of the construction phase, from laying the foundations, digging of the sewerage and water systems, the utility connections, and several other features of how the German house construction system operated.

By the time the tour was over, Bentley had noticed that the Duke seemed elated at the thought he could offer his advice on what he had seen to any British building companies who would care to listen.

They barely had time to return to the *Kaiserhöf* for a light meal before getting changed once again and escorted to the opera. Predictably, it was a work by Richard Wagner, much favored by the Nazis for his supposed anti-Semitic leanings, despite being born in the Jewish quarter in Leipzig.

The opera was an amateur production performed by manual laborers in a workers' playhouse. The Duke and Duchess appeared to enjoy the performance, but, like most Wagnerian operas, it seemed interminably long, and they did not linger after the show. Bentley, not an opera fan, especially of never-ending ones, sat a few rows behind the couple and pretended to be giving the opera his undivided attention. In reality, his mind was elsewhere most of the time, and he would have been hard-pressed to give even a précis of the plotline.

The following day, they went to meet Hermann Göring at his hunting lodge at Carinhall. The widower was effusive in his praise of his English guests.

"My dear friends, thank you so much for coming to my humble home. It is such a joy and a pleasure to have you here." Göring's home was not as modest as he suggested. Although originally a small building when he acquired it, since his tenure, he had extended it to incorporate several more rooms, with the newly extended reception room being over twenty meters long and ten meters wide. He had also converted his attic into a giant miniature train set room, with overhanging aircraft dropping little wooden bombs onto the tracks. Reaching the converted roof space, Göring revealed, "I have had this constructed for my little nephew, to let him see how our Luftwaffe will drop real bombs onto British trains. It will be quite instructive for him, don't you think?" Edward said nothing. Göring was, after all, discussing with him the prospect of raining missiles down onto the railway system of his own country. Had these people no finesse, he thought? With his arm around Edward's shoulder in an avuncular fashion, he continued, "I have instructed the kitchen staff to prepare what you English call 'high tea.' I hope this will make you feel more at home."

Edward and Wallis smiled warmly at their host while Edward, who spoke fluent German, translated for his wife, and Bentley stayed discreetly in the background. At least, there were no signs here of the sinister men who had seemed to be everywhere that the couple went. They dined with Hitler's Reichsminister of Aviation before engaging in more serious discussions in Göring's study. These talks went on into the evening before Göring decided that everything that had to be said had been deliberated.

The Duke noticed a large new map of Germany pinned to one of the study walls. He was surprised to see that the chart did not show Austria as a country in its own right with its own borders. Instead, the map had been redrawn to indicate that it was now a part of Germany, absorbed into the Greater German Reich. This alteration contravened the Treaty of Versailles, which forbade unification of the two countries. Edward was too timid, and Wallis too discrete to react to this astonishing chart. Seeing the expression on their faces, Göring replied, "It is the wish of the Austrian people to be subsumed into the German state. They have shown this by their growing support for our cause in the country and their enthusiasm for our progressive policies. I think that is all that needs to be said on the subject."

Edward acknowledged this statement with a smile and a bow, but said nothing.

They finished their tour by looking at an exhibition of Göring's art treasures, of which he was proud. The couple had heard rumors of where he had obtained many of his artworks, having stolen them from Jews who had used them to buy their freedom from the Reich or simply looted other works when their owners mysteriously disappeared. Once again, neither visitor pursued this matter.

Göring was a larger-than-life character, and by the time the Duke and Duchess had returned to their hotel, they were grateful they had no further engagements that evening. Bentley, also, was happy that they had no plans to go out. Although barely a couple of days into their schedule, it was already beginning to take its toll on them all. It was only the fourteenth.

They still had another ten days to go. And, to Edward, the greatest prize, the highlight of his entire tour, would be a meeting with the Führer himself, Adolf Hitler, at a date and time still to be decided. They had much to discuss, and Edward was looking forward to meeting the man who would restore him to his rightful place as the King of the United Kingdom, with Wallis by his side as his Queen.

CHAPTER 24

Berlin and other locations, Germany, October 1937

Bentley was convinced that there were no listening devices secreted in the Windsors' suite, but was almost certain that their phone calls from the room were being monitored. This made sense to him. The only people likely to visit them in their rooms would be representatives from the government and senior Reich ministers to whom Edward would hardly voice his displeasure at anything. Calls to outside individuals were another matter entirely. Who knew to whom the Duke might be expressing some disquiet at any aspects of his visit? It was far more likely then that anyone listening in on his conversations would be doing it through his hotel apartment telephone.

Although he was positive he was correct in his assumption, he took no chances. Speaking softly to the Duke, he said, "Your Royal Highness, I have conducted a thorough search of your suite and can find no trace of any hidden microphones. That does not mean, of course, that there are none. Maybe they are just cleverer than I am and have secreted them in places I have not found, so I would still caution you to be discrete in all you say and do. It is far more likely that any telephone calls you make will be of interest to them, so, once again, please mind what you say and to whom you say it. Do I make myself clear?"

"Crystal clear, Inspector, and once again, I thank you for looking out for our interests."

"If your Royal Highness is to achieve his ambitions, it is of paramount importance that you do nothing which might upset those who can bring these aspirations to fruition."

"And I thank you once again, Detective Inspector, or should I say, 'Assistant Chief Constable?'" Edward winked.

"You've no idea how long my wife has been nagging me to apply for promotion, Sir."

"Well, she won't have to nag you for much longer, once... well once things change, eh."

"No, Your Royal Highness, she won't."

"It's the least we can do. Just make sure that things go to plan, and your elevation will be assured, I promise you."

Assistant Chief Constable, thought Bentley. Yes, 'Assistant Chief Constable Alan Bentley' did have a nice, comforting ring about it. Was he really made for such lofty heights? Time would tell.

Edward sought out his protection officer again the following day. "Inspector, Wallis and I are due to inspect some barracks or other later today. Why on earth they are taking us there, I have no idea, but Dudley tells me that this site, whatever it is, may not be what it appears to be. He seems to believe it is a detention base for political dissenters. What do you think I should do?"

Bentley scratched his ear thoughtfully. "Well, Sir, if they have already planned this part of your schedule, you can hardly refuse to attend. I'm sure your hosts won't let you see anything which you may find... distasteful. I don't think you have any other option than to go.

"Yes, I suppose you're right. It's just... well, it would hardly be appropriate for me to be seen there if it is such a camp, don't you think? It will be on all the newsreels, of course. What will they say back home if I'm seen at such a place? It'll look as if I'm endorsing political suppression."

"If that's what they really are using these barracks for, I'm quite sure that any inmates will be well out of view of the cameras, your Royal Highness. Our hosts aren't that stupid."

"Yes, I suppose you're right. It's just...."

"May I speak freely, Sir?"

"Yes, of course. What do you want to say?"

"Well, Sir," Bentley began hesitantly. "It's just that, well, the British public and the government have already made their feelings quite clear about your decision to abdicate and to marry the Duchess. They seem to have taken to your brother rather more than, forgive me, Sir, they took to you. I do not see why you should care what they think back in Britain. It is no longer your home, at least for the time being. What happens in the future is, of course, another matter, but by then, they'll have more important things to worry about."

"By Jove, Bentley, you're absolutely right. No, dammit, I'll go. After all, Forwood is only surmising that is what the barracks are being used for. He hasn't come up with any evidence or anything. It might just be so much eyewash."

Bentley could see that Edward had convinced himself of his obligation to attend whatever venue his Nazi hosts had planned. He could hardly do otherwise.

The Duke and Duchess were accompanied on their visit by their host, Dr. Robert Ley, who gave them a conducted tour of the site. As they were inspecting the grounds, Edward noticed some concrete silos off to the side of the main buildings. Curious about their nature, the Duke turned to Ley and asked, "What are those structures over there, Doctor Ley? May we see inside them?"

Ley was nonplussed for only a second, before replying, "I doubt your Royal Highness would gain much from going inside. They are empty at the moment. Looking away from the Duke and Duchess, he continued, "That is where they store the cold meat." Ley's assistant had to stop himself from sniggering at his superior's flippant remark. The 'cold meat' Ley was referring to was not the butchery of animals. It was altogether something far more sinister and disturbing.

"As you will see, Your Royal Highness," observed Ley, the whole area is laid out just like a military quadrangle. Eventually, it will house Reich troops who will defend the Fatherland should it come under attack from Bolshevik forces."

"Oh, I thought it was..." was as far as Edward spoke before being discretely nudged by his equerry. "Sorry, I only meant..." he faltered as his voice trailed off to a whisper.

The rest of the tour was conducted without incident before the Windsors were escorted back to the *Kaiserhöf*. Although there was nothing apparent or obvious, Edward had the distinct impression that Ley was somehow having fun at his expense. It wasn't anything he could define, but somehow the feeling would not leave him. The leader of the DAF was turning out to be something of an inhospitable host. Often the worse for drink, he slurred his words and made several unpleasant comments, often within the Duke's earshot, of what he would like to do to the Duchess given the opportunity. Edward affected not to hear them, but they angered him nonetheless.

The following day, Edward alone made the trip to the Mercedes plant by way of Munich. Once again, a drunken Ley drove the Duke on the six hundred-kilometer journey to the Bavarian city, paying scant attention to the road and pressing his car horn at any drivers who were impeding his progress. They completed this leg of their journey in under five hours, despite the rain and mist that accompanied them for much of the trip. Sir Dudley Forwood, seated beside the Duke, said, "S... sir, I... I don... don't know how much m... more of this... this man's driving I... I can take. H... he dri... drives like a... a m... adman."

Despite Forwood's fears, they arrived safely at the factory they were scheduled to visit. The road trip did not, however, end without incident. Ley, still intoxicated, failed to notice that the plant gates were locked and drove straight through them, causing damage to the limousine. Undeterred by this accident, he continued to drive around the factory yard at high speed, almost careening into several workers. This state of affairs was intolerable, and Edward said to his equerry, "I don't care what you have to do, Sir Dudley, but when, no, if we get back to Berlin in one piece, that man will not drive for the Duchess or me again. Do you hear me?" to which Forwood was only too happy to reply that he did.

Bentley, who was following in the car behind, also could not fail to notice Ley's erratic maneuvering and was afraid that he was going to drive his vehicle off the road. There might be a great deal of sadness and grief in Germany if this was the case, thought the protection officer. However, in the United Kingdom, he was sure the reaction would be much more muted and restrained.

Despite the traumatic journey, the party recovered well, and the tour went ahead with no input from Ley, who was, they presumed, sleeping off his drunken binge.

Although he was still intoxicated, Ley insisted on driving them to their next destination, the Mercedes factory at Stuttgart, almost two hundred and fifty kilometers away. Surprisingly, they reached Untertürkheim safely, and after introducing the Mercedes management to the Duke and his party, Ley unobtrusively slipped away. Bentley surmised that their driver had more schnapps hidden in his limousine and considered following him. He reasoned, however, that even if he did catch him drinking again, there was little he could do about it without causing a scene. He would just have to hope that Ley could drive drunk as well, or as badly as he could when he was sober.

Edward met Richard Seaman, who discussed with the Duke his recent recruitment to the Mercedes racing car team. Sir Dudley Forwood cautioned the intemperate Duke to be cautious in his meeting with the thirty-four-year-old racing driver. Three months earlier, during the second stage of the European Championships at Nürburg, Seaman had been partly responsible for the death of fellow racing driver Ernst von Delius in an accident during the race. Seaman's own injuries had prevented him from taking part in the Monaco Grand Prix one month later. He had, however, compensated for this disappointment by coming fourth in the Italian stage of the competition a few weeks earlier.

Mindful of not saying anything indelicate, Edward was guarded in his conversation, and the dialog between the two men was stilted. After he met with Seaman, the Duke toured the rest of the factory before driving back to Berlin.

It appeared that Bentley's fears were unfounded. Ley had recovered, and the return drive was uneventful. Nonetheless, Ley did not drive for the Duke again. Forwood had done as the Duke had directed him through diplomatic channels, and that duty was assigned to Hermann Göring by Hitler himself.

The next few days were taken up with visits to other locations with which the Nazi government wished to impress the Duke and the Duchess. These included visits to a Hitler Youth camp, and the Krupp works at Essen. This time, Edward did voice mild concerns when he witnessed the production of weapons that the Versailles Treaty banned. As he was being shown around the factory, the Duke turned to his guide Alfried Krupp, the son of the current owner Gustav. "I understood that these weapons are not permitted under the terms..." before he could say any more, Sir Dudley Forwood stepped in. "Wh... what the Duke m... means is that he b... b... believed th... that the a... armaments he has s... seen being man... manuf... factured are n... not con... consistent with the ba... ba... ballistics we understood you to be in possession of. There is no offense meant." Forwood looked pointedly at the Duke as he tried to allay Alfried Krupp's surprise.

"None taken, I assure you," replied Krupp jovially. "I was not aware His Royal Highness was so well informed as to the armament restrictions placed on the Fatherland." Despite his affable retort, Forwood did not fail to notice the look of concern on their host's face. Edward had done it once again, saying the most injudicious thing he could to foment clouds of mistrust out of a clear blue sky to an otherwise ordinary event. He hoped his employer's *faux pas* did not come back to haunt them before they finally left their Nazi hosts.

Being aware of Wallis's fondness for fine china, the tour organizers also arranged a visit to the Meissen porcelain works. While this was an interesting call for the Duchess, the Duke's attention was constantly elsewhere, much to the chagrin of his wife and their hosts.

As interesting as all these visits were, there was only one appointment uppermost on the Duke's mind; his forthcoming discussions with Hitler. This meeting had now been confirmed to take place the day before the Windsors were due to leave Germany. It was all he could think about, and it was coming closer and closer, day by day. The real reason for their invitation to the country, a reason he could not disclose to anyone. He had been loyal to Hitler. It was now time for the Führer to reciprocate his fidelity.

CHAPTER 25

Berchtesgaden, Bavaria, Germany, October 1937

The meeting with Hitler was scheduled for October 22nd., the day before Edward and Wallis were due to return to France. It was to take place at the dictator's retreat at *Berchtesgaden*, on Germany's southeast corner just across the Austrian border. After briefly greeting the distinguished couple on the steps of his mountain retreat, Hitler disappeared.

"Where on earth did he go to?" asked an exasperated Edward. "He knows how important this meeting is to me, to both of us. We're due to return to France tomorrow, for goodness' sake. I hope he doesn't expect us to stay the night."

"Now, now, dear, don't take on so. I'm sure Herr Hitler has much to occupy him. It can't be easy, running a country almost single-handedly. You should know." she finished tartly.

"Yes, I suppose you're right. Still, it is rather disrespectful of him to...."

"Be quiet," hissed Wallis. "You don't know who might be listening. Just calm down. I'm sure he'll be here shortly."

Finally, an hour after they arrived, Hitler reappeared to welcome them again. Without apologizing for his tardiness, he ushered the couple, together with Alan Bentley, Sir Dudley Forwood, and his interpreter, Paul-Otto Schmidt, into his study. Already seated was the deputy Fuhrer, Rudolf Hess, who rose to meet them. After Hess had formally greeted the couple, Hitler suggested that Wallis should take tea with his deputy. "But I had rather hoped...." Wallis started to object before Hitler interrupted her. Through Schmidt, Hitler replied, "Your husband and I have matters of import to discuss, my dear. I'm sure they would not interest you and would only starve you of the company of one of the most charming men in Germany." Hitler smiled.

It took Hess a few seconds to realize that his Führer was addressing him. Startled by Hitler's out-of-character compliment, the deputy Führer took Wallis by the arm as he led her out of Hitler's sanctum. Bentley, also, would be surplus to requirements. "Who in their right mind would even dare to try and harm a hair on the head of the Duke or his wife in my presence?" So the detective was obliged to leave his charge to the tender mercies of the German leader. Hitler then turned to Edward's equerry, suggesting that he, too, should quit the room. "Alas, H... Herr Hitler, I c... c... annot do that."

"And why ever not?" asked a querulous Chancellor. This was an awkward moment for the Duke's equerry. The Duke spoke flawless German and did not require any translator, let alone two.

"It w... w... was a condition of H... h... is M... majesty's Government that the Duke cou... could not confer alone wi... with the head of s... s... state of a f... foreign country, e... especially one who has no c... c... command of the Eng... english language. Mis... mistransla... lations can ha... have unfor... fortunate r... r... reper... percussions, I f... fear. It was thought th... that it w... would be to ever... everyone's b... benefit i... if another p... p... person was present to c... c... confirm all that was said a... and agreed."

"Are you suggesting that our host's interpreter is not good enough? Why was I not made aware of this, Sir Dudley? This is an intolerable position you have put me in. Do you see how this must look to Herr Hitler? I would remind you that this is a private visit, and it is not the business of H.M.G. who I see or what we discuss. Now, you will leave us alone. That is an order." Demanded a furious Edward.

"I... I'm s... sorry, Sir, b...but I m... m... must insist. I was i... instructed to advise you th... that your refusal to obey this e... edict could have f... financial as w...well as diplomatic c... c... consequences," his equerry replied uncomfortably.

So there it was – a naked threat directed squarely at Edward's allowance from his brother. Heed Sir Dudley's advice or suffer the humiliation of having to go begging to Albert to reinstate his stipend. This possibility would not be as easy as it sounded. Edward had already tried many times since his abdication to have his allowance increased, only to be met by a blank refusal on each occasion by the new King. It was an intolerable situation, but what else could he do? No longer considered part of the Royal family, he and the Duchess were denied any money from the Civil List. Despite his other investments, without the income he received by installments from his disposal of Sandringham and Balmoral, bequeathed to him by his late father, and transferred to the new King, his revenue would be greatly reduced.

Clenching his fists to conceal his anger, he agreed to the British government's terms. "Very well, Sir Dudley, but they have not heard the last of this. I will have plenty to say about this state of affairs when I get home."

"S... sir, I regret to r... remind you, but England i... is no longer your home."

Only for the time being, thought Edward.

While Schmidt translated Sir Dudley's faltering explanation, Edward turned his face away from his equerry, fearful that he would say anything that would make his already precarious position even worse. Hitler's face also darkened. As well as discussing various political affairs, there was also the other matter, and no one, no one, apart from the two of them, would be permitted to be a party to these discussions.

"Very well," Hitler agreed. "I do not wish to cause any further bad feeling between our guest and his family or his government. Sir Dudley may be permitted to stay, with one condition. He may not interfere in any discussions between the Duke and me. He is here only as an observer and will stay quiet. Is that understood?"

Sir Dudley remained silent, which Hitler took as acquiescence to his demands.

For the next hour, the two men discussed various issues, including the United States' attitude to the European situation. America was still an isolationist country, and it was important to Hitler's plans that they remain so. The last thing he needed was U.S. interference in affairs that did not concern them. The Chancellor also used Edward's extensive knowledge of the British government and its new leader to sound him out about how it might react should he attempt to annex any more of his geographical neighbors' territory. Edward told Hitler what he wanted to hear, much to the alarm of Sir Dudley Forwood. Did Hitler even now consider himself so unassailable that he cared little about who knew of his territorial ambitions?

The meeting finally broke up, but before anyone could leave the room, Hitler made an announcement. "The Duke and I have concluded what I might term the public part of our discussions. There are certain matters that I would now wish to talk to him about that must be done in private."

The Duke's equerry made to rise in protest, but Hitler held up his hand to forestall him. "I have been gracious enough to agree to your government's terms up to now, Sir Dudley, but I must insist that the last part of our conference will be conducted strictly between the two of us. You may make of this decision as you wish, but this is my house, and that is my final word. Do I make myself clear?"

"A... abun... bundantly clear, Ch... chancellor."

"Very well. Otto, you may leave now, and please escort Sir Dudley to be with the Duchess. Rudolf is a charming man, but he does have a rather annoying tendency to repeat himself. I'm sure she would welcome Sir Dudley's presence, although whether she would prefer the company of an eloquent stutterer or a pleasant bore, I cannot say." Hitler smiled without humor.

After the two men had vacated the room, Hitler wasted no time in addressing the subject both men had been desperate to discuss. "In under three years from now," Hitler began, "I expect our troops to be in London. This prediction is not just idle speculation, you understand. I am as sure of this as I am of my own name. It seems that the British government has disregarded my overtures to ally themselves to us in a common cause to fight against the Communists. Well, they had their chance and they chose to ignore it. So be it. My strategic planners have assured me that by that time, we will have amassed enough weaponry to supersede even British military superiority. Already, we are almost a match for the other European powers, and very soon, those who denounce our territorial ambitions will find they cannot stop our inevitable expansion. We must be able to exploit those other countries to the east as a buffer against Soviet aggression and hegemony.

"But it will be Britain that will be the greatest prize. Once we have defeated their army, we will re-educate them to understand who the greatest threat is – Comrade Stalin and his horde of Bolsheviks. With British troops fighting alongside our own glorious army, we will defeat the scourge of Communism forever.

"However, for all this to happen, the British public will need a figurehead they know and can trust. They will need someone who can persuade them that it is all for the common good that we fight this pernicious enemy together. Democratic governments are fleeting and can be replaced at the whim of the electorate. What they need is stability; someone who will continue to lead his country not just for a few years until the public tires of them, but someone who will still be a figure of authority decades from now. That is what is required, and I cannot think of a more able and suitable candidate than someone who has already fulfilled this role, however briefly. A person with clarity of vision; a person with purpose and determination. Someone like you! Will you undertake this journey with me? Will you be remembered a thousand years from now as the King who swept away the yoke of Communist tyranny? Who helped to free the world from oppression and despair?"

Edward waited a few seconds to be sure Hitler had finished his peroration. There was an almost messianic fervor in his eyes, as, in his mind, he could see the shining future that awaited them. Hitler as the supreme leader of a united Europe stretching from Great Britain in the west to the farthest reaches of the Soviet Union, with Edward as his British counterpart. It was even more than he could have expected."Yes, Führer, how could I say otherwise? To be crowned King of my country once again, with a people united in one destiny? It is the only thing I have dreamed about since abdicating. I will show those who doubted my ability to rule, including my brother, who the true ruler of his country is. They will all pay the price for their treachery and betrayal. There is only one thing I would ask..."

"Do not concern yourself, my friend. A good King needs a good Queen to reign by his side. Wallis seems to be a perfect match for you. It could not be better. In time, your subjects will come to love you, both of you, as they seem to have taken to your brother. But he will be gone by then and will be but a footnote in history. It will be you who will be remembered, my dear Edward, long after Albert is forgotten."

Edward grinned from ear to ear. This was exactly how he had envisioned the conversation would go, in fact, even better than he could have imagined it. But Hitler was not finished. "For the time being, let us pursue a different tack. To achieve our goals and have you re-established as the head of state, it will be necessary to employ some subterfuge, perhaps even some intrigue. It is important to make our future adversaries believe that we seek only peace and harmonious relationships with them. As I have already stated, our only common goal should be the destruction of the Soviet Union. If we can make them believe this, it will be all the easier to do what has to be done when the time comes."

"Yes, I..."

As if he hadn't heard Edward, Hitler continued, "and this is where you can prove invaluable to us. With your influence on the world stage, people will listen to you. You and others like you who can persuade those governments who mistrust our motives not to harbor any sentiments of hostility toward us. If they will only see things from our perspective, it would be so much easier. Do you think you can do this?" If Edward had any doubts about his ability to agree to Hitler's proposals, he did not express them. His overriding passion was to re-ascend the British throne, and he would do anything to accomplish this aim.

Hitler looked Edward straight in the eye and said, "You are so important to our long-term plans that I do not want you merely to be part of this strategy; I want you to lead it. You will be the figurehead, the beacon whose light will shine out to all the other like-minded parties who believe in our cause. You will raise such a groundswell of opinion in our favor, my dear Edward, that governments will disregard our aspirations at their peril."

Once again, Edward saw the absolute certainty with which his host was speaking. This was a man, the leader of his country, who would brook no opposition to his ambitions. His strength of character and force of will alone would make great leaders tremble. He would do it. He would do all he could to support this incredible human being. Hitler was correct. His brother would soon be forgotten, and it would be he, Edward, who the history books would remember. The Duke was so emotional over Hitler's praise and his faith in him, he could not return his gaze. Casting his eyes downward, he replied, "Führer, it will be an honor and a privilege to serve you in any way I can. Together, we will make this world a far better place."

Resting his hand on Edward's shoulder, Hitler replied, "Yes, my dear Edward, that we shall surely do." Then, glancing at his wristwatch, the Reich chancellor commented, "I believe we have concluded our discussions, and I have no wish to detain you any longer. I do not want your equerry to be any more suspicious of our private meeting than he must already be. Let us find your charming wife so we may all have tea together."

They found Wallis in animated conversation with Rudolf Hess and Sir Dudley Forwood, with Ernst Bohle interpreting. English-born Bohle was a member of the SS and a close colleague of Hess. Hitler ordered refreshments for Edward, Wallis, and himself. They spent another short while talking, with this time Edward playing the role of the translator.

Finally, it was time for the couple to depart, and Hitler bade them a fond farewell as they left the *Berghof*.

It had been so easy to dupe this weak and vainglorious man, but Hitler had yet more ways of convincing the British than he was willing to share with his acolyte. He would assure them that he would not seek any territorial gains from its empire in return for granting him a free hand in Europe. He was sure this accommodation would meet with the approval of its government. No one, least of all the British, and especially their new Prime Minister, Neville Chamberlain, wanted another European conflict.

His scheme was proceeding according to plan. By autumn nineteen-forty, Hitler would be in Downing Street, and Edward... well, he had other ideas in mind for him.

CHAPTER 26

Château de la Croë, Cap d'Antibes & Verdun, France, April 1939

The telephone rang six or seven times. Both Wallis and Edward heard it ring, but it was not their job to answer it. That was the function of the staff, and if they would not perform their duties properly, they could find employment elsewhere. Finally, the maid, Mathilde, knocked delicately at the conservatory door. Edward, she could just about tolerate. He was mostly pleasant when he deigned to acknowledge her at all; his wife, however, well, she was prone to black moods, even when there was no justification for her wrath. Perhaps it was the frustration of her lack of French, and her trouble communicating with the help. Whatever her problem was, it was not fair that she should vent her ill-humor on them. Had jobs been more plentiful in the area, she would certainly have found alternative work by now. Curtseying as she entered the room, Mathilde walked the few paces until she reached the couple. "Madame, M'sieur, there is someone on the telephone. He wishes to speak to the Duke. It is a long-distance call – from the United States."

Wallis and Edward looked quizzically at each other. They were not expecting anyone to phone them, least of all from across the Atlantic. "Did he say who it was?" Wallis asked.

"Oui, Madame. He said his name is Lenox Lohr. He runs a radio station in New York."

"What on earth does he want?"

"There's only one way to find out, dear."

Turning to the maid, Edward instructed her to tell Lohr that he would be there shortly." Mathilde hesitated. "What is it, girl? Can you not understand a simple instruction?"

"Of course, M'sieur. It's just that Monsieur Lohr is calling from a long distance, and...."

"And I am not paying for the call. Whoever this Lohr person is, he will wait until I am ready to receive him."

"Very good, M'sieur. I shall let him know." This was the last straw. Mathilde could tolerate this couple no longer. She would hand in her notice on Friday, job or no job. The minuscule pay they gave her did not entitle them to treat her like this.

After she had left, Wallis asked, "Who do you think it might be? A radio station? Maybe they want you to give a talk on the wireless over there. It would be nice to go back for a while."

"Don't get ahead of yourself, my dear. Maybe they want me to advertise some dreadful product that I would never use. Still, if the money's good, I might consider it."

Lifting the instrument, Edward introduced himself.

"Your Royal Highness, thank you for taking my call. My name is Lenox Lohr. I'm the president of NBC. How do you do, Sir?"

"I'm very well, thank you. What can I do for you, Mr. Lohr?"

"Excuse me for being so intrusive, but would I be right in saying that you served with the British forces in the European conflict?"

"Well, yes, I was with the Grenadier Guards but saw little active service, unfortunately. The government thought it would harm public morale if I were injured or killed or captured by the enemy, so they made sure I was kept well behind the lines. That's not to say that I did not experience trench life, but not as much as I should have done. Why are you asking me about my war experience?"

"We, that is my company, were thinking about doing a radio broadcast from one of the fiercest and bloodiest battle sites of that conflict, Verdun in France. In these uncertain days, it might remind people just how devastating such a war can be, not only in terms of military losses but with the inevitable impact on the civilian population as well. I know you think we were a bit tardy in not coming in until nineteen-seventeen, but we lost many good men, nonetheless. We thought that someone with your influence, albeit with limited first-hand experience, might alert the people to the consequences of perpetrating another catastrophe on such a grand scale. Would you consider giving such a speech?"

Edward was unprepared for such a conversation and did not know how to respond. His silence prompted Lohr to continue, "There would, of course, be a fee for your services, and we would naturally defray the expenses of your visit."

It was not the cost of the trip or even his payment that was uppermost in the Duke's mind. He had already caused considerable controversy by his earlier visit to Germany, considering himself fortunate that his brother did not stop his allowance after his private interview with Hitler. Did he want to court even more conflict between himself and the British establishment? Would giving a talk on the horrors of the Great War be seen as capitulation to the forces of appeasement? But hadn't he made a Faustian pact with the German Chancellor back in October nineteen-thirty-seven to do just what Lohr was now asking him to do? It would certainly serve Hitler's cause and would, in all likelihood, help to cement even further his relationship with the German leader. And he could not help but remember how the combined forces of the British government, the Roosevelt administration, the American labor movement, and the Jewish lobby prevented him and Wallis from visiting the United States just after his return from Germany. This would be the ideal opportunity to redress that atrocious decision and show them he was not a man they could treat in that fashion.

He was now living in France, with little likelihood of him or Wallis being welcomed back to Britain any time in the foreseeable future. And, he convinced himself, he still had a living to earn. When he weighed up all the advantages and drawbacks in agreeing to Lohr's proposal, he concluded there was only one course of action he could take. "Although I did not see much service during the previous conflict, nonetheless, it left me with an abiding sense of the utter horror and futility of war, especially war on such a large scale. I believe we must see that our generation and the generations yet unborn do not make the same mistakes committed by our fathers twenty years ago. Very well, Mr. Lohr. If you would be kind enough to wire me the details, I would be more than happy to visit Verdun on behalf of NBC."

* * *

Edward gave his speech on May 8th., having made the thousand-kilometer journey a few days earlier. He had not taken much part in this conflict, but was all too aware of the carnage suffered by both sides. It was part of the reason why he had become a pacifist in his anti-war beliefs and his conviction that warfare on such a grand scale should never happen again. He began his broadcast by explaining to the listeners where he was. "*I am speaking tonight from Verdun,*" before going on, "*and as I talk to you from this historic place, I am deeply conscious of the presence of the great company of the dead.*" He declared he was convinced that if they could make their voices heard, they would be with him in what he was about to say. "*I speak simply as a soldier of the last war. The supreme importance of averting war will, I feel confident, impel all those in power to renew their endeavors to bring about a peaceful settlement....*" He went on to say that it was his most earnest prayer that such a cruel and destructive madness should never again overtake mankind and concluded his speech by asserting that there was no land whose people wanted war. Well, he had done it now. He could not have made his sentiments plainer. Avoid war at all costs, even if it meant giving Hitler what he wanted and subjecting the peoples of Europe to Nazi domination whose despotic ruler and his autocratic government would tolerate no political, moral, ideological or philosophical opposition.

Alan Bentley accompanied the Duke on his visit and had listened to the Duke's discourse. Like most of the British public, he believed that war with

Germany was almost certain. Would Edward's speech have done anything to avert such a disaster? In his opinion, not only would it have done nothing to further the cause of peace, but it would have only emboldened Hitler even more. No, rather than prevent another war, Edward's speech would probably be the catalyst that would propel the world into another conflict of unimaginable proportions once again.

CHAPTER 27

London, England, September 1939

On September the first, the German army drove into Poland from the west, while Soviet forces invaded from the east. The Luftwaffe mercilessly bombed Polish cities inflicting unprecedented carnage, misery and death on the country's civilian population. Having no choice but to honor their treaty obligations with Poland, Great Britain and France, after Hitler's flagrant disregard of Poland's allies' insistence to cease hostilities, declared war on Germany.

This, then, was Hitler's intention all along. To antagonize his adversaries into declaring war on his country, on his terms, a war he was sure his country would win. His invasion of the Rhineland, the annexation of Austria, and Germany's territorial demands in the Sudetenland were all designed to test the Allies' resolve. They would tell themselves that these incursions were, well, in Hitler's back yard, and he did have the right, however tenuous, to achieve his demands that these areas should be subsumed into the German Reich. Anything to prevent the carnage of two decades ago.

But Poland was a step too far for those countries who had allowed Hitler to humiliate them before the world. He had ignored and flouted every treaty to which his country had been a signatory, and the French and British could disregard his warlike intentions no longer.

Not only Edward's brother, King George VI, was concerned about his sibling. The Duke had also been taxing the minds of the British government. He was still living in France, and although the establishment would have preferred that he remained in that country, they realized that, inevitably, he would need to return to the United Kingdom. The King arranged a confidential meeting at Buckingham palace between himself and his new Prime Minister, Neville Chamberlain.

"It seems my brother continues to be a thorn in my side as much in war as he did in peacetime. I honestly don't know what to do for the best. Do we keep him in France or bring him back? My instinct is to leave him where he is, but I expect you will have other ideas, Prime Minister." King George VI smiled wanly.

"I believe we have no other alternative but to arrange for his passage back to these shores, Your Majesty. I have no doubt our French compatriots will give a good account of themselves should Herr Hitler turn his attention toward them, but I fear their armies will be no match for the German forces, now we have seen what they are capable of. I don't mind telling you that I wish we had listened to Winston all those years ago. Had we done so then, we might not be in this situation today. Be that as it may, if Hitler overruns France, he would undoubtedly hold your brother to ransom over us. I would not wish to be in Your Majesty's shoes if he were put in that invidious position. 'Surrender to us, or we will imprison the Duke.' I doubt they would actually harm him, but then again, if Hitler's back was to the wall, who knows what he might do...?"

The King gave Chamberlain's words a few seconds to penetrate. "Yes," he replied resignedly, "I suppose you're right. Very well, Prime Minister, can I leave it to you to make the necessary arrangements?"

"Yes, Your Majesty. I believe Captain Mountbatten is on standby to carry out the Duke and Duchess's evacuation."

"Very well. Thank you, Prime Minister." And with those final words, the decision to bring Edward and Wallis back to Britain was taken, and Chamberlain's audience with his King was over.

* * *

The Duke and Duchess of Windsor sailed back to Britain from Le Havre on September 12th on Mountbatten's ship, HMS Kelly. They immediately drove to see the King, and Edward wasted no time in discussing the current situation with George and what he could do to help the war effort.

"Well, now you've dragged Wallis and I back from France, I suppose I must do something to help the country. Perhaps I..."

"You will return to France, this time in uniform, where you will be under the auspices and protection of the army. You are to join the General Staff of the British Military Mission there as liaison officer with the French. I suppose your command of the language will be sufficient by now, seeing the time you've spent there."

"That's not what I...."

"This matter is not up for discussion. It has already been decided. You will receive the rank of major-general with...."

"Major-general?" shouted Edward. "I must remind you that I have already attained the rank of field marshal. What, am I now to be demoted because of the dereliction of my royal obligations? Is that it? How dare you? By what right...?"

In an uncharacteristic display of anger, his brother shot back, "What right? What right, you ask? I'll tell you by what right, my dear brother. By your refusal to accept your royal duties, to blithely go off with that American... woman, to give up the greatest throne on earth, to refuse to accept your responsibilities to your country... do I need to go on? I should never have become King! I did not wish to become King. As the eldest son, that was your birthright, which you absolved yourself from so cheaply and easily. I would have been as loyal a subject to you as any of the other millions of British citizens had you but allowed me to be so. And now it is I, who should never have been the monarch, who must carry the burden of Kingship and steer this country through yet another war, a war which was started, may I remind you, by your friend across the Channel. So yes, my dear brother, I do have the right. The right you thrust upon me!"

"Do you think it was easy for me to do what I did? I..."

George held out a restraining finger against Edward. Quivering with emotion, he retorted, "Don't you dare! Spare me your sanctimonious hypocrisy. You no more wanted to be King, than I did. You who was too busy cavorting about with all the married women you could seduce, who cared for nothing but your own selfish, hedonistic pleasures, who could not even be bothered to come home from Africa when we thought our father was dying?"

Seeing the astonished look on his brother's face, George smiled humorlessly, "Oh, yes, Tommy Lascelles told me all about it. You truly are a despicable character, my brother. To be honest, perhaps it is as well you are no longer ruler. God help us all had you still been on the throne."

Edward had no answer to the accusations his brother had fired at him. Instead, he said something George did not expect. "Congratulations. After all these years, it is gratifying to see that you have come out of your shell at last. I'm glad to see you've finally lost that awful s...s...stammer." Edward goaded him. "It's just a pity that you had to express all your vitriol at me, but I suppose I should have expected it. You were always so timid and in my shadow and now look at you. I think rather than be angry with me, you should be thanking me for finally bringing out the man in you."

Without rising to his brother's bait, George said, "You will accept your posting as I have ordered, with the appropriate rank. You are a serving officer in His Majesty's forces and subject to military discipline, just like every other soldier. If you refuse to accept this command, I will see you court-martialed and imprisoned if the tribunal believes this is the correct punishment. You will receive no preferential treatment just because of who you are. Do you understand me?"

The former King had underestimated his brother. This was a new Albert who stood before his brother. One with a purpose, a resolve, and a determination which Edward had not seen before. This was a brother who had come into his own. A monarch who would be a good King. For the length of a heartbeat, Edward felt a pang of regret. Perhaps his family, his advisers, his government, his ministers, his church, his subjects, had all been correct. Maybe he should not have insisted on marrying Wallis at the expense of his crown, but it was too late now. What was done was done. The die had been cast, and he had made his choice. His brother would not be deterred from the decision that they had taken about his immediate future. Things might change in time, but for now, he had no choice but to obey his brother's instructions. Edward adopted a military stance before saluting his brother. "Yes, Your Majesty."

The King did not disclose the other reason why he was sending his brother back to France. He and the government were already aware of Edward's close ties to Hitler's Germany, and especially the Nazi hierarchy. They could not be sure that any confidential or classified papers that came under his purview would not find their way to the *Abwehr*. He was just too dangerous to be left unsupervised. They made sure that despite his posting as liaison officer, his would be a sinecure position only. He would not see or handle any documents that could be of benefit to the enemy. At least, that was the plan.

While the Duke of Windsor was speaking to his brother, a different discussion was being held in Thames House, headquarters of Britain's intelligence services. Present at this meeting were the head of the security organization, Colonel Vernon Kell, and his deputy, Sir Eric Holt-Wilson, together with Alan Bentley. The security chiefs decided not to include Bentley's other superior, Lieutenant-Colonel John Carter, who had succeeded Sir James Whitehead. Carter did not know the double role being played by Bentley, and now, with the advent of war, they felt it better if the fewer people who knew of Bentley's espionage activities, the better.

"Welcome home, Detective Inspector, or should I say future Assistant Chief Constable?" ventured Kell, smiling. "I can't believe they actually thought you'd gone over to their side. I still don't understand quite how you managed that trick."

"Well, for a start, I wouldn't sell myself so cheaply. A bloody Assistant Chief Constable? I would accept nothing less than the job of the Home Secretary." Bentley answered, tongue firmly between cheek. "Actually, it wasn't so difficult to gull them once I got the measure of these people. Like most Nazis, they are arrogant and self-obsessed. They are stimulated by flattery and sycophancy and hear what they want to hear. And, of course, there's my wonderful manly charm and exceptional wit."

"I think the less we say about your 'manly charm,' the better. Still, I expect it's nice to be back in London again, although I wish it could have been in more favorable circumstances. I suppose it was only a matter of time before the balloon went up, as they say. Hitler's been planning this for years, of course, but our silly-assed politicians buried their heads in the sand, and now look where we are. I don't mind telling you, Alan, but if Hitler decided to cross the Channel tomorrow, there's damn little we could do to stop him. That's how unprepared we are. We're going to have to ramp up war production pretty quickly if we're to have any hope at all of forestalling an invasion. I tell you, Alan, it scares me like I've never been scared before. And I don't scare easily."

Bentley knew of the bravery of Colonel Vernon Kell. This man had seen action in the Boxer Rebellion War in nineteen-hundred while serving in China and had been mentioned in dispatches later in his career. His courage was a byword in military circles, as were his intellect and his integrity. If he was frightened by the inevitable war to come, they should all be worried – very worried indeed.

"I assume you will have been getting my reports, gentlemen. I'm sure Edward's up to something, but what that something is, I don't know. I believe he wouldn't think twice about betraying his country if he felt it was in his best interest to do so, but what form that treachery would take, I leave to your imagination."

"What about this secret meeting with Hitler a couple of years ago? The one that even the interpreters were barred from? Do you think they may have been playing the long game? What if all they planned everything that's happening now at that meeting?"

"With the greatest of respect, sir, I don't believe Hitler would have disclosed his war plans to Edward. Not in detail, anyhow. I just can't see Hitler discussing his invasion priorities with someone who, quite frankly, isn't very bright. The Duke, unfortunately, was not blessed with an intellectual brain, and certainly not one capable of understanding complex military strategies."

Both men chuckled. "Thank you for that assessment, Alan. In these dark days, we all need a bit of cheering up. I've heard that Edward is to be posted back to France as part of the Military Mission to that country, so hopefully, that'll keep him out of harm's way in all senses of the word. Which means he'll no longer need his minder. Not if he's got the British army to protect him. So it's back to regular duties for you, I'm afraid, and I'm sure you'll have more than enough on your plate in the coming months. But I'd still love to know what he and Hitler were chatting about so secretly. What was so important to him that he would only discuss it with the Duke?"

"Well, seeing as there were only the two of them in the room, I think it's safe to assume that whatever it was concerned Edward himself. There's only one possible explanation as far as I can see."

"Yes," agreed Kell, "He's probably promised Edward that he would reinstall him as King with that awful Simpson woman as his Queen should he set foot on British soil. It doesn't bear thinking about."

"Everything I found out and my suspicions have all been in my messages. Except..."

"Yes? What is it you want to say?" prompted Holt-Wilson.

"Well, I think it's safe to say that my assumptions concerning Edward's re-succession to the throne are correct, but now that I think about it further, I believe that there's more to it. For Edward to become King once again, he would need to do more than just agree to Hitler's terms. He would need to be an active participant in Hitler's aims of invading this country. In other words, Edward would be, is, a traitor – a traitor to the very country of which he was once its King!"

CHAPTER 28

Adlerhorst Castle, Hesse & Berlin, Germany – Mechelen, Belgium, January 1940

Hitler sat with his generals around the large table in the war room on which lay a map of Western Europe. Its scale allowed everyone to see the terrain, woodland, population centers, and topography of the area in detail. Although the castle had not yet been completely restructured to meet the designs of its architect, Albert Speer, it had been modified sufficiently for the purposes of the General Staff. All that mattered now was Hitler's overriding ambition to be the conqueror and sole ruler of Europe, and he would tolerate no further delays.

Although Britain and France had upheld their political and military obligations to Poland, they were still reluctant to wage actual war on its aggressor. This *Sitzkrieg*, or Phony War as the British called it, could not last much longer. Having declared war on Germany after the invasion of Poland, there had been very little actual fighting between the belligerents. The Allies seemed content enough to blockade neutral merchant ships from reaching Germany to deprive them of war materiel. This action did not worry Hitler too much, as he could still procure much of what he needed from those neighboring countries still trading with him either willingly for economic reasons or out of fear of retribution if they refused. The time was coming when he would show the British what a blockade could really do. Not yet, but soon.

Sitting with Hitler were, among others, General Franz Halder, the OKH Chief of Staff, and Walther von Brauchitsch, Commander-in-Chief of the German Army. Although it would not have been considered unusual for both men to have been part of the strategic planning conference, they had concerns nonetheless. These officers had been part of the plot to depose Hitler just before he signed the Munich agreement, afraid that his premature invasion of Czechoslovakia might trigger a military response from the Allies, a response which Germany was not yet ready to repulse. Brauchitch particularly had already infuriated Hitler a couple of months earlier when he suggested that German forces were not yet in a state of mental preparedness for battle. Some lower ranks, he declared, had even been insubordinate to their superior officers. Hitler dismissed Brauchitch and other senior officers as traitors and cowards. Had Hitler had gotten wind that these same generals had planned a *coup d'etat*? Were they there merely as military leaders, or did their Fuhrer know of their intended treachery? Would this be their last meeting before Hitler signed their death warrants?

The discussions had been heated regarding from which direction the German army should advance into France. The officers debated the three most effective ways. Either through the lowlands of Belgium into northern France, travel south, and invade around the heavily fortified Maginot Line, or drive their tanks through the deeply wooded Ardennes Forest. Opinions differed, but eventually, a battle plan was reached on which all present could agree.

Finally, Hitler spoke. Without even looking at Halder or Brauchitch, he declared, "Very well; it is settled. Our forces will advance through the middle of the Belgian lowlands into northern France. You will draw up the order of battle and see that it is delivered to the necessary commanders. I need hardly remind you that these documents will be classified to the highest level and must not fall into the hands of our adversaries under any circumstances. Let us now go and prepare to engage the enemy."

* * *

On the morning of January 10th., Major Erich Hoenmanns was flying his Messerschmitt Bf 108 single-prop light aircraft toward Cologne when a low fog bank descended, obscuring his view of the terrain below and confusing his usually well-honed navigational skills. His only passenger was Major

Helmuth Reinberger, who had cadged a lift from Hoenmanns for the trip, ostensibly for nothing more urgent than to attend a routine staff meeting.

Hoping to return to his intended course, the pilot flew in the direction of what he assumed would be a familiar landscape – the Rhine. Not realizing he was already crossing over it as he altered his aerial maneuver, Hoenmanns flew instead toward the River Meuse, which straddled the Belgian/Dutch border. He did not want his passenger to see him so agitated and engaged in small talk to divert the Major's attention from his disorientation. As the temperature plummeted, the cold weather caused the Messerschmitt's twin Sun carburetors to ice over, preventing its Argus As 10 engine from getting the correct fuel mixture to ignite the airplane's fuel. As the aircraft stalled in mid-flight, Hoenmanns panicked, accidentally nudging the fuel control lever with his elbow. This inadvertent action made the aircraft lose power entirely, causing it to plummet toward the ground. Unaware of the reason for the sudden loss of control, the pilot shouted, "Hold on!" as he veered his plane downward, attempting to bring it into a gliding pattern toward the terrain below.

Praying to a God he soon expected to meet, Hoenmanns steered the Messerschmitt, managing to lever out the airplane as it hit the open ground, speeding toward the edge of a clump of Canadian poplars. Its speed and momentum were so great that the aviator could not stop the Messerschmitt in time, causing it to lose both wings as it sliced into the trees. Hoenmann's plane was severely damaged, probably beyond repair, but by some miracle, neither he nor his passenger was badly hurt. They were alive. That was all that mattered. Both men quickly released their safety harnesses before pushing back the cockpit's glass canopy.

Crisp virgin snow blanketed the surrounding fields while their breath formed visible vapor as they exhaled. As the men were about to leap out of the airplane, a young farmhand, Engelbert Lambrichts, who had seen the airplane's German and Luftwaffe insignia, ran through the snow toward them as his farm boots left tracks behind him. He held his pitchfork in his hands with the prongs facing outward as he approached the downed aircraft. Assuming they were still in Germany, Hoenmanns called out, as they descended from the craft, "Where are we?"

"Belgium," Lambrichts shouted. "You're in Mechelen, just across the Dutch border. Now get over here slowly. No tricks or I'll skewer you."

Although Mechelen was on the Belgian side of the river, Lambrichts, like most of the locals, spoke Dutch, a language with which Hoenmanns was familiar. "We don't want any trouble. Just..."

"You're Germans, and you're my prisoners. Now move over here, slowly."

Before Hoenmanns could respond, he felt Reinberger tugging at the elbow of his flying jacket. "I need to speak to you," he hissed. "I must get...."

"What's he saying?" asked the farmhand suspiciously.

"I don't know. I think..."

"My briefcase. I must have my briefcase," Reinberger whispered urgently. Lambrichts gestured at the major with his makeshift weapon. "What does he want?"

"He says he needs his briefcase. He left it in the cockpit. Is it O.K. if he...?"

"Fine, but no tricks. If I see anything funny, you know what'll happen." Nodding to Reinberger, he allowed the soldier to climb back into the cockpit. Almost immediately, the major reappeared, clutching his briefcase to his chest like a protective father. "What's so special about that satchel? You got money in it, or something?" Reinberger did not speak Dutch, so Hoenmanns translated each man's conversation.

"No, it's only some papers for my meeting; nothing important."

"Well, it looked pretty important the way you were carrying on a minute ago. Open up your bag. Let me see."

Reinberger undid the hasps of his briefcase, turning the open mouth toward Lambrichts. "See, only papers. Nothing important." At that minute, all the men heard sounds coming from across the fields. It was two Belgian border guards. As the farmhand was momentarily distracted, Reinberger spoke softly, "These papers must not fall into the Belgians' hands. They contain the battle plans of our imminent invasion of their country and the Netherlands. I must destroy them before...."

"For God's sake. Now, you tell me this?"

"It may have escaped your attention, my useless pilot friend, but thanks to you, we nearly became fertilizer for this man's crops. I was just glad to get out of that cockpit in one piece. Now, are you going to...?"

"Oh, for fucks sake," breathed Hoenmanns, barely audibly at his passenger. "When I shout 'now,' run." The pilot and his passenger slowly walked toward their captor, then, after taking a few steps, Hoenmanns suddenly sprinted to the right, immediately attracting Lambricht's attention. "Now!" he screamed.

At that second, Reinberger raced back toward the Messerschmitt, but rather than climbing into the cockpit, he loped past it, running behind a hedge. Pulling out his cigarette lighter, the officer tried to set the papers on fire but could not get a spark. Then, suddenly, he managed to get a light, and the documents started to smolder.

By this time, the two patrol guards had arrived, one of whom saw the smoke and ran to find its source. Seeing Reinberger trying to fan the embers with his hands, he held his rifle up. Reinberger attempted to flee when two shots rang out over his head. "The next one will be in your arse, you Kraut bastard, and don't think I wouldn't shoot a German in the back. Now stop!" The guard barked as his breath vaporized in the still morning air.

Reinberger knew it would be useless to run anymore. This man was only looking for an excuse to kill him, and the army major was certainly not willing to oblige him. Hoenmanns, too, was being held at gunpoint, accepting the unwelcome fact that they were now both prisoners of war, two of the first Germans to be captured in this latest conflict.

The border guards marched their captives to the whitewashed brick guardhouse on the outskirts of the town. There they were interrogated by the commandant, Captain Arthur Rodrique, who held the burned remnants of Hitler's battle plans in his hands. Reinberger had only partly succeeded in destroying his precious intelligence, and many of the sensitive papers were still legible.

"Well, gentlemen, what do we have here? Adolf's shopping list, if I am not mistaken. So, he intends to invade us and our neighbor next door, eh? What, is Austria, the Rhineland, and Sudetenland not enough for that stinking man, eh? Is our little country so important to him that he must have it also? Ah, well, I suppose we must face reality. We are not strong enough to resist your forces by ourselves, but we expect Great Britain and France are well aware of his intentions, and if they are not, they soon will be. Once this evidence reaches the two governments, it will give them all the justification they need to bring your country to its knees. I still have not forgotten the carnage you caused here twenty years ago. No Belgian has. If it were up to me, I would take you both out the back and shoot you two bastards myself and send your bodies back in bits to your Führer. Let's see how he'd like that, eh?"

While he was ranting, he did not notice the look that passed between his two prisoners. Even Hoenmanns now realized the importance of what these documents signified. They had to be destroyed. Turning around to face his captors, he asked, "Could I use your toilet? This man's rant has made me want to pee." The two guards shrugged their shoulders. As they were helping him up, Reinberger suddenly shot forward, grabbing the remains of the battle plans from off Rodrique's desk. He bolted toward the room's wood-burning stove intending to destroy them in the flames.

Rodrique was startled by Reinberger's impulsive action, but only for a second. As the two guards were also reacting to the Major's abrupt actions, the guardhouse commander sprung after him, just as Reinberger was about to complete his intentions. Burning his hands in the process, Rodrique pushed the German's hands away from the stove, saving the incriminating plans. Rifle butting Reinberger, the guards quickly subdued him while Rodrique snatched the papers, quickly securing them in the adjoining room. Meanwhile, Hoenmanns was making for the outside door but stopped when he heard the snick of the guard's K98AZ bolt-action rifle. He would be gunned down before he could reach the door handle.

Reinberger wasn't finished. Just as Rodrique was starting to compose himself, he made a grab for the Belgian's gun. As both men were wrestling for control of the weapon, Rodrique punched the German to the ground. "I'll say this much for you Krauts. You don't give up easily. So now we can add attempted murder to the other charges. I think for you, my friends, the war is over."

"Attempted murder?" Reinberger echoed. "I wasn't going to kill you. I was going to shoot myself. When the High Command finds out what I've done, a bullet in the head will be a blessing. They'll make sure I die a much slower and more painful death."

"I wouldn't worry about that, Major. We'll keep you well away from your fellow soldiers," Rodrique smiled casually.

"Yes, until we invade your country and they free the jails. I never thought I'd hear myself say this, but I hope you defeat us. If you don't, I'm a dead man, anyway."

* * *

It did not take long for Reinberger's disastrous flight to come to Hitler's attention. The dictator was incandescent with rage, venting his anger at whoever was in his company for no reason other than they were a convenient outlet for his fury. "All our strategies, our schemes, our weeks and months of planning, all for nothing. Thanks to that idiot major and his incompetent pilot, we do not know if our plans have fallen into enemy hands. Even that information would be something. It's not knowing what the Belgians, and I presume the other Allies know or don't know that's so frustrating. Did the Major manage to destroy the battle details before they captured him? How can we alter our strategies and prosecute our military objectives, eh? I will have his head when we get him. The pilot too. I want to know his name. I will personally put a gun to that man's head and pull the trigger myself. I cannot accomplish this yet, but I can punish those who are their commanding officers. Turning to his adjutant, Hitler ordered him, "Get me General Felmy and Colonel Kammhuber. I will fire them myself, personally."

Eventually, the dictator calmed down to the point where one of his senior military advisors, General Alfred Jodl, the head of the *Oberkommando der Wehrmacht*, or OKW, asked him tentatively, "Well, *mein Führer*, what do we do now?"

Hitler looked at Jodl for several seconds, digesting the question inwardly. As he turned away, he replied softly, "We wait, General; we wait."

CHAPTER 29

Habarcq & Paris, France, January 1940

Edward had reluctantly accepted his assignment and reported for duty at the British military camp where he was to be stationed. He made himself known to his commanding officer, General Lawrence Plenderleith, on his arrival. As the two men shook hands and saluted, Edward stated, "Of course I won't be billeted here, you understand. Somehow, I don't see myself fitting in with the other ranks. I will base myself in Paris, where I believe I will be of more use."

"I beg your pardon, Your Royal Highness, I was not made aware of your intentions, but I must say, this is highly irregular."

"Well, be that as it may, this is my decision, and it is final. I will, of course, keep you apprised as to my whereabouts. You do not have to worry about my fulfilling my military obligations. I assure you I will be as assiduous in my duties as you would wish from any soldier under your command." Edward turned to leave, but the General was not finished. Royal title or not, it did not give Edward the right to be so insubordinate to a superior officer, and Plenderleith was not about to allow the Duke to walk out in such a high-handed manner. "It may have escaped your attention, Major-General, but this country is at war. We cannot have any of our troops, no matter their rank, or sense of entitlement, to consider themselves above the army or its disciplines and procedures, especially when it would take you three hours by car to get here. I am instructing you to find quarters in this camp and be on call immediately. I cannot have my men chasing around Paris trying to find you. Do I make myself clear?"

"Oh, yes, General, very clear, but I will remind you that there is nothing in King's Regulations that requires senior officers to be billeted with their men, save in combat conditions. As far as I know, not only are we not in that position but in my opinion, neither will we be."

Plenderleith was now becoming annoyed with his junior officer and his arrogant manner. "And pray tell me why you do not believe we will soon be at war, despite all the overwhelming evidence to the contrary." He bristled.

"Because even at this late stage, I believe our government will come to its senses and see that it is not Hitler who is the real enemy, but Stalin and the Soviet Union whom we should be fighting. They are the ones toward whom we should be directing our efforts. You mark my words, you'll see."

"Until I am given orders to the contrary, my enemy is Germany, not the Soviet Union. Now, I may not be able to prevent you from living in Paris, but I will tell you this. If you fail to arrive for duty, even once, I will have you up on charges of dereliction of duty and insubordination. That is all. You may go."

Edward was about to reply with some tart response but thought the better of it. He quickly saluted once again before leaving Plenderleith's office.

* * *

The Duke of Windsor had arranged a suite at the Meurice in Paris, where he soon settled in. He was determined that his military responsibilities would not prevent him from continuing his hedonistic lifestyle and shamelessly used his title to ensure he received the best attention.

A short time later, as he was leaving the Meurice to go to Habarcq, he met Charles Bedaux, who was just entering the hotel. Bedaux affected shock at the encounter. "My dear Edward, *quelle surprise*! I did not know you were in Paris. When did you arrive? The last I heard, you and Wallis were on your way back to England, I presume to meet your brother. How did it go? Did you manage to reconcile your differences? I do hope so. It is not so good when families quarrel with one another."

"I'm sorry, Charles, I'm in rather a hurry. Got to get to my day job. I've been enlisted to the British Military Mission. Can't say much about it. Hush-hush, you know. Perhaps we can meet for a drink later. I'll be back around eight. I can fill you in, then, if you're free."

"There's nothing I'd like better, my old friend. Shall we say eight-thirty for drinks at the bar here?"

"Certainly. Sorry, I need to rush...."

"See you later," Bedaux said to the back of Edward's head as the Duke hurried to his car.

* * *

It was just after their pre-arranged time when Edward met Bedaux in the bar of the Meurice, with its large shades-of-pink and lapis lazuli bas-relief mural adorning the wall behind the bar. "You look harassed, Edward. Please calm yourself. Let me buy you a drink." Without waiting to hear what his guest would prefer, Bedaux ordered two glasses of Glenfiddich grand cru single malt whisky. "There," he smiled once the barman had laid down the drinks. "This should make you feel better. Rough day, was it?"

"They believe I don't know what they're up to, but I'm not as stupid as they think I am, you know." Edward confided.

"What do you mean? I don't think you're stupid at all. Just the opposite, in fact."

"That's very kind of you, Charles, but it's them. They don't trust me. They won't let me see any papers that are sensitive or classified. They're frightened I would betray them to the Germans. It's so frustrating. I never wanted this war, you know. I told them no good would come from it. We should be joining forces with Hitler, not fighting him. I thought it back then, and I still believe it now. It's ludicrous, even more so for me. I've got German blood in me, for God's sake! Why will no one listen to me?" Edward had drained his glass while he was speaking, and Bedaux had signaled for another.

"Yes, it must be quite discouraging. I can see that. Here, don't let it get cold," he joked, pushing the amber liquid toward Edward. "Sadly, I don't think there's much you or I can do about it. All we can hope for is that when it comes, as it will, it won't drag on for four years like the last time. The sooner it's over, the better it will be for all of us, and we can start to get on with our lives again."

"Yes, I suppose so," Edward agreed gloomily. "Do you know, I've sent report after report telling our people back in London that France just isn't ready to go to war with the Germans. Their state of preparedness is woeful; in fact, I'd go so far as to say that it's pathetic. Yet, what do they say in London?" As Bedaux was about to answer, Edward continued, "They say, 'that's fine, Your Royal Highness, just keep sending reports. We know what we're doing.' And they don't, Charles; honestly, they don't. Our military command is sleepwalking into an unmitigated disaster. Hitler is far stronger than they think."

"Well, you've done all you can, I'm sure. Drink up; there's still the best part of a bottle to get through." Edward drained his glass and allowed Bedaux to order a refill.

"You and I speak the same language, Charles. It's just a pity our stupid politicians don't see it the same way. Yes, I know Hitler can be a bit... aggressive at times, but he's done a first-rate job of getting Germany out of the mire he found it in. You know the old saying about omelets and eggs. I just hate the fact that I have to fight against him instead of fighting on his side."

"Yes, I know what you mean. Here, let me get you another of those." Motioning the barman over, he pointed at the glasses, holding up two fingers; the universal language of ordering more of the same. "You know, there might be... no, I don't suppose...."

"Suppose what?" Edward asked as he tilted the refilled glass to his lips.

"Nothing. Forget it. I shouldn't have mentioned it."

"Now you've got me intrigued. What were you going to say? Come on, spit it out."

"No, I can't. You don't want to hear it, I promise you."

"Charles, you were kind enough to lend me your beautiful home to have my wedding in. That's more than just a casual friendship. Wallis and

I are very fond of you, both of you. There's nothing you can say that will upset or offend me. Now, what's this all about?"

"I think you'd better have another drink," and without waiting for Edward to finish the one he was nursing, Bedaux ordered two more. By this time, the Duke was feeling light-headed, and the pressures of the last few hours now seemed like a distant, bad memory. "Not now, my friend. We'll talk again about this matter but for the rest of the evening, let's turn our minds to other happier things. How's Wallis, by the way...?"

* * *

"Well, how did it go?" asked the man on the other end of the telephone line. It was an older voice, belying his fifty-four years, cultured and erudite, but with a trace of anxiety in its delivery.

"Early days, my friend; early days. But I don't think there'll be too much trouble getting him to see things from our viewpoint. Another week or so should do it. He trusts me. Why shouldn't he? As he said, I even gave him my house in which to hold his nuptials. You can bet your life savings on this. It won't be long, I assure you."

"It had better not be. If you knew the pressure I'm under to get this done, you'd be glad your name is not Julius von Zech-Burkersroda."

CHAPTER 30

Paris & Habarcq, France - The Hague, Netherlands, January - February 1940

Bedaux saw Edward the following evening, taking up his conversation from the night before. The Duke was still bridling at the army's refusal to allow him to view to papers he believed he should have access to, as a former King of the realm. He lost no time in venting his indignation at Bedaux while his friend listened patiently and sympathetically. "What do they say when you demand to see the documents? They cannot keep rebuffing you like that. It's outrageous. You should take a stand. You should..."

"Do you not think I've already done that? And every time I insist on doing something concrete, something worthwhile, they give me papers that are hopelessly out of date or worthless in their own right. I've a good mind to write to my brother and tell him to either allow me to do the job he's sent me to do or bring me home. It's becoming intolerable, and I don't know how much more I can take."

"Do you know, it's a terrible thing to say, but I honestly believe the Reich values you more highly than your own country. Isn't that a shocking thing to even think?"

Edward nodded his head in agreement. Gulping down his third glass of whisky, he said, "They have the barefaced cheek to call me a traitor. I'm the one who tried to prevent this beastly war; I'm the one who tried to negotiate with Hitler, to let him see that I, at least, understood his motivation. If I had still been the monarch, I'm convinced we could have reached an understanding to avoid this impending catastrophe. It seems the government is hell-bent on giving Hitler the war he wants, much good may it do them. Germany is unstoppable, you know. I've heard things that... oh, I mustn't say any more. Top secret stuff, you understand."

"You know, going back to what you said a minute ago, I'm quite sure things would have been very different if you had still been King." Bedaux dropped his voice, so he was barely audible. "I hear that may still become possible," he whispered. "My sources tell me that if Britain falls, there is every likelihood that Adolf will reinstall you as King, with Wallis as Queen. Now, wouldn't that be something, eh?"

"Your sources are very well informed, Charles. I don't wish to say too much about it, but, yes, the Führer and I did have a conversation after this fashion. It's only a matter of time now. If the government chooses to prosecute this war, it is one they will surely lose. Then my position as King will be assured." Edward gulped down the last inch of scotch just as Bedaux pushed another full glass in his direction. Without breaking stride, he swallowed that one as well.

"You know, the time is coming, in fact, I would say the time has arrived when you are going to have to choose which side you are on. Before you answer, let me summarize your position as I see it." Bedaux slid yet another glass of Glenfiddich toward Edward as he continued, "What has Britain done for you? I mean, you personally, you and Wallis. Your Prime Minister, your government, your church, your family, your own brother, would not allow you to marry Wallis and remain King, all because of some silly, outdated religious rule about not being permitted to wed a divorced person whose spouse is still alive. We are living in the twentieth century, my friend. This is not the middle ages. Surely, as monarch, you had the right to choose your own wife without the interference of church or state."

"Don't fool yourself, Charles. You know as well as I do that her divorced status was only the excuse they needed to get rid of us. They were well aware of our pro-German sentiments and were worried that I would exert my influence as King to persuade the country to enter into a pact with Hitler. That's the reason they wanted us gone; nothing else." Edward retorted bitterly.

"Whatever the reason, your country has let you down very badly, very badly indeed. I understand they also turned a blind eye to the assassination attempt on you a few years ago. You owe them nothing, Edward. They would not even afford Wallis the royal status to which she is entitled. And, as I am led to believe, they did not even send a royal car for you when you arrived back in England, nor would they let you stay in the Palace. Is that any way to treat a former King of his country? Now, compare that with the reception you both received in Germany. Could they have done any more for you? They treated you with more respect and dignity than the country you once ruled. No one could have done more to make you feel welcome than Adolf, is that not so? Did they not treat Wallis as the Queen she should have been? Here, your glass is almost empty. Let me get you another." Bedaux caught the barman's attention, calling him over to refill Edward's tumbler. "So I will ask you. If it comes down to it, who do you think will act in your best interests?"

"By Jove, when you put it like that, I don't see there's any decision to be made. I owe Britain nothing. They virtually hounded us out like two common criminals, only calling me back to fight in their ghastly war. No, Charles, you are quite right. My allegiance should be to the country that supports me, not the one who dismissed me so ignominiously. I know where my loyalties lie."

"And the sooner we win this war, the sooner you can reclaim your rightful place as King. They need never know how you came to be re-crowned. That will be our little secret, eh?" Both men raised their glasses in an unspoken toast, saluting the time when Hitler would be the ruler of the United Kingdom with Edward, his obedient monarch.

Now he knew where Edward's true fidelity lay, Bedaux leaned forward. Although the bar had only a few patrons, he did not want anyone to overhear what he was about to say. "I'm going to tell you something, but for God's sake, keep it to yourself. Do you understand?"

Edward bent his face forward to meet Bedaux's. "Yes, of course. What is it?" he whispered.

"The Germans believe the Allies may have captured documents that show plans for a full-scale German invasion of Belgium and Holland. Don't ask me how I know this. The information is classified, but I have sources high up in the top echelon. The problem for Hitler is he can't be sure whether they have them or not, or how much they know, and he cannot proceed with his objectives if he believes the enemy will be waiting for him."

"Yes, I understand that. But what can I do? You know how they keep things from me, I don't see...."

"You must try, my dear Edward. Whatever it takes, we must know if the Allies have got these plans, and what their counter-measures are likely to be. The High Command cannot prosecute this phase of the war until we know what they know."

"I will do my very best, Charles. After all, it is in our common interest that there should be a successful German outcome. Leave it with me. I won't let you down."

Pushing another glass of scotch toward Edward, Bedaux replied, "I know, my friend. I know you won't."

* * *

"Well, how did it go? Did he agree to do as you suggested?" asked the refined, almost manicured voice on the other end of the line.

"It was even easier than I had thought it would be. He is so asinine and gullible, I almost felt guilty at how simple it was to deceive him. He is a vapid, vain, and vacuous individual. My, I never realized how alliterative I am." Bedaux laughed into the mouthpiece.

"So, he has agreed to help us, as you asked?"

"Agreed? Once I showed him which side his bread was buttered, as our English friends say, it would have taken a force of will stronger than mine to stop him. What a dreadful man he truly is. God help Britain once he is back in Buckingham Palace."

After they ended their call, von Zech-Burkersroda sent a coded message to Berlin. Von Zech-Burkersroda was the German ambassador to the Hague and a confederate of Charles Bedaux. The message read, in part, '*Through personal relationships, I might have the opportunity to establish certain lines leading to the Duke of Windsor. He does not feel entirely satisfied with his position...and at some time, under favorable circumstances, I believe his estrangement from the current British government might acquire a certain significance.'* The ambassador hoped that this secret communique might take some of the pressure off him. He had done his part. The rest was now up to Bedaux and the Duke.

* * *

For the next few days, Edward surreptitiously tried to gain access to prohibited documents, only to find himself constantly stymied. It seemed to the Duke that his suspicions had been vindicated. The rest of the Intelligence staff had been made aware of Edward's questionable patriotism and had been ordered to ensure no sensitive papers were left in his purview. Then, almost by accident, Edward came across the papers Bedaux had asked him to find.

A few days after his meeting with Bedaux, he was summoned to his commanding officer's office. On his arrival, Plenderleith's adjutant told the Duke that the General had been delayed but would return shortly. Against the adjutant's orders, Edward entered Plenderleith's room, leaving a flustered junior officer not knowing how he should handle Edward's lack of discipline. Rather than sit at Plenderleith's desk, the Duke walked around it, hoping to see some intelligence that would be of interest to his German friends. Almost immediately, he realized he had found material related to Hitler's planned invasion. Sitting atop his c.o.'s desk was a War Office memorandum headed 'Imminent Danger from German Forces.' The memo reiterated much of what Bedaux had revealed earlier and confirmed that the Allies had, indeed, recovered the Nazi's intended offensive strategy. More importantly, the document laid out what this was and how the Allies would counter it. Edward could not believe his good fortune. This information was exactly the intelligence he had been tasked to find.

Just as he had finished re-reading it, he heard a commotion outside. Quickly laying the memorandum down on Plenderleith's desk as he had found it, he took his seat as his commanding officer stormed into his office. "What the blazes...?" he shouted. "I gave specific instructions that no one was to enter this room in my absence, yet here you are, disobeying my orders once again. I could have you on a charge for this, Major General. Did you read any of these documents? Come on, now, and don't lie to me. Do you know the contents of any of the papers on my desk?"

The Duke stood up, replying casually, "I am not in the habit of reading anyone else's correspondence without their permission, Sir," giving false emphasis on the final word.

"These papers are highly confidential and are not to be seen by anyone outside of this office. Now, I will ask you once again, have you read any of these documents?"

"And again, I repeat, no, I have not," Edward lied. "And I should point out, General, that if these files are so sensitive, you should have locked the door."

"How dare you be so insubordinate?" Plenderleith shouted. "My instructions should have been sufficient enough for you to comply with them. This is a deplorable show, damn it! I will let this episode go without further comment, but if you ever disobey any more of my commands again, I will have you cleaning the latrines, Duke of the realm or not. Now, get out!"

"I came here because you ordered me. May I ask why you sent for me?"

"It's gone out of my head, but doubtless, it was nothing important. Just make sure you don't wander off without letting me know. Now, go. I have important work to do." Glancing at his documents without looking up, Plenderleith dismissed Edward with a peremptory wave of the hand. Edward stood to attention and saluted before quickly leaving his commanding officer. He, too, had work to do. Work of a very different kind.

Walking briskly to his own office, Edward sat at his desk and notated as much as he could remember. It wasn't everything, but it would be enough. He would soon put Plenderleith in his place, and others like him. Thanks to him, Germany would now be able to invade Belgium, and the Low Countries, even France itself, and there would be nothing the French or British could do about it. He would make sure of it.

CHAPTER 31

Adlerhorst Castle & Berlin, Germany – Paris & Biarritz, France, June 1940

A few months earlier, thanks to Edward's duplicity and treachery, the German High Command knew that the Allies had, indeed, compromised their war plans. A further coded telegram from Julius von Zech-Burkersroda had confirmed as much. '*The Duke of Windsor has said that the Allied war council devoted an exhaustive discussion at its last meeting to the situation that would arise if Germany invaded Belgium. Reference was made throughout to a German invasion plan said to have been found in an aeroplane that made a forced landing in Belgium.*'

Gathered around the war room of the almost restructured castle, and armed with the knowledge that his plans had been discovered, Hitler and his senior generals considered their revised strategy. "Well, now we know that the Allied powers are aware of our intentions, what do you propose we do about it?" Hitler asked the room at large.

"Perhaps we should postpone...." Colonel-General Wilhelm Keitel, Chief of Armed Forces High Command, ventured timidly.

"Postpone?" screamed Hitler, enraged. "If I hear anyone use that word again concerning this operation, I will have them taken out and shot! For the purposes of this offensive, the word 'postpone' is not in our vocabulary. Do I make myself understood?" No one dared speak, not even to acquiesce to Hitler's demand. Turning to the source of his anger, the German dictator shouted, "I gave you the position you hold, *Generaloberst*, because, despite your sycophancy – don't think I don't see how you fawn at my every suggestion - I consider you a good soldier. Do not disappoint me like that again. If you have nothing better to contribute to this conversation, keep your mouth shut!"

Keitel felt himself blush. To be upbraided by his Führer in front of his peers was almost more than he could stand. Keitel bowed his head as all eyes turned in his direction. He decided to stay quiet for the rest of the briefing and only speak if asked a direct question. Maybe silence really was golden, he thought bitterly.

"Perhaps we could double bluff the Allies," suggested Alfred Jodl. "Now that we know they are aware of our battle plans, the last thing they will be expecting is for us to adhere to this offensive. They will anticipate for us to break through elsewhere and will undoubtedly reposition their forces accordingly. Or..."

"Yes?" questioned Hitler.

"Well, what if... what if we use the third and fourth Panzer divisions as diversions, fooling them into thinking we still intended to break through from Belgium, but stormed the Maginot Line with our main forces instead. I know the French consider it impenetrable, but I'm sure...."

"Wouldn't it be better to outflank them and go around the fortifications?" asked Walther von Brauchitch.

"That would take our forces too far to the south and would mean splitting our army in two. Let's not underestimate the enemy, gentlemen." Responded Hitler in a more conciliatory tone. At least these officers were thinking positively, if not tactically. "They know we're coming, and they'll be ready for us, but you're quite correct. A diversionary ploy will be necessary if we are to succeed in our objectives." Hitler studied the map once again, slowly running his forefinger along the contours of the French defenses. No, he would not risk his troops trying to break through such strongly fortified garrisons. However, the Allies did not necessarily know that. "We can use their own barricades against them. Let us make them believe we are indeed going to try to engage them there." Hitler stabbed his finger at the map. "There. Kehl is virtually on the French border. Although their defenses are strong here, I believe this is where our diversionary force should be. Meanwhile, our main thrust will be through the Ardennes Forest. It is the last place they will be expecting us to come from."

"With good reason, *mein Führer*. The forest is practically impenetrable. It is a natural barrier. What you are suggesting is...." Jodl stopped, remembering how Hitler responded to his colleague's previous negative remarks. "Yes, I see how we can outmaneuver the Allies if we...." He, too, studied the map, concentrating on the Ardennes region. Slowly nodding his head, Jodl concurred. "It is a brilliant strategy, *mein Führer*, if I may say so. You are quite right. They will never expect an attack to come through such a densely wooded area."

Hitler smiled to himself at Jodl's abrupt *volte-face*. But then again, what else could he do? And it was a good plan, even if Hitler thought so himself.

* * *

That had all been back in February, and now German troops were poised to take Paris. The British and Allied forces were in retreat and had been routed at Dunkerque. Lord Gort, the British Expeditionary Force commander, was grateful that Hitler had stopped German troops from advancing to engage his men, preferring to leave the impending defeat of the Allied forces to Hermann Göring's Luftwaffe. This strategy gave the Allies the time they needed to regroup and for the survivors to make their way back to safety across the English Channel.

As the German army drew nearer to the French capital, Edward understood that it was no longer safe for him to remain in his hotel. Turning to Wallis, he said, "I think the time has come for us to leave. Enemy troops will be here soon, and I'm not sure that even our relationship with the German government will save us. I think it would be better for us both if we left Paris for a little while. Just until the dust settles."

"Oh, really, must we go?" whined the Duchess. "We're so settled here and near all the shops. Is there no way...?"

"I don't think you understand, my dear. In all likelihood, they'll put us under house arrest at the least, so I'm afraid your free-spending days are over anyway. I have an idea where we should go. I've been thinking about it for a while, and if I'm to be honest with you, I've been expecting this to happen for some time. Don't worry, everything's arranged."

"Where are we going? Where are you taking me?" Wallis demanded.

"We're heading south; that's all I'm prepared to say for the time being. I can keep secrets if I want to, you know."

"Talking about secrets, shouldn't you be joining your Intelligence unit? Everyone seems to be evacuating to the ports, trying to get out before it's too late."

"Well, they don't seem to have missed me much up until now, so I don't expect they'll notice I'm not there. Who cares? I'm done with all of them, especially after the way they've treated you, my sweet."

"Yes, I know. Maybe it's all for the best. Things have a habit of working out, don't they?"

"I suppose so. I'm not sure when we'll be able to return, so leave nothing behind, at least nothing of value. Now come on, we've got a long drive ahead of us...."

* * *

The couple arrived at their destination, the Hotel du Palais in Biarritz, thirty kilometers from the Spanish border just before midnight.

"It seems very nice," Wallis commented on their arrival. "Not a patch on the Meurice, of course, but beggars can't be choosers, I suppose."

"If it was good enough for my grandpapa, it's good enough for us," countered Edward. "There is a war on, you know. He got them to improve the drains, I believe. Kept getting wakened in the night with the dreadful smell, so I understand. Well, at least he did one useful thing in his life."

"How long do you intend for us to remain here?

"Not long; a few days, perhaps a week. Just until..."

"Until what?"

"Until I can find somewhere more permanent for us to stay. As I already told you, I saw this coming a long time ago. We're no match for Hitler, not now, and he'll soon be across the Channel. Mark my words, he'll be in London sooner rather than later. All we have to do until then is bide our time. Now, come on, it's late. You must be exhausted after such a long drive. Let's get a good night's sleep and take our bearings in the morning."

"You go on up, darling. I'll be with you shortly."

"You'll be what? It's almost one in the morning. What are you up to?"

"The bar's still open. I thought I might have a nightcap before I turn in. It helps me to sleep." She smiled.

"I'll join you. Wouldn't mind a snifter myself, come to that."

"No," she responded more harshly than she meant to. "I mean, I would just like some time alone, that's all. We seem to have been in each other's company so much lately, not that I mind, of course; it's just that I'd like a little time to myself if that's alright."

"Well, if that's what you want," he answered huffily before turning away and entering the lift.

Wallis ordered a gin and tonic, which she sipped slowly. The Duchess had given Edward fifteen minutes to return. When he did not, she left her drink and went up to the reception desk. Pinging the bell to attract the night attendant's attention, she asked, "Can I send a telegram from here just now?"

When the receptionist confirmed it was possible, Wallis replied smiling, "Very good. Now I need you to dispatch a message...."

* * *

The Reichsminister of Foreign Affairs, Joachim von Ribbentrop, sat back languidly in his chair. He suspected that Edward knew of his continuing relationship with Wallis, but even if that were true, what could or would he do about it? Any other man would have confronted their wife's lover, demanding that such a liaison should cease immediately. Perhaps, in the more extreme cases, even some violence might be involved. But in Edward's case, this was highly unlikely. He had shown himself to be a man of straw, willing to overlook Wallis's indiscretions as long as she returned to him in the end. Besides, it would look bad for Edward himself if word got out about his wife's infidelities. No, in his case, it was better to let sleeping dogs lie.

Ribbentrop was well aware that Wallis, too, was playing a double game. She enjoyed the company of other men as well her husband's, and the more powerful, the better. Powerful men like him. There was no doubt their affair would continue, even after Hitler had her husband re-crowned King. She couldn't help herself. It was who she was. And while he had her under his sway, he would use her, just as she was using him.

There was only one place the Duke could be taking them; across the border into Franco's Spain. Where else would he be as safe as in a country which, although professing neutrality, had secretly allied itself with Germany? It was working out better than they had imagined. Thanks to Edward's poltroonery, it would be even easier for them to execute their plans than they had calculated. They would now have to revise their strategy accordingly. Although he did not know it, the former King of England was playing straight into the hands of very dangerous, unscrupulous, and determined men, men to whom the ultimate prize was the throne of the greatest empire in the world – the British Empire, his Empire.

CHAPTER 32

London, England – Biarritz, France – Madrid, Spain, June 1940

"He's where?" roared Winston Churchill down the telephone line. Churchill had taken over from Neville Chamberlain as Prime Minister a few weeks earlier when the former incumbent of 10 Downing Street lost the confidence of most members of the House of Commons. "What the bloody hell is he doing in Biarritz? Why is he not with his unit? No, on second thoughts, perhaps it's best if he's kept as far away as possible from secret... no, damn it! He's a serving officer in the British army in wartime. No matter what his political sympathies are, right now, he should be with his men. He's the former King of this country, for goodness' sake! What sort of example is he setting to the rest of our troops? While they've been fighting tooth and nail to keep the Nazis from our doorstep, he's swanning off without a care in the world. What he did was tantamount to desertion. Had it been anyone else, they'd have been dragged back to Britain and court-marshaled. It's only because of what it would do to public morale and the Royal Family's reputation that prevents me from doing just that. It's damn well not good enough. I must have a word with his brother about this intolerable situation; several choice words, in fact!"

"Yes, Prime Minister, and I would advise as soon as possible. We can't have a loose cannon like Edward wandering all over France as if he's on a sightseeing tour."

The recipient of Churchill's ire was Colonel Stewart Menzies, Director of MI6. Since the start of hostilities, Menzies and Churchill had formed a close working relationship that had developed into an amicable friendship.

This bond did not stop the Prime Minister from venting his anger at his Intelligence chief:

"How do we know where he is? That detective's still not with him, is he?"

"No, Prime Minister. It was his equerry, Major Metcalfe. Apparently, he returned to find Edward gone with all his belongings. No word of thanks or farewell. It was only because he found some sort of paper advertising the Hotel du Palais that he surmised where the couple had decamped to. He's not very happy with the Duke; I can tell you that."

"He's not very happy? How does he think we all feel? We need to get him out of harm's way for his own sake as well as the country's. Leave this with me, Colonel. As if I don't have enough on my plate as it is." An exasperated Churchill ended the call, considering the best way to handle this new and troublesome situation. An idea was forming in his mind, but he would have to take soundings before he could put his tentative plan into operation.

* * *

Edward knew he could not stay in Biarritz for too long, correctly surmising that the government would soon discover his location. After a few days enjoying the warm summer sunshine, he announced to Wallis, "We'll need to move again, my sweet. We can't risk them finding us and forcing me to go back to Britain. That's the last place I want to be right now."

"I'm sorry, David, but I refuse to keep behaving like some poor refugee. First Paris, which wasn't so bad, I suppose, now here; where to next?"

"Spain, my dear. We're going to be the guests of General Franco. He's arranged lodgings for us in Madrid."

"Lodgings? My dear, you should know me well enough by now. I don't do 'lodgings.' You make us sound as if we are some itinerant peddlers begging for shelter. You may wish to live in lodgings, but don't expect me to."

"Oh, I think Francisco will do better than that, my sweet. In fact, I know he will."

* * *

The Duke surprised Wallis. She expected to drive into Spain from their hotel in Biarritz, but Edward had other ideas. "I told you, my sweet, I've had this planned for a while. We'll send the other cars south from here while we enjoy the sights of Biarritz for another day or so. I have a feeling that they're watching us, and if I'm right, they'll try to stop us at the Spanish border. They'll have to get up earlier in the morning if they want to catch me, my dear. I'm too smart for them. I'm going to do something they'll never suspect...."

The following day, ensuring there were no vehicles following them, Edward and Wallis set off before dawn, traveling southeast. Their destination was Perpignan, a road journey of over five hundred kilometers. "Yes, I know it's an awfully long road, but it's the safest. The Germans haven't got this far south yet, and the British will never think we'll drive this way. We'll stop at Perpignan for the night in some little guest house."

Wallis looked at him aghast. "In some little guest house?" she echoed. "Did you not hear what I said the other day? I do not put up in guest houses, bed-and-breakfast places, or shabby hotels. Now...."

"It's only for one night, my sweet," begged Edward as they sat together in the rear of Edward's Buick. "Besides, think how romantic it will be. We can book in under the names Mr. and Mrs. Jones. I doubt anyone will recognize us, and if they do, we can give them some financial inducements to forget they ever saw us. It'll be fun, and besides...."

"Besides?"

"It'll make you appreciate the place we're going to in Spain all the more. Desperate times call for desperate measures and all that."

* * *

It was not the landlord of the little auberge or his customers that the Windsors had problems with the following day. The Spanish consul had not been made aware of the couple's arrival and their intended stay in his country. "I regret, Señor, that I cannot issue you with the necessary travel papers. Perhaps you could...."

"Do you know who I am, you jumped-up dogsbody?" fumed Edward. "I am the Duke of Windsor, and this is my wife, the Duchess. "I must insist you provide me with the necessary documents immediately. Now, do I have to inform your superior of your intransigence, or are you going to do your job?"

The official refused to be cowed by Edward's bombast. "Señor, perhaps in other circumstances, it would not be too much of a problem, but you must understand the situation. Your country is at war with a government with whom we have non-belligerent relations. I cannot authorize any visas to you or your wife without the approval of my government. If you would care to...."

"Never mind. I'll take care of this myself. Do you have access to a telegraph machine?"

"But of course, Señor."

"Very well. I want you to send a message to the British ambassador. Can you do that?"

"Yes, I can."

Edward dictated the message, which the consul immediately wired to Madrid. He did not have long to wait. Within a few hours, the consul received a reply authorizing him to issue the necessary transit papers. This would mean that the British government would know where he was and where he was likely to go. To the Windsors, it made no difference. He had virtually severed ties with his native country and would only return once England was in German hands.

In the late afternoon, Edward and Wallis crossed into Spain and drove to Barcelona, where they spent the night. The following day, they traveled the six-hundred-and-fifty-kilometer journey to the Spanish capital. Franco had arranged a suite at the Ritz Hotel, and Wallis once again lost no time in alerting von Ribbentrop to their whereabouts.

Things had not gone to plan when the establishment would not accord her the royal title she craved, but she would soon rectify this situation. With her husband as Hitler's puppet King, and her as Queen, she would have dominion over all she surveyed and more besides. Hadn't Ribbentrop promised her as much? She had been good to him in ways his wife would not. There was no reason why this liaison could not continue whenever the Foreign Minister was in London. Society may have shunned her for who she was, but they would soon be jostling with each other to ingratiate themselves with her.

Spanish Intelligence had advised Franco that the couple had arrived, but the Spanish dictator was in no hurry to meet them. They had all but imposed themselves on him, putting him and his government in a difficult position. He had wanted to maintain an air of neutrality, but for how long could he keep up this pretense when such a well-known supporter of Hitler had decided to make Spain his temporary refuge rather than return to England? He decided to speak to the British ambassador, Sir Samuel Hoare, the former British foreign secretary. As well as being a friend of the Duke of Windsor, he knew Hoare to be in the same camp as Chamberlain, who wanted to avoid war by appeasing Hitler and capitulating to his European ambitions. Here was a British diplomat he could negotiate with to try and find a way out of the political situation into which Edward had plunged his country.

CHAPTER 33

London, England - Madrid, Spain – Berlin, Germany, June 1940

"It's no use," Churchill decided, speaking to his Deputy Prime Minister, Clement Attlee. "We'll have to get him out of there. While he's in Franco's clutches, there's every likelihood the Germans will try to capture him. It wouldn't even surprise me if he didn't put up much resistance to a Nazi abduction. He's never made any secret of his admiration for that abominable little man. As much as I supported Edward through his abdication, my affection for him has sadly diminished. I warned him not to go to Germany, but he was determined to give Wallis a taste of what she felt she had been deprived of here. And what he did in France was unforgivable, but we can't leave him in Spain. He's too valuable a prize for them. We need to get him as far away as possible and keep him out of trouble. I've spoken to the Colonial Secretary, and we're agreed. Edward is going on a nice long holiday at the taxpayers' expense...."

"I'm intrigued, Prime Minister. This country is at war, and you're sending the Duke of Windsor on a vacation, which we're all paying for. I assume there's a method in this madness."

"Quite so, Mr. Attlee; quite so."

"Where are you sending him, if I may ask?"

"Sadly, we cannot yet travel outside our own planet, so I'm sending him to the next best place. He's going to be Governor of the Bahamas."

"Very nice. I may tender my resignation and become his next Principal Private Secretary."

"No, you bloody well won't," rejoindered Churchill. Both men smiled, but this was no laughing matter. Whether he liked it or not, Churchill had to make Edward's hasty departure from Spain his number one priority. His former monarch had a lot to answer for. Churchill hoped that when the conflict was over, he would be able to confront Edward with his misdemeanors. Churchill had been one of the few public figures who supported Edward during the abdication crisis four years earlier. Not only had the Duke of Windsor deserted his country during its time of peril, he had betrayed his friend. In his own mind, Churchill could not decide which was the worst misdeed.

* * *

"He has put us in a very difficult position, Ramòn. As much as I am grateful to the German leader for his assistance in our successful struggle against the Republican forces, I do not want to incur the wrath of the British. I fear that even yet, they may give Hitler a surprise or two. Then where would we be? They would not be in a hurry to forgive us for harboring Edward."

Franco's Minister of the Interior, and his brother-in-law, Ramòn Serrano Suñer, replied, "*Caudillo*, if I may be permitted to speak freely, I do not believe we have anything to be worried about. Hitler is unstoppable and is growing stronger almost by the day. See how he chased the British out of France, and even now, his forces are poised to cross the English Channel. The British may put up fierce resistance, and I have no doubt they will fight well, but ultimately, it will be the Germans who will prevail. Of that, I am utterly convinced. Then, it will not matter in the slightest."

"Perhaps you are right. Time will tell, eh?"

"And in the meantime?"

"In the meantime, I will speak with Beigbeder. He is close to the German Foreign Minister, von Ribbentrop. Let's see what they come up with."

"And by distancing yourself from the discussions with the Nazis, if anything goes wrong, you can deny any culpability."

"You have a Byzantine mind, Ramòn. I see I shall have to keep a closer eye on you than I have done up until now." Franco smiled. Sũñer knew his Generalissimo meant him to take his flippant remark as a joke, but behind the jest, Franco was making a serious point. Never try to outsmart or out think your leader. At least, not to his face, even if he is your brother-in-law.

* * *

In his office within the Hotel Adlon on the Unter den Linden, von Ribbentrop read the communiqué sent by the Spanish Foreign Minister, Colonel Juan Beigbeder y Atienza. So, little Edward and his wayward wife had made it into Spain, had they? The flies had become entangled in the spider's web, from which there would be no escape. The Führer would be pleased, no, more than pleased – he would be delighted at how well their plan was working out. It would take a little while to marshal all the strands together. The Spanish authorities would need to 'persuade' Edward and Wallis to stay in their delightful country for just a little longer. The Duke loved the good life and all the trappings that went with it. Together with the other inducements the Reich was prepared to offer, von Ribbentrop would see that he was made a proposal he could not refuse. These propositions would buy them time until they could put the next phase of their scheme into operation.

* * *

"Unfortunately, the stars seem to have aligned themselves with the Nazis," Churchill spoke gloomily to George Lloyd, his Colonial Secretary. "I wanted to get Edward and Wallis to Portugal post-haste, but Salazar has prevented this from happening. With all that's going on, I had forgotten that Prince George is currently there on a goodwill visit. Salazar does not want anything to interfere with this, and the Duke of Kent certainly does not want to come into even close proximity to his brother. He is not scheduled to leave Portugal for another few days. This is not good."

Churchill sighed. "It appears fate has decreed that Edward should fall into their hands. If that's the case, I fear there is nothing we can do about it."

"Could we not get Sir Samuel to insist that Edward stays in the embassy? That would certainly keep him away from the Germans."

"That's a good idea, George. I'll signal a message to him, instructing him to do just that. It's bad enough that I have to spend so much of my valuable time answering his asinine messages. If it's not him still wanting a royal title for his wife, it's his demand that he be allowed to visit the Palace. This is something that both the King and I and the rest of the cabinet are vehemently against. He says he wants to do something more useful and constructive to help the war effort. As if publicly supporting the Nazis, fleeing in the face of the enemy, deserting his men, potentially demoralizing the nation's spirit, and thinking of no one but himself has already been helping the war effort! I'm sorry to say this, George, but the best thing that man did in his whole life was to abdicate. He is not fit to run a haberdashery shop, never mind rule this country. The sooner we're shot of him, the better."

* * *

Sir Samuel Hoare met with Edward at his suite in the Ritz Hotel to discuss Churchill's instruction that the Duke should take up residence at the embassy.

"Why should I do anything they want me to do?" asked a truculent Edward. "Winston has not agreed to any of my requests and seems to want everything in return."

"With all due respect, Your...."

"Isn't it strange?" interrupted Edward, "That when someone says 'with all due respect,' it's just before they show you no respect whatsoever. What were you going to say?"

A slightly disgruntled ambassador replied, "As I was about to say, the Prime Minister has not refused to accede to any of your requests. He only thinks it would be better to discuss them once you are safely back on British soil rather than through diplomatic cables. And I have to say, I agree with him."

"Of course you do, Sir Samuel; of course you do. Especially if you want to retain your nice safe billet here, eh?"

Hoare was astounded by Edward's sanctimonious hypocrisy. He was living in one of the finest hotels in Spain while his fellow Britons were fighting in a war against a brutal dictator. "Your Royal Highness, we have known each other for a long time, and I would like to think that a friendship had developed between us. That remark was most unworthy, even from you!" Sir Samuel retorted angrily. "Franco could decide to align himself with Hitler any day now. That would put my staff, my family, and myself in the most precarious position. I must insist that you withdraw that remark immediately!"

Edward looked at the ambassador for a few seconds, deciding what to do. He had overstepped the mark; even he recognized that, but to apologize would be to capitulate, and the former King felt he had given enough ground already without ceding more. Without saying a word, he turned around abruptly and left the room, leaving a hurt and angry ambassador staring into empty space. Had this event happened in former times, Sir Samuel thought, he would have had no compunction in slapping the Duke with his glove, demanding satisfaction on the dueling field. Sadly, those days had long gone, and personal disputes were now settled by more peaceful and less bloody means.

The British ambassador followed Edward into the other room. He was still enraged at what the Duke had said, but he was a professional statesman and politician. He had a job to do and had to rise above petty sentiments like indignation and pride. "Your Royal Highness, I have tried to be courteous and patient, but my exasperation is now beyond my control. I must insist that you leave this hotel and accompany me back to the embassy, where suitable quarters will be found for you and your wife. I have been asked to remind you that your financial well-being is at the discretion of your brother, who may choose to cut off your substantial allowance should you refuse to comply with the instructions the government has given me."

Edward merely smiled at this not-so-veiled threat to the retainer his brother had provided for him. The last time this matter had been raised was when he was in Germany visiting Hitler. There was little he could do about it then, but times had moved on, and the world had changed. He could not tell Sir Samuel that the German government had recently offered him fifty million Swiss francs to betray his country and agree to become King for the second time under a Nazi administration. The subsistence he received from his brother was miserly in comparison.

"I have already been offered a far nicer billet than the stuffy British embassy," countered the Duke of Windsor. "Señor Beigbeder has offered us the use of his villa in Andalucía. I'm sure Wallis and I would find his hospitality far more conducive to our standards than anything you have to offer. We shall go there instead."

"No, Your Royal Highness, you will not. This matter is not up for discussion or negotiation. I must remind you, although I hardly need to do so, that it is well-known where Señor Franco's loyalties lie. We cannot risk that the former King of England should be in the home of a senior Spanish diplomat should the Generalissimo decide to declare for Germany openly. It would be a disastrous and intolerable situation."

For you, perhaps, thought Edward. Still, by refusing to accompany the ambassador to the British residency, it may raise some awkward questions. Without referring to his last outburst, Edward announced, "Very well, Sir Samuel. I will arrange for our things to be sent to the embassy as soon as possible. You will kindly leave us now while we make our preparations. I'm sure you have more urgent matters to attend to."

Hoare was not sure whether Edward was deliberately being unpleasant or if this was just his natural personality. And his reference to the Royal 'We' was most vexing. Did he really believe he was still the King, or was he referring to himself and his wife? Who knew what was going through his former monarch's mind? And the way Edward had dismissed him so indifferently. Even in his dispute with a former prime minister, David Lloyd George, he had never been treated in such a cavalier fashion.

To make Edward and Wallis feel welcomed in their new temporary home, Sir Samuel arranged a lavish cocktail party a couple of days later.

Among the five hundred or so guests was the United States ambassador to Spain, Alexander Weddell, next to whom Edward found himself seated. After the customary introductions, the Duke, who had already had several drinks, said, "You know, Alexander – I may call you Alexander? – this war is totally unnecessary. If I've said it once, I've said it a thousand times. All that Herr Hitler is asking for is the territory that rightfully belongs to Germany. I'm sure if we can accommodate his justifiable demands, he will not seek to expand Germany any further. All this talk of him wanting complete European domination is just so much hogwash, as you Americans say. The United Nations League and the Peace Pledge Union have been in touch with me, you know. They are aware of my feelings on the matter and want me to become involved in their cause. Of course, I've already done some work on that front myself, you understand. I would do anything to avoid another war on the scale of the previous one. The most important thing we can do now is to stop this conflict before it escalates any further."

Just as he was about to continue, another guest tapped him on the shoulder, and Edward turned from Weddell to address his new companion. Weddell was not particularly pro-British, but even he was alarmed at what the Duke had confided. He knew he should make his British counterpart aware of Edward's sentiments but reasoned that Sir Samuel must surely already be aware of his former King's views. There was one thing that he could do, however, and do it as soon as possible. He would contact his President, Franklin Roosevelt. Better still, he would contact the Secretary of State, Cordell Hull. Firstly, this would be going through the correct diplomatic channels, and secondly, while he did not know Roosevelt that well on a personal level, he was on friendly terms with Hull. Yes, that's what he would do. He would contact Cordell; then the matter would be out of his hands.

* * *

Von Ribbentrop could not rely on glamorous incentives alone like large sums of cash or beautiful homes to entice Edward fully over to the Nazi cause. He would need to find other means to ensure that Edward was committed to the Reich. More subtle methods would have to be employed, and he knew the very person to assist him in this endeavor. His Reichsminister of Public Enlightenment and Propaganda, Joseph Goebbels.

"My dear Joachim, I have often said that if you are going to tell a lie, tell a big one rather than a small one. People are more likely to believe large untruths than insignificant ones. However, sometimes the secret of a successful factual misrepresentation is not to overstate it. You do not want to burden the subject with too much data; otherwise, they will become confused. Where there is confusion, there is uncertainty, where there is uncertainty, there is doubt, and where there is doubt, there is the possibility the subject will become so bewildered, they will not believe anything. You have to focus your distortions to prey upon your subject's fears, even his paranoia. In Edward's case, this should not be too difficult a task. I am in the middle of a couple of urgent projects at the minute, but I know the Führer treats this situation with the utmost importance. Give me a little while, and I will get back to you."

"Please, Reichsminister. The sooner, the better. We cannot allow him to slip through our fingers now we have him in our grasp."

"Don't worry, Joachim. Little Edward isn't going anywhere."

* * *

Winston Churchill was about to go into a meeting with the War Cabinet under the Treasury building in Whitehall when he was approached by his Assistant Private Secretary, John Colville. "Prime Minister, I'm sorry to trouble you, but we've just received a cable from the American President. He thinks there's something you should be aware of...."

"If he's telegraphing to inform me that we're at war with Germany, tell him I already know," answered Churchill gruffly. "Well, what is it, Jock? What is so urgent that you would come rushing in like a bull at a gate?"

Colville hesitated before answering. "It's, er, it's about the Duke of Windsor, Sir."

"Oh, for God's sake!" Churchill thundered. "What now, and how come whatever it is, I'm hearing it from Roosevelt and not from our own people?"

"He's had a report from his Ambassador to Spain. It seems the Duke has been rather indiscreet again, I'm afraid."

Churchill visibly slumped, and his shoulders sagged as Colville explained, "It appears Edward has got himself mixed up somehow with the Peace Brigade. He doesn't say much more than that, but he felt you ought to know."

"Yes, we know all about that lot. They mean well, I'm sure, but don't they understand what we're fighting for? If they got their way, the very freedoms they enjoy to protest about wars and suchlike would be taken from them by that despot, Hitler. I get regular reports from the security branch. Fortunately, support has dropped off quite a bit in recent months. Perhaps they've finally woken up to what's happening across the Channel. But if the Duke has thrown in his lot with them, who knows what might happen? This just makes it even more urgent to get Edward as far from their influence as possible."

Churchill had been walking as he was making his way to the War Room but stopped abruptly, causing his Assistant Private Secretary to take a few steps forward before he, too, came to a halt. As Colville turned to face his superior, Churchill said, "Remind me to call Franklin after the conference. There are a few things I need to discuss with him, Edward notwithstanding. That man is becoming a thorn in my side."

* * *

A couple of days after Edward's argument with Sir Samuel Hoare, he was visited at the embassy by his old friend, the Spanish diplomat Don Javier Bermejillo. "I heard you were in Madrid," Bermejillo began. "Why did you not get in touch? There is so much for us to catch up on, but perhaps not in this city. There is far too much intrigue going on here at the moment." Then, as if he had just thought of it, Bermejillo suggested, "Why don't we take a drive, eh? Toledo is only about an hour away, and it is such a lovely city. It would be my pleasure to give you a guided tour of the historical sights, and we can get a bite to eat at my favorite restaurant. What do you say? Are you busy?"

"No, not really. It's just...."

"There. Then it's settled. Please do bring your lovely wife also, of course. I'm sure she, too, will find the city an interesting place to visit."

Edward did not wish to offend his old friend by declining his offer. Bidding Bermejillo to wait in the library, The Duke went off to find Wallis. The Duchess was not pleased by this interruption to her day. "Really, David, must we go out with that dreary man? I find him so dull and uninteresting. Why don't you two go on your own? Then you'll be free to indulge in talk that women should not hear. It will be nice for us to be apart for a little while."

"I'm sorry, my dear. I've already accepted his invitation on your behalf. Cheer up. I believe Toledo is a delightful place, and I'm sure there are plenty of shops there for you to explore. Come on, just for me, eh?"

Wallis sighed audibly as she shook her head. "The things we do for our men. Just let me find my jacket...."

The journey to Toledo took just under ninety minutes, with Don Javier providing a running commentary on many places of local interest as they drove past. They finally arrived at their destination just before midday. "I think we should leave the car here in the town center and walk around on foot. The city dates back over a thousand years and many of the streets are too narrow to accommodate modern vehicles. Let's explore some of the more fascinating parts of the area, then we can stop for a bite of lunch." The statesman did not notice the look of despair that passed from Wallis to Edward. The Duchess was only happy strolling when she was shopping on the wide boulevard of the *Champs Élysées* or Madrid's *Calle de Serrano*. She had not thought to wear flat-heeled shoes, but smiled in agreement at Bermejillo's suggestion.

After walking for half an hour, they found themselves in the Jewish Quarter, where the former synagogue of *Santa María la Blanca* was located. "Alas, it has not been used for Jewish worship for hundreds of years now," explained their guide. "Hence the Catholic name now ascribed to it.

There was a thriving Hebrew community here once, and they lived peacefully alongside their Muslim neighbors, but the Expulsion ended all that. Quite a shame, I suppose."

"Oh, really?" asked the Duke huffily. "If you don't mind my saying so, Don Javier, it's because of the Jews, the Reds, and even our own Foreign Office that we're in the mess we are now. I don't care what anyone says, you can be sure that where there's any mischief in the world, the Jews are almost certainly behind it."

Bermejillo smiled benignly at Edward's display of anti-Semitism. "I have no love for the Jews either, but I think you go too far. And by the time our German friends are finished, they will never be in a position to make mischief again."

"Well, let us hope you are correct." Edward was warming to his theme. "If I had my way, all the Jew-lovers in the cabinet, and I'm sorry to say, even Winston, would be put up against a wall…" and the Duke crooked his right elbow, while extending his left arm straight out in front of him. The mime was obvious. "Do you know, the more I think about it, the more I'm convinced that if the Luftwaffe turned their attention to British cities instead of just attacking military air bases, the war would be over by Christmas. British people just will not stand for their houses and factories being bombed, I believe. An action like the one I'm suggesting will force the government to sue for peace before the public hound them out of office."

Bermejillo did not respond to Edward's rant, but noted his remarks nonetheless. Here, from his own lips, Edward seemed to be hoping for a German victory. This was the best news he could give his Nazi associates. Now, more than ever, they had to get him to Berlin as soon as possible. It would be a battle of wits between them and the British to see who could get the Duke over to their side, but at the final reckoning, the British were amateurs. It would be the professionalism and dedication of the Germans that would see Edward working for the benefit of the Third Reich.

* * *

Joseph Goebbels had, indeed, given thought how they could ensure the Duke's loyalty. After deciding on a course of action, he contacted von

Ribbentrop with his ideas. Once he had heard his suggestions, the Reichsminister of Foreign Affairs contacted the German ambassador to Madrid, Baron Eberhard von Stohrer. Their discussion lasted for almost an hour until von Stohrer knew what he and his staff needed to do.

The following day, Edward received a call at the embassy from Ramòn Suñer inviting him to lunch at his former hotel. The British ambassador was not happy about Suñer's offer. "Your Royal Highness, I must caution you against meeting with the Spanish Interior Minister. He is a well-known advocate for the Nazi cause, and I fear...."

"You fear what, Sir Samuel? That I may hear things you would rather I didn't? That Spain is as much against this idiotic war as I am? That they, too, see that all Hitler wants is what is rightfully his? Well, Germany's, at least. No, my mind is made up. I intend to dine with Señor Suñer, and that is the end of the matter, and I shall be going with Wallis." Hoare could only shake his head. It was like dealing with a petulant and spoiled child. Perhaps he could not stop Edward and Wallis from going to the Ritz, but he would ensure they would not be alone.

Suñer was already seated when the couple arrived and rose to greet them as they walked into the dining area. His kiss on Wallis's cheek lingered just a second too long for Edward's liking, but the Duke was discreet enough to pretend not to notice. After the introductions, the Spanish Minister of the Interior invited them to sit. The trio engaged in small talk for a few minutes while Suñer summoned a waiter. As the couple perused the menu, their host leaned across the table. "Do not turn around," he whispered, "but I believe you have been followed here. Two men are sitting behind you who are trying so hard not to glance in our direction; their attempts at subterfuge are almost laughable."

"I expect Sir Samuel has sent a couple of his staff to keep an eye on us, well, me, to ensure I don't do anything stupid."

"Well, there is no doubt that they are British. Who else would wear such drab clothes on a beautiful day like today and in a city as lovely as Madrid?" Suñer quipped. "But I do not think they are from your embassy. I am familiar with all the personnel who work there. It is my job to know these things, you understand, and I am sure they are not part of the regular retinue. I fear these men are here for an entirely different purpose."

"And what purpose is that?" asked Edward curiously.

"I'm afraid your government considers you too much of a liability to be allowed to continue to advocate appeasement. They are in the middle of prosecuting a war. A war against the very country whose policies you espouse so openly. Look at it from their perspective. Their ex-King, who has left his country in a time of great peril, speaking passionately about wanting to avert war. As I understand it, your government is aware of your association with the Peace Brigade. Sadly, they believe these groups have been subverted by certain elements with other, less reputable motives for seeking peace. By your perceived affiliation with them, they now consider you too dangerous to be allowed to continue to voice such dangerous sentiments. At the very least, they would arrest you for high treason should you find your way back to Great Britain unscathed."

The Duke became alarmed at what Suñer was implying. "You don't mean...?"

"I doubt they would try anything here in this hotel, especially when you are in my company, but...." Suñer let the rest of his sentence hang in the air.

"But that's an outrageous thing to say," Edward spluttered. "No, I refuse to believe it. I know I've let the side down a bit, but Winston would never contemplate doing anything like that. It's inconceivable."

"Do you doubt the evidence of your own eyes? Two men are sitting not a few meters away who might beg to differ with your optimism. It's not safe for you to return to your embassy. I suggest you take up Beigbeder's offer of his villa in Andalucía. You will be quite safe there, I assure you. I will arrange for your things to...."

"No, I've had enough of this. Yes, I'll take Beigbeder up on his offer but not before I've had this out with Hoare. He must know what was going on. How dare he not tell me that my life was in danger? I may no longer be the King, but he had no right to...."

Suñer did not expect Edward, whom everyone knew to be so easily impressionable, would take this very opportunity to assert his limited fortitude in so forceful a manner.

The Duchess quickly stepped in. "Edward, my dear, are you sure it will be safe for us to return to the embassy? Would we not be better to take Señor Suñer's advice, and...?"

"No, I have made up my mind." Turning to the Spanish Interior Minister, Edward declared. "I've quite lost my appetite, I'm afraid. If you don't mind escorting us back, I would be most grateful for your company." Edward stood up without waiting for Suñer's reply, pushing his chair back, noisily scraping against the polished floor as he rose. He failed to notice the look of resigned hopelessness that passed between his wife and his host. They had been so close, but it would be no use now. Suñer had overplayed his hand. He had made Edward so incensed at this unbelievably monstrous news, he was determined to confront the British ambassador. As he passed the two men to whom Suñer had referred, Edward gazed sharply in their direction. The agents merely looked straight ahead, not meeting his penetrating stare. Suñer shook his head almost imperceptibly at them. Their plan would have to wait a little longer to come to fruition.

Edward's sudden recalcitrance would undoubtedly cause Sir Samuel Hoare some consternation, not to mention problems for Suñer himself. He had to act quickly to prevent Edward's indignity from developing into a major diplomatic incident. As Edward and Wallis were leaving the Ritz, the Interior Minister rushed after him. "Your Royal Highness, please. Just a minute. Before you do anything hasty...."

"Do anything hasty?" Edward exploded. "Two men are sitting not twenty feet from here who, if you are correct, have been sent by my government to kill me, and possibly Wallis, too. And if not to murder me, to drag me back to face charges of treason. In wartime, that offense carries the death sentence, so either way, my life expectancy is rather short at the moment. Do you not think I have every right to be angry and have it out with Hoare? Would you not do the same in my position?"

"Very possibly, but he will only deny any knowledge of this situation and accuse you of being an alarmist or having lost your mind apart from anything else. Believe me, Your Royal Highness, I've been in diplomatic circles long enough to know how the game is played. It really would be better if...."

"No! I am determined to have this death sentence removed, and I cannot do that from Andalucía. I must discuss this with the ambassador. I have no choice."

"If I cannot persuade you not to return to the embassy, I must beg of you not to disclose where the information came from."

"And why not? Surely I...."

"You must be aware of how things stand between your government and General Franco. Unlike President Salazar, he is not, how shall I say, too disposed toward Great Britain. Any disagreement between the two nations would only push my leader more firmly into the German camp. I'm sure this is the last thing you would want, despite what has just transpired, not to mention the awkward position into which it would put me. I must beg of you not to bring my name into your dispute. Please." Suñer implored him.

In the time between Suñer's plea and his response, Edward calculated the best course for him. Suñer was an experienced enough diplomat to look after his own affairs. Edward had himself and Wallis to consider, and that issue would be his main concern. The Duke merely nodded in feigned assent. The Interior Minister could make what he wanted from it.

The entourage climbed into their automobiles, making a stately cavalcade of vehicles as they drove in procession down *Calle de Alfonso XII* past the *Puerta de Alcalà* before heading toward the British Embassy in *Calle de Fernando El Santo*. As they sat in the back of their limousine, Wallis asked Edward, "Do you still intend to talk to Sir Samuel about this state of affairs, despite Señor Suñer's appeal?"

"What would you do if you were in my position?"

"I suppose in a way I am. If he is correct, there is no telling what those men might do. They might even use me to get to you. In that case, despite what Señor Suñer asked, then, yes, I probably would want to get it into the open."

"Well, there you are, then; my sentiments exactly. Hoare has a lot to answer for, and he better answer me, or there'll be hell to pay, I can promise you."

They sat in silence for the rest of the short journey. Wallis knew better than to try to engage her husband in further conversation when he was in one of his moods.

After returning to the embassy, Edward lost no time in seeking out the British ambassador. He had been nurturing his wrath and did not want to lose the momentum he had gained. Without going through the usual formalities, the Duke burst into Sir Samuel's private office to challenge him. A bewildered and angry ambassador looked up from his correspondence to find Edward staring down at him, his eyes flashing with disdain. "Don't try to deny it. I know all about your dastardly plot to get rid of me or send me back to be tried for high treason," he fumed.

Sir Samuel stared at Edward in amazement, not believing what he had just heard. "I'm sorry, Your Royal Highness, I haven't the faintest idea what you're talking about. What do you mean 'get rid of you?'"

"You know, Sir Samuel. Don't sit behind your desk and play the innocent party. You know damn fine well what I mean."

"I can assure you, Your Royal Highness, I haven't the foggiest clue what you're talking about. If I may be so bold, how much have you had to drink? It's a bit early, even for you."

"I shall ignore that remark, but I have it on good authority that H.M.G. plans to have me eliminated one way or another."Despite himself, Sir Samuel laughed out loud. Did this fool of an ex-King think he was important enough for His Majesty's government to arrange to have him killed? "Where did you hear this allegation?"

"I... I'm not at liberty to say, but it comes from a very good authority, I can assure you."

"And does this 'good authority' have a German name?"

"No, as a matter of fact, he does not."

"Well, assuming that to be true...."

"How dare you?" Edward shouted. "Do you think I'm making this up? Of course, it's true. I saw the evidence with my own eyes, dammit." At first, Hoare assumed Edward had spotted the MI6 agent he had sent to keep watch on his recalcitrant charge.

Feigning ignorance, Sir Samuel said, "Now I'm intrigued. I'm sorry, Your Royal Highness, but you cannot come storming into my office making such baseless allegations without revealing who told you this nonsense. And as for the 'evidence' you claim to have seen, I, too, would like to examine this alleged evidence. I can assure you categorically, no one from the government wants you dead... officially."

"Well, if you must know, I heard this information from the Spanish Interior Minister not half an hour ago. And the evidence was two British agents who I assume were sent from S.I.S. to murder me sitting almost as close to me as I am to you right now."

Relieved that whoever Edward had seen was not his intelligence officer, Hoare retorted, "So what you are telling me is that two operatives from our intelligence service have been sent to kill you and were sitting at the next table to you at the Ritz? Is that what you're telling me?" Sir Samuel laughed as he repeated Edward's allegation. "Can you not see how absurd this sounds? Do you honestly believe that two highly trained officers would be so unprofessional and amateur as to sit at the next table to the person they were sent to dispatch, in full view of one of the most powerful men in Spain? I'm sorry, but this is pure fantasy. He has spun you a yarn, and you have fallen for it."

"No! This is not a 'yarn', as you put it. My life, and possibly Wallis's, is in danger. I cannot stay here any longer. Señor Suñer has arranged safe accommodation for us at the home of Señor Beigbeder in Andalucía. I shall go there, where I will be safe."

"No, Your Royal Highness, you will go nowhere without my permission." Hoare shook his head impatiently. "Can't you see this is just a ruse to get you out of the embassy? Look, I've no doubt the Prime Minister has enough on his plate at the minute, but if it eases your mind, I'll send him a cable asking him to confirm there is no plot to assassinate you or drag you back to Britain to stand trial for treason. In the meantime, I must insist you stay within the confines of this building. Do I make myself clear?"

"And do you know to whom you are speaking?" Edward countered.

"Yes, Your Royal Highness, I am very well aware who I am addressing, and I must insist you obey my orders. You are in no danger here, I promise you, but if you continue to defy my instructions, I will have no option but to place you under house arrest for your own protection. Now, you will please leave me to get on with the rest of my duties. I will send for you when I receive a reply from Downing Street. Good day, Sir." With that abrupt end, Sir Samuel returned to his documents leaving a frustrated and incensed Duke standing before him, like a schoolboy being dismissed by his headmaster.

After the Duke had left Sir Samuel's office, Hoare lifted his internal phone. "Under no circumstances is the Duke or the Duchess to leave these premises. If anyone calls for them, you will take their credentials and say they are indisposed for the moment. Do not enter into conversation with anyone, no matter how insistent they are." After listening to the response, Hoare sighed. "Well, as a last resort, and only as a last resort, I suppose you will have to summon me. Be firm, Mason. That's what you're being paid for."

* * *

Joachim von Ribbentrop read the cable from Ramón Suñer before throwing it down in disgust. His displeasure was twofold. Firstly, because the Spanish had failed to secure the Duke of Windsor as they had planned. He was also contemptuous that the Spanish Interior Minister was too cowardly to tell him over the telephone, preferring to relate the news by a coded telegram. They're as useless as the French, the German Foreign Minister thought. No one had the organizational skills of the Germans. That was the true secret to victory – the ability to be better prepared than your enemy. Didn't this idiot realize that all their designs for conquering Britain and the glorious aftermath of Britain's humbling defeat rested with Edward? Without him, their scheme would be all for nothing. They would have to do much better if they wished to share the spoils that his country would provide. They would have to try again, and this time, failure would not be an option.

* * *

Sir Samuel, too, had received a coded communiqué from London. Churchill had made clear that while Edward was not in any physical danger from his government, he was still a serving officer in a time of war, and therefore had duties and obligations to fulfill. He read Churchill's telegram to the Duke. "*Your Royal Highness has taken active military rank and refusal to obey direct orders of a competent military authority will create a serious situation...*" Edward left the room rather than listen to any more, but could not have failed to understand the message it entailed. Failure to comply with these responsibilities could render him liable for court-martial.

It was now too dangerous for Edward to remain in Spain any longer. His brother would be leaving Portugal within seventy-two hours, and Edward and his wife needed to arrive there as soon as the Duke of Kent was no longer on Portuguese soil.

The Prime Minister had not lied when he asserted that his ex-sovereign was not in any immediate danger. He did not wish to see Edward killed by any means, but it was absolutely vital that the Duke should not fall into enemy hands. Churchill had already taken the appropriate steps and signed the necessary warrant. At the last, if all else failed, it was better that his former King, his friend, should die.

CHAPTER 34

Berlin, Germany – London, England – Lisbon & Cascais, Portugal, - Madrid, Spain, July 1940

"I would suggest we start with his fear for his own personal safety. After all, is this not something we all take seriously? Let's not forget the half-hearted attempt made on his life some years ago. That must surely still prey on his mind, even at the subconscious level. If our intelligence sources are to be believed, even MI5 were implicated in this. What if...?"

"I see where you are going. If we...."

"I haven't finished," Goebbels interrupted him. This has to be a two-pronged attack. As I said, there must be an immediate fear for his safety, but there must also be a further provocation to complete his anxiety. Edward knows he has done badly, even if he will not admit it to himself. As well as convincing him that his life is in danger, if we can persuade him that Churchill will have him arrested for high treason if he sets foot back in Britain, this will make him so fretful, he will practically beg us for sanctuary. It cannot fail. Edward is as good as ours."

Von Ribbentrop ruminated on the conversation he had had with Joseph Goebbels a few days earlier. He was right. It was a good plan, marred only by Suñer's incompetence. Placing two Spanish security men dressed as British agents at the next table was stupidity beyond belief. The fact that the Duke of Windsor was gullible enough to believe the Interior Minister did not say much for Edward's intelligence or his common sense. Time was running short if their plan was to remain on schedule. Within the next couple of weeks, Luftwaffe warplanes would be flying over R.A.F. bases to incapacitate British air defenses before a full amphibious and airborne invasion of the country. If that pompous ass Göring was to be believed, his air force was far superior to the British. Having spent time in London a few years earlier as ambassador, von Ribbentrop was not so sure but kept his thoughts to himself. The Führer forbade anything other than total and complete confidence in Germany and its armed forces. To believe otherwise was considered treasonous, and the British Royal Air Force would have to be defeated before Führer Directive Number Six For the Conduct of the War could be achieved – '*to win as much territory as possible in Holland, Belgium, and northern France to serve as a base for the successful prosecution of the air and sea war against England.*'

But before all that could happen, the Reich had to secure Edward's cooperation, and, despite all their enticements, they could not be certain of his total compliance unless they had him in Berlin. The Spanish had failed, and Edward was due to travel to Portugal within the next few hours. The Portuguese president, António de Oliveira Salazar, was not as disposed towards the Nazi regime as his Spanish counterpart, and it would be harder to extract the Duke of Windsor once he was there. However, there was one man who could still pluck little Edward from right under the noses of the British and the Portuguese. He had already proven his worth by infiltrating secret peace negotiations between the British and dissident German military and government officials at Venlo in Holland. This subterfuge resulted in the capture and interrogation of two British secret agents. If anyone could get Edward and Wallis out of the hands of the British, it was *SS Sturmbannführer*, Walter Schellenberg.

* * *

"Whether he likes it or not, he's going to have to go to Portugal to bring the Duke back. I can no longer trust Edward to return of his own volition." Churchill was talking to his Colonial Secretary, George Lloyd. "I know it will be dangerous, but we're at war, and with war comes hazards. He won't be on his own, anyway. I'm sending someone with him, who'll take care of him, and the Windsors should the Germans try anything funny." The

Prime Minister had been discussing sending Edward's friend and legal advisor, Sir Edward Monckton, to bring him back to London.

"When are they leaving?" Lloyd asked.

Churchill glanced at his wristwatch. "They should be on their way within the hour," Churchill replied confidently.

* * *

Walter Schellenberg stood to attention before Hitler in his office within the *Reichschancellery*. "You are clear of your duties, *SS Sturmbannführer*? Nothing must be left to chance. This will be our final opportunity to seize the Duke."

"*Jah, mein Führer*. I have worked out a strategy to remove our quarry with our intelligence operatives. It has been planned down to the last detail. We have left nothing to chance."

"Let us hope you are as successful in Portugal as you were in Holland, then."

"I understand the importance of the mission. It will not fail."

Hitler opened the top drawer of his desk and pulled out an envelope. Handing it to Schellenberg, he announced, "This document will give you all the assistance you need. I have signed it personally, and it gives you authority far above your present rank. The next time we speak, I shall expect to have the Duke of Windsor standing beside you."

He knew this was Hitler's way of dismissing him. Schellenberg clicked his jackbooted heels together as he gave the '*Heil*' salute before turning smartly around and leaving his Führer's inner sanctum.

* * *

The two Englishmen traveling to Portugal had little in common, save their nationality. One was a top-ranking lawyer, highly regarded in legal circles and within the government. The other was a security operative, focused and dedicated to his job and his country. Neither felt like talking on the flight to the Iberian coast except for necessary discussion. The flight would be on a civilian Boeing 314 Clipper rather than a Royal Air Force airplane, which would be a target for any German warplanes in the area.

Spain had closed off its air space to flights from Britain, so the flying boat would have to fly further west over the Atlantic before turning in to land in the sea off Lisbon. Both men knew the dangers involved, and Monckton barely spoke until the aircraft coasted in to land safely at *Cabo da Roca*, forty kilometers from the Portuguese capital.

The British ambassador, Walford Selby, had arranged an embassy car to meet them. Bad news awaited them when they arrived at the embassy in *Rua San Francisco de Borja*. Edward was not there. As Selby explained, "Salazar does not wish to antagonize the Germans by officially recognizing the Duke of Windsor to be in the country. It's quite ridiculous, really. I know he's here, you know he's here, and the Nazis certainly know Edward is in Portugal. But Salazar is trying to walk a very thin tightrope. While his sympathies are undoubtedly with Great Britain, he cannot be seen to be supporting us openly. Especially when Franco has all but made his sentiments on the matter perfectly clear."

"Yes, well, I suppose from his point of view, it makes sense of a sort." Monckton agreed. "If he's not here in the embassy, then where is he staying?"

Selby hesitated before answering. "That's the other piece of news that's not so good. Salazar has him holed up at Cascais with a banker called Ricardo do Espírito Santo Silva. It's about an hour's drive away along the coast to the west. We've no proof, but we think he might be working for the opposition."

Monckton was perturbed by this disturbing revelation. "What are we doing about the situation? We can't allow Edward to be influenced by anyone who might be sympathetic to the Reich. We know how easily impressionable he is. For all we know, they may be making plans as we speak to spirit him out of the country."

"You're quite right, of course." agreed Walford Selby. "Unfortunately, I cannot make this an official visit for the reasons I have already explained, so you will have to go on your own. I'll telephone Señor Espírito Santo to arrange a suitable time for you to visit and give you directions on how to get to the house. You can't miss it. It's a rather imposing structure with an equally pretentious title. It's called '*Boca do Inferno.*'"

Monckton struggled with the description. "My Portuguese is a little rusty, I'm afraid. *Boca do Inferno*? 'Hot House,' perhaps?"

"Close, but no cigar, as our American cousins say. I don't want to worry you unduly, but '*Boca do Inferno*' translates as 'Mouth of Hell!'"

"Let's hope that's not a portent of what's to come, then."

"Quite so, Sir Walter; quite so."

* * *

The Duke and Duchess had arrived at their new temporary home in Cascais. It was Espírito Santo's summer home, and an ideal location for the couple, secluded from the outside world and curious onlookers. The banker was on hand to greet them upon their arrival. He was an unwilling host, only accommodating them as a favor to his friend, António de Oliveira Salazar. After settling themselves in and taking a tour of the palatial grounds, Edward commented, "What a beautiful place you have here, Señor Santo."

"Thank you," beamed Espírito Santo, "but please call me Ricardo. "I want you and your charming wife to feel as much at home here as you would in your own house. *Minha casa é sua casa*."

"*Muito obrigado*," Edward replied graciously.

"Please do not be alarmed, Your Royal Highness...."

"David," the Duke interrupted him. "My friends call me David."

"As I was saying, David, I do not want you or the Duchess to be alarmed, but for your personal wellbeing, the President has arranged protection for you while you are here. Officers from the *Polícia de Vigilância e Defensa do Estado* will be patrolling the grounds. It is for your own safety, you understand. We would not want any harm to befall you while you are on Portuguese territory. Or anywhere else, of course," Espírito Santo quickly appended. "They will be as discrete as possible, but it may be inevitable that you run into them. I'm just making you aware in advance, so you do not get worried if you see men with guns."

"Thank you for alerting me, Ricardo. I shall try to keep out of everyone's way as much as possible. Especially those who are carrying firearms." The Duke added dryly. "It's a pleasure to be in such a quiet spot. As much as we loved Paris and Madrid, it's nice to be able to hear the birds singing by themselves, instead of having to compete with all the traffic noise."

"Yes, we love it here. Sadly, we can only come occasionally, usually during the summer months. Fortunately, I have good business partners. Señor Goldfarb is..."

"I didn't realize there were any Jews in Portugal. They get everywhere, don't they? I hope you don't leave the safe open when he's around, eh?" Edward laughed.

Espírito Santo's eyes narrowed. "Señor Windsor, Michel Goldfarb has been a good colleague for many years and is a valued and trusted friend as well as a loyal partner. I do not take kindly to anyone who disparages him because of his religion, and I would point out to you that my wife also has Jewish ancestry. You will kindly moderate your language when you are in my presence, or I will have to ask the President to find you alternative accommodation. Do I make myself clear?"

The Duke blushed. He was not prepared for such a response from someone reputed to be a Nazi supporter. Stammering as he spoke, Edward replied, "I... I'm sorry, Señor Santo. I... I had no idea. I did not... I... meant no offense, I assure you."

"You have offended me deeply, Señor Windsor. I will not deny it, but it is over now. We will not speak of the matter again." Espírito Santo turned around abruptly, leaving a contrite and chastened Duke standing alone in the courtyard. He was thankful that at least Wallis had not been present to witness his tasteless remarks. She was forever berating him over his lack of verbal discipline, and this episode would only be another lump of coal to add to the glowing embers of his other lapses of judgment. He shook his head in self-reproach. Who would have thought it? A Jew-loving Nazi. If ever there was a contradiction in terms, this was surely it.

* * *

Walter Schellenberg flew to Madrid where he lost no time in contacting the German ambassador, Eberhard von Stohrer. Hitler's emissary did not go alone, but took with him one of the foremost Nazi psychiatrists currently practicing, the Austrian national, Maximus de Crinis. After the introductions were over, Schellenberg explained why he had brought de Crinis. "I need to know, Baron von Stohrer, what Edward's frame of mind was like. How did he seem, especially after that botched attempt to rattle him at the Ritz?"

The German ambassador sighed. "That was none of my doing, *Sturmbannführer*. I assure you, had...."

Schellenberg cut him off in mid-sentence. "I am not here to apportion blame, Ambassador. I merely wish to know how Edward behaved when Suñer told him he was sitting across from two British agents who had been sent to kill him."

"I was not present at that meeting, you understand, but..."

"Please address your remarks to Herr Crinis, if you would be so kind," Schellenberg instructed him.

Turning to face the Nazi psychiatrist, von Stohrer continued, "To the best of my knowledge, he wanted to leave the hotel as quickly as possible. He was certainly afraid for his safety, as you can imagine. That much I do know."

"He actually believed two British agents were sitting at the next table?" de Crinis asked incredulously, almost laughing as he spoke.

Von Stohrer nodded as he replied. "Yes, *Herr Doktor*."

"If he is as susceptible as that, I'm not even sure you will need me to coerce him further psychologically. He really is quite stupid, isn't he?" Neither man spoke, each content to consider de Crinis's assessment of Edward in their own minds. The three men discoursed for a further few hours, considering the best strategy to lure Edward and Wallis into German hands.

Finally, Schellenberg ended the conversation. "Well, gentlemen, all I can say is that if we do not get the Duke into Berlin within the week, I will change my name to Emmanuel Goldstein and let Reichsführer Himmler do with me as he pleases." Schellenberg went on without waiting for an invite from the Ambassador, "We will stay here for the night and fly to Lisbon first thing tomorrow. There is much to be done, but nothing, I think, we cannot manage. I think we have said enough about Edward. Let us now drink a toast to our inevitable success." Hitler's words echoed in Schellenberg's mind. Failure was not an option. The Führer had made that quite plain. If he could not secure Edward with or without his cooperation, he knew the fate that awaited him on his return to Berlin.

* * *

Despite their apparent pleasure in seeing their old friend, Edward and Wallis were guarded in their greeting to Sir Walter Monckton. They were also curious to see who he had brought with him. It was their former security guard, Detective Inspector Alan Bentley. After their initial pleasantries were over, Edward pulled the lawyer over to one side, away from the rest of the assembled party. "I know why you're here, of course, Sir Walter, but I did not believe you would stoop so low in your efforts to get me to return to England with you." The Duke whispered.

Monckton looked bemused as he answered, "I'm sorry, Your Royal Highness; I have no idea what you're talking about. Surely you knew we were coming. Selby called Señor Santo to let him know we were in Portugal and would naturally wish to see you. I don't understand...."

"No, it's not that. Of course, he told me you were here. It's the stone-throwing...."

The lawyer's eyebrows shot up to his forehead.

"The... what?"

"You know." Glancing toward Bentley, Edward demanded, "Why did Inspector Bentley deem it necessary to lob small pebbles at our bedroom window the other night? That was most uncalled for."

Monckton was so surprised by the Duke's outburst, he spoke louder than he intended, causing the rest of the room to look round at the couple. "David, are you losing your mind? Why on earth would Detective Bentley do such a thing? He is a Metropolitan police officer, not one of Mosley's Blackshirts who rely on intimidation to cow their subjects. What gives you the idea that he was anywhere near this house until today? Did you see him?" Without waiting for Edward's response, Monckton called Bentley over, repeating the allegation. Bentley smiled gently. "Your Royal Highness, I think you know me better than that. Do you honestly believe I would drive all the way out here from Lisbon just to lob a few stones at your bedroom window? To what purpose, might I ask?"

Even Edward could now see the foolishness of his argument, but he would not give in yet. "To... to... frighten Wallis and me into returning to London. Why else?"

"Do you honestly think we would resort to such childish behavior? Really? Because if you do, quite frankly, I don't know what else to tell you."

"No, I suppose you're right," sighed a despondent Edward. "It's just that one hears all sorts of wild rumors so that one doesn't know what to believe."

"All the more reason for you and the Duchess to return to Lisbon with us right now. We can be out of the country tonight, and you can be dining in your club this time tomorrow. The Prime Minister has given me a letter for you. I suggest you read it now." Saying which, Monckton proffered a sealed envelope for the Duke to accept. Edward took it from him with trembling hands. By his actions, he had made an enemy of his former friend, and whatever message the letter contained, it would not make comfortable reading. He tore open the envelope and read, "*Many sharp and unfriendly ears will be pricked up to catch any suggestion that Your Royal Highness takes a view about the war or about the Germans or about Hitlerism which differs from that adopted by the British nation and parliament...*" he crumpled up the missive without bothering to read the rest. It would, no doubt, be more humbug in the same vein, and Edward had already had enough sermonizing and sanctimony from the Prime Minister without needing any more.

"There are one or two things I have to finish up here. I'll be free in forty-eight hours. There. So, why don't you and Inspector Bentley come back in two days or so, and Wallis and I will be more than happy to accompany you both back to England?"

"I'm sorry, Sir, but I must insist that you pack your bags and come with us now. There is no time to lose. I'm sure whatever you have to finish doing can wait until you arrive back in Britain."

"Look. It's Wednesday the twenty-fourth today. I simply cannot come with you sooner than Friday the twenty-sixth. Now, that is my final word, and I will not deviate from it."

"May I ask what is so important that you cannot just bid your hosts a courteous farewell and drive back to Lisbon with us?" Monckton asked with asperity. He was now becoming frustrated with Edward. Didn't he realize the danger he was in, or did he simply not care? A few minutes ago, he seemed to be in fear for his life, and now he was behaving as if he were being asked to visit a leper colony. Short of dragging him by the lapels of his jacket, there was little Monckton could do. "Very well, Your Royal Highness, it shall be as you wish, but I must make this point perfectly clear. If you fail to accompany us back to Britain on Friday, the matter will be out of my hands, and you will have to answer to a much higher authority. Do you understand me?"

The Duke of Windsor did not reply but merely walked away. This was going to be much more difficult than anyone imagined. Without saying goodbye to Espírito Santo, Monckton and Bentley left *Boca do Inferno*.

Once they were out of sight of the house, Bentley said, "If you don't mind, Sir Walter, I think I'll stay here for a bit and admire the scenery. It's a lovely coastline, don't you think?"

"Never mind the scenery, Detective Inspector. What's on your mind?"

"Call it a 'copper's instinct,' but something's not right. I don't know what it is. It's just a feeling; that's all. You drive back to the embassy. I'll make my own way there later."

"Well, as long as you're sure, Detective Inspector."

"That's just it, Sir Walter. I'm not sure at all."

From an upstairs window, Schellenberg watched as Bentley and Sir Walter drove away. Edward had delayed his departure as instructed. The rest was now up to him and Max de Crinis. It would not be long now until they had the Duke and Duchess. Everything was going according to plan – his plan.

CHAPTER 35

Cascais, Portugal – London, England, July - August 1940

Heinkel HE 111, Dornier Do 17 and Juncker JU 87 bomber aircraft supported by Messerschmitt Bf109 and Bf110 fighter-bombers relentlessly pounded R.A.F. bases, reconnaissance posts, gun emplacements and radar stations in the south of England, causing heavy losses to British air defenses. Despite Spitfires being more maneuverable, and able to fly faster at higher altitudes than their Messerschmitt counterparts, the superior Daimler-Benz engines in the yellow nosed Me's and the overwhelming numbers of Nazi aircraft were too much for the R.A.F. pilots to contend with. The Spitfires carried a greater number of weapons in total, eight wing-mounted 7.69mm machine guns, but the Luftwaffe compensated for their lower number of two machine guns, with two wing-mounted MGFF cannons, each capable of firing 20mm caliber projectiles with explosive shells at the rate of a thousand per minute. Where the R.A.F. pilots needed to expend a great number of bullets to cause serious damage to the Messerschmitts, a single hit by one cannon shell was enough to seriously injure or destroy a Spitfire or Hurricane.

Luftwaffe tactics of attacking with the sun behind them disrupted the Spitfire teams' formation patterns, causing them to split up into single units, making it easier for the Messerschmitts' pilots to fire upon individual enemy aircraft. All these strategies eventually weakened the morale and the resolve of the British defense squadrons until they finally realized that it was only a matter of time before they could no longer function effectively against their superior German adversaries.

Wehrmacht intelligence soon discovered where the Spitfires and Hurricanes were being manufactured, and air bombardments destroyed the factories in Castle Bromwich, Birmingham and at the Supermarine facility in Woolston, Southampton. Spitfire production was deployed to other factories in the area, and other manufacturing bases were quickly converted to war production. Despite the best efforts of the local population, as quickly as these factories were retooled, so they were obliterated by increasingly accurate shelling by German aircraft. The Hawker company factory at Langley in Slough was also severely damaged together with its other main production facility at its Gloster works in Cheltenham.

The continual bombardment of aircraft production factories and R.A.F. airfields finally proved too much for the overwhelmed and beleaguered British workforce and air crews, and by late August, despite reciprocal but ineffectual aerial bombing of German aircraft bases, and the Messerschmitt production facility at the Erla Maschinewerk factory in Leipzig, the Luftwaffe had complete control over the skies of Britain. Phase One of Hitler's Directive Number Six for the invasion and conquest of Britain had been achieved.

* * *

A few weeks earlier, while Bentley kept watch on the Espírito Santo household, Schellenberg put his scheme into operation. It seemed that fate was smiling on the Nazi officer, with Sir Walter Monckton being accompanied by Edward's former protection officer, Detective Inspector Alan Bentley. Rather than having to fabricate a false danger scare, using de Crinis's psychological assistance, here was a Heaven-sent opportunity to utilize a scenario that Edward would have no choice but to accept. His former security agent now sent to neutralize him before he could defect to the Nazis. "Isn't it obvious, Your Royal Highness? Why else would your government send an agent who has not only been trained to protect, but who is also prepared to kill? Someone you know, and have put your trust in. It is the perfect choice, and if I were the head of British Intelligence, I could think of no better person."

"But... but..." the Duke stuttered. "Sir Walter? I've known him for years. As well as being my senior lawyer, he's a trusted friend. I simply cannot believe he would have any part in this. It's... why, it's inconceivable!"

"I agree. That is why I do not believe he has any idea about it. It's more likely that your government is merely using him as an unwitting dupe to lull you into a false sense of security. I'm quite sure that Monckton would have no part in this despicable subterfuge if he knew the real purpose of Bentley's role in accompanying him to Portugal."

"What do you think I should do?"

"Well, Your Royal Highness, it's not really for me to say, but..."

"But..."

"Well," Schellenberg began, feigning reluctance to continue, "if I were you, I'd be looking for a safe place to stay until we can deal with Sir Walter and Detective Inspector Bentley."

"But surely, it's safe enough here, in *Boca do Inferno*. They wouldn't try anything now, would they?"

"Sadly, Your Royal Highness, these are parlous times. I cannot offer you any assurances on that score. I will do my best to protect you and the Duchess, of course, but..."

"Then what do you suggest? How can you keep us safe?"

Schellenberg smiled. "I have an idea, but for the moment I will keep it to myself. Do not worry, Your Royal Highness, I have the situation well under control."

It was just after 10.30 p.m. and twilight in Cascais. Bentley had waited patiently in the small village for night to fall while he considered what to do about Edward. The Duke was deliberately stalling for some reason, and to the detective's sharp and agile mind there could only be one explanation. He had already been importuned by agents of the Reich, who were probably hidden in the house, and it was just a matter of time, possibly only a few hours before the ex-King would no longer be in Portugal, but would be on his way to Berlin. Bentley walked back to the retreat along the quiet streets taking care to watch out for any late-night strollers or passing cars.

He soundlessly scaled the wall, dropping down onto the patio. Listening for the sounds of any patrols, he took out his retractable telescope. With this instrument, Bentley gazed up at the second-story windows, hoping to catch a glimpse of Edward or Wallis. He did not spot them, but did see someone else which confirmed for him the urgency to get the Duke out of the spacious hacienda tonight. He spied someone he believed to be a high-ranking member of the *Schutzstaffel*, the SS. The image MI6 had of this individual was not clear, and slightly out of focus, as the cameraman's main objective was to get a picture of the person in the foreground – Reinhard Heydrich, Director of the feared RHSA, or Reich Security Main Office, and the former head of the Gestapo. Although he was not in uniform, there was no doubt in Bentley's mind; the person in the illuminated upper floor window was the same individual in the grainy picture – Walter Schellenberg. There was no time to get back to the embassy or even phone them from some call box. By the time help arrived, Edward might be gone. He would have to do whatever it was to rescue Edward, assuming he wanted to be rescued, by himself.

Creeping forward, the detective made his way to the side, then the rear of the spacious property. He located a door, but on trying the handle, found it locked. Extracting his set of lock picks, he tried various tools until he found the ones he needed. Within thirty seconds, he had opened the door and made his way inside. The whole of the downstairs seemed to be in darkness. Allowing his vision to become accustomed to the gloom, Bentley prowled around the various rooms, intending to disable anyone he came across. Finding no one and remembering the layout from his earlier visit, the Englishman slowly climbed the stairs, keeping to the side next to the ornate wooden banister to avoid making the floorboards creak beneath him. As he ascended, he heard several voices coming from a room at the top of the landing. He stopped and listened. Yes; it was unmistakable. One of those voices definitely belonged to the Duke of Windsor. He considered his options. He would have the element of surprise, it was true, but even supposing he managed to extricate the Duke at gunpoint, how far did he think he would get, especially with the grounds presumably being patrolled by Portuguese or German operatives? One call out of the window could see ten or more guards rushing in, all with their weapons drawn, and their safety catches off. There had to be another way.

On his earlier tour of the downstairs rooms, he had come upon the kitchen. He nodded slowly as the kernel of an idea came to him. Making his way back down the stairs, he headed for the cooking area. Scouting around in the dark, he found the items he was looking for, taking them from their hanging places, and putting them in a deep food cupboard. He then sought out the cooking ranges. There were three separate hobs, each with four burners of differing sizes. One was near a curtained window. The police officer gently opened the casement window and used his cigarette lighter to ignite the gas jet nearest the curtain. He then brought the curtain to the flame where it instantly caught alight, the air from the open window helping to accelerate its combustion. Within a few seconds, a patrolling officer noticed the burning curtain and rather than deal with the situation himself, he rushed into the house to alert the occupants. Bentley had banked on the man's reactions and it had worked. Had the officer been smart, he would have extinguished the small fire before it could develop into something more serious. His decision to warn the other members of the household caused the fire to increase in intensity, and by the time everyone had rushed downstairs the kitchen was well alight. Schellenberg instructed his men to enter the burning area to put out the blaze with the fire extinguishers.

As everyone was busy trying to deal with the situation, Bentley raced upstairs to where the Duke and Duchess waited in concerned safety. Under cover of his diversion, Bentley charged into the room, his gun drawn. Edward looked in amazement as the detective quickly summoned the Royal pair with his gun hand to follow him. Edward gripped the sides of his chair, unwilling to follow Bentley's command, while the Duchess looked on in mild amusement. "Detective Inspector Bentley, do you really think you are going to make us go with you? Are you so naïve or so stupid, that you do not know what is going on? Within the next few weeks, German troops will be in London, and my husband will regain his rightful place as King. Why on earth should we accompany you back to Britain now, that is, if you can even get back, as things stand? We will shortly be making our way across the Channel at the behest of the country's new rulers, not clandestinely like some weary refugees. I'm afraid you've had rather a wasted journey, not to mention causing damage to this fine house. I don't think Señor Espírito Santo will be very pleased with you." With those words, Wallis rose from her chair and went to stand resolutely beside Edward. Bentley leveled his Colt at them. "Really, Detective Inspector, has it come down to this? You would commit regicide? Really? From guarding Edward to becoming his murderer? I hardly think so. Now, put your gun away and don't be so foolish."

"Duchess, I have been given orders by my government. They are to get the Duke and you, if possible, back to the United Kingdom. Those instructions have not changed. If I am unable to accomplish this objective, I am to ensure that under no circumstances must Edward be allowed to go to Germany, even if it means killing him. I don't want to do this, but believe me, I will if I have to." Edward stayed immobile while Wallis put her hand to her mouth in astonishment.

From behind him, Bentley heard the laconic drawl of a German accented tongue speaking good English. "How very noble of you, Detective Inspector. We could do with dedicated people like you in the SS, but I doubt I could convince you to change sides at this stage in the game. It was very resourceful of you to hide the fire extinguishers before starting the blaze, but I am sure my men will soon have everything under control. Now, you may or may not intend to shoot the Duke, but please understand I shall most assuredly shoot you if you do not lay down your weapon right now." Bentley did not move. "I know what you are thinking, Detective Inspector. Could you fire off an accurate round before I killed you? I doubt it very much. There might only be milliseconds between your leveling your gun to fire and my own pressing of the trigger, but my weapon is already aiming at your back, and there would be at least one, if not two well-aimed bullets in your lungs before you could squeeze the trigger. Give it up, Detective Inspector. No cause is worth dying for that much."

"I'll remember to convey your sentiments to Herr Hitler when I see him in hell," and Bentley fired his gun at the precise moment Schellenberg discharged his Luger. The detective's shot missed Edward's head by mere millimeters, as the bullets from the SS officer's gun tore through Bentley's body, killing him instantly as the impact threw him forward into the arms of the Duchess of Windsor. She screamed as the collision pushed them both backward against the wall. Bentley's lifeless and bloodied body slowly slid down the front of her dress as the Duchess tried to straighten herself upright. No one said anything for a few seconds as the couple came to terms with the shock of what had just happened.

As the smell of cordite hung in the air, it was Edward who broke the silence. "Did... did you see that? He... he tried to kill me, the treacherous bastard. He was assigned to protect us, and he very nearly blew my head off. I... I..." The Duke could not finish his sentence as reaction to the events began to set in, and he realized how close to death he had just been.

"It is now more imperative than ever that we get you and Wallis to a place of safety. There may be more Bentleys out there, but even if there are not, things will quickly come to a head when he does not return to the embassy. Monckton may not wait until Friday and when he does return, he will not come alone. We cannot delay our departure until tomorrow as I had planned. We need to get you and the Duchess out of here tonight."

Meanwhile, the sounds of the combined gun blasts caused two of Schellenberg's men to come bounding up the stairs with their pistols out. They stood behind their leader at the threshold as they took in the sight which confronted them. Without turning around, Schellenberg spoke to his junior officers. "The Duke and Duchess are leaving tonight. We must be out of here and away within the hour. Find Max de Crinis and see the cars are fully fueled and ready. I will make the necessary preparations." Both men nodded and smartly turned about before hastening to fulfill their duties. "Come, Your Royal Highnesses, we have no time to lose. You must pack your things immediately," the SS officer instructed the Royal couple.

Despite the trauma and stress of what had just happened, it did not escape Wallis that their savior had deferred to her as 'Royal Highness.' Gripping Edward's hand, she smiled gratefully as they passed him in the doorway. Looking down at her bloodstained dress, Wallis remarked, "I'll need to change, if you don't mind, *Sturmbannführer*."

"Of course, Your Royal Highness, but please be quick. Time is of the essence."

No, she hadn't misheard him. He had said it again. How good it sounded. As they made their way to their bedroom, she mouthed it to herself over and over. 'Your Royal Highness,' 'Your Royal Highness.' What a pity, she thought, it had taken the life of a former lover, brief though he was, to finally attain the rank she craved.

As they left, Schellenberg walked over to the body of Alan Bentley. Standing over his corpse, the SS officer said, "Why did you do it, Detective Inspector? As I told you, no cause is worth dying for, although, of course, I would never repeat this thought in certain quarters. While you were still alive, you might have done some good, but now you are dead, what use are you to anyone?" He shrugged his shoulders before saluting his slain adversary and leaving the room.

While Wallis was changing into more appropriate traveling attire, Schellenberg returned to the fire-ravaged kitchen. The household staff and his men had managed to bring the blaze under control, although a considerable amount of damage had been caused. Espírito Santo stood at the kitchen door in his pajamas with his arm around his wife. Neither spoke as their staff tried to put the kitchen back into order. Everything else would have to wait until morning, but they were grateful that the conflagration did not spread to other parts of the house. Schellenberg turned to the couple. Before he could speak, the banker asked, "Was anybody hurt?"

"Only the perpetrator, Señor. He will cause no more trouble."

Espírito Santo nodded in understanding. Schellenberg continued, "We are all leaving your house now, within the hour. If you wish to say your 'goodbyes' to the Duke and Duchess, I recommend you do it now."

Neither of them turned or acknowledged his suggestion, remaining silently where they stood. Their meaning was perfectly clear.

* * *

In London, the War Cabinet was in a crisis meeting. The air battle for Britain had been lost and it would only be a matter of time before airborne troops and German warships and amphibious vehicles were crossing the English Channel. The government had to prepare now for the inevitable conflict that would take place on British soil, the first such action since the

Battle of Culloden in 1746, and the first land invasion since the French assault in the Battle of Fishguard in 1797.

"It's just as well we managed to get as many of our soldiers back from Dunkerque as we did." Churchill considered thoughtfully. "I fear, however, we have only brought our forces out of the Nazi frying pan and into the Nazi fire. Churchill had summoned Sir Hugh Dowding, the Air Chief Marshall, and head of Fighter Command. Dowding was a reserved individual, who felt awkward in company and who found small talk difficult. His reluctance to share a beer with his men had earned him the nickname 'Stuffy.' Despite his reluctance and bitter resentment of having to take valuable time off from running Britain's air defenses, Churchill made it abundantly clear that Dowding's attendance was not a request. "How are the fortifications going along the south coast?" he asked Dowding. "Not well, Prime Minister." Dowding answered in his Scottish burr. "It seems that as soon as we finish digging gun emplacements, the Germans fly over and bomb them out. I reckon for every ten we finish, we are lucky if we keep two or three intact. And I'm afraid that's not all."

"Go on," Churchill answered glumly, expecting the worst.

"German intelligence must be better than we thought. They may not know exactly what our RDF masts are for but they've worked out that they are critical to our air defenses. Most of the Chain Home towers have been destroyed and of the few that remain, only a fraction are in working order. Not enough to be able to maintain an effective communications system, but even if we could..." His silence worried Churchill even more than anything Dowding had just said. "Even if they hadn't knocked out the towers, they would have been useless anyway. They've discovered where our Fighter Command nerve center is. They've all but obliterated Bentley Priory. We can no longer spot German war planes as we could before. Where once we could determine the number of their bombers, their speed and altitude from a distance of sixty miles, we are now in the invidious position of not being able to spot them until they are practically right over our heads, giving our air crews no time to intercept them or mount a counter-attack. They have all but blinded us."

"I wonder if I should have taken my own counsel earlier, Air Chief Marshall, when I allowed you to dissuade me from sending some of our fighter planes to assist the French. Maybe we might not be in the position we are in now, but we must not dwell on what might, or might not, have been. Time is running out, gentlemen. I expect we shall soon be coming to grips with the might of the German army at close quarters. We must be ready to meet them. If we cannot stop them on the beaches, we must stop them inland. We have to muster every resource available to us to defeat this cruel and implacable foe. I do not need to remind you all seated here that in this struggle, we are not only fighting for our own survival, but for the survival of democracy and the freedom of peoples all over the world. Our actions in the coming weeks and months will determine the fate and the future of mankind, and in this mission, we will not fail."

The cries of "hear, hear," echoed around the War Cabinet rooms. He knew some of his cabinet feared the approaching battle was already lost, and sought to regain the initiative that was beginning to wane. He hoped this speech would re-galvanize them and motivate them to levels above which they had never before aspired.Despite his cabinet's support, Dowding was seething at Churchill's comments. Did the Prime Minister forget, or simply choose not to remember, why he was reluctant to send his badly needed warplanes across the Channel? Everyone knew that the fall of France was imminent, and no amount of the limited aid that Britain could spare, would save the French military from defeat. The Luftwaffe had five times the amount of war planes as the Royal Air Force. He had five hundred aircraft under his control, against Göring's two thousand five hundred. What was the point of committing such badly needed aircraft to a cause that was already lost?

As the clamor died down, it was Lord Beaverbrook, the Minister of Aircraft Production, who voiced the thought of many of the cabinet. Despite their rousing approval of his speech, there was the inevitable doubt about the final outcome of what lay ahead. "Prime Minister, I pray with all my heart that right will prevail, and that we can remove and expunge the threat of this godless Nazi menace for good. However, if, despite our best efforts, we cannot stop them from gaining and increasing a foothold on

British soil, we must consider the alternative. We know that they have drawn up a list of our people they wish to capture, not least of which are all of us here. I believe they call this document, their 'Special Wanted List.' 'Wanted,' I should imagine, is their euphemism for liquidate. We must have a strategy for escape and a government in exile, should the worst happen. We can be of no use to anyone if we're dead."

Churchill slapped the palm of his hand down hard on the War Room table. "I told the House that we shall fight this insidious and evil enemy on the beaches, the landing grounds, the fields, the hills and the streets. And I meant every word. I cannot expect the people of this country to fight as I believe and expect they will, while I and my cabinet conduct the course of the invasion from a safe haven. Their Majesties have had every opportunity to leave London for safer places, and they have refused to do so. How, gentlemen, can we do any less? While it is true we will perhaps no longer be able to remain in the nation's capital, I will not leave this country while one enemy soldier remains on its soil. It will be a great hardship for all of us, but at least we will be able to sleep at night with a clear conscience. However, in the present situation, I cannot demand any of you to remain in Britain while there is still an opportunity for you to depart with your families to the safer shores of Canada or the United States. I would only ask that any of you who are considering such a course of action do so now, so the rest of us can work on keeping our country free." He waited for a few seconds while the rest of his War Cabinet stayed silent. No one moved or spoke. "Very well, gentlemen. I will take it that your refusal to budge from your seats means I have your full backing and support." He stood up, glancing at each member of his wartime government. "There is much to do. Let us roll up our sleeves and get to work."

CHAPTER 36

Ciudad Rodrigo, Spain – Washington, D.C. – Berlin, Germany, August 1940

The entourage drove through the night, stopping at Coimbra to refuel. The garage patron was not happy about being woken at such an ungodly hour, but the promise of being paid far more than the cost of the gas for his trouble mollified his displeasure. They arrived at their intended destination, The *Palacio de Montarco* in Ciudad Rodrigo, just over the Spanish border, a little before six o'clock in the morning.

The Conde, Eduardo de Rojas Ordóñez, had arranged an early but sumptuous breakfast for them after their long journey. The Conde was a Falangist, and a supporter of General Franco. It was the Generalissimo to whom Schellenberg had turned to ask where they might be safely installed for the short sojourn before making their way to Berlin. Franco hastily called his friend, Ordóñez, who had a house situated in the ideal location, a mere thirty kilometers across the Portuguese border.

"Eat up, Your Royal Highness. We have a busy few days ahead of us," Schellenberg commanded his charge.

Edward replied testily, "If you don't mind, my wife and I would like to rest first. It has been a long and arduous journey, and we are both tired. Give us a few hours to refresh ourselves and we will be more than happy to do whatever you require of us."

Schellenberg nodded in pretended agreement. "Yes, it must have been tiring for you, but I had assumed you would have been used to long car journeys by now. After all, you drove from Paris to Biarritz, then across to

Barcelona. And, of course, there was the tedious drive across Spain to Madrid, then a further road trip into Portugal. Surely such a seasoned traveler as yourself must be used to long journeys by now."

The German's barbed observations were not lost on Edward. "I shall ignore those comments. They are not worthy of you, *Sturmbannführer*, but I will remember to mention them to your superiors once we reach Berlin. I am sure they will be less than impressed by your insolence."

Had this ungrateful swine already forgotten that it had been only a few hours since he had saved Edward from getting his royal head blown from off his shoulders? "You may do as you wish, Your Royal Highness. I would just urge you to remember who organized your breakout and successful trip across Portugal to where we are at present. Now, can we please stop all this verbal jousting. It is tiresome and is getting us nowhere. Have your rest as you wish, then we shall get down to work."

"Work?"

"Oh, yes, Your Royal Highness. We did not extricate you from Portugal solely for the good of your health. If you wish to regain your throne, there are some things we have to accomplish first."

"And those are...?"

"All in good time, Your Royal Highness. All in good time."

* * *

In the United States, a crisis meeting was taking place in the Blue Room of the White House between the Canadian Prime Minister, William Lyon Mackenzie King, and President Franklin D. Roosevelt. "Mr. President, I am begging, I am imploring you to do something, anything, that will help Britain. The German army is poised to cross the English Channel any day now, and..."

Roosevelt sighed wearily. "Prime Minister, I am fully aware of what is happening across the Atlantic. Do you not think I am every bit as concerned as you are? Unfortunately, my hands are tied. With few exceptions, much of Congress, including, I am ashamed to admit it, many in my own party, not to mention most Americans, are against becoming embroiled in another European conflict. Many questioned why we entered the last one, and what we gained by doing so. Over one hundred thousand families did not see their husbands and fathers again, not to mention the two hundred thousand troops who came back wounded and broken. The American people have no appetite for another war, at least another war in which they do not personally feel threatened. I'm sorry, Prime Minister, as much as I would like to, I cannot help you. And there's one other factor for me to consider. This is an election year. I cannot go to the American people on a platform of preparing them to become involved in another conflict. They just wouldn't wear it, and if Willkie gets elected, you can be sure he'll never agree to join in any war that does not directly affect American interests."

"And I'm sorry to tell you, Mr. President, the war may be closer than you think."

"What do you mean? The Nazis don't have the technology – yet – to reach our shores with ballistic missiles. They just don't have the capability, as far as I know, to be able to threaten us, so what's your point?"

"Yes, it's true they can't touch you, or us, directly by military means, but they are being much more devious than I think you know. They are fomenting anti-American feeling in central and South America. Their agents are all over the sub-continent, Mexico, Argentina, Peru, Uruguay, and so on pushing the Nazi agenda. And as you know, many of these nations have right-leaning governments who are already favorably impressed at how successful the Nazis are at suppressing any opposition to them, not to mention their military superiority on the battlefield. I honestly do not want to see you fall into the trap of languid complacency, Mr. President. I honestly don't."

"You need hardly worry on that score. I am keenly aware of what is happening 'south of the border.' We have agents there who are keeping us apprised of the situation."

King chose his next words very carefully. It was all about semantics and inference. "Are you aware that there may already be hundreds of German troops stationed in some of these countries?"

Roosevelt raised his eyebrows in amazement. "Go on," he said tonelessly.

"I believe that several hundred troops, if not more, of the Third Reich were landed secretly by submarine in one of the countries I have just mentioned. I have no proof of this, but my agents, also, have been busy."

"I wasn't aware that U-boats had that range."

"Yes, indeed, Mr. President. Some of their submarines can travel well over ten thousand nautical miles without refueling. Sailing back and forth across the Atlantic from Germany would not pose too much of a problem for them."

"A thousand enemy troops on the American continent, you say?" Roosevelt stared thoughtfully into the middle distance. "If you are correct, this puts an entirely different complexion on things." The President nodded. "With your help, I may yet make a case for coming to Britain's aid, Prime Minister."

"If I may venture an opinion, it would not look good for you or your intelligence agencies if you admit you got this information from Canada. It would appear as if the Germans had caught you on the back foot," King cautioned.

"Perhaps you're right, Prime Minister. I won't mention you or your country. Besides, if I did, my team would assume you might be exaggerating, eh?"

King smiled without responding. "There is one other troubling issue which, once again, I believe you must be cognizant of."

"And what is that?"

"Well, it would be bad enough if German soldiers were already embedded on these shores, but there's another matter that's equally troubling. Many pro-German societies are operating here openly, some masquerading as patriotic to America, and merely demanding that the country remain neutral, but who are actually right behind Hitler. Again, I have no direct evidence, but it is more than possible that German senior officers and members of the pro-German lobby here have already been in contact with each other. If this is true, it would certainly be a worrying development."

"As you say, Prime Minister, it would, indeed, be a very troubling state of affairs. There is no time to lose. I will call an emergency meeting of my cabinet for tomorrow, and try to force the issue. I will let you get back to Ottawa. I'm sure you have much to do."

King rose, shaking Roosevelt's hand as he did so. "I'm sure you won't mind if I don't get up," the President smiled.

"Not at all, Mr. President. If you don't mind, there is something I'd like to say before I leave."

"What's on your mind?"

"It's not so much what's on my mind, as what I'd like to get off my chest."

"Now you've got me intrigued. I hope I didn't say anything to offend you."

"No, you didn't." King took a deep breath. "Some years ago, I gave a speech in London, in which I said that my country would not support Britain in another military misadventure, unless Britain, herself, was threatened or attacked. I said other things as well, for which I feel deeply ashamed. I also met with Hitler in nineteen-thirty-seven, and called him a great man, equal in stature, if you care to believe it, with Joan of Arc. I stated that, his treatment of the Jews aside, he loved his fellow-man, and would make any sacrifice for their good. I see now how wrong and foolish I was. He has to be eradicated, Mr. President, by any means open to us. If we fail to do this, I fear for the future of the world. We will enter a new dark age from which we may never recover."

"Thank you for being so candid, Prime Minister. I assure you I will do all in my power to see that right prevails, no matter what sacrifices we must make to achieve it."

After King had left the White House, Roosevelt reflected on the meeting he had just had with the Canadian Prime Minister. He was not fooled by King's words. He had trained as a lawyer and was used to the way words could be used to convey different meanings. Innuendo, suggestion, conjecture, all fabricated as 'evidence' without actually saying so. He knew what King was up to, but could not disagree with his sentiments. There may or may not be German troops on the American continent, who may or may not be communicating with Nazi groups in the United States. Whatever the situation, Hitler had to be stopped. He hoped he could convince his cabinet as easily as King believed he had fooled the President. His powers of persuasion might be all that stood between a future of freedom and democratic prosperity or a thousand years of Nazi tyranny.

* * *

"We may have beaten the Royal Air Force, but their navy is still a force to be reckoned with." Declared Grand Admiral Erich Raeder, Head of the Kriegsmarine at a meeting of the German General Staff which included the Führer himself. "Especially after the losses our navy suffered at Norway. It will be a difficult challenge for us to defeat their ships as easily as we did their air force."

"And I'm telling you, Raeder, that it can be done, despite those losses. Don't forget, the British also lost several warships, including an aircraft carrier," argued Hitler. They were all sitting around a large-scale map of the north coast of France, the English Channel, and the south and east coast of England. "I had hoped it would not come to this. I said it before many times, and I repeat it now. The British are not our enemy. It is the Soviets we should be concerned about. I do not trust Stalin any more than I would trust a venomous snake. With the combined resources of both our forces, we could easily see off the Red Army, and work for a peaceful outcome afterwards. Sadly, that does not now seem likely, not with that pompous ass Churchill and his Jewish backers. Well, they have made their bed and now they must lie in it. I do not want reasons why this cannot be done. I want ideas how it can be achieved. Is that clear?"

All the assembled officers mumbled their assent. It was Göring who spoke. "Perhaps a seaborne invasion may not be necessary, at all, Führer."

"What do you mean, Hermann?"

"It was the Duke of Windsor who gave me the idea, actually. Reichsminister von Ribbentrop told me about von Stohrer's report concerning Edward's visit to Toledo with the Spanish statesman, Don Javier Bermejillo. He seems to think that a sustained bombing campaign of British cities would make the people more amenable to our proposals, not to mention blaming Churchill and the government for allowing all the devastation and loss of life in the first place. A focused aerial assault on London, Manchester, Birmingham, and so on would make the British more accepting of the terms we would impose."

"If I am to inherit London, I do not want a bombed-out city full of rubble and dead civilians, not to mention all the displaced citizens who would not welcome us as liberators of their warmongering government. I have nothing but contempt for their stupid politicians, but I have always admired the architecture. Are we going to have to rebuild a devastated city from the ruins of such an imposing landscape?"

"Well, we will not be short of manpower, that's for sure. They may hate us for what we did, but they will still have to eat. They will work for whatever we wish to pay them." Göring observed.

"I have already said we should do to them what they tried to do to us. Blockade our ports, and areas of food production. In other words, starve them into compliance. I have no issue with attacking ports, harbors, airfields, and so on, but I am not sure our cause would be served by bombing them into submission."

"If we have to destroy London to own it, so be it. At least it will be rebuilt to German architectural designs rather than the decadent and self-indulgent buildings which are so wasteful of space and indifferent to functionality."

"Enough!" barked Hitler. "We have wasted enough time on this matter. Very well, we will embark on a limited, and I mean limited blitzkrieg of their cities, at least, to begin with."

"They are a stubborn people, *mein Führer*, led by an even more determined Prime Minister. We may need to increase our methods of persuasion to make them see sense."

"Then that is what we shall do. In the meantime, I want you to target their food supply and materiel delivery routes. This should be our priority. No sea vessel must be allowed to land at any port or harbor in the United Kingdom. We must make their docks inoperable. Together with restricted, but strategic bombardment of their cities, this will sharpen their minds. I want them at the negotiating table no longer than eight weeks from today."

The General Staff commanders glanced at each other. It was not impossible to achieve the Führer's directive, but it was not going to be easy. The British were, indeed, a proud and stubborn race, and would fight every inch of the way. They all stood to attention, as they gave the Nazi salute. "Heil Hitler!" they exclaimed in unison.

* * *

In the library at the *Palacio de Montarco*, Edward sat at the Conde's escritoire, preparing to draft a speech composed for him by Max de Crinis, Joseph Goebbels, and from notes supplied by Joachim von Ribbentrop. "I trust you are now relaxed, Your Royal Highness. The moment has come for you to publicly disavow your country's policies towards Germany. If you are to regain the throne, you must show allegiance to those who will reinstall you to this exalted position. Do I make myself clear?"

For the first time since leaving Paris a few weeks earlier, Edward lost his resolve. Everything he had said and done up until now had led to this very moment. Once he did what his hosts required of him, there was no going back, and things would never again be the same. He glanced up at the Duchess who was standing beside him, her hand resting gently on his shoulder. She nodded encouragement as his Montblanc Meisterstück fountain pen trembled in his hand.

"Very well, Your Royal Highness, if you are ready, I will dictate the letter you will now write, which will be broadcast to Britain in a few days once we reach Berlin. We are doing this now, so that you may concentrate on other matters once we are safely in Germany."

Edward nodded slowly without looking up, as he focused on the blank foolscap page in front of him. Schellenberg began to speak as Edward took his dictation. After a few minutes, it was over. Edward carefully rolled the Herbin rocking blotter over the handwritten document. The German carefully lifted the pages and blew gently on them to complete the ink drying process. Just a few short days from now, Edward would read his speech on German radio, which would be broadcast in Britain. Once the British saw that even their former King was suing for peace, how much longer would they continue to fight?

CHAPTER 37

London, England – Washington, D.C., U.S.A. – Berlin, Germany, September 1940

It had been six weeks since Hitler issued his directive to blockade British seaports and aerial bomb its cities. With little resistance from the few remaining R.A.F. aircraft, the Luftwaffe lost no time in asserting its dominance over English skies. Felixstowe, Liverpool, Harwich, London, and the Clydeside in Scotland, were mercilessly attacked by German airplanes. Meanwhile, U-boats were patrolling the Atlantic. Although they took great care not to torpedo vessels flying the American flag, any ship bearing British or Canadian emblems were attacked without warning, and thousands of tonnes of shipping, together with their crews, went down in the cold and unforgiving waters of the North Atlantic. Although British destroyers and Royal Navy submarines scored a few notable successes against their German adversaries, and some supplies were reaching what remained of British ports, the tide was gradually and inexorably turning in favor of the Nazi fleet. Britain was slowly being deprived of the food and the material it needed to continue to prosecute the war.

"They are trying to starve us into submission," Churchill declared to his cabinet, "and regretfully, they are succeeding. Although I will not make such a statement to the British people just yet, I do not know how much longer we can hold out at this rate. Unless we find a solution to the problem, I fear the worst will soon be upon us."

"How much longer do we have?" asked Ernest Bevin.

"Truthfully?"

"Truthfully," responded the Minister of Labour and National Service.

"A few weeks, a month at the most."

"And since they started bombing our cities, morale has plummeted. Maybe we should..."

"No!" shouted the Prime Minister. "While I have the keys to Number Ten, I will not bow down to that evil, vicious, malignant, psychopathic, anti-Semite. I will not!"

"But...?" began Lord Halifax.

"'But me no buts,'" Foreign Secretary. "I will lay down my life, and be happy to do so, before one Nazi jackboot struts down the streets of London. And I am steadfastly sure the British people are right behind me. We fight, gentlemen! We fight and we fight and we fight until we can fight no more. Then we shall fight all the harder, because that is all we can do."

Those sitting around the War Cabinet table thought the same thing. "How do we fight, and expect our people to fight, on empty stomachs, and many already bombed out of their homes?" Many members thought it, but not one said it.

* * *

In the United States, President Roosevelt made an impassioned speech to Congress, which he concluded by saying, "*...and so, let me be clear, we cannot afford to sit in complacent indifference while our allies across the Atlantic fight for their very existence. Poland has fallen, France has fallen, Belgium has fallen, the Netherlands has fallen, Norway has fallen, Denmark has fallen, Luxembourg has fallen, Czechoslovakia has all but capitulated. Slowly, one by one, the lights are going out again all over Europe. How long will it be before they begin to dim even on our shores? Make no mistake, we are not immune to the evil banditry that is sweeping through Europe at this very moment. On our streets as we speak, groups are gathering who show greater loyalty to the Third Reich than they do to our own democratically elected government. Is it not better to confront this menace now before it reaches our continent? Even today, German U-boats patrol off our shore, keeping watch on our navy's movements. Why are they doing this if they have no malicious intent against us?*

"Let me make it abundantly clear. I have no intention of asking this House to declare war on Germany. We may yet find that, even at this late

stage, we have enough common ground to avoid conflict between us, but that does not mean that we cannot, should not help our allies. Would we want them to sit idly by while we faced such a great threat to our existence, our way of life? Is it not now time for our Neutrality Act to be repealed, so we can legitimately give the assistance they so desperately need to our closest cousins across the sea?"

Despite his heartfelt plea, Congress believed it was reflecting the will of the American people when it voted not to repeal the Neutrality Act. Moreover, it felt that this was Britain's problem and Britain's alone. She had declared war on Germany and now must pay the price for her presumptive folly. The United States would not become embroiled in a situation that had nothing to do with her. Britain was on her own.

* * *

The Windsors and their Nazi entourage drove the one hundred and twenty kilometer journey to Salamanca airdrome where they boarded a Ju-52/3m transport aircraft specially chartered for them by the German government. They completed the nineteen hundred kilometer journey to Tempelhof airport in just over eight hours, and Edward and Wallis finally landed in Berlin just after two p.m. They were greeted by Hitler himself, such was the importance the Nazi government attached to the Duke and Duchess's arrival. "My dear Edward, your Royal Highness," the Führer deferred toward Wallis, "Welcome back to Berlin. It is a pleasure to see you both once again. You must be tired after your long flight. We have much to discuss, but first, I think, a little celebration is in order. Let us go back to the city." Wallis preened visibly at being addressed in the regal manner.

On the way back to the German capital, sitting in Hitler's limousine, the German leader asked Edward if he had prepared and written the speech he would give on German radio. "Yes, Führer," he replied. "It is all ready. When would you like me to relay it?"

"Soon, Your Royal Highness; very soon."

CHAPTER 38

Berlin, Germany – London, England - Washington D.C., U.S.A., September 1940

It was three nights after the Windsors arrived in Germany that Edward gave his speech on German radio from the main RRG station on Masurenallee in Berlin's Westend. The speech was broadcast on medium wave to the United Kingdom and on short wave to the United States.

If there had ever been any doubt as to where Edward's loyalties truly lay, his oration had put those doubts to rest. "*I am speaking to you tonight from Berlin, where the Duchess and I are the guests of the German government. The German people offered the British people the hand of friendship, and continue to offer the hand of friendship, to avoid the bloodshed which sadly both sides endured in the previous conflict. Even now, they are willing to put aside all feelings of animosity and bitterness if the British government accepts that it would be foolish and destructive to carry this strife on any further. Britain has already suffered enough brave young men to be killed in this unnecessary war. Germany, too, has lost much of the cream of its generation, and to what end? Have we learned nothing from the carnage of twenty years ago? Are we so blind to the devastation and loss of life that will undoubtedly ensue in a protracted conflict which Britain cannot win? I implore the British people and the government of the United Kingdom with all my heart not to allow any more blood to be spilled in a useless war.*

"The German leadership is more than willing to offer favorable terms if only the British people renounce their antagonism towards Germany and its allies, and to withdraw their forces with honor from the battlefield. Let us not

repeat the mistakes from the previous conflict, mistakes which would not be played out in the fields of Flanders, Ypres, The Somme, and Verdun, but on the beautiful and peaceful countryside of Britain.

"Is it worth sacrificing so many young lives, full of so much promise and of hope, to fight in such a pointless and futile war? Let us cease this hostility now, while there is still time. Let our two countries reach a mutually acceptable accommodation which will permit both nations to move forward together in the spirit of peace and harmony.

"Thank you, and God bless you all."

* * *

Churchill had never felt such dismay and feelings of hopelessness in his life. Tears rolled down his cheeks, as he whispered, almost to himself, "He was my friend, my King. How could he betray the country he once ruled? Betray it with such utter contempt and indifference? He could not have done more to hurt me if he had stuck a dagger through my breast. But he has also done something else. Now, more than ever, he has hardened my resolve. To see that man re-anointed as King and sit on the throne of this great country of ours is more than I can bear. Despite what I said earlier, I might have been prepared to come to terms, no matter how unfavorable, with Germany, but no longer. It is as if the Almighty has given me a sign. From this moment on, if I have to fight this war on my own, with nothing more than a pistol in my right hand, while I draw breath, that man will never set foot back in Britain!"

* * *

On the other side of the Atlantic, American public opinion was divided. The mainly German-run pro-Nazi organizations, and most isolationists were delighted. Edward was giving Britain the opportunity to surrender, while not appearing to do so. They were in a hopeless situation. Germany could easily invade and conquer the country, then where would they all be? The Duke made a lot of sense, and would make a good King once his brother was ousted. His insight, and aversion to another war, not to mention his warning of the devastation of the English countryside, was to be applauded. Many remembered tales their fathers and grandfathers told them of the Civil War, and the destruction and havoc it had wrought upon their own communities. This was, by far, the best, the only option open to the British. Peace with Honor.

Roosevelt, and many in his cabinet were not so sure. If the American people were made aware of how evil Hitler and his regime were, maybe their reaction would not be so favorable. Jewish organizations were giving the President all the intelligence they could on the deteriorating situation in Europe regarding Jews. As well as the thousands who were being publicly persecuted and beaten in the streets, many were simply disappearing, never to be seen or heard from again. What was happening to them? There were a few rumors, mostly unfounded, of camps that had been built in the occupied countries, to house the undesirables, Jews, Gypsies, Catholic priests, homosexuals and others who had spoken out publicly against the Nazis and their disgusting policies of racial purity. Attempting to create a racially pure and perfect society was an anathema to the President, especially when those at the head of the Reich itself, were anything but perfect. Others, too, had gone missing, those with low intellect or physical deformities. Some had told of unspeakable experiments which were conducted in these camps, many on children, most of whom did not survive them. But until he and his government could get actual evidence of the existence of these camps, and what they entailed, their hands were tied.

He considered calling in Germany's *Chargé d'affaires* in Washington, Hans Thomsen. Thomsen, however, would only deny any such allegations, and blame them on an American-Jewish attempt to discredit his country.

There was one thing Roosevelt could do. He did not know if it would do any good, but he would do it, anyway. Doing anything was better than doing nothing.

* * *

All the leaders of the Reich came in to congratulate Edward after his historic speech. He had delivered it with just the right amount of diplomacy, aplomb, and empathy.

"I was glad to hear that you made so much use of the notes I was able to send to *Sturmbannführer* Schellenberg," beamed Goebbels. "It is gratifying to see one's work utilized in such a positive way."

Not to be outdone, Hermann Göring stepped in. "Yes, Your Royal Highness. With the success of our glorious Luftwaffe pilots over the R.A.F., it will not be too long before the final victory."

After the backslapping that Edward reluctantly endured, he was approached by Hitler's aide-de-camp, Julius Schaub. Taking Edward gently, but firmly, by the elbow, Schaub spoke quietly into Edward's ear. "Your Royal Highness, you need to come with me right now."

Although he was not happy at the physical demonstration of appreciation of his speech, he enjoyed the adulation. "Why do we have to leave so suddenly? Surely...."

"I do not wish to worry you unduly, but there are rumors that British agents are in the area. Now you have shown your true colors, so to speak, they have been instructed to...."

"Oh my God!" Edward squealed. "Yes, of course." Turning to his hosts, Edward hastily bid them a happy farewell before leaving with Schaub. Six SS guards, flanked the Duke as he made his way from the radio station. He hunched down as he left the building to make his stature as small as possible. For all anyone knew, they could be hiding in any of the adjoining buildings, the telescopic sights of their rifles trained on his crouching body. He ran to the waiting limousine, quickly ducking down as he stepped inside. With Hitler's a.d.c. sitting beside him, Edward asked, "Where are we going?"

Turning to look at his charge, Schaub replied, "For security reasons, it is better you should not know until we arrive. The Duchess is on her way, and will be there by the time we reach our destination. There is nothing more to worry about."

Edward sat back and allowed himself to relax in the comfortable leather seats of the armored Mercedes. He was safe now, and it would not be long before Britain capitulated one way or another. Despite his earlier funk, Edward dozed off in the car. He dreamed the Archbishop of Canterbury was placing the crown on his head, the ceremonial ring and scepter already in his hands. In his mind, the Archbishop was saying, "You have arrived, Your Royal Highness. Welcome to...." And then he awoke to find himself in a large, enclosed courtyard. "Welcome to..." he heard the voice saying again, only it was not the Archbishop of Canterbury, but his fellow passenger, Julius Schaub. "... Schloss Köpenick, Your Royal Highness. This will be your new home for a while. It is well guarded, and apart from those who need to know, no one else knows you are here. You will be quite safe."

Edward smiled easily. Schaub stepped to the side and whispered into the ear of an SS officer who was nearby. The officer gave the Nazi salute, as he acknowledged the instructions he had been given. Returning to Edward, Schaub introduced him to the SS guard. "This officer will escort you to your quarters. I understand the Duchess is already there. You did well, Your Royal Highness. We are all very proud of you."

Edward gave a small backward wave as he allowed the guard to lead him away.

CHAPTER 39

Washington D.C., U.S.A. – London, England – Berlin, Germany, September - October 1940

Three men occupied the Oval Office. Behind the desk sat the President. Seated in front of him were Henry Morgenthau Jr., and Henry L. Stimson. Morgenthau was the U.S. Secretary of the Treasury, and Stimson, the Secretary for War. After the usual formalities, it was to Morgenthau that Roosevelt spoke first. "Henry, I've asked you to come here on a matter which is not related to your responsibilities in the Treasury. You're a prominent member of the Jewish community here, and I need to know what you know about what is happening in Germany right now regarding the Jewish population there. I've heard reports that terrible, dreadful things are going on that, as a Christian, I find hard to believe. I just need to know if they're true."

"I've also heard the rumors, Mr. President, but I know no more than you do. It's a terrible worry for us all here. If even half the stories are true, I fear the worst."

Turning to Stimson, Roosevelt enquired, "Is there nothing we can do to ameliorate the situation by military means? Surely there must be something we can do. It frustrates me that we must sit on our hands while that madman rapes Europe."

"Sadly, Mr. President, Congress has made its position abundantly clear. Unless we, or our interests are directly threatened, there is no desire to become involved in another European war. People have long memories, Mr. President, and, quite frankly, I can't say I blame them. After what I witnessed as an artillery officer in France, I would not wish my sons, if I had any, to go through the same thing again."

"So, what you're both telling me is that there is nothing we can do to help these poor people in any way?"

Both men shook their heads in unison. It was Morgenthau who spoke for both of them. "Sadly not, Mr. President. Barring a divine miracle, I am afraid to say that in the not-too-distant future, not one Jew will be left in the whole of Europe."

* * *

Churchill addressed his War Cabinet, wearing his spectacles on the bridge of his nose, and clutching a document in his hand. "We have had a communiqué sent to us via the Swiss embassy. It is from the German government listing the terms we must accept to avoid an invasion. They have made it quite clear that there will be no room for negotiation, and failure to comply with all their demands will result in a German assault on Great Britain. Never did I think it would come to this, gentlemen. Never did I think in my wildest dreams I would have such a perfidious document in my hands. But we have to live with the situation as it is, not as we would wish it to be."

"What are their terms, Prime Minister?" asked Lord Beaverbrook.

"Just what you would expect. Our armed forces should stand down and be demobilized. Police and security forces are to be under the control of their State Police organization, that is, the Gestapo. Dissolution of both Houses of Parliament, and replaced by direct rule from Berlin, with only a token government to execute orders and statutes imposed by the Reich, and so on. I and my cabinet are to present ourselves to the incoming parties to be arrested and indicted for war crimes. There are many other conditions, of course, but what I have just read out to you are the salient points."

Without exception, every minister shook their heads in disbelief, resolute defiance showing on their lined faces. It was Clement Attlee who stood to respond to Churchill's statement. "Never, Prime Minister; never in a thousand years can we possibly succumb to these imperatives. I am not a belligerent person by nature, but, by God, I will not see my family, or the people of this nation, go the same way as those poor souls on the Continent. I think I speak for all of us when I say 'we fight on.'"

Every member banged their fists on the War Cabinet table in agreement. "Very well, gentlemen. You have given me your answer. I will draft a reply to the Nazi government opposing their demands. The Germans will pay a heavy price for their arrogance and conceit. We will mobilize every man, woman, and even our children. No German will be safe on British soil. If necessary, we will form guerilla armies and fight them on every street corner, from around every rock and stone we will harry them, there will be no let up from us, no peace for them, while one Nazi soldier remains in our land. Let us go forth, gentlemen, and prepare for battle!"

* * *

Within the heavily fortified walls of Schloss Köpenick, Edward paced up and down his suite impatiently. "It's been almost six weeks, Wallis. Why won't they tell us what's happening? When are we to go back to Britain for my coronation? They are all being very civil and polite, and showing us every courtesy, but whenever I ask the question, all I get in reply is 'Soon, Your Royal Highness.' Why won't they tell us anything?"

"You must learn to compose yourself, my sweet. It will most likely be any day now. If I were you, I would make the most of the peace and tranquility we are currently enjoying. Once we are back in London, there will be a lot to occupy our time, I've no doubt."

"Yes, I suppose so. It's just a feeling I've got that something isn't right. I can't put my finger on it, but...."

Wallis put her forefinger to her husband's lips. "Hush, my darling. What can go wrong? I'm sure they've got everything in hand. You're darting at shadows, as usual." She took his hand and led him out onto the balcony. Despite the chill in the Autumn air, the sun was shining brightly.

Yes, of course everything would be alright, he reassured himself. Why wouldn't it be?

* * *

It was on Sunday, October 6th. that air raid sirens sounded all across England as hundreds of Luftwaffe airplanes dropped thousands of airborne paratroops onto British soil and German warships sailed across the channel, carrying amphibious assault vehicles and many more soldiers of the German army, together with their allies. The invasion of Britain had begun.

CHAPTER 40

London, England – Berlin, Germany, October - December 1940

Despite fierce fighting and unparalleled resistance from the British army on the shores of England's south coast, German forces, supported by Göring's Luftwaffe, eventually gained a bridgehead on English beaches before their troops moved gradually north and eastward. The British fought rearguard actions valiantly as they retreated, causing massive losses to the advancing enemy host, but their counteraction was weakening as the *Wehrmacht* penetrated ever more inland.

Churchill's cabinet had reluctantly fled London in the early stages of the battle for the nation's capital, and conducted their campaign of defiance from wherever the enemy had not yet gained a foothold. Speaking on portable short wave radio equipment, the Prime Minister exhorted his people to fight on, assuring them that the tide of battle would soon surely turn in their favor. His powerful speeches became less ardent, and fewer and further between as German technology became more sophisticated and able to quickly locate the source of the broadcasts.

The Royal Family had not been so fortunate, unwilling to leave their subjects, hoping to give them the courage they themselves were displaying by remaining in Buckingham Palace, despite pleas by Churchill to decamp to safer accommodation. They had been captured a few weeks after the siege of London, as Luftwaffe airplanes bombed the city from above, as the prelude to the German troops who stormed the barriers and defenses erected by the army and their civilian allies. The King and Queen, and the other members of the Royal Household were taken to the Tower of London while the German High Command decided what to do with them.

Edward's speech still echoed in the minds of much of the British population. Many had fathers, sons, brothers and uncles killed in the butchery of the previous conflict, and still more men bore testament to the intolerant savagery of warfare. These were the young men who had volunteered to fight for King and Country, and had gone gladly to engage the enemy on foreign shores, only to return with missing limbs, permanently blinded by mustard gas and physically and psychologically broken. And that same enemy had now landed on British shores. This time the fighting would be in the fields and streets and villages of England.

The former King was quite right, many thought. Was it all really worth it to see their beautiful country with its golden fields, ripe orchards and picturesque villages churned up by tanks and other heavy vehicles? Was it all worth it to have their towns, villages and hamlets desecrated by mechanical behemoths and their hail of lethal ordnance? Was it all worth seeing this generation of young men cut down and die as their fathers did not even a generation ago? Especially when they faced a much stronger and mightier foe? As the population became more dispirited and demoralized, more and more people realized the unpalatable truth. It was over. The Germans had won.

* * *

In a schloss on the outskirts of Berlin, an SS officer knocked deferentially on the door which led into an ornate suite of rooms. Without waiting for a response, he entered, his hat tucked into the crook of his elbow, and saluted as he stood in front of the man he had come to find. "It is time, Your Royal Highness."

CHAPTER 41

Berlin, Germany, February 1899

Kaiser Wilhelm II strutted up and down the richly carpeted floor of the library in the Royal Palace, shaking his head vehemently from side to side. "No, it will not do," he announced to no one in particular. "It simply will not do. I cannot have a serving officer in the British army as next in line to one of the most prestigious Houses in Germany. I know the Duke of Connaught. He is a good man, and I have nothing against him personally, but I will not have an English army officer ruling the House of Saxe-Coburg and Gotha. Can you not see the conflict of interest that would arise if ever we should find ourselves at war with them? His position would be intolerable, as would ours."

The Kaiser and his officials were discussing the Line of Succession of the Saxe-Coburg and Gotha Dukedom. The current incumbent, Prince Alfred was gravely ill with throat cancer, and was not expected to survive. His only son, and next in line to the title, also named Alfred, had died in mysterious circumstances two weeks earlier. Alfred junior's four siblings were all females, three of whom had married into other European royalty. The fourth, Princess Beatrice, was fourteen-years-old, with no claim to the title.

The Dukedom should have been inherited by Edward, Prince of Wales, Prince Alfred senior's older brother, and the eldest son of Queen Victoria and her late consort, Prince Albert. Edward renounced the title because of his own conflict of interest, as heir to the British throne, thus causing the current dilemma for the German monarch.

"Your Imperial Majesty, is it not rather indelicate to be discussing such a subject so soon after the young Prince's death, and while his father is still alive?" commented the Kaiser's Secretary of State for Foreign Affairs, Bernhard von Bülow.

"No, it is not, von Bülow. One does not solve problems by pretending they do not exist. Is it not better to conclude the matter now, than wait until the issue is forced upon us? The man is dying and there is nothing that you, or I or anyone else can do about it."

"The Duke of Connaught has a son, I believe..."

"Ach!" spat the Kaiser. "I have already broached this subject with the Duke, but we have reached an impasse. I have insisted that the young man must have a German education. How else can he know how to rule his subjects if he has not been grounded in our laws and customs? But the Duke is adamant that he will not permit it. He is being stubborn and foolish as only the English can be. I doubt we shall reach an agreement over this, so it seems we must go further down the line." The Kaiser lifted a document from his desk. "The next in line to the title would have been Prince Leopold, but he has sadly died. Therefore, it will be his son, whose first name is also Leopold, but whom they call Carl Edward, who will be the new Duke of Saxe-Coburg Gotha."

Von Bülow asked, "Do you need me to do anything, Your Imperial Majesty?"

"No, thank you. It has all been arranged. The boy and his mother are currently living in England. He speaks no mother tongue, so that will be the first order of business. He is only fifteen years old, so his young mind should still be pliable enough to absorb our language. He will be of no use to anyone if he cannot understand his subjects, nor they him."

"Quite so, Your Imperial Majesty."

"He is still young, and will require guidance. See to it that he gets the necessary instruction he will need. Everything will be strange to him at first, but we must see that he is made to feel as much at ease here as he does in England. After all, once the current Duke dies, this will be his new home."

CHAPTER 42

London, England – Berlin, Germany, January - March 1941

The Gestapo-GB was slowly homing in on Winston Churchill. The new Reich government had issued an edict forbidding anyone to aid, give succor or support, shelter or provide any other assistance to the former Prime Minister or any of his cabinet under penalty of death. His broadcasts had now stopped entirely, and many citizens believed he had been caught, secretly tried and executed.

As the country slowly adjusted to life under the new Nazi regime, it soon became clear that things were changing, and not for the better. Food already rationed became even more scarce, and many shops had closed due to the shortages. They simply had nothing to sell, and grocery store owners found themselves in the same precarious position as their customers. Jews, and those with Hebrew-sounding names were being rounded up, to be taken to secret facilities that had been quickly erected in remote parts of the English countryside. These premises had been fenced off with barbed and razor wire, with electrified cables running through them. Access to the approach roads had been sealed off, and only those with special clearance were permitted through the heavily guarded command posts. Ominous smokestacks could be seen from a distance but no one dared to ask what could cause such acrid emissions. Anyone who did question what was happening to the Jewish population was told to mind their own business, or they, too, would disappear. The message was clear, and people soon learned simply to stop enquiring. It was safer that way.

* * *

The Duke was driven to the *Reichschancellery* and was immediately escorted up to the Führer's private office. A smiling Hitler warmly welcomed his guest. "Your Royal Highness, how good to see you again. I am sorry I have not been to visit you in a while, but pressure of work, you know...."

"Absolutely, m*ein Führer*, no apology is necessary. I fully understand."

"And are you ready to fulfill your role, your destiny?"

"Yes, *mein Führer*, and I owe it all to you. If you don't mind my saying so, you have engineered everything so well, down to the last detail. You have been magnificent."

"Thank you, Your Royal Highness, but as I recall writing to you some time ago, I could not have accomplished all that I have without the assistance of people like you. It is now time for me to repay my debt of gratitude to you."

"But despite our previous conversations on the subject, I do not see how the British people will accept me as their sovereign. I am not in the Line of Succession."

"And you still do not see, my dear Carl Eduard, that their constitution, or what was their constitution, allowed for the monarchy to be decided, not only by hereditary title, but by the discretion of their parliament. Well, I am now the leader of their parliament, if somewhat remotely, and it is I and I alone who will decide who will be on the throne of England."

"But surely, the Duke of Windsor...."

"You begin to sound as if you do not want the title I wish to confer upon you."

"No, of course not, but the Duke of...."

"The Duke of Windsor is weak, vain and vacuous, everything I despise in a man. He was prepared to betray his country, his government, his people, his friends, and his family to further his own ends. Would he not also be willing to forsake me, if the situation, however unlikely, should arise? No, my dear Carl, it has always been you who I have determined should rule in my stead. It is your birthright, as I have ordained it. Edward did as he was asked to do, and has now fulfilled his purpose. Do you honestly believe that the British people would accept him as their King again after the speech he gave, much less have the American woman as their Queen?"

"No, *mein Führer*, I suppose not."

"Of course, they would not. You have been faithful to me from the beginning. You supported me, and encouraged others to do so. In the election where we came to power, you raised funds, you have been a good and loyal National Socialist, and you even sheltered us at Veste Coburg when our fortunes were not as they eventually became. What loyalty do you owe a country who stripped you of your titles and royal heritage due to circumstances that were out of your control? Go now, and be their King to rule in my place."

The Duke of Saxe-Coburg and Gotha could not contain himself any longer. "Thank you, *mein Führer*, thank you a thousand times over. I will not let you down. I will reign over them as I know you would wish me to."

"I know you will, Carl Eduard. I know you will."

* * *

After being held incommunicado for several more weeks, a lieutenant knocked on the door of the suite of rooms occupied by Edward and Wallis in Schloss Köpenick. Holding his cap deferentially in his hand, he asked the couple to accompany him.

"Where to, now?" the Duke asked testily. "We've been cooped up in this castle for months, not knowing what's going on in the outside world. We haven't even been provided with a radio. How is the war going? Are we, that is, the British still fighting on? When will the Führer invade the country? Britain must surely be in a parlous state by this time. Why will no one tell us what's happening? No, dammit, it's not good enough." Pointing his finger at his military escort, Edward shouted, "I demand to see your superior. Where is Julius Schaub? Why has he not been to see us for weeks? I must insist...."

The lieutenant interrupted Edward's diatribe. "I'm sorry, Your Royal Highness; I should have explained. I believe your airplane is being fueled. It will be ready to depart as soon as you arrive at the airport."

"At last!" beamed Edward, all further thoughts of dissatisfaction quickly forgotten. Grabbing Wallis's hand, Edward allowed the young officer to escort them along the hall and down the stairs to the limousine already waiting at the front of the schloss.

"Wait!" shouted Wallis. "We're not ready. We need to pack our cases. We can't return to England without our things."

"There is no time," the officer replied. I was instructed to tell you that your belongings would be sent on but it was a matter of some urgency that you board the plane as soon as possible. There is a strict timetable to adhere to. Please, follow me quickly."

"What on earth could be so imperative?" asked Wallis quietly.

"I don't know, but whatever it is, we'll just have to make the best of it. Don't worry, my sweet, I'm sure everything is under control. You know how these Teutons are. Everything has to be done to a schedule. It won't be long now, my love. Everything we've striven for, worked so hard for, it's almost here. I can practically taste it." As the chauffeur opened the rear passenger door, Edward ushered Wallis in front of him, then climbed in behind her.

Their excitement was so palpable, they did not hear the soft snick as the doors locked. Neither spoke as the large Mercedes drove off, each of them engrossed in their own private thoughts. It was several minutes before Edward realized they were not going toward Tempelhof Airport. His attempt to open the glass partition failed as the window would not slide apart. Rapping at the glass partition, he tried to get the driver's attention. "I say, you're going in the wrong direction. You need to turn around and..."

Despite his frantic banging at the window, the chauffeur affected not to hear him. The Duke of Windsor banged even louder but still the uniformed guard did not respond. "What's going on?" Wallis asked, slightly perturbed.

"I don't know. This oaf won't answer me. Doesn't he know the way to the airport? We should have turned off a mile back. God knows where he's taking us."

"Maybe he knows a shortcut. These locals usually know ways we don't. I wouldn't worry. Just sit back and don't be so flustered."

"Flustered be damned! Good manners cost nothing. He hasn't even acknowledged me. It's just not good enough. Does he not know who I am? By George, I'll have plenty to say once we get to Tempelhof, don't you worry."

They drove on for almost half-an-hour before even Wallis started feeling twinges of unease. "Where on earth is he taking us? We should at least be able to see signs for the airport by now." Edward tried knocking on the window again, but to no avail. Just as he was about to remonstrate once more, the driver began to slow the car down. They were in a part of the city Edward was not familiar with, nor would he wish to be. It was a run-down area with dilapidated, soot-blackened three-story apartment blocks, all in need of serious repair, and boarded-up shop windows, many with Jewish names above the doors. These wooden slats had been daubed with anti-Semitic slogans and painted with large yellow Stars of David and caricatures of Jews with obscenely long noses and nooses around their necks.

The first thing that struck Wallis was the absence of people. At first, it looked as if there were no signs of life at all. Then, from out of the doorway of one of the abandoned apartment blocks came four men, all attired in high-ranking SS uniforms. Now, both of them were severely alarmed. Why had the driver brought them to this dreadful place? What was going on, and who were these officers? The passenger door locks snicked again, this time the sound being heard by the frightened couple. As their situation slowly dawned on them, it was Wallis who gave voice to their fears. "I don't think we're going to the airport, my love."

As the true horror of their position finally sank in, Edward screamed in panic. "No! No! No! You cannot do this! It's monstrous! I am to be the King of England, proclaimed by the Führer himself. Get the Führer! He will confirm what I've said. How dare you countermand his orders? Have you taken leave of your senses? He will..."

Wallis sighed resignedly. "I'm afraid it's no use, my dear. We've been duped royally, if you'll forgive the pun. Now that we've fulfilled our function, we're of no use to them; in fact, we're more of a liability, especially you."

"Oh my God!" Edward screamed, as his hands went up to cover his face. "All this time..."

"All this time, they were leading us on. Hitler had no intention of re-installing you, us, as monarchs. We've been good little Nazis and done as we were told, but we've now outlived our usefulness. Still, it was a good run, eh?"

Edward shook his head violently from side to side, unwilling to believe what was happening. His eyes bulged from their sockets as he looked in vain for help around the close confines of the limousine. The driver still sat motionless in front of them, like an automaton waiting for a command. There would be no aid, no assistance, no one to come to their rescue.

Outside the Mercedes, the four SS officers stood with their arms folded. They would wait another minute or so for the couple to exit the car. Then they would wait no longer.

* * *

It was a muted and somber crowd that watched their new sovereign as he rode through the streets of London in the Gold State Coach with his wife, Princess Victoria Adelaide of Schleswig-Holstein. This had been a coronation like no other and a public holiday had been declared. Nazi authorities permitted the distribution of foodstuffs that had not been available for several months. Under the propaganda division of Reich-GB, newspapers published special editions proclaiming the new King and Queen.

After the celebration, work would recommence on the rebuilding of London, with German architects overseeing the construction. No expense would be spared, as London would become the showpiece of the new Greater German Reich, second only to Berlin in its magnificent architecture.

* * *

A few weeks after the coronation, RRG Radio in Berlin broadcast a brief and terse announcement. 'The German nation and the peoples of the Reich mourn the passing of the Duke and Duchess of Windsor who were killed in a motoring accident near their temporary home at Schloss Köpenick in Berlin. No one else was involved in the incident.'

* * *

It would take time, but the people would eventually become resigned to their austere way of life and welcome their new rulers. After the current population had passed, future generations would know of no other form of government. Life would go on, but only for those whom the state deemed it should. The degenerates and subnormal would eventually be eliminated or bred out of existence and from the survivors would emerge a new superhuman Aryan race.

With each generation, an even stronger population would arise, whose destiny would be nothing less than world domination. The Third Reich would no longer be a dream; it would become a reality. In the future, the only history that would be taught was one where the Reich had always been, was of the moment, and would always be. There would be no trace, no record of there ever having been any other race, any other society, any other culture. All was subservient to the Reich. *Heil Hitler! Heil the Reich!*

THE WINDSOR CONSPIRACY/ EPILOGUE

On a cold, rainy Autumn day in November 1951, the female occupant of a house in Barnet, North London, opened her front door in response to a staccato of three sharp raps. She found a tall, handsome but frail-looking, well-dressed man standing in front of her. He doffed his trilby as he asked her in a cultured English, but accented German accent if she was Mrs. Deborah Bentley. Cautiously, she replied, "Yes, that's right. What...?" Before she could ask anything more, the man requested if he might come inside.

"Please believe me, Mrs. Bentley, I am not trying to sell you anything, nor do I mean you any harm. Quite the opposite, in fact." He smiled.

Against her better judgement, she stood aside to allow him to pass. Once he was inside, she showed him into the front parlor. "If I may be permitted to sit, I won't take up too much of your afternoon." She slowly nodded in acquiescence as he took a seat. Knowing his time was short, he said quickly, "I have come here today, Mrs. Bentley, because I knew your husband. I feel it is only right that you should know what happened to him." The woman felt the blood drain from her face as she reluctantly motioned him to continue. "Our acquaintance was very brief, and I only met him once for a few minutes in a house in Portugal in nineteen-forty." He stopped talking to allow her to process what he had just revealed.

"Please go on," she told him in a dry, hoarse voice. He did not have to. She knew what he was going to say, but needed to hear it from his own lips.

"I was responsible for your husband's death, Mrs. Bentley." And he told her what had happened on that fateful night.

As tears began to well in her eyes, Deborah Bentley responded, "If you've come here to ask for my forgiveness...."

"No, Mrs. Bentley, I have not come to ask for your forgiveness or absolution for what I did. I was a serving officer in the German army and did what I had to do. I came here today, because... because I feel you have a right to know how brave your husband was. Knowing he faced certain death, he still carried out his duty. Or tried to. We may have been on opposite sides, but I respect and admire the courage that your husband displayed in the moments before I... before he died. He was a man of exemplary spirit and heroism. I just thought you should know that he died bravely in the defense of his country."

"Why now? Why so many years after the war have you decided to come here and tell me this?"

"No more lies, Mrs. Bentley. I am dying and have only another few weeks, or months to live. They tell me it is liver cancer. Untreatable, incurable and inoperable. It is only a matter of time."

"And you wanted to make your peace with God through me before you die. Is that it, Mr....."

"Schellenberg, Mrs. Bentley. Walter Schellenberg. And no, I did not come here to find salvation either through you or anyone else. God does not exist, Mrs. Bentley, and I should know. After all the things I did during the war, the... things I was responsible for, believe me, if God ever did exist, he left long before. At least, that is what I tell myself, because if there is a God and a Heaven, then, surely, there must also be a Satan and a Hell. If that is the case, then I will never find redemption, I assure you. My place for eternity will be in everlasting darkness. No, I came here only out of a sense of duty. One professional soldier to another, although I believe your husband was not in your armed services. Nonetheless, as I said, I feel you have a right to know what happened. The Duke and Duchess of Windsor were also present, of course, but they are no longer in a position to discuss those events, as I am sure you are well aware. So, it is up to me, alone." He made to rise, but the widow laid her hand on his shoulder. "Was it all worth it, do you think? All the lost lives, all the devastation, all the fear, the misery, the destruction. What did you really accomplish in the end?"

Schellenberg sighed audibly. "The fact that my country now rules over yours should answer that question, Mrs. Bentley, and as history is written by the victors...." Schellenberg raised his eyebrows as if in unspoken affirmation of his statement. "As for the people who lived through it and survived...?" he shrugged his shoulders. "Who knows, Mrs. Bentley? Who knows?" He half-rose with effort, using the arm rests to prop himself upright. As he got to the front door, he turned around to face her. "I cannot apologize for what I did, but I am sorry that it happened. I'm not sure if you understand, nor even if this makes any sense." He turned the latch and pulled the door open. Without turning around again, he said quietly, "Goodbye, Mrs. Bentley."

She watched him walk down the path with his head bowed against the wind. He turned left as he walked out of her gate, and she waited until he was out of her sight before she returned indoors.

THE END

AUTHOR'S NOTE

Although this novel is primarily a work of fiction, it draws heavily from actual historical events and real contemporary personalities. As I have taken certain dramatic license with many of these incidents, however, this book should not be used as a resource for anyone studying this period of history.

The fact that Edward was, indeed, an ardent admirer of Adolf Hitler, and his anti-Semitic views were largely hidden from the public. This situation changed after his and Wallis's visit to Germany in October 1937, and more people began to question his loyalties to his country and the Crown.

The incident of the 'bogus' assassination attempt on the life of King Edward VIII is recreated here almost exactly as it happened. I have, however, added my own imagination to this event. Bannigan/McMahon is not recorded as having shouted any pro-Nazi or Irish Republican slogans during his botched attempt on the king's life. Likewise, in a later chapter, Bannigan/McMahon's trial is also a reasonably accurate, if abridged account of the proceedings as they happened.

Charles Bedaux and Axel Wenner-Gren were well-known acolytes and supporters of the Nazi regime, and both were involved in dubious practices and suspicious fund-raising activities for the Reich.

Edward was, indeed, approached by Lenox Lohr of NBC to give a speech from Verdun, which was broadcast on May 8th. 1939 and which I have reproduced, almost word-for-word in the novel. The broadcast was banned from being aired on British and Canadian radio. Many newspapers, however, carried a textual account of what was said much to the chagrin of both the British and Canadian governments.

The incident at Mechelen is reproduced from historical records and eyewitness accounts. Documents purporting to detail Germany's invasion plans for the Low Countries, Belgium and France were allegedly discovered during the capture of the pilot and his passenger. It is believed that Edward somehow got hold of these papers during his tenure as liaison officer, and passed those details to Britain's enemies.

The Duke and Duchess's flight from Paris to Biarritz is much as I have described it, although why Edward chose to drive a further five hundred kilometers to Perpignan rather than enter Spain via Irun, a mere thirty kilometers from the French/Spanish border before heading to Madrid is unclear. Perhaps it was for the reason he states, i.e., to throw off any British surveillance, but his true motive for making this journey may never be known.

Several incidents which occurred while the Duke and Duchess were in Spain and Portugal are recreated in this novel, however, for dramatic purposes, I have used some creative license to fictionalize these accounts.

If Edward had really been spirited away to Germany instead of finally sailing to the Bahamas, it is highly likely that on his return to Spain, en route to Berlin, he would have stayed in the palatial home of the Conde de Montarco, Eduardo de Rojas Ordóñez, a Falangist and supporter of General Francisco Franco, at his *Palacio de Montarco* in Ciudad Rodrigo. These details may be found on the following YouTube video https://www.youtube.com/watch?v=tHgtUNVlFJc.

Air Chief Marshall Hugh Caswall Tremenheere Dowding, 1st. Baron Dowding, GCB, GCVO, CMG, was born in Moffat, Scotland in 1882. He enlisted in the British army in the early 1900s before joining the Royal Flying Corps (forerunner of the R.A.F.) at the start of World War I. He rose through the ranks of the service to become Air Member for Supply and Research in September 1930. In July 1936, he was appointed as chief of the newly created R.A.F. Fighter Command. Worried about German warplane re-armament, he enacted a series of measures to counter the threat of a Luftwaffe bombardment. Although the novel sees the R.A.F. defeated by the Luftwaffe, it is in no small part thanks to the measures he took before and during World War II that the R.A.F. was, indeed, able to defeat the Nazi air menace. Despite his victory in what would come to be known as the Battle of Britain, he was dismissed by Churchill in November 1940 due to tactical differences between himself and other senior members of the R.A.F. High Command. His interest in spiritualism following the death of his first wife also raised fears that he was not emotionally sound enough to continue in his job. He retired from the R.A.F. in July 1942. He died in

February 1970, almost unknown and barely remembered for his extraordinary part in keeping Britain free from the scourge of Nazi-ism.

Carl Eduard inherited the title of Duke of Saxe-Coburg and Gotha in July 1900 in the manner I have described. He was an ardent Nazi and supporter of Adolf Hitler, and gave aid and succor to the embryonic National Socialist movement, providing shelter for its members in his Castle Veste home. After WWII, he was initially charged with crimes against humanity. These indictments were later reduced to lesser crimes, and he lost much of his property after the trial. He died in relative poverty and obscurity in 1954.

Had Hitler conquered Britain, would he really have re-installed Edward as monarch with Wallis as his queen, or would he, as I have suggested, have been suspicious of someone who was prepared to betray everyone and everything he was meant to stand for in order to satisfy his own selfish and self-serving ends? Thankfully, we will never know the answer to this conundrum.

THE DUKE OF WINDSOR CONSPIRACY REFERENCE SOURCES

Charles Edward, Duke of Saxe-Coburg and Gotha - Wikipedia

https://lineofsuccession.co.uk/1930-08-21

http://www.unofficialroyalty.com/charles-edward-duke-of-saxe-coburg-gotha/

https://www.thesaurus.com/
https://en.wikipedia.org/wiki/Mussolini_Cabinet#:~:text=The%20Mussolini%20Cabinet%20was%20the,8%20months%20and%2025%20days.
https://en.wikipedia.org/wiki/Galeazzo_Ciano
https://en.wikipedia.org/wiki/Pact_of_Steel
https://www.britannica.com/place/Rhineland
https://www.nationalarchives.gov.uk/education/resources/germanoccupation/#:~:text=On%207%20March%201936%20German,France%20and%20Britain%2C%20into%20confusion.
https://en.wikipedia.org/wiki/Spanish_Civil_War

https://en.wikipedia.org/wiki/Fascist_Italy_(1922%E2%80%931943)

https://en.wikipedia.org/wiki/Konstantin_von_Neurath

https://thecritic.co.uk/assassinating-edward-viii/

British state 'covered up plot to assassinate King Edward VIII' | Espionage | The Guardian

The Irishman who tried to assassinate King Edward VIII (irishtimes.com)

Were MI5 told of plot to kill Edward VIII then let it go ahead? | Daily Mail Online

https://en.wikipedia.org/wiki/Dino_Grandi

https://en.wikipedia.org/wiki/George_McMahon_(failed_assassin)

https://en.wikipedia.org/wiki/John_Simon,_1st_Viscount_Simon

https://en.wikipedia.org/wiki/Vernon_Kell 'K' interesting site

https://www.historyireland.com/volume-26/issue-4-july-august-2018/on-this-day-42/

https://en.wikipedia.org/wiki/July_1936#July_16,_1936_(Thursday)

https://en.wikipedia.org/wiki/Special_Branch#Heads_of_the_Metropolitan_Police_Special_Branch

https://www.britannica.com/topic/Scotland-Yard

https://en.wikipedia.org/wiki/James_Whitehead_(police_officer)

https://www.google.com/search?q=Who+was+the+President+of+the+Irish+Free+State+in+1936&rlz=1C1CHZO_enAU900AU903&oq=Who+was+the+President+of+the+Irish+Free+State+in+1936&aqs=chrome..69i57.16080j0j15&sourceid=chrome&ie=UTF-8

https://en.wikipedia.org/wiki/Pope_Pius_XI

https://en.wikipedia.org/wiki/British_Union_of_Fascists#:~:text=This%20is%20the%20latest%20accepted%20revision%2C%20reviewed%20on%2025%20March%202021.&text=The%20British%20Union%20of%20Fascists,in%201932%20by%20Oswald%20Mosley.

https://www.tutor2u.net/history/reference/build-up-to-the-abyssinian-crisis-1935

https://www.tutor2u.net/history/reference/the-stresa-pact-1935

https://en.wikipedia.org/wiki/Stresa_Front

https://www.fbi.gov/news/stories/photo-gallery-fbi-reference-firearms-collection#:~:text=Shown%20is%20the%20Colt%20Police,armed%20with%20in%20the%201930s.&text=The%20majority%20of%20firearms%20in%20the%20collection%20are%20from%20adjudicated%20cases.

https://www.google.com/search?q=colt+.38+police+positive&rlz=1C1CHZO_enAU900AU903&oq=Colt+.38+&aqs=chrome.4.69i57j0l9.9456j0j15&sourceid=chrome&ie=UTF-8

Home Secretary - Wikipedia

Second Italo-Ethiopian War - Wikipedia

https://en.wikipedia.org/wiki/World_War_I

Walter Monckton - Wikipedia

BBC NEWS | UK | Profile: Walter Monckton

https://en.wikipedia.org/wiki/Secretary_of_State_for_the_Colonies

Churchill tried to suppress Nazi plot to restore Edward VIII to British throne | Monarchy | The Guardian

https://www.open.edu/openlearn/history-the-arts/history/world-history/former-king-wanted-england-bombed-and-anglo-german-alliance-archives-reveal?active-tab=review-tab&all-comment=1

https://en.wikipedia.org/wiki/Munich_Agreement

https://en.wikipedia.org/wiki/Johanna_Wolf

https://en.wikipedia.org/wiki/List_of_wars_involving_the_United_Kingdom

https://en.wikipedia.org/wiki/Harry_Dixon_Longbottom

https://en.wikipedia.org/wiki/Pol_Roger

https://www.wine-searcher.com/find/pol+roger+vintage+brut+champagne+france/1921/uk#t5

https://en.wikipedia.org/wiki/Secret_Intelligence_Service

https://www.sis.gov.uk/our-history.html

https://www.anderson-sheppard.co.uk/about-us/our-history/#:~:text=The%201930s%20were%20a%20golden,continued%20in%20the%20next%20decade.

https://medicalsciences.stackexchange.com/questions/4398/why-do-medical-professionals-tap-syringes-before-injecting-somebody#:~:text=By%20holding%20the%20syringe%20vertically,harm%20to%20a%20normal%20person.

http://jmu-journalism.org.uk/did-hitler-really-visit-liverpool/

https://en.wikipedia.org/wiki/List_of_prime_ministers_of_the_United_Kingdom

https://en.wikipedia.org/wiki/Leo_Amery#Opposition_to_appeasement_of_Germany

https://en.wikipedia.org/wiki/Harrow_School

https://www.harrowschoolonline.org/about-admissions/about-fees-and-scholarships

Harrow School - Wikipedia

https://en.wikipedia.org/wiki/Joseph_Goebbels
https://www.pinterest.co.uk/gunboat69/british-cars-of-the-1930s/

https://en.wikipedia.org/wiki/Division_of_the_assembly#House_of_Commons

who was the German ambassador to Britain in 1936 - Bing

Boodle's - Wikipedia

https://www.pinterest.co.uk/pin/326722147952437360/

https://en.wikipedia.org/wiki/Buckingham_Palace#/media/File:Plan_of_Buckingham_palace.gif

https://londonmap360.com/london-boroughs-map

https://en.wikipedia.org/wiki/Forms_of_address_in_the_United_Kingdom#Peers_and_peeresses

https://en.wikipedia.org/wiki/The_lady_doth_protest_too_much,_methinks#:~:text=%22The%20lady%20doth%20protest%20too,father%2C%20the%20King%20of%20Denmark.

https://www.isleofwight.com/incarcerated-isle-isle-of-wight-prisons/

https://en.wikipedia.org/wiki/HM_Prison_Camp_Hill

https://en.wikipedia.org/wiki/Keble_College,_Oxford

https://en.wikipedia.org/wiki/DSMA-Notice

https://en.wikipedia.org/wiki/Attorney_General_for_England_and_Wales#1900%E2%80%932001

https://en.wikipedia.org/wiki/Donald_Somervell,_Baron_Somervell_of_Harrow

https://en.wikipedia.org/wiki/Walter_Greaves-Lord

Longstanding royal courtier Sir Alan 'Tommy' Lascelles' hatred of King Edward VIII | Daily Mail Online

A brief history of the British Royals and their alleged Nazi connections | Guide (sbs.com.au)

Will We Ever Know Why Nazi Leader Rudolf Hess Flew to Scotland in the Middle of World War II? | History | Smithsonian Magazine

https://en.wikipedia.org/wiki/MI5#Early_years

Axel Wenner-Gren - Wikipedia

Alfred Blunt - Wikipedia

http://forwoodpictures.blogspot.com/2006/02/sir-dudley-forwood-3rd-bt-obituary.html

Château de Candé - Wikipedia

(70) Edward VIII the traitor king - complete documentary - YouTube

https://www.unofficialroyalty.com/wedding-of-prince-edward-duke-of-windsor-and-wallis-simpson/

http://www.unofficialroyalty.com/may-28-daily-featured-royal-date/

https://www.goodmorningamerica.com/culture/story/wallis-simpson-love-man-marriage-edward-vii-historian-52931591

https://en.wikipedia.org/wiki/Deuxi%C3%A8me_Bureau

https://en.wikipedia.org/wiki/Candid_photography

Fruity Metcalfe - Wikipedia

https://www.britannica.com/topic/Morse-Code

https://www.nobility-association.com/etiquetteaddressingroyals.htm

https://www.factinate.com/people/43-scandalous-facts-edward-viii-king-lost-crown/

https://en.wikipedia.org/wiki/Robert_Anderson_Jardine

https://www.express.co.uk/news/uk/1210129/robert-anderson-jardine-windsor-history

https://sites.google.com/site/allenproqatardoha/residences-of-the-duke-of-windsor/chateau-de-la-maye-versailles

https://en.wikipedia.org/wiki/Ch%C3%A2teau_de_la_Cro%C3%AB

https://www.thenorthernecho.co.uk/history/15325027.darlington-vicars-starring-role-greatest-royal-sensation-century/

https://en.wikipedia.org/wiki/Deuxi%C3%A8me_Bureau#:~:text=The%20SCR%2C%20headquartered%20at%202,run%20by%20Commandant%20Guy%20Schlesser.

https://earth.google.com/web/search/Gendarmerie+Nationale,+171+Avenue+de+Grammont,+Tours,+France/@47.3777803,0.6936313,57.39088305a,687.75964402d,35y,0h,45t,0r/data=CqcBGn0SdwolMHg0N2Zj

ZDVkMmEyM2JkNThmOjB4MWNlMTNiMTg1ZDFkYjYzYxlaydga
W7BHQCFBbJ9EOjLmPyo8R2VuZGFybWVyaWUgTmF0aW9uYWx
lLCAxNzEgQXZlbnVlIGRlIEdyYW1tb250LCBUb3VycywgRnJhbmN
lGAMgASImCiQJ4H0Gb-
PLR0ARcohkKQOeR0AZfBnuiXGY9T8hMGgqZ6kUyD8
http://carstylecritic.blogspot.com/2016/05/styling-variety-1930s-french-cars.html

https://en.wikipedia.org/wiki/Capital_punishment_in_France#1939_onwardshttps://en.wikipedia.org/wiki/Capital_punishment_in_France#1939_onwards

https://www.consam.com/a-brief-history-of-two-way-radio/#:~:text=In%201933%2C%20the%20Bayonne%2C%20New,transceivers%20installed%20in%20police%20cars.

https://en.wikipedia.org/wiki/Servizio_Informazioni_Militarehttps://en.wikipedia.org/wiki/Servizio_Informazioni_Militare

marcel dupre - Bing

http://www.historygrandrapids.org/photoessay/4345/charles-bedaux-the-duke-and-du

https://en.wikipedia.org/wiki/Time_and_motion_study#:~:text=A%20time%20and%20motion%20study,book%20Cheaper%20by%20the%20Dozen).

https://en.wikipedia.org/wiki/Le_Meurice#Early_20th_century

Former King wanted England bombed and an Anglo-German alliance, archives reveal (theconversation.com)

(111) King Edward VIII - Professor Vernon Bogdanor FBA CBE - YouTube

https://en.wikipedia.org/wiki/Robert_Ley was an alcoholic

https://en.wikipedia.org/wiki/Duke_and_Duchess_of_Windsor%27s_1937_tour_of_Germany

https://www.thetrendspotter.net/trilby-vs-fedora-how-to-wear/#:~:text=The%20style%20first%20debuted%20during,tweed%2C%20wool%20or%20straw%20design.

https://en.wikipedia.org/wiki/Horcher_(restaurant)

https://www.restaurantehorcher.com/eng/historia.html

https://www.theguardian.com/uk/2002/jun/29/research.monarchy

https://en.wikipedia.org/wiki/Albert_Speer

https://en.wikipedia.org/wiki/Salon_Kitty

https://en.wikipedia.org/wiki/Daimler_Motoren_Gesellschaft

https://en.wikipedia.org/wiki/Neuk%C3%B6lln#History
https://en.wikipedia.org/wiki/Richard_Wagner#Operas_2

https://web.archive.org/web/20190708150347/http://www.wagneroperas.com/indexparsifal.html

https://en.wikipedia.org/wiki/Hermann_G%C3%B6ring

https://digitalcosmonaut.com/2018/herrmann-goering-carinhall/

http://www.usmbooks.com/carinhall_story.html

https://www.historyofroyalwomen.com/wallis-simpson/the-duke-and-duchess-of-windsors-tour-of-germany-1937/

https://www.biography.com/news/edward-viii-wallis-simpson-nazi-sympathizers-hitlerhttps://www.biography.com/news/edward-viii-wallis-simpson-nazi-sympathizers-hitler

https://en.wikipedia.org/wiki/1937_German_Grand_Prix

https://en.wikipedia.org/wiki/Ernst_von_Delius

https://en.wikipedia.org/wiki/1937_Italian_Grand_Prix

https://en.wikipedia.org/wiki/Alfried_Krupp_von_Bohlen_und_Halbach

https://en.wikipedia.org/wiki/Berghof_(residence)#:~:text=The%20Berghof%20was%20Adolf%20Hitler,near%20Berchtesgaden%2C%20Bavaria%2C%20Germany.

https://en.wikipedia.org/wiki/Paul_Schmidt_(interpreter)

https://en.wikipedia.org/wiki/George_S._Messersmith

https://en.wikipedia.org/wiki/Ernst_Wilhelm_Bohle

https://en.wikipedia.org/wiki/Edward_VIII#Second_World_War

https://military.wikia.org/wiki/Edward_VIII

Operation Willi - Wikipedia

https://en.wikipedia.org/wiki/Lenox_R._Lohr

https://www.youtube.com/watch?v=pG4bu5LJUTo

https://en.wikipedia.org/wiki/Battle_of_Verdun

https://en.wikipedia.org/wiki/December_1939

https://en.wikipedia.org/wiki/Louis_Mountbatten,_1st_Earl_Mountbatten_of_Burma

https://www.lordmountbattenofburma.com/hms-kelly

(222) Britain's Nazi King-Edward VIII - YouTube

https://en.wikipedia.org/wiki/Julius_von_Zech-Burkersroda

https://www.wikiwand.com/en/John_Carter_(police_officer)

https://en.wikipedia.org/wiki/Belgium_in_World_War_II

https://en.wikipedia.org/wiki/F%C3%BChrer_Headquarters#Headquarters_locations

https://en.wikipedia.org/wiki/Adlerhorst

https://en.wikipedia.org/wiki/German_General_Staff#World_War_II

https://www.history.org.uk/publications/resource/9689/the-phoney-war-teaching-wwii

https://en.wikipedia.org/wiki/Phoney_War

https://en.wikipedia.org/wiki/Blockade_of_Germany_(1939%E2%80%931945)

https://en.wikipedia.org/wiki/Franz_Halder#Invasions_of_Poland_and_Western_Europe

https://en.wikipedia.org/wiki/Mechelen_incident

https://en.wikipedia.org/wiki/List_of_Belgian_military_equipment_of_World_War_II#Rifles https://de.wikipedia.org/wiki/Schloss_Wasserleonburg

https://en.wikipedia.org/wiki/Berchtesgaden
https://en.wikipedia.org/wiki/Alfred_Jodl

https://www.google.com/search?q=what+height+could+a+messerschmitt+bf+108+taifun+go&rlz=1C1CHZO_enAU900AU903&oq=What+height+could+a+Messersmit+Bf108+taifun+&aqs=chrome.1.69i57j33i10i160l4.37529j0j15&sourceid=chrome&ie=UTF-8

https://aerocorner.com/aircraft/messerschmitt-bf-108-taifun/#:~:text=The%20Bf%20108B%20has%20a,is%201%2C200%20feet%20per%20minute.

https://www.google.com/search?q=what+altitude+can+a+crow+fly&rlz=1C1CHZO_enAU900AU903&oq=&aqs=chrome.0.69i59i450l8.533347313j0j15&sourceid=chrome&ie=UTF-8

https://www.nam.ac.uk/explore/british-army-ranks

https://en.wikipedia.org/wiki/John_Vereker,_6th_Viscount_Gort#Death

https://www.dorchestercollection.com/en/paris/le-meurice/history/#1936

https://www.dorchestercollection.com/en/paris/le-meurice/meetings-events/salon-jeu-de-paume/

https://www.dorchestercollection.com/en/paris/le-meurice/meetings-events/salon-jeu-de-paume/

https://www.glenfiddich.com/au/

https://www.youtube.com/watch?v=dhnrnh3KLbk

https://encyclopedia.ushmm.org/content/en/article/wilhelm-keitel

https://en.wikipedia.org/wiki/Wilhelm_Keitel#Criticism_of_capabilities

https://en.wikipedia.org/wiki/Maginot_Line#German_invasion_in_World_War_II

https://en.wikipedia.org/wiki/Kehl#History

https://en.wikipedia.org/wiki/Dunkirk_evacuation

https://en.wikipedia.org/wiki/H%C3%B4tel_du_Palais

https://en.wikipedia.org/wiki/Neville_Chamberlain

https://en.wikipedia.org/wiki/Winston_Churchill

https://www.smithsonianmag.com/smart-news/newly-released-documents-reveal-churchills-efforts-suppress-details-nazi-plot-180964131/

https://en.wikipedia.org/wiki/Operation_Willi

https://www.mi5.gov.uk/brigadier-oswald-allen-harker

https://en.wikipedia.org/wiki/Fruity_Metcalfe

https://www.justabouttravel.net/2012/07/11/biarritz-queen-of-resorts-and-resort-of-the-kings/

https://warfarehistorynetwork.com/2016/11/08/operation-willi-the-nazi-plot-to-kidnap-the-duke-of-windsor/

https://medium.com/lessons-from-history/when-nazis-tried-to-kidnap-the-ex-king-of-britain-operation-willi-7d8acdf6ee6b

https://www.history.com/this-day-in-history/italy-declares-war-on-france-and-great-britain https://www.youtube.com/watch?v=6q2_DHoYC3E

https://www.youtube.com/watch?v=oTMRDovfKQ8

https://www.army.mod.uk/who-we-are/our-people/ranks/

https://spartacus-educational.com/SSmenzies.htm

https://en.wikipedia.org/wiki/Stewart_Menzies#First_World_War_action

https://www.vaguelyinteresting.co.uk/to-kidnap-the-king/

https://nationalinterest.org/blog/buzz/remember-when-hitler-tried-kidnap-ex-king-england-133207

https://royaltyrobertwriter.home.blog/2020/05/17/plots-and-intrigues-the-duke-and-duchess-of-windsor-in-madrid-june-1940/

https://en.wikipedia.org/wiki/Samuel_Hoare,_1st_Viscount_Templewood

https://spartacus-educational.com/2WWkentD.htm

https://www.sbs.com.au/guide/article/2017/08/28/brief-history-british-royals-and-their-alleged-nazi-connections

https://en.wikipedia.org/wiki/Prince_George,_Duke_of_Kent

https://en.wikipedia.org/wiki/Ram%C3%B3n_Serrano_Su%C3%B1er#Involvement_in_World_War_II

https://journals.openedition.org/rfcb/1415

https://en.wikipedia.org/wiki/Peace_Pledge_Union#Attitudes_towards_Nazi_Germany

https://en.wikipedia.org/wiki/League_of_Nations_Union

https://en.wikipedia.org/wiki/Secretary_of_State_for_the_Colonies#Secretaries_of_State_for_the_Colonies_(1854%E2%80%931966)

https://en.wikipedia.org/wiki/NSDAP_Office_of_Foreign_Affairs

https://en.wikipedia.org/wiki/Hotel_Adlon#First_Hotel_Adlon

https://history.state.gov/departmenthistory/people/hull-cordell

https://en.wikipedia.org/wiki/Joseph_Goebbels

https://en.wikipedia.org/wiki/War_cabinet#Second_World_War

https://en.wikipedia.org/wiki/Churchill_War_Rooms

https://en.wikipedia.org/wiki/Churchill_war_ministry#14_May_1940_to_30_April_1941

https://en.wikipedia.org/wiki/Jock_Colville

https://roomfordiplomacy.com/spain-madrid/

https://www.google.com/maps

https://en.wikipedia.org/wiki/Juan_Luis_Beigbeder_y_Atienza

https://en.wikipedia.org/wiki/Operation_Sea_Lion

https://en.wikipedia.org/wiki/Walter_Schellenberg

https://military.wikia.org/wiki/Walter_Schellenberg

https://en.wikipedia.org/wiki/Ant%C3%B3nio_de_Oliveira_Salazar

https://en.wikipedia.org/wiki/Venlo_incident

http://www.rafweb.org/Biographies/Chamberlayne.htm#top

https://en.wikipedia.org/wiki/Walford_Selby

https://roomfordiplomacy.com/portugal-lisbon-oporto/

https://en.wikipedia.org/wiki/Boeing_314_Clipper

https://en.wikipedia.org/wiki/Ricardo_Esp%C3%ADrito_Santo

https://www.bhsportugal.org/uploads/fotos_artigos/files/DukeofWindsor%26RESanto.pdf

https://en.wikipedia.org/wiki/State_Surveillance_and_Defense_Police

https://www.jstor.org/stable/44327333?Search=yes&resultItemClick=true&searchText=Walter+Schellenberg&searchUri=%2Faction%2FdoBasicSearch%3FQuery%3DWalter%2BSchellenberg%26filter%3D&ab_segments=0%2FSYC-5910%2Fcontrol&refreqid=fastly-default%3A785e39872bcbf9fe09bce4e90ac269f5&seq=2#metadata_info_tab_contents

https://en.wikipedia.org/wiki/Max_de_Crinis

https://earth.google.com/web/search/Vilar+Formoso,+Portugal/@40.6138151,-6.8349271,758.56351793a,8823.5710218d,35y,0h,45t,0r/data=CoEBGlcSUQokMHhkM2M0NWUwNjA2YjM0ZjM6MHg0YTJkZDcxNGVhNzVmNTMwGQnLjkOzTkRAIUpbXOMzWRvAKhdWaWxhciBGb3Jtb3NvLCBQb3J0dWdhbBgCIAEiJgokCe3vft-CWENAEbceyBxwWENAGWzS0sb02yLAIa5VtwIV3CLAKAI

https://en.wikipedia.org/wiki/Vilar_Formoso

https://www.generalblue.com/calendar/1940

https://qz.com/423449/king-edward-was-apparently-pro-nazi-wanted-england-bombed/

https://earth.google.com/web/search/Calle+de+Serrano,+Madrid,+Spain/@40.42289902,-3.6882671,655.31663407a,0d,60y,356.08808536h,84.78834214t,0r/data=CigiJgokCe-TE8XhN0RAEYQjPjCYNERAGYh1yRVIYw3AIfq-qUphgQ3AIhoKFjZNcEExSEJBZWdsOVlTYTNESTFpNmcQAg

https://en.wikipedia.org/wiki/Synagogue_of_Santa_Mar%C3%ADa_la_Blanca

https://en.wikipedia.org/wiki/Aircraft_of_the_Battle_of_Britain#Main_types:_Hurricane,_Spitfire_and_Bf_109

https://en.wikipedia.org/wiki/Messerschmitt_Bf_109

https://en.wikipedia.org/wiki/Messerschmitt_Bf_110

https://www.southampton.gov.uk/arts-heritage/history-southampton/spitfire/

https://en.wikipedia.org/wiki/Hawker_Hurricane#:~:text=The%20first%20Hurricane%20built%20at,produced%20in%20England%20and%20Canada.

https://en.wikipedia.org/wiki/Hawker_Hurricane

https://airpages.ru/eng/uk/hurr1.shtml

https://airpages.ru/eng/uk/spitf1.shtml

https://airpages.ru/eng/elw_main.shtml

https://www.luftkrieg-ueber-europa.de/en/comparison-of-the-supermarine-spitfire-mk-ia-with-the-messerschmitt-bf-109-e/

https://en.wikipedia.org/wiki/Ernest_Bevin

https://www.bbc.com/news/uk-politics-52588148

https://www.youtube.com/watch?v=HY9DAD0BGPM

https://www.youtube.com/watch?v=KY_AUdtvhY8

https://www.timeanddate.com/sun/@2264396?month=7&year=1940

https://second.wiki/wiki/palacio_de_montarco
https://second.wiki/wiki/eduardo_de_rojas_ordc3b3c3b1ez

https://www.google.com/maps

https://en.wikipedia.org/wiki/William_Lyon_Mackenzie_King

https://history.state.gov/milestones/1937-1945/american-isolationism

https://en.wikipedia.org/wiki/United_States_non-interventionism#Isolationism_between_the_World_Wars

https://en.wikipedia.org/wiki/Foreign_policy_of_the_Franklin_D._Roosevelt_administration

https://en.wikipedia.org/wiki/Type_IX_submarine#List_of_Type_IXA_submarines

https://en.wikipedia.org/wiki/Franklin_D._Roosevelt#cite_note-AHD-2
https://en.wikipedia.org/wiki/Neutrality_Acts_of_the_1930s
https://en.wikipedia.org/wiki/Executive_Residence

https://en.wikipedia.org/wiki/Operation_Weser%C3%BCbung

https://en.wikipedia.org/wiki/Montblanc_(company)

https://en.wikipedia.org/wiki/The_Antiquary

https://www.e-ir.info/2012/05/20/roosevelts-path-to-the-second-world-war-interventionist-or-isolationist/

https://www.airports-worldwide.com/spain/salamanca_spain.htm
https://www.galenleather.com/blogs/news/ink-blotting

https://www.airmilescalculator.com/distance/slm-to-txl/

https://online.norwich.edu/academic-programs/resources/6-important-battles-of-world-war-i

https://en.wikipedia.org/wiki/Reichs-Rundfunk-Gesellschaft

https://en.wikipedia.org/wiki/Hans_Thomsen

https://en.wikipedia.org/wiki/Coronation_of_the_British_monarch

https://en.wikipedia.org/wiki/Chain_Home

https://www.youtube.com/watch?v=BV1ZuJbTlus

https://www.google.com/search?client=firefox-b-d&q=Sir+Hugh+Dowding

https://en.wikipedia.org/wiki/RAF_Bentley_Priory
https://en.wikipedia.org/wiki/Ground-controlled_interception

About the Author

David Philips was born in Glasgow, Scotland, in 1953 and emigrated to Perth, West Australia with his wife, Adele, in 2009. He has two adult children who still live in Scotland. He has had several careers, including being the anonymous human half of a comedy double-act with an irreverent, mischievous, keyboard-playing robot called Mr. Hairy, and it was always a matter of some chagrin that the robot continually stole all his best lines and got more laughs than he did. In his spare time, David plays folk harmonica, swears at the T.V., and reads. His favourite authors are Scottish crime fiction writers Ian Rankin and Craig Robertson. He is also a fan of the works of Robert Harris and the late author Robert Ludlum, from which he draws inspiration for his own books. As well as authoring conspiracy novels, David also writes short horror fiction and is an occasional contributor to *Schlock Horror*, an on-line sci-fi and fantasy magazine. His anthology of thirteen short tales of mystery and the macabre, entitled *The Finest Thread*, is available online. He has also written a comedy novella based in his home city of Glasgow, and set in 1972, called *The McBrides*, which is also available on the web.

David's first novel, *The Judas Conspiracy*, which was published in September 2022, is a personal interpretation of the JFK assassination, inspired by his experiences as an adolescent, and contains his unique insight into this tragic event.

His second book, *The Errol Flynn Conspiracy*, which became an Amazon #1 bestseller for historical fiction, was published by Black Rose Writing in March 2023.

The Duke of Windsor Conspiracy is his third novel.

For more details on David's current activities, please visit his website, www.davidphilipsauthor.com.

Other Titles by David Philips

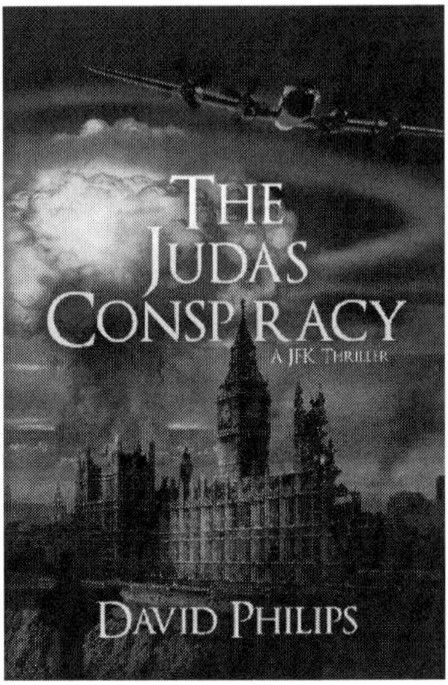

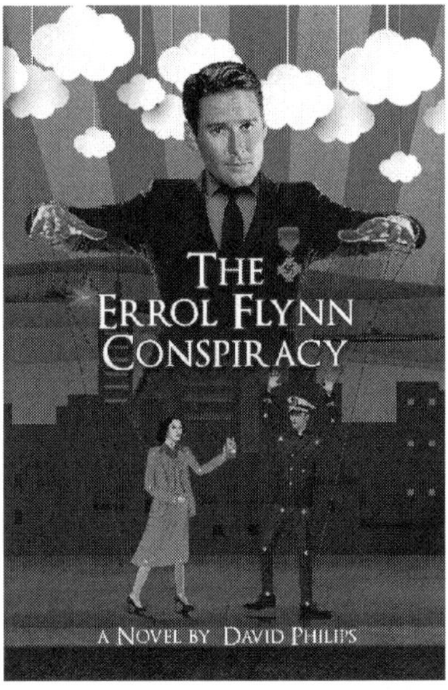

Note from David Philips

Word-of-mouth is crucial for any author to succeed. If you enjoyed *The Duke of Windsor Conspiracy*, please leave a review online—anywhere you are able. Even if it's just a sentence or two. It would make all the difference and would be very much appreciated.

Thanks!
David Philips

Printed in Poland
by Amazon Fulfillment
Poland Sp. z o.o., Wrocław

34339583R00192